# Diamonds And Dreams

"Dammit, Saber!" she whispered vehemently. "I'm bein' an improper lady for you, and you don't even have the decency to be in bed waitin' on me! Now what the hell am I supposed to do?"

No sooner had the question left her lips than strong hands caught her shoulders. Arms pulled her against a torso that was both hard and soft at once.

Warm lips met hers in a kiss that demanded everything she had to give. Searching fingers fumbled with the ribbons at the neck of her night rail, and a satisfied groan hit her ears when the filmy gown skimmed down her body, pooling at her feet.

"Tell me something, my improper lady," Saber murmured, his lips nuzzling the sweet hollow of her throat. "Do you want me to be an improper gentleman? Shall we cast aside all the rules and make this night highly improper? Shall I do improper things to you, Goldie? And may I expect you to do improper things to me in return?"

"Yes." She pulled at the sash of his robe, quivering when the garment fell to join her nightgown on the floor. She leaned into him, desire pulsing through her veins. "Yes, yes," she repeated breathily.

Saber laughed and swept her into his arms.

*Other Books in*
**THE AVON ROMANCE** *Series*

FIRE LILY *by Deborah Camp*
HIGHLAND MOON *by Judith E. French*
LOVE ME WITH FURY *by Cara Miles*
SCOUNDREL'S CAPTIVE *by JoAnn DeLazzari*
SURRENDER IN SCARLET *by Patricia Camden*
TIGER DANCE *by Jillian Hunter*
WILD CARD BRIDE *by Joy Tucker*

*Coming Soon*

CONQUEROR'S KISS *by Hannah Howell*
ROGUE'S MISTRESS *by Eugenia Riley*

# Diamonds And Dreams

## REBECCA PAISLEY

AVON BOOKS ◆ NEW YORK

DIAMONDS AND DREAMS is an original publication of Avon Books. This work has never before appeared in book form. This work is a novel. Any similarity to actual persons or events is purely coincidental.

AVON BOOKS
A division of
The Hearst Corporation
1350 Avenue of the Americas
New York, New York 10019

Copyright © 1991 by Rebecca Boado Rosas
Inside cover author photograph by Kent McCarty
Published by arrangement with the author
Library of Congress Catalog Card Number: 91-92040
ISBN: 0-380-76564-0

First Avon Books Printing: October 1991

AVON TRADEMARK REG. U.S. PAT. OFF. AND IN OTHER COUNTRIES, MARCA REGISTRADA, HECHO EN U.S.A.

Printed in the U.S.A.

RA  10  9  8  7  6  5  4  3  2  1

I remember your intimate perfume, your platinum nail polish, and your silver charm bracelet; your frosted hair, those full-skirted dresses, and your high heels. Did you know I thought you were the most beautiful mother walking this earth?

I remember your tears when Daddy died. I remember your courage, too. Did you know I thought you were the bravest mother in the world?

I remember the nights when I didn't come home on time. You waited in bed alone, listening to sirens and fearing the worst. When I did come home, did you know I couldn't believe it when you didn't kill me?

But most of all I remember your love. It never wavered. Even when I deserved it least, you wrapped it around me. Did you know how much I loved you, too?

I still do. With all my love, Mama, I dedicate this book to you. You're the best.

# Chapter 1

**"Y**ou're going to find a plain man and turn him into a *duke?*" Big repeated incredulously. "Goldie, you're an *American,* and you've only been here in England for nine days! What do you know about the English nobility? How can you possibly make some commoner into this . . . this Royal Lordship Duke Tremayne, or whatever the hell it is he's called! You've never even *seen* the fellow!"

Goldie looked at the tiny man and smiled. Big Mann was her very best friend and a midget. And it was in that order that she saw him. His real name was Beauregard Irwin Grover Mann, but ever since she'd noticed his initials spelled "Big," that's what she'd called him. She slid her hand across his whisker-studded cheek, then spooned more oat mush into her toothless nag's mouth. "You like this, don't you, Dammit?" she asked the old horse, watching him gum it.

Big stomped his foot. "Did you hear me, Goldie Mae?"

"I heard you, Big. Great day Miss Agnes, folks back in America probably heard you. Y'know, when you scream like that, you remind me of Elvin Moots back in Green As a Gourd, Virginia. Uncle Asa and I lived in Green As a Gourd about two years before we met you. Anyway, Elvin Moots never talked soft, but only yelled. One day he opened his mouth to scream, and no sound came out at all. I'll swannee, not even as much as a low murmur, Big, and I'm not makin' that up. Daddy's honor. He—"

She broke off and cocked her head. "Did I ever tell you why I say 'Daddy's honor'? Most folks swear on the Bible,

1

but see, my daddy—God rest his soul—was the most honest man in the world. So when I say 'Daddy's honor' it's the same as swearin' what I say to be the Gospel truth. I *never* lie against Daddy's honor, Big.''

"Goldie, I've been with you for four years. Don't you think that's time enough for me to learn why you say 'Daddy's honor'? Besides, we're discussing the *duke.*''

"No, we're discussin' Elvin Moots," she corrected him, still spooning mush between Dammit's smacking lips. "Leonie Bradshaw said he'd busted up his throat from so many years of hollerin'. He was the preacher, y'see, and loved the sound of his own voice. Sundays came, and we all brought dinner and supper with us to church. Nobody thought it'd be proper to faint from hunger in the Lord's house. Reverend Elvin Moots didn't mind us eatin' durin' the sermons, but heaven help the poor soul who went to sleep.

"Anyhow, after he lost his voice, we didn't go to church anymore because there wasn't a minister. Duncan Gilmore tried preachin' for a while, but nobody in town trusted a man who wore a skirt and went around with naked knees. He said he was Scottish and that his skirt was part of his heritage, but folks didn't believe that for one minute.''

She looked at Big from the corner of her eye. "So you better watch that screamin', Big, or you'll turn into another Elvin Moots.''

She picked up the tin bucket, slid the handle into the crook of her elbow, and proceeded down the meandering path that led to her newest home, an ancient stone cottage. "Uncle Asa and I left Green As a Gourd soon after that," she continued as Big trailed along behind her. "Myra Carney caught Uncle Asa tryin' to steal her corset right off the clothesline. See, Uncle Asa had had too much to drink, and when he saw the corset he wondered if it would make him look thinner. He didn't mean any harm.''

She stopped for a moment to examine a spiderweb floating from a wooden post. A small moth was caught inside it. With a gentle touch, she freed it. "Anyway, we packed up and left that night because the townsfolk said they were gonna string him up for what he did to Myra Carney. It near about did her in to look out her window and see a man wearin' her corset. Doc Burpy had to stay with her all afternoon. But I'll tell you the truth, Big—I think Myra Carney and Doc Burpy were more than just doctor and patient, and that the only reason he stayed at her house for so long was because they were lovin' up on each other.

"Uncle Asa and I went to Tennessee after that. Little town called Pickinsville. I liked it there. Thought maybe we'd finally found somewhere we could send down some roots, y'know, Big? But we didn't fit in there either. Hadn't been there even a month when Uncle Asa got drunk and proposed to Hank Cooper's wife, Nellie. I don't think Hank would've run us out of town if Nellie hadn't accepted Uncle Asa's proposal. After Pickinsville . . . well, you know the story. I've been everywhere."

She arrived at the cracked wooden door of the dilapidated cottage. After setting down her bucket, she picked a handful of bright yellow dandelions, caressed her chin with them, and looked out at the green hills around her. "And now here I am in the royal country of England. I know we've only been here for nine days, Big, but I *am* part English, y'know. On Daddy's side. I feel bad that Uncle Asa's runnin' from just about every lawman in America is what brought us over here, but I'm glad we're here. And I'm glad you came with us, Big. And I'm glad—"

"Goldie, I'm glad you're so glad about everything, but about making a duke . . . You—"

"And just think, Big! This cottage belonged to my great-aunt Della Mae! I forgot to tell you that a few days ago I found her diaries hidden up in the ceilin' rafters. I was cleanin' down spiderwebs, and they were right there in a burlap sack. A lot of 'em have gotten wet from rain seepin' through the roof, and you can hardly read 'em. But some are all right. Anyway, I read a few of 'em, and Aunt Della wrote that she was born right here in this cottage. Imagine how nice that would be, stayin' in one place for your whole life. I bet the roots Aunt Della sent down here go clear through the earth and out the other side. She must have fit in here real good. I can't believe she died only a month ago. I . . . I never even got to meet her. If only we'd gotten here sooner."

Big watched her eyes mist and waited before continuing. He knew her tears would be gone soon, for she never allowed herself to cry for long. Just as he suspected, she was smiling in the next moment. "Goldie—"

"England." The word came from Goldie on a long, contented sigh. "Wonder when I'll get to visit Queen Victoria? Wonder if anyone ever calls her *Vicky?* I bet you a trillion dollars that's her nickname. Mildred Fickle back in Sparrow Nest, South Carolina, made it her business to know everything there is to know about royalty, and she said Queen Vicky has a special crown for everything she does. An eatin' crown, a walkin' crown . . . she even has a soft crown to wear to bed. I'll swannee, I bet the poor woman spends half the day tryin' to remember which crown she's supposed to wear."

Big kicked a rock across the yard and stuffed his hands into his pockets. "Goldie, I don't know a thing about Queen *Vicky* or England. Neither did Mildred Fickle, and neither do you. This idea of yours about making a duke out of a commoner is the craziest thing I've heard in my entire life."

"But it's the only solution to the problem." She sank to the dirt, her gaze directed at the horizon.

Big squatted beside her and noticed she wouldn't look at him. His suspicions grew. "Well, would you mind telling me *what* the problem is, and *why* this plan of yours is the only solution? I've been trying to drag the information out of you for a half an hour already."

Her gaze moved from the horizon to a nearby shrub. "I wonder what kind of bush that is, Big? We don't have that kind in America."

Big's eyes narrowed. "Goldie, you're hedging, and—"

She laughed. "Oh, Big, how funny! I saw that shrub, wondered what kind of bush it was, and then you said I was *hedgin'*. Did you mean to make a joke, or was it just one of those lucky things?"

Big won the battle not to smile. He knew if Goldie saw him grin, she'd feel less pressured to tell him about her outrageous plan. He realized also that whatever that scheme was, he wasn't going to like it. Otherwise, Goldie would have told it to him from beginning to end. "Goldie," he said, forcing a note of warning into his voice, "I'm waiting."

She finally looked at him, blinking several times and wondering how to explain things to him. "I—Well, y'see, Big . . . last night, Uncle Asa drank too much at the—"

"I knew it! I knew Asa was somehow connected with this wild idea you've come up with! He's done it again, hasn't he, Goldie? Done something that has made the villagers hate him, and now these people are taking it out on *you!* It's always been that way! *He* makes the trouble, and *you* pay for it! He—"

"Big, settle down. I haven't even explained—"

"Well, you're taking so long to do it, I'm already imagining the rest!"

Slowly, she swirled her finger in the soft dirt by her feet. "All right. Uncle Asa drank too much at the village saloon—I mean *pub*. Did y'know that's what these English villagers call their saloon?"

Big laid his forehead on his bent knees and prayed for patience. "No, I didn't know that. If I promise never to forget it, will you *please* tell me your reasons for needing this Royal Tremayne fellow?"

She realized she'd just have to come out with it. "Well, Uncle Asa got fallin'-down drunk last night, and some of the men threw him out of the pub. Uncle Asa worked himself into a snortin' rage and told 'em a pack of lies."

Big raised his head and stiffened. "Such as?"

She fiddled with a gold ringlet before answering. "He told the men that when we first got here to England, we went to London and met Duke Tremayne himself, and that we introduced ourselves as Della Mae's family from America. He said that when the duke learned who we were, he entertained us in his town house for a few days and promised us his assistance if we ever need it."

"Lord," Big whispered.

Goldie picked up another yellow curl, watching it twist around her finger as if by its own volition. "Then Uncle Asa swore to the men that he was gonna tell the duke about the way he was bein' treated here in Hallensham, and added that it wouldn't surprise him a bit if the duke came and demanded the villagers treat us with more respect. He even said the duke was sweet on me, and that if anyone could get him to come back, I could. Great day, Miss Agnes, imagine a duke bein' sweet on *me!*''

"Oh, Lord."

Goldie nodded and watched her piglet, Runt, come waddling toward her. Tenderly, she scratched his pink hairy ears, smiling when he grunted with contentment. "Uncle Asa's lies wouldn't have been so bad if the men hadn't halfway believed 'em. But they *did.*"

Big closed his eyes, dread skidding down his spine. "And why did they halfway believe him?"

"Well, y'see, Aunt Della used to be the cook at that Ravenhurst mansion there."

She paused, her gaze sweeping up the grassy hill and settling on the awesome manor house. Though she'd stared at it almost continuously since arriving in Hallensham, it was so grand that it still made her breath catch in her throat each time she studied it.

It was the biggest, most beautiful place she'd ever seen, a castle in her eyes, a home fit for royalty. It even had towers, and she wondered if any princesses in distress had ever waited inside them for rescuing knights on white chargers. She let out a small sigh.

"Goldie?"

She looked blankly at Big. "Uh . . . Yeah. That mansion up there belongs to Duke Tremayne, and he's called the Duke of Ravenhurst. I read that in Aunt Della's diaries. And accordin' to Aunt Della, she used to spoil the puddin' out of him when he was a little boy. She loved him, and he loved her. I made the huge mistake of readin' that part of her diaries to Uncle Asa. He remembered it, and that's why he told the villagers what he told 'em. That's why they gave him the benefit of the doubt, too. Seems folks around here remember how close the duke and Aunt Della used to be, and since Uncle Asa went on about how hospitable the duke was when he learned we were related to Della Mae, the lies made some sense to the men."

"Lord, Lord," Big repeated, shaking his head in his hands.

Goldie fed a few dandelion leaves to Runt and tossed the rest of the flowers into the breeze, watching it scatter them around the yard. "So now the villagers think Uncle Asa and I know the duke personally, and they want us to get him to come here to Hallensham. And they threatened to run Uncle Asa out of town if they find out he was lyin'. Said they didn't want any dishonest, drunken troublemakers in their peaceful village. And y'know if Uncle Asa goes, I go too. I—He—I know he's gruff sometimes, Big, but only when he's drunk."

"Which is most of the time," Big muttered, dislike for Asa thickening his voice.

Goldie bent her head and struggled to forget hurtful memories. "He paid your way to come over here with us."

"With money he stole!"

"Big, he's the only real family I've got. I know he's not a saint, but—He—I love him."

Realizing her distress, Big tried to calm himself. "I know you do, and such love is rare, Goldie Mae," he said, taking her hand. "Now, back to Aunt Della and Royal Tremayne, if you please. Tell me—"

"Shhh!" she hushed him when she saw a dark-haired, buxom girl approaching, her round hips swaying. "It's Dora Mashburn."

"Lord, I hate that girl," Big whispered, frowning. "She's been mean to you ever since we got here, and I—"

"G' mornin', Goldie," Dora said, ignoring Big. "Wot are ya still doin' in Hallensham? The whole village is talkin' about how yer uncle said yer goin' ter bring back Lord Tremayne. Why ain't ya already left ter get him?"

Goldie bristled at the gleam of animosity in Dora's eyes and the patronizing tone of her voice. "Mornin', Dora," she said, and didn't bother to comment on the rest of what the girl had said.

Dora smiled. "Some's sayin' they're sure ya can bring back the duke, and they're already plannin' a village festival fer when he arrives. Others only *hope* ye'll bring him back. The rest o' us are positive yer Uncle Asa be lyin'. Lord Tremayne's been gone fer twenty years, an' he ain't never comin' back here, I vow. Asa Mae ain't nothin' but a bleedin' drunk, an' the two o' ya should go back ter where ya came from. An' take *him* with ya,'' she added, glaring at Big. "Midgets, drunks, an' sluts ain't welcome here in Hallensham, an' I told Mr. Hutchins that this mornin', I did. I told him all about how yer uncle says yer goin' ter bring back His Lordship. Him bein' the estate manager an' all, it's his business ter know.''

"Pay her no mind, Goldie,'' Big said. "She wants you out of Hallensham because she's jealous.''

"Jealous!'' Dora exploded. "I'm not—''

"Yes, you are,'' Big argued. "You're jealous that Goldie knows the duke, and you don't. It infuriates you that Goldie's going to be Hallensham's heroine. You can't sleep at night for thinking about the statue the villagers will probably erect in her honor,'' he gushed, too angry to stop himself from elaborating on all the lies. "You've had it in for her ever since that Hutchins fellow started watching her, and that's why you call her a slut. You're sweet on the man yourself, and when you saw him staring at Goldie, it almost killed you!''

"Big,'' Goldie said, "Mr. Hutchins is not sweet on me.''

"He bloody well ain't!'' Dora agreed shrilly.

"Goldie, never you mind this screeching shrew,'' Big cooed, and patted Goldie's hand. "When you bring Mr. Ravenhurst back, she'll—''

"Why, ya bloody little bugger!'' Dora screamed. "I'll have ya know that the duke is me friend from way back! I used ter play with him! Once he even gave me half his apple, he did!''

Big laughed. "Then give up, Goldie,'' he said merrily. "Dora here ate half the duke's apple twenty years ago. So since she has more of a claim on him than you do, let *her* get him back!''

Dora shuddered with anger and glared at Goldie. "I almost choked when I heard it said Lord Tremayne's got eyes fer ya! Wot would His Grace see in ya? Ya don't even come up ter me shoulder, an' wot with yer chest bein' as flat as it is . . . ya look like a *child!* There's nothin' about ya ter attract a man's eye, there ain't. An' the only reason why Mr. Hutchins stares at ya is because he ain't never seen an uglier girl!''

Big watched Goldie flinch and bring her knees up to cover her breasts. "Goldie's perfect in stature!" he roared, more for Goldie's sake than Dora's. "She—"

"Well, o' course ya'd say that," Dora interjected. "Yer a *dwarf!* Ye'll be gone soon, I vow, Goldie Mae," she warned spitefully. "Yer uncle's already bein' watched real careful, he is at that. Aside from bein' a drunk, the man's a thief. He stole Miz Crawton's pie from her window, an'—"

"I made her another!" Goldie reminded her.

"Ten times better than the one Mrs. Crawton made in the first place!" Big added vehemently.

Dora smirked. "An' nobody's fergittin' the way the friggin' sop staggered inter that freshly plowed field the other day neither! Dancin' an' fallin' all over . . . He made such a bleedin' mess o' things, the men had ter plow all over again! Lost a day's wages, they did, an' all because o' yer stinkin' uncle! When the duke don't come, he'll be tossed out o' Hallensham on his bloomin' arse!"

With that, Dora turned and began to walk away.

Big stood and shook his fist at her. "Oh, yeah?" he called loudly. "Well, when Goldie brings back His Dukeship, we'll just see who has the last laugh, you . . . you—"

"Great day Miss Agnes, Big, calm down," Goldie admonished. "Dora doesn't bother me," she lied.

Big looked at her, not missing the glint of hurt in her golden eyes. "I can't help it, Goldie. It's the same old story, over and over again. Asa finds trouble; you suffer for it. When is the man going to straighten himself out, for God's sake? And the way he screams at you all the time! The things he says to you! It makes me furious. He—"

"Big—"

"Look, Goldie," he huffed impatiently, "I just told Dora you'd be Hallensham's heroine. Now I want to know just how the hell that outrageous prediction will come about. Tell me the whole story about this Duke Ravenhurst."

She took heart over his growing willingness to understand and gave him her most brilliant smile. "All right. Aunt Della's diaries say this duke is the landlord here. All

that land out there? What you can see and even further
than that? Well, he owns all of it. Owns all those farms
too. But he hasn't been back since his parents died when
he was ten. His daddy was killed in a huntin' accident,
and his mama just sorta wasted away after that. So his two
aunts came and took him to London. But before he left,
he sobbed in Aunt Della's lap and told her he'd never come
back here because the memories would make him too sad.
He wanted her to go with him, but she said she just
couldn't leave her home. That was twenty years ago.''

Big felt impatience rise again when she paused for a
moment to rub her baby pig's back. ''Runt, go away!'' he
snapped.

Goldie continued to stroke Runt and went on with her
story. ''About five years ago the duke got engaged to some
girl named Angelica Sheridan. Aunt Della wrote that this
Angelica came here one day. Duke Ravenhurst didn't come
with her, but she had one of those lady companions that
rich folks always have. Aunt Della said the lady was old
and slept all the time. Angelica told everyone here that she
was gonna be the duke's bride, and that he'd consented to
make Ravenhurst their home. Aunt Della wrote that he
must have really loved Angelica to agree to that. Aunt
Della and the villagers were so excited about seein' their
duke again. Anyway, Angelica stayed on here for a while.
Things were kinda run-down, just like they are now, so
she decided to fix up some stuff. She started plantin' a
huge rose garden. Aunt Della wrote that the garden was
gonna be a surprise weddin' present for the duke. Since
he hadn't seen this place for so long, Angelica wanted it
to look real nice for him.''

Big saw her eyes fill again. ''What's so sad about a
surprise rose garden?''

She gathered her piglet in her arms and held him as if
he were a baby. ''Well, Big,'' she sniffled, ''on the very
day Angelica finished plantin' the roses, she fell down the
big staircase inside that mansion and died. She broke her
neck. That lady friend of hers took her body back to London. I reckon the duke buried her there. That was five
years ago, and Aunt Della wrote that all those roses Angelica planted up there have never bloomed. Not a damn

one of 'em. Aunt Della believed the roses won't bloom until the duke falls in love again. Oh, Big, isn't that the saddest story you've ever heard? The poor roses. Poor Angelica. The poor, poor duke.''

Big watched her tears spill down her freckled cheeks and onto Runt's belly. He thought her own plight was a lot sadder than the duke's. "Goldie, the man's obviously wallowing in money and most likely leads a glittering, carefree life in London. He probably has other estates and no need whatsoever to come back to Ravenhurst. And he's probably already replaced Angelica Sheridan with another English beauty. A man like that certainly doesn't need anyone's pity, and yet here you are feeling sorry for him.''

"But he loved her, Big. Then he lost her.''

Big tried to find some sympathy for the man, failed, and realized he would have to feign it if he was to get any more information out of Goldie. "The poor man. The poor, devastated man. Lord have mercy on the poor, poor man. All right, we've mourned over his sorrows. Now can we continue unraveling this mystery you keep tying into knots?''

Goldie set Runt back on the ground and dried the last of her tears on her apron. "Well, from what I understand, Big, these villagers miss havin' their duke. Aunt Della wrote that there's been a Ravenhurst duke livin' up there in that duke mansion for some five hundred years. Now the only one up there is that Dane Hutchins. That estate manager fella. He's not the duke, so—''

"Well, judging by the way he struts around here, you'd think he was,'' Big commented. "You should have seen him yelling at some of the farmers the other day, Goldie. He had them scared to death of him, and he thought their terror was funny! And I have to tell you, Goldie, I don't like the way he watches you.''

She waved away his words. "Oh, Big, he stares at everybody. Maybe that's what an estate manager is supposed to do. We've never seen one, so we really don't know how they act. But the fact remains that there's no duke up in that mansion. It kinda breaks up the tradition, I reckon, and Mildred Fickle said that traditions are sorta like the Ten Commandments to the English.''

She stared at the huge, rambling manor house again, remembering snatches of what she'd read in Della's diaries. "Everybody doted on the duke when he was little. See that tree house in that tree over yonder? It was his. The village men built it for him. I'm gonna climb into it one of these days. Anyway, Big, I guess havin' the duke back would mean the world to these folks."

"But Goldie, you don't know the man! How can you—"

"I told you I'm gonna find someone who looks like him, and make him into a duke."

Big tried to subdue his rising vexation and worry. "Goldie," he said, his voice deceptively calm, "this is never going to work."

She lifted her face to the sky and closed her eyes for a moment. The sunshine heated her cheeks and her determination. "I gotta try though, Big. It's like that expression, 'I'm damned if I do, and I'm damned if I don't.' If I *don't* try, Uncle Asa's gonna get run out of Hallensham. And if I *do* try and get caught, we're still gonna get run out. So why not try? Y'know I've been movin' around with Uncle Asa ever since Mama and Daddy died. Big, I'm just plain weary of it. I want to *belong* someplace. This is such a purty little village, and I *am* part English, so it's right for me to be here. And Big, if I *do* get away with my plan and convince the villagers that the duke is our friend, we won't ever get sent away. We'll have found a place where we can fit in and be happy for the rest of our days."

Big almost choked on the compassion he felt for her. *A place where we can fit in.* He wondered if that would ever happen for her. "Goldie," he whispered, his throat strangled with emotion, "I—"

He broke off at the sound of hoofbeats. Looking up, he saw Dane Hutchins cantering toward them upon a fine horse. "My, but we're having some grand company this morning, aren't we?" he asked sarcastically. "Here comes God."

"Miss Mae," Dane greeted her as he reined in his horse.

Big stared up at the overweight man. "What the hell do you want, Hutchins?"

Dane kept his gaze on Goldie. "Inform your uncle I am here."

"You got an appointment?" she asked, shielding her eyes from the glare of the sun as she peered up at him. "I heard English folks *always* make appointments before comin' to visit. Y'see, I had this friend named Mildred Fickle. Mildred knew everything about—"

"Cease!" Dane thundered.

"Now wait just a damn blasted minute!" Big responded. "Don't you talk to Goldie that way! You—"

"We don't say *cease* in America," Goldie decided to tell Dane. "Well, maybe some folks do, but most of us just say *shut up.* 'Course, even if you told me to shut up, I wouldn't. I'd shut up if I knew I was bein' ugly to you, but I haven't said anything to have to shut up over, so—"

"Where is your uncle?" Dane asked, his tone suddenly much less strident. He reached up to his snowy neckcloth, touching the glittering stickpin there, then smiled at Goldie.

Big scowled. The man was strange—angry one second, and sweetness itself the next. "Asa is sleeping, if it's any of your business. Now what do you want?"

Dane ignored Big altogether. "Your uncle's behavior in the pub last night has come to my attention, my sweet. There are people here who are not inclined to accept the three of you among them."

"You're not real popular around here either," Goldie dared to inform him. "And I'm not your sweet anything."

At the slight stir of the breeze, Dane hurried to smooth his hair. "Is my hair mussed?" he asked worriedly.

Big and Goldie frowned at each other, neither of them answering, then looked back up at Dane.

"Why are you staring at me like that?" he asked. "Is there something wrong with me?" He brushed at his coat sleeves and gave his hair another pat. "Do you have any idea *who* I am?"

"Do you have any idea how little we care?" Big countered, his question making Goldie giggle.

"I have the power to make you care very much," Dane answered coolly, fondling his stickpin again.

"Look, Mr. Hutchins, we know you're the estate boss," Goldie said. "You live in the duke house, dress in fancy clothes, ride that fine horse . . . but you're *not* the duke, y'know, and we don't have to treat you like you are."

"Do not ever say that to me again."

Goldie stared at the fat, middle-aged man. She decided he had mean eyes and a cruel mouth. His extreme calmness made her feel slightly nervous.

"It has come to my attention," Dane said, licking his bottom lip, "that you are going to attempt to bring back Lord Tremayne. Is there any truth to this, my sweet?"

"She's not your sweet!" Big exploded. "And you—"

"Answer me," Dane commanded Goldie.

"Yeah, I'm bringin' him back."

Another gust of wind swept through the yard, causing Dane to glower. "I must return to the house. I don't like wind. I don't like dust either."

"Why do you live in the duke's house?" Big asked.

Dane turned and looked at the mansion in the distance. "I wish the roses would bloom."

Goldie cocked her head to her shoulder. "You'll have to get out of that house when I bring back the duke. He won't let you stay in it."

Dane looked back down at her. "When do you leave for London?"

Goldie stared at his smile again. It made her feel as though ants were crawling on her. "In about two weeks."

Dane smoothed his hair once more. "Indeed," he drawled. "Then we will all have to wait and see what happens, shan't we? Good day." He pulled on the reins and sent his horse galloping down the dirt road.

"Great day Miss Agnes," Goldie murmured, fanning dust away from her face. "That's the strangest man I believe I've ever met."

Big looked at her and smoothed an unruly flaxen curl back from her face. "Goldie, forget about His Highness Hutchins. Tell me the plan from beginning to end with no more interruptions."

She heard the quiet resignation in his voice, and decided

to take full advantage of it. "I was up almost all night thinkin' it over," she assured him excitedly. "It's purty obvious that this Lord Duke Tremayne Ravenhurst fella's never gonna come back here. And I can understand his reasons. His daddy, mama, and sweetheart all died here, Big. The place would only remind him of those tragedies. That and the fact that he hasn't been here in twenty years . . . why would he up and come back now? So what I'll do is have *my* duke come for just a few hours or so. He'll talk to the villagers, and then explain that he has to get back to London. It won't be *my* fault that he can't stay. I'll have done exactly what folks want Uncle Asa and me to do by gettin' him here."

With a sigh, Big sat back down, leaning against the stone wall of the cottage. "But Goldie, you don't know what the man looks like. I realize these people haven't seen this Ravenhurst duke in years, but they'll expect to see some kind of resemblance between *your* duke and the real duke's parents."

She tossed her bright hair off her shoulders, rose, and ambled around the small yard, kicking pebbles, picking leaves, and taking deep breaths of the fresh air. "Late last night, I snuck into that big ole mansion up there," she admitted, staring at the wonderful castle-like estate again. "I crawled right through the window, and—"

"Good Lord, what if that Hutchins bastard had caught you?"

She bent to examine a rotten log. "He wasn't there. I saw him leave with my own eyes. Dora was gone, too. Did y'know she's all the time up there? Maybe she's his servant. Besides, Big, I didn't go in to steal or anything like that. I just went to see if there were any family paintin's linin' the walls. Rich people do that, y'know. Mildred Fickle said so. Big, in one closed-up room there were dozens of paintin's. Dane must've taken 'em down and stashed 'em in there. All the portraits had little brass plaques under 'em that told who the paintin's were of. The duke's mama and daddy were there, and so was he. His name is Marion Tremayne. His middle initials are W. S., but I don't know what they stand for."

She strolled back to where Big sat. "You ever heard of

a man bein' named Marion, Big? Wonder what his mama was thinkin' when she named him that? I reckon maybe she wanted a daughter so bad, she gave her son a girl name. Poor Duke Marion. Poor, poor Duke Marion.''

"Goldie, Marion is a boy's name too."

She stuck a leaf stem in her mouth and chewed on it, grimacing at its bitter flavor. "Sounds like a girl's name to me. Anyhow, little Marion was only about three years old when his paintin' was done, but after starin' at his parents' paintin's along with his, I think I've figured out what he looks like now. He's gotta be over six feet tall because both his mama and his daddy looked tall. His hair is black and wavy, he's got a strong jaw, high cheekbones, and a long straight nose. I couldn't tell too much about his mouth because it was sorta pinched up. Looked like he was antsy about havin' to stand there and get painted. And I wasn't sure about the color of his eyes either because he was wearin' a hat that shaded 'em. His mama had blue eyes, his daddy brown ones, so I was gonna take my chances and do eenie meenie miney mo.''

She smiled at the look of dismay in Big's eyes and turned to walk back out into the yard again, her hands clasped behind her back. When she'd traveled a few yards, she spun around quickly. "But lo and behold, Big, Aunt Della's diaries say the duke's eyes are green! They're probably a throwback or somethin' to one of his kin. That or his mama was messin' around with some green-eyed milkman. Mildred Fickle says rich people *always* have lovers. That must be another one of those English customs. And I think Duke Marion's real strong too, Big, because his daddy was all muscle if that paintin' was tellin' the truth. Muscles *are* inherited, aren't they?''

Big stared into her tawny eyes and shook his head in exasperation. "And what are you going to do about fancy clothes, a carriage, and horses? You can't dress your duke in tattered clothing, and you can't have him saunter into the village with dust all over his boots. He has to dress—"

"I'm gonna borrow some clothes that are already up there in his duke house. I found some in a closet in one of those upstairs bedrooms. It was a real dusty bedroom, so I'm sure the clothes have been there a long time, and they don't belong to Mr. Hutchins.''

"If they've been there that long, they'll be outdated," Big pointed out.

She stared at him for a long time. "Why do you have to make so many problems, Big?"

"*Me?*" he asked in utter disbelief.

She continued to stare at him, her mind at work on the point he'd brought up. "Hell, Big, beautiful clothes never get outdated," she decided out loud. "They stay in fashion forever. Everybody knows that. And great day Miss Agnes, you've never seen the kind of clothes up there in that house! I was so excited I almost set 'em on fire when I dropped my candle! Satins and silks, and some even had gold buttons! Fancier'n anything I ever saw Amos Hicks back in Shakin' Pines, Georgia, wear. He—"

"Goldie, you are off of the subject again. I asked you not to interrupt yourself anymore."

"Oh, all right, ill-box."

"And don't call me that. I'm not crabby, only impatient."

She walked back to him, dragging the toes of her shoes in the dirt behind her. When she reached him, she looked over her shoulder at the lines her dragging feet had made. "As far as gettin' a carriage and horses for the duke . . . I'm not that far in my plans yet."

"What?" Big asked, pretending astonishment. "You mean there are actually some *holes* in this grand scheme of yours?"

"Not many, and I'll fill them in later."

Big fashioned a steeple with his fingers and laid his chin upon it. "Hole number two, Goldie: how are you going to get this poor common man you find to *agree* to these wild plans?"

She patted his shiny bald head. "I've got about five pounds of money. Uncle Asa bought some stuff the other day, and he told me that people here pay for things in *pounds*. I reckon they have to weigh the money before they can pay for stuff with it. I don't know how in the world these English folks manage to carry more than, say . . . ten or twelve pounds around with 'em. Wonder what they do when somethin' costs over a hundred pounds? Y'know, Big, now that I think of it, that might be why the duke's daddy had so many muscles. A person would *have* to be strong to tote around so many pounds of money. Anyway, I have a whole pile of silver coins that I figure weighs about five pounds, and I'll offer my duke three pounds of 'em for doin' the job. I've been savin' all these years, and Uncle Asa doesn't know. Don't tell him.''

Nothing Big could think of would induce him to tell Asa Mae about her savings. The bastard would steal it from her and spend it all on drink. ''All right, Goldie, let's pretend your plan is foolproof. Just where do you propose to find your Marion W. S. Tremayne?''

''Well, at dawn tomorrow—''

''Tomorrow? You just told Hutchins it would be two weeks before—''

''I lied because he yelled at me.'' She tilted her chin up and folded her arms across her breasts. ''Y'know how I hate it when folks yell at me, Big. He deserved to be lied to. We're leavin' tomorrow mornin'. We'll just keep on travelin' till—''

''*We?*'' Big shouted, scrambling up from his seat on the ground. ''Goldie—''

''Big, you have to go with me. What if someone tries to get me while I'm on the road? They have lots of highwaymen here in England. Mildred Fickle told me all about 'em. Would you be able to sleep at night knowin' I was out there at the mercy of those dreaded English highwaymen? They wear these black capes and boots, ride black horses, and they carry these long, vicious swords! What if one gets me? What if—''

''All right, all right! But—''

''We'll have a weapon too, Big. Diaries aren't the only things Aunt Della kept. She's got her own sword in there, and I mean to tell you it's the biggest thing you ever saw. She wrote that it's a Scottish claymore. Belonged to somebody in her family. The thing's so big, I can't hardly lift it. But see, the size alone will scare any dreaded English highwaymen who try to get us. I'll just sorta let it hang off Dammit's saddle in a warnin' kinda way.''

"Thank you, Goldie. You've laid all my fears to rest."
Big shook his head again.

She nodded and tapped her chin with her finger. "I'll
leave a note to Uncle Asa tellin' him that we went to get
ole Marion. It's better that he doesn't know about my real
plans because of the kind of mouth he has when he's
drinkin'. I've gotta find the man somewhere far away from
here, y'see. I can't take the chance of pickin' some commoner that one of the villagers knows. When I find him,
I reckon I'll need about two months or so to teach him
duke stuff. Then I'll—"

"Which brings me to another question. How can you
give him duke lessons when you know nothing about the
English aristocracy?" Big sat back down and drummed
his fingers on his knee.

Goldie sighed at Big's picky questions. "Mildred Fickle
knew, and so did Aunt Della. There are all sorts of noble-
folk descriptions in her diaries. See, other dukish people
used to come visit the Tremaynes. Aunt Della wrote all
about 'em. 'Course, a lot of what she wrote is messed up
by those water stains I told you about, but I can guess at
what I can't read. Y'know what a good guesser I am, Big.
And Mildred Fickle said noble people sniff each bite of
food before they eat it. She said that custom probably came
from back when noble people were always gettin' poisoned by their enemies. Smellin' his food will be the first
thing I teach my duke. Yeah, food-sniffin' is high on the
list for duke requirements. And 'course we'll get glimpses
of *real* dukes when we get to London."

"London!" Big bolted to his feet again.

"Well, of course *London!*" She turned toward the fields
and held her arms open wide as if embracing the distant
city. "Big, we have lots of duke research to do! What
better place to do it? All those bluebloods congregate
there, and—Do you think their blood is really blue?"

Big was so exasperated he couldn't answer.

Goldie hugged herself, supremely proud of her grand
plan. "After we've learned all we can from our duke-spyin'
in London, we'll come back here. By that time I hope I'll
have figured out what to do about a fancy carriage and
horses to pull it. We'll—"

"Goldie!" Asa shouted from inside the cottage. "Where the hell are you, you worthless, good-for-nothin' twit! I want my damn dinner, and I don't see a blasted thing in here cookin'! Goldie!"

Big's heart lurched when he saw pain fill her eyes. "Goldie, don't you listen to him. You—"

"It's all right, Big," she squeaked, turning away so he wouldn't see her tears. "I gotta go. He's probably got him one of his day-after headaches, and y'know how frenzied he gets when he's feelin' low and hungry at the same time." She hurried to the door, but turned back to Big before she opened it.

"Big," she began, chewing her bottom lip. "I've got to find my common man just as fast as I can. There's just no tellin' what kinda trouble Uncle Asa'll get into while I'm gone. I'll have to get back to Hallensham as soon as I've got Duke Marion. Big . . . I could really use your help, but you never did say if you'd give it to me or not. I'm gonna go through with the plan no matter if you go with me or not, but—Big, will you help me?"

He gazed into Goldie's huge, amber eyes, and saw her hope spilling from them. "We'll find your Duke Ravenhurst, Goldie. If we have to scour all of England, we'll find him."

She let go of the doorknob and gave him an impulsive hug. "Now, now," Big said, embarrassed, "go get Asa's dinner or there'll be hell to pay."

She smiled and turned back to the door. "Oh, by the way, the new word for the day is *risible*. It means 'capable of laughing.' So if someone has a sense of humor, I reckon you could say he's *risible*." With that, she disappeared into the cottage.

Big sighed. Goldie loved learning new words, and found a new one every day in her precious dictionary. She made Big learn them too. It was rare when either one of them remembered to use the words, but that never deterred Goldie. "Risible," he muttered down to Runt, who was nipping his pant leg. "I wish I were *more* risible. It would make these wild plans she's dreamed up a whole lot easier to take."

He looked out at the countryside and thought about all she'd told him. "Duke lessons, Runt. *Food-sniffing* of all things! Lord have mercy, I don't know who to feel sorrier for—Goldie or her duke."

# Chapter 2

Saber cringed. The loud, grating noise of the curtains being jerked across their brass rods sounded like great shards of shattering glass crunching into his eardrums. Sharp swords of bright sunlight stabbed through his eyelids, blinding him. His head felt like a ripe melon that had just been smashed on the ground, and the more he concentrated on that thought, the more vivid it became in his mind.

"The weather's set fair, Saber. Perfect for traveling."

Saber didn't have to open his eyes or even recognize the voice to know who was speaking to him. Only Addison Gage would dare disturb him in such a rude fashion. "Addison, get out," he ordered, his voice muffled in his satin pillow.

Addison grinned and released the dark blue velvet drapes. He picked up a porcelain pitcher, and sauntered to the thickly carpeted dais upon which Saber's bed stood. Reaching for a corner of the downy blue coverlet, he yanked it off. "I say!" he exclaimed, chuckling. "Look at that! Lord Marion Westbrook Saberfield Tremayne, the wealthiest, most powerful, most envied, most sought-after bachelor in all of England. There he lies in all his naked, noble, and *painful* splendor. Could it be that you had a night that wasn't at all the thing?"

"Get out," Saber repeated, searching without success for his covers.

Smiling, Addison raised the pitcher of cold water. With one swift motion he emptied it upon Saber's bare flesh.

"What the—" Saber bolted out of the bed, water streaming from his hair and into his eyes. He shuddered both with anger and cold. "Addison, I swear—"

22

"It's one o'clock, Saber, and you're yet lying in. You're supposed to be dressed and prepared to depart. The boys will be here straightaway, and I fear they will not show the same benevolence I have. They'll drag you naked and screaming into the coach. Unless you've the irresistible desire for all of London to witness such a spectacle, I'd suggest you show a leg and put yourself right."

Saber struggled to understand what his friend was talking about, but the only thing he could comprehend was that every nerve in his body was throbbing with a dull and constant pain only more sleep could alleviate. "Addison, you are a thundering nuisance. If this is your idea of a lark, I must warn you it is most assuredly not mine. I'll give you five seconds to remove your obnoxious person from my room. Go a second over that time, and I'll—"

"Tsk, tsk. My, how you do take on. You've obviously forgotten that you are under *my* command now. Mine and the boys'. Beginning at noon today—which was an hour ago—you are to be our slave for two weeks. We'll be spending those fourteen delightful days at Leighwood. And that, Saber, my friend, is the top and bottom of it."

Saber yanked his robe on and frowned. Leighwood was one of his four country estates, the others being Ravenhurst, Wellsbourne, and Mellenshire. Two weeks at Leighwood with Addison, Winston, Kenneth, and David, the rowdiest bunch of noble jokers in all of England? He couldn't think of a more irritating way to spend a fortnight.

Massaging his temples, he sat on the bed, the slight bend of the mattress reminding him of a vessel on a storm-tossed sea. He wished he could bury himself in the sheets again, but was now wide awake, his mind already working on what he had planned for the day. "Addison, I have no idea what you're talking about, I've no intention of going to Leighwood, and as far as my being your slave . . . I cannot remember the last time I heard anything as ludicrous. Aside from that, I cannot leave London now. I've a meeting with several people concerning an investment in—"

"I'm afraid you'll be forced to give it a miss, old boy," Addison said, patting his blond hair. "Really, Saber, you've got so much money now that you couldn't spend it all in three lifetimes. But if it's an even grander fortune you want, why not let others earn it for you? Making it yourself is rather like keeping a dog and barking yourself, is it not? And it's so unseemly for a gentleman of your status to work.''

Saber narrowed his eyes. ''I know of no one in this entire country who would so much as *whisper* an insult concerning anything I choose to do. No one, Addison, except you. And I don't make my investments to earn money. I do it to keep boredom at bay, and I don't consider it *work*. Unlike you, I find little diversion in attending endless and monotonous Society assemblies.''

''Saber, my friend, you've forgotten what real diversion is. You've been hiding behind that stuffy facade of yours for five years. Hence, it's been five years since I've heard you laugh, five years since—''

''Get out.''

''I see I must refresh your memory about who is giving the orders now.'' Addison swiped at a speck of dust on his coat sleeve and proceeded to a small table, upon which two cups sat, one filled with his tea, the other containing black coffee for Saber. After taking a sip, he brushed at his sleeve again, set the cup down, and burst into loud laughter. ''God, this is rich! You, the Duke of Ravenhurst, slave for two weeks!''

''Addison—''

''Last night at Winston's—You *do* remember supping there with us, do you not?''

Saber snatched his sheet from the floor and dried his face with it. He strode to a huge, glit-framed mirror and grimaced at his reflection. Black strings of his hair were plastered to his forehead and cheeks. His green eyes were bloodshot. He closed them against the sting for a moment, then turned and faced Addison again. ''I remember arriving and eating. Judging by that telltale twinkle in your eyes, I imagine much more went on as the evening progressed, but I cannot fathom the final outcome.''

''We were all in our cups, Saber. *You* were deeper in yours than the rest of us. You were fairly drowning in it, actually. And since you rarely indulge, it didn't take much to get you completely sodden. You cannot imagine the good it did me to see you in such a state. It was positively topping to see you without your starched shirt on.''

"Why do I have the feeling that it did *me* no good at all?" Saber asked suspiciously.

"Well, you were itching for a bet and said you didn't care what it entailed. Good friends that we are, we thought one up and bet you couldn't make Winston's Uncle Horatio laugh. You accepted the challenge and—''

"I bet no such thing. There's no one in the entire world who can make that cantankerous man *smile*, much less laugh. I did not bet—''

"Ah, but you *did.* You said you'd make him laugh. The wager was that if you did, the boys and I would be your willing slaves at Leighwood for two weeks. If you lost, *you'd* be the slave. You were deliriously excited about the prospect at having the four of us at your beck and call, but to be perfectly honest, Saber, we knew you'd lose. It was almost four o'clock in the morning when you stumbled up the stairs and staggered to Lord Alders' bedroom. Once you were hovering over his bed your candle wavered, and you dropped hot wax on his very tender . . . very bare backside. He sleeps in the buff. A fact you revealed to us all last night.''

Saber's eyes widened in disbelief. "Addison, tell me you're making this up, and that it's only another one of your annoying pranks.''

It was a moment before Addison could stop laughing. "It's the t-t-truth!' he sputtered merrily. "And while Lord Alders was busy peeling the wax off himself, you stood there and told him stupid jokes. He was, needless to say, far from amused. And people who are not amused do not laugh. You therefore lost the bet quite completely. Now get ready, slave. We're off to Leighwood. You obviously like working, so it is work you will do. As much as we can possibly wrench out of you.''

Saber closed his eyes again, willing memories of the previous night to come to him. None did. "Were there any witnesses to this outrageous bet?''

"Is Lord Alders himself good enough for you? If not, Lady Alders was there too. You woke up the entire household as a matter of fact.''

"God," Saber groaned. He picked up his coffee, didn't notice the steam rising from the dark brew, and promptly burned his mouth. Deeply aggravated, he stared at Addison, who was in the throes of more hysterical laughter. "You and the boys planned this, didn't you? The four of you are forever badgering me to go to the countryside with you, and now you've finally—"

"It was an honest bet, and you gave your word to keep your end of it, Saber. I've known you to do a lot of things during our many years together, but I've never known you to break an oath."

"Then let it be recorded that I'm breaking this one."

"You'll regret it."

"I sincerely doubt that."

Addison smiled. "Refusing to go to Leighwood or disobeying us while there will cost you dearly. You'll be obliged to escort your Aunt Lucy and Aunt Clara to Paris, not to mention whichever friends they decide to invite along for the trip. I've already discussed it with the aunties, and they're praying you won't honor the bet you made with the boys and me. You know how long they've been wanting to see Paris again. And since they're unable to travel by themselves anymore, they're quite anxious for you to take them."

Saber curled his hands into fists, realizing he was thoroughly trapped. Backing out of the bet with Addison and the boys was one thing, but disappointing his Aunt Lucy and Aunt Clara was quite another. He couldn't do that. It would hurt them terribly.

However, escorting a bevy of elderly ladies to Paris was about the worst thing he could think of himself doing. He loved his two aunts dearly, but they and their friends had a way of driving him to distraction. Being a slave for two weeks at Leighwood was definitely the lesser of the two evils. "You and the lads have tricked me into some outlandish wagers during the years, Addison, but this one—"

"Is by far the best," Addison finished for him. "Better even than the time you lost a bet and had to escort Prudence Weatherby to the Marlborough ball."

Saber groaned again, remembering that not only was Prudence Weatherby the homeliest girl in all of London, but she also had some sort of deformity in her nose that caused her to snort like a sow. The Marlborough ball had been one of the longest, most irritating nights of his life.

At the look of revulsion on Saber's face, Addison grinned and strolled to the door. "Give over, Saber. You've well and truly lost. And if you could possibly see your situation in a more positive light, you would be thanking the boys and me for all we've done and still plan to do. You need to be ruffled on occasion. Your life is boring and uneventful, and a trip out of London is just the thing for you. I cannot remember the last time you joined us for a holiday in the country. The only times you ever go are when you slip away for those passion-filled trysts with the Frost Queen. And don't try sending word to her of your whereabouts for the next two weeks, Saber. Jillian's not invited. If she dares to show up, I will personally—"

Saber set down his cup, the loud rattle cutting off Addison. "I was under the impression that Leighwood belongs to *me*. Are you saying I am forbidden to invite—"

"Exactly. The agreement was that you would do exactly as the boys and I say, and we say she's not invited. Whatever it is you see in that female serpent is beyond me anyway."

Jillian Somerset's image came to Saber's mind. The young and extraordinarily beautiful widow of an elderly earl, her hot body sheltered a cold heart, and that suited him perfectly. He made no promises to her, saw no future with her, and he'd made that clear from the very beginning of their relationship. He suspected she harbored the secret desire to become his duchess, but if she ever brought the subject up he'd dismiss her from his life in an instant.

Addison saw the faraway look in Saber's eyes and realized he was pondering Jillian. "You'll never meet anyone else if you insist on spending what little free time you allow yourself with her, Saber. Granted, she is a beautiful woman, but hers is a cold beauty. I confess to shivering when she looks at me with those glacial blue eyes of hers. There are dozens of other lovely women who—"

"I've seen most all of them, care for none, and have no desire to meet any others." Bejeweled vultures, all of them, he mused angrily. He was the prime piece of meat, and he did everything he could to avoid their sharpened talons. "None are any different than Jillian, Addison, so I fail to see the importance of my becoming acquainted with them."

"But—"

"At any rate, my love life is my own concern, and I will not discuss it with you. I'm in no need of your match-making anyway, and thank God I'm not. The last girl you arranged for me to meet didn't know what two plus two equals, and could speak of nothing but her talent with napkins. For two solid hours I had to sit and watch her fold a square of linen into different shapes. One of them, as I recall, was my own profile. Now why she thought I would enjoy wiping my mouth with my own face goes quite beyond my lowly comprehension."

Addison smiled. "Dulcie was beautiful though, and if you'd married her, the place settings at your dinner parties would have been the talk of London. I bet Jillian doesn't have such a unique talent."

Saber raised a black brow and couldn't resist irritating Addison. "No, but I thoroughly enjoy the ones she *does* have."

"She's after your title and fortune."

*So is every other unmarried female in London,* Saber raged silently. "She'll get neither, and this discussion is over."

Addison tipped his imaginary hat and grinned again. "I'll meet you downstairs. I've already informed your staff to prepare you for the trip, and I've sent a messenger to Leighwood as well. It *will* be Leighwood rather than Paris, will it not?"

"You know perfectly well it will be," Saber snapped. "You made sure of it."

Addison couldn't stop smiling. "Smashing! I'll be in the drawing room with your dear, sweet aunties. When I left them they were having a discussion concerning the poor unfortunate street girl who will be living with them. Sheltering, teaching, and finding honest employment for destitute lasses is the newest mission of mercy among the older ladies of the nobility. From what I gather, Ladies

Roth, Baldwin, Ainsworth, and Chapman already have their little paupers.''

Saber's shoulders sagged. A thieving street waif in his home was just what he needed, he thought sardonically. God. What other obnoxious bits of news were going to come to him today? ''I suppose Aunt Lucy and Aunt Clara are anxious to have one of these lasses of their own?''

'' 'The most ignorant and needy soul in all of England.' Those were their precise words. They have consented, however, to wait until you return from your trip. I'll go now and inform them you've chosen to go to Leighwood rather than Paris.''

''Addison, I swear I'm going to get back at you. I'll have you on toast for this!''

''The deuce, you say?'' Addison exclaimed, feigning fear. ''Cheer up, old chap. The bet could have been for higher stakes.''

Saber made a growling sound. ''What, besides going to Paris with Aunt Lucy, Aunt Clara, and a group of their companions, could be worse than being a servant to you and those three idiots I'm confused enough to call friends?''

Addison was silent for a moment. He looked at the floor, then back up at Saber. ''We could have stipulated the fortnight be spent at Ravenhurst instead of Leighwood. God knows *something* must get you back to your ducal lands.''

Though Saber was a master at hiding his emotions, Addison did not miss the fleeting look of rage in his eyes and felt a wave of frustration and sadness. ''You'll have to return one day, Saber,'' he said quietly. ''And when you do, it should be with your duchess on your arm.''

Like a giant wave, grief gathered, swelled, and crashed through Saber. He felt as though he were drowning in it. ''Addison—''

''If you won't be told by me, your closest friend, who will you listen to?''

''And you never let an opportunity pass to tell me, do you?''

''Then you'll hear me out?''

''Short of shooting you, I cannot think of a way to dissuade you. Besides, it is not the purpose of your life to run mine?''

Addison was undaunted by his friend's sarcasm. He loved Saber like a brother and there was nothing he wouldn't do, dare, or shoulder in order to help him set his life right again. "Five years, Saber. Five years or sixty months, or two hundred and sixty weeks, or . . . How many days is that? Well, no matter. However you look at it, it's a very long time to hide from the world.''

"I do not hide.''

"Very well,'' Addison conceded. "Five years is a long time to pretend you have no feelings for the world and the people who live in it.''

"I have feelings, and the ones I am experiencing at this moment are impatience and anger.''

"Lord Marion Tremayne,'' Addison continued, rocking from toes to heels. "Once a man of charm and laughter. But that man met his death when Angelica Sheridan did. Yes, as I live by bread, the truth is that he's turned his face to the wall.''

"Addison, I will hear no more!'' Saber stormed to the window and glared out of it. Gripping the draperies, he watched black smoke rising into the sky, casting a grayish film over the city. The sight suited his mood. "Do not speak of Angelica. She is the one subject I forbid you to ever try to discuss with me.''

"She's dead,'' Addison went on heedlessly. "You are *alive*. You have a life, and you must live it.''

*Not without her,* Saber responded silently, his hold on the curtains tightening.

"You are not unlike Winston's Uncle Horatio, Saber.''

"And I have the utmost respect for the man,'' Saber countered. "Granted, he appears rather sour at times, but—''

"*Rather?* My God, Saber, the man was weaned on a lemon! You said yourself he's the most cantankerous man in all of England! And not only that, he's quite the most fastidious man I've ever had the extreme misfortune to know. You, Saber, come in second. What do the two of you do before starting your day? Wallow in a tub of starch?''

"Are you implying that I should abandon all civilized modes of behavior and become a tearabout as you and the boys—"

"We are not tearabouts. We simply find ways to bend the rules without breaking them. You used to enjoy that also, Saber. But now . . . now you are as stuffy as—"

"Addison, you are trying my patience sorely."

"You're angry because I speak the truth, and you don't care for the way it sounds. I realize you have specific moral obligations as the Duke of Ravenhurst, Saber. As the Earl of Aurora Hills, I have similar ones. There are certain codes of decorum we must observe. But we are not required to be so indifferent to life that we have neither the time nor inclination to seek diversion. To laugh. To notice whether or not it is raining. To sing a song! When was the last time you sang out loud?"

"What bearing does that have on—"

"I'll keep asking the question until you answer it."

Saber sighed and laid his forehead against the window pane. "When I was a child."

"Perhaps you should try it as an adult."

"Perhaps you should leave this room before—"

"But perhaps I shall stay until I've finished what I'm saying."

"I believe you've already said more than enough."

Addison crossed his arms in front of his chest. "Quite the contrary. I called on you yesterday morning. Did the aunties inform you of that? No, of course not. How could they? You were locked away in your office. And I knew why, Saber. Yesterday would have been your fifth wedding anniversary. You do the same thing each year. You lock yourself—"

"I was working."

"You were not working. You were mourning. And that is why the boys and I came and dragged you to Winston's last night."

"I should have had the lot of you arrested."

"But you didn't. Because as much as it goes against your grain to admit it, you harbor a deep fondness for us. We are your friends, and if you won't help yourself it is our obligation to—"

"I am in no need of help."

"Ah, but you are." Addison walked back into the room, his hands clasped behind his back. "You think to mask what is inside you, Saber, but the boys and I have known you for too long to be fooled so easily. Ever since Angelica's death, you have been the epitome of social grace. Your manners are so utterly spotless that you are quite the most boring member of the nobility. Yes, I believe you even surpass Horatio Alders. You are definitely and positively His Perfect Lordship, the Duke of Ravenhurst."

Saber's gaze narrowed until he could see London's gray haze only through the slashes of his eyes. "I assume you mean that as an insult."

"I do. Because there was a time, Saber, when although you were the Duke of Ravenhurst, you were first and foremost Saber Tremayne. And therein lie your many problems."

Saber spun from the window. "I have no problems, and this discussion has reached its conclusion. Take yourself from this room, or I shall—"

"You have many problems, and lucky for you, I not only know what they are, I'm willing to divulge them." Addison straightened his lapel before continuing. "As the eleventh Duke of Ravenhurst, a man devoid of all feeling, it is your duty to marry, produce an heir, and instill in your little son an abiding love for the Tremayne lands. To do that, you will have to raise the boy at Ravenhurst."

"Addison—"

"But as Saber Tremayne, the man filled with very human emotions, you have vowed never to return to Ravenhurst. Moreover, you refuse to enter into a loveless marriage. After having loved Angelica, you—"

"Get out."

"And so we come to the problems," Addison continued smoothly. "The Duke of Ravenhurst is duty-bound to marry a woman who will provide him with a son. But Saber Tremayne, who will not marry without love, has sworn never to search for it either. Instead, he has buried all emotion, and has sought refuge behind his lofty title. The duke. That man is your facade. The indifferent air, the authority . . . those are your shields against the possibility of ever loving again. But in truth, you are Lord

Tremayne in name only. Down deep, lies Saber Tremayne. A man who cares very much. You're afraid of love. You've loved and lost so many times, that you—''

''Addison—''

''That's why you spend time with the Frost Queen. She warms your body but does nothing at all to melt the ice around your heart. She doesn't even try. Jillian's *cold,* and that's the way you want to be too. Ice can be with ice, and they'll both stay frozen. But put ice in contact with heat, and it melts. You don't attend any of the social activities because it's possible you might meet a warm woman at one of them, and her warmth might reach your heart. And then you'll be vulnerable, won't you, Saber? Opening your heart means taking another chance on life, and you might lose again.''

Saber ran his fingers through his hair. Words he didn't want to speak came to his lips. ''Those women you speak of, Addison . . . they—Not a one of them—How can you say there is any warmth in them?''

Addison took a moment to dwell on Saber's question. ''Ah, I begin to see.''

''You see nothing. If you did, you would realize the depth of your misconceptions.''

''So you are denying everything I have said to you? Lie to others if you must, Saber, but do not lie to me. Or to yourself. I understand you. If I didn't, I would never dare to presume that I could waltz in here and throw a cat in with the pigeons as I have done.''

Saber raised his chin. ''But you're wrong about the women. They want only to be the Duchess of Ravenhurst. They see nothing in me but my title and fortune. What warmth is there in that?'' he snapped.

Addison realized he was receiving a rare glimpse of what Saber carried inside him. The realization made him want to embrace his friend. ''You've given them no other choice but to see you that way, Saber,'' he said softly. ''You hide your true nature behind the Duke of Ravenhurst facade.''

Addison walked back to the door and opened it. ''You're going to Leighwood with us today. There, you cannot be the Duke of Ravenhurst. You will be our slave. I really have no earthly idea if our fortnight will do you any good, but I'm praying for some kind of miracle. You will be forced to shed the role of duke . . . so who knows what might happen? It could be that you'll have a little fun. Maybe you'll laugh. Maybe you'll look up and be astonished at how very blue the sky is."

*How blue the sky is,* Saber thought. Couldn't Addison see that the sky was gray? He straightened, looked his friend in the eye, and felt his irritation return. "The only miracle that might occur at Leighwood, Addison, is that the end of the fortnight will find me with my wits still about me. If I have to spend two weeks listening to your incessant lectures, I fear I'll go insane. Out of courtesy, I have allowed you to rant and rave to your heart's content today, but be forewarned that I will not tolerate such behavior again. Have I made myself clear?"

"Indubitably."

Saber didn't miss the twinkle in his friend's bright blue eyes. As usual, it tempered his aggravation. "Addison, you are as incorrigible now as you were when we met."

"It was at some opera, was it not? We were twelve."

Saber smiled. "We were eleven, and it was at your mother's birthday party."

"Ah, yes. You had filched Lord Warton's snuffbox and put pepper in it. You swore me to secrecy."

"*You* stole his snuffbox and put pepper in it. *You* swore *me* to secrecy."

"Yes, I do believe you're right. It was but the beginning of many pranks to come. It was then, too, that I gave you your nickname. I thought it rather clever, lifting 'Saber' from 'Saberfield.' "

"I think it is rather unseemly."

"Now why doesn't that surprise me, *Your Grace?* But you must admit, 'Saber' does suit you. You can be as cold and hard as steel. You've a sharp wit, you're to the point, and your slashing anger can draw blood as well as any weapon I can think of."

"Are you trying to antagonize me again?"

"I am merely indulging in what no one else in England would feel safe doing—pushing you beyond your limit. I confess to feeling a tremendous amount of pleasure at being cheeky in your presence and living to tell about it.''

"You are implying that I am a beast?"

"Say you nay to the charge, sir?"

Saber grinned. "I'm supposed be angry at you right now, Addison. Get out before I decide I like you again."

"As you wish." Addison made a low, exaggerated bow, and then looked Saber in the eye. "But do ponder the things I told you, Saber. They came from a friend, not an enemy." With that, he quit the room.

When he was gone, Saber removed his robe and sank into the tub of steaming water he realized Addison must have ordered for him. Lying back, he closed his eyes and dwelled on Addison's accusations.

*Your life is boring and uneventful.*

*The indifferent air, the authority . . . your shields against caring.*

*Opening your heart means taking another chance on life, and you might lose again.*

*You've loved and lost so many times . . .*

Saber remembered each charge. They were true. All of them.

But there was nothing Addison or anyone could do to change them, he knew. Addison was daft for hoping a fortnight in the country was the answer to such unsolvable problems. "For hoping for a miracle," Saber whispered, bathwater lapping at his lips.

A miracle. Saber shook his head at the absurdity. No help from heaven had ever come to him, and nothing miraculous whatsoever was going to occur at Leighwood either. The fortnight would end and then he could come back to London and get on with . . .

Get on with what? he asked himself. With his life?

He didn't have one.

# Chapter 3

**B**ig wiped his forehead with the back of his hand and surveyed the surroundings. "I have no idea where we are," he snapped in answer to Goldie's question concerning their location. "For all I know we've journeyed in a perfect circle, and Hallensham is right over our shoulders."

Goldie watched the ripples dance on the clear, clean pond they'd found hidden in a dense thicket, and breathed deeply of the crisp woods-scented air. "Big, we've been travelin' for days. Hallensham is a long way away from here."

He threw her a sour look. "I'm going to go see if I can snare some kind of supper for us. Don't you dare wander off while I'm gone."

As soon as Big left, Goldie pulled a sliver of soap from her dress pocket, shed her clothes, and waded into the fresh water. "Maybe when Big gets back, he won't be such an ill-box," she commented to the big gray mongrel, who sat watching her from the sandy bank. "It really set him off when I gave you all our food the day I found you. But what was I supposed to do, Itchie Bon? You were lost and starvin'. 'Course, now Big and I are lost and starvin' too," she added.

Itchie Bon barked loudly, his wagging tail sending sand flying in all directions.

"Well," Goldie continued, "I thought for sure we'd come across some town where we could get more food. It's not my fault these English people didn't build villages along the route we're takin'." Rolling the soap in her hands, she examined the pretty and peaceful place they'd come to. "I wonder which route we *are* takin'?"

36

She shrugged and lathered up her body and hair. Tossing the soap bar to shore, she watched as it landed beside her claymore, then waved to Itchie Bon before submerging to rinse. While beneath the shimmering surface, she remembered "Mermaids," a game she and her friend used to play. Keeping her legs tightly together, she moved them as a mermaid would her tail and propelled herself through the water. After coming up for a breath, she splashed and squealed loudly before diving again, her "tail" beating the water with powerful flapping motions.

Opening her eyes as she swam deeper, she watched the water plants flow. They looked like long, green fingers conducting an underwater orchestra. The pond pebbles, smooth, colorful, and illuminated by the strong sunlight that touched them from above, twinkled up at her from the sandy bottom. A silver fish swam past her. She chased it, thinking to catch it with her bare hands, but just as she reached for it she heard a loud splash. Before she could investigate it, something very strong and unyielding grabbed her from behind.

For a moment she froze, unable to understand what was happening to her. But as whatever had her tightened its hold about her waist and began pulling at her, she struggled to escape. Reaching for the pond creature, she closed her fingers around it and sucked in a mouthful of water.

It was a man, she realized, terror spinning through her. And it wasn't Big. It was very large, extremely strong man, and he was trying to drown her! She squirmed violently, managing to get her mouth near his upper arm.

"Blast it!" Saber shouted underwater, his voice a loud, gurgling sound. "Don't bite me!" Bubbles made by his yelling rose around his face and irritated his eyes. He grabbed a handful of her long hair and yanked her head away from his arm. Her watery scream made him let go immediately. He hadn't meant to hurt her, but she was going to drown him too if she didn't cooperate with her own rescue! They were about a foot from the surface, and it would only take a few seconds to reach it if she would only stop fighting him! "Stop!" he tried to tell her.

Goldie understood nothing of the man's gargled shouts, but took full advantage of his loosened hold. She twisted suddenly, and brought her right foot up behind her as forcefully as she could. The water slowed her kick, but she did manage to find her mark successfully.

Again, Saber groaned. His arm was still smarting where she'd bitten him, and now his groin was on fire from her well-aimed kick. The pain radiated up to his belly, and he clenched his teeth against it. Very well, he thought angrily. He'd tried to be gentle with her, but she wouldn't let him. So now he would just have to save her life with brute force.

Goldie felt what little breath she had left rush out of her when the man crushed her to him. Her lungs felt as though they were going to burst. She panicked, knowing with absolute certainty that if she didn't get away from her would-be killer, she was going to die. She struggled against the hard, thick arms wrapped around her, but lightheadedness set in, weakening her.

The girl in his arms went limp just as Saber broke through the surface. With strong, sure strokes, he swam to the shore, pulling her with him. He carried her to the warm leaf-strewn bank and knelt down beside her. His eyes grew round in astonishment as they took in her full length. He'd already realized she was nude, but had been under the impression she was no more than ten or eleven years old. She'd felt so slight, so very tiny while fighting him in the pond. The sight he had now, however, proved she was by no means a child, but a fully grown woman.

He stood, raking his fingers through his dripping hair. "Miss?" he inquired loudly, unable to decide if he should look at her or not. After all, she *was* naked. Still, she was half-drowned too. She wasn't dead; he could see her chest rising. But it worried him that she wouldn't wake up. "Miss, are you all right?" he asked again, carefully keeping his gaze centered on her face. "Can you open your eyes? Speak? Miss?"

A low growl made him spin around in the sand. For a moment he saw nothing, but in the next instant, his eyes widened. "Good God!" he yelled when a great, gray beast came charging toward him.

The huge, ugly mongrel took a flying leap, hurling himself directly at Saber. Saber lost his balance immediately and landed flat on his back, the dog's body lying full-length upon him. He tried pushing the beast away, but its weight and violent contortions prevented success. While Saber rolled in the sand, the dog clinging to him, tufts of stiff gray hair poked him in his eyes, and long sharp claws dug into his midriff. But by far the worst thing about the attack was the dog's hot, sour breath. Accompanied by furious growling, it blew onto Saber's face in great, moist puffs.

"Get him, Itchie Bon! Great day Miss Agnes, get him!"

Saber, still battling his canine assailant and trying his best to keep from being bitten, twisted and saw the girl. She was standing only a few feet away, the hilt of a huge claymore in her hands, its point stabbing the ground. *"Get him?"* he yelled at her. He'd saved her wretched life, and she wanted him dead! he raged, groaning when the dog nipped his shoulder. As hard as he tried, he couldn't seem to get the mongrel off long enough to stand. God, he fumed, if he didn't get away from here, he'd either be torn to bits by the dog or slashed to pieces by the girl's huge, silver blade.

Summoning strength, he finally managed to grab the growling animal. Rising, he staggered to his feet, and tossed it into the pond. No sooner had the furry beast left his hands than the girl came at him, dragging her claymore behind her. When she reached him, he watched her face contort as she struggled slowly and shakily to raise the point of the great sword.

God, Saber thought. The evil, foul-smelling dog, the naked girl, the huge claymore . . . Nothing like this had ever happened to him before, and he didn't know how to react. Panting, he said, "Miss, kindly lower your weapon. I am—"

"Make one more move, and I'll run you through," Goldie warned, her gaze traveling down his tall, muscular form. Taking in his black breeches, the black boots thrown behind him, and the black horse pawing the sand nearby, a terrifying thought came to her. She trembled so violently, the heavy sword she held made it difficult for her to keep her balance. But she refused to drop her weapon, and for a few moments she staggered and stumbled around, her claymore leading the way. She finally righted herself and glared at the huge man before her. "You're one of those dreaded English highwaymen Mildred Fickle told me about, aren't you?''

Saber stared at her, so many observations running through his mind, he couldn't decide which one to concentrate on. She was an American. Her speech told him that. She looked ridiculous holding the claymore. It was almost as tall as she was, and he knew it weighed more. She'd lifted it up to the height of his groin, and the thought of her running him through *there* was highly disturbing. She'd accused him of being a highwayman. He, the Duke of Ravenhurst, a common thief! She'd spoken of one Mildred Fickle as if he were supposed to know the woman.

But by far the most interesting observation he made concerned the girl herself. She was the tiniest woman he'd ever seen, and he knew if she were to stand in front of him, the top of her head would barely reach his chest. But as small as she was, her body was flawlessly proportioned, and he could make *that* observation quite correctly since she was still naked.

Her hair fell just past her shoulders, and although it was still wet, a few strands were beginning to form soft, gold ringlets around her face. Her thickly fringed eyes were large, round, and tawny. Right now they were filled with anger and fear, but he suspected they twinkled brightly when she was happy. He didn't understand why he'd come to that conclusion, but there was just something about her that made him think it. Her nose, small and pert, was covered with freckles, as were her delicate pink cheeks. Her mouth was a deeper pink and pushed out into a slight pout, as if she were on the verge of tears. He decided it was definitely a mouth made for kissing, then immediately wondered why he'd thought of that.

His gaze caressed her slender throat, and slid to her breasts. They would fill his cupped palms perfectly. Though they were little, they were full, supremely shaped, and crowned with delightfully proud and rosy nipples. Her waist was so small he was sure he could wind his hands around it with room to spare. Her hips, too, were slim, but nicely rounded. There was a slight matting of curls as blonde as her hair at the apex of her dainty, white legs, and her feet were so small he wondered if she had to wear children's shoes.

She was beautiful, but that didn't really describe her. She was so golden. So tiny. She reminded him of a delicately painted figurine. She really was quite . . . lovely. No, that wasn't the right word either.

His gaze took a delightful journey down her body again. He felt himself grow hard. Hot, deep waves of desire shot through him, and he was astonished at his strong and immediate reaction. It had been a long, long time since any woman had affected him the way this freckled, claymore-wielding elf did. Not even Jillian made him feel the way he did now.

He shuffled his feet in the sand. His tight riding breeches were wet, making them cling to him all the more, and he knew she would soon notice what was happening to him. Any sudden movement on his part might frighten her into thinking he was going to assault her, and if he shielded himself with his hands he would only succeed in drawing attention to his problem. Not knowing what else to do, he decided to explain himself in the most genteel manner he could. "Miss, I apologize profusely for . . . for—That is to say, I don't mean to stand before you with such obvious—I'm—It's certainly not your fault. But miss, you *are* without clothing, and *I* didn't get you that way."

Goldie gasped. In her attempt to protect herself, she'd forgotten to put on her dress! Her cheeks grew warm; she leaned forward a bit, closing her elbows together in attempt to hide her front. "Get your eyes off me, you . . . you woman-drownin' ravisher-highwayman! Big! Big, where the hell are you?"

Saber kept a wary eye on the dog who'd just emerged from the pond. "Miss, I am no ravisher of women," he informed her sternly. "I am—"

"You are so!" Goldie shouted, her hands turning white around the hilt of her sword. "If I didn't have my claymore, you'd be—"

"I would not!" Saber exclaimed. "I—"

"Oh, Lord!" Big yelled, running into the clearing and seeing Goldie's bare body. "What's happening here? Who is that man? Why are you naked with him? What—"

"Big, find my dress! I can't get it and hold my sword at the same time! Great day Miss Agnes, I forgot I was naked, and this dreaded English highwayman is turnin' into a ravisher right before my eyes!"

Big threw down the rabbit he'd snared and panicked when he didn't see the dress. "Where is it?" he screamed desperately, charging all around the bank of the pond as he looked for it. "Oh, good Lord, I can't find it anywhere, and that man is going to—"

"I am going to do nothing at all," Saber tried to assure them. "Miss, if your performance in the water is any indication of your fighting abilities, I wouldn't attempt to ravish you even if you paid me to try."

Goldie let the point of the claymore drop. "Paid you?" Her eyes misted.

At the sight of her sudden tears, Saber was thoroughly confused. He couldn't understand why she was crying, why he felt an almost desperate determination to mend her wounded feelings. "Miss," he said gently, his hands outstretched, "I'm—"

"Where the hell is that damn dress?" Big shrieked. "Where did you throw it?"

Goldie's gaze never left the huge man before her. "Do you really think I'd have to *pay* a man to ravish me?" she sputtered. "That's the meanest thing anyone's ever said to me. If I'm ugly, just say so. You don't have to taunt me like that. Get him, Itchie Bon," she instructed her dog.

Saber tried to shield himself from the shower of water Itchie Bon shook on him. "I didn't say you were ugly. I only meant that—"

"You didn't say it, but you *did* mean it!"

Saber shook his head in dismay. The Duke of Ravenhurst certainly didn't ravish women on pond banks, but since he'd never had to convince anyone that he didn't resort to such behavior, he found himself lacking the right words. "I meant nothing of the sort. I was merely trying to convince you that I won't hurt you. That's all."

Goldie sniffled and dried her eyes with the back of her hand. "Never mind all that. Ugly is as ugly does, and I'm a kind person inside. At least I try to be. But sometimes things set me off. Gettin' ravished is somethin' that would really set me off. Where's your black cape? Did you lose it in the water?"

Saber's mind whirled. "Cape?"

"Mildred Fickle said dreaded English highwaymen ride black horses and wear black capes and boots. Your black horse and boots are over there, but you're missin' your cape. I don't see a sword either. Are you just startin' out in the dreaded English highwayman business? Is that why you don't have all the necessary equipment yet? And why were you tryin' to drown me? Mildred Fickle didn't say anything about dreaded English highwaymen doin' their dirty work in ponds. I thought they only did it on dark, deserted roads. Big, where the hell are you and my dress?"

Saber sighed in exasperation. "I'm not a highwayman, and I wasn't trying to drown you. I was trying to *save* you from drowning, but you—"

"Save me?" Goldie yelled. "I—"

"I found it!" Big hollered, running to her. "Here," he said, and handed her the dress. He moved in front of her, shielding her from the towering man who stared at her. "You may have gotten an eyeful, you great big bastard, but that's all you're getting!"

Saber clenched his jaw. *No one* had ever insulted him in such a fashion. "Sir, you—"

"I didn't need to be saved," Goldie announced, her voice muffled as she pulled the dress over her head. "I—"

"You may be five times my size," Big continued to the giant in front of him, "but I'll fight you to the death if you try to lay one paw on her, you horny wretch, you . . . you lustful hooligan!"

"Great day Miss Agnes, I been swimmin' since I was little!" Goldie finished explaining as her dress fell into place. "I learned when I was—"

"You take my warning, Mr. Two-Ton Tom cat?" Big demanded.

Saber decided to ignore the feisty midget. The Duke of Ravenhurst did not engage in verbal battles concerning rapes that weren't even going to happen. With practiced ease, he dismissed the little man from his mind and concentrated on the girl instead. "If I may ask, who is Miss Agnes?"

Goldie frowned. "Who is she? Well, how the hell should I know? I didn't make up that expression." She stepped around Big and heard him mutter a profanity.

"Then who is Mildred Fickle?" Saber asked.

"The question, I think, is who are you?"

"Yeah!" Big blasted, peering out from behind Goldie.

Saber kept his gaze directed at the girl. "I thought I was a dreaded English highwayman."

"You said you weren't."

"So you believe me now?"

Goldie wrinkled her nose. "Say Daddy's honor you aren't."

"Daddy's honor?" Saber felt totally bewildered. The girl certainly used some strange expressions. "Is Daddy somehow related to Miss Agnes and Mildred Fickle?"

Despite her wariness, Goldie smiled.

Her smile made Saber feel like grinning back. He folded his arms across his chest and tried to discern what it was about the girl that made him feel so attracted to her. She was quite unpolished. Certainly not the sort of woman with whom he'd ever taken up company.

"What self-respecting dreaded English highwayman would be without his sword and black cape?" he queried, still feeling that urge to smile at her. "As you pointed out, I have neither. Now, if you weren't drowning, what were you doing in the water? I was riding through the woods and saw all your splashing, heard you screaming, and I was sure you—"

"It's none of your damn business what she was doing in the water!" Big exploded. "Get out of here!"

Saber stiffened, anger curling through him. The little man was actually trying to throw him off his own land! "Sir, you will cease ordering me about. I am—"

"You're a dead man if you don't get out of here!" With that, Big made fists and began prancing around. "Go ahead! Put 'em up! I may be little, but dammit, I'll—"

"I will not fight you," Saber informed him. Good God. Imagine the Duke of Ravenhurst engaging in fisticuffs with a belligerent midget! The thought was utterly absurd.

"Why won't you fight?" Big taunted. "Afraid?"

Again, Saber dismissed the man. He looked back down

at Goldie. "If you weren't drowning, miss, what were you doing in the water?"

"I was playin' 'Mermaids.' " Goldie let her stiff shoulders relax and dropped the sword. Her hunger and exhaustion were making her shaky, and she sat on the ground, bringing her knees up so they touched her chest. Looking at the man looming above her, she decided he wasn't a dreaded English highwayman and felt relieved she didn't have to kill him. "Big, put your fists down. This man's not the ravishin' kind. If he were, you'd be knocked out, and I'd be ravished already."

Sullenly, Big complied. He planted his feet directly behind Goldie, folded his arms across his chest, and kept his gaze centered on the black-haired giant's face.

"Gladys Shoat and I used to play 'Mermaids' all the time out in Ninny Creek back in Weaverville, Georgia," Goldie explained. "I heard the creek got its name because so many girls went skinny-dippin' in it, showin' their ninnies to anyone who came wanderin' by."

"Ninnies?" Saber felt amusement bubble in his throat. He'd never heard a girl say that word before. He sat near her, but not too near, for the dog she called Itchie Bon was watching him with shining black eyes, and the expression on her diminutive guardian angel's face was equally ferocious. "I see. Weaverville, Georgia, you say? Interesting name."

Goldie sighed deeply. "That's where my beloved is. Fred Wattle. He never loved me, but I loved him with my every breath. He kissed me once, but later I found out he only did it to win a bet with his friends. He broke my heart. But he was the handsomest fella in Weaverville, and I didn't really deserve—I mean . . . I—He was in love with Velma Wiggins anyway. She was tall. Tall and so purty. I still think about Fred though."

Saber hadn't missed what she'd almost said. Did she think she didn't deserve the handsome Fred Wattle? And was it really possible that Velma Wiggins was prettier than this golden imp?

"You didn't have to pull my hair so hard," Goldie said quietly.

"What?" Big roared. "He pulled your hair? Put 'em

up!'' he ordered the huge man and made fists again. "No-body touches her and gets away—"

"Big, stop that," Goldie said. She twisted and took hold of one of his fists. "I'm all right, Big. Nobody ever died from gettin' their hair pulled."

Saber watched the little man return to his guard post behind the girl. "I apologize if I hurt you," he said softly, and felt genuine remorse. He stared at the riotous mass of flaxen curls shimmering around her face and had to sup-press his odd urge to touch them. He'd never seen such wild hair allowed such freedom. Most women he knew would have taken drastic measures to tame it. They'd an-chor it down with a hundred pins if necessary.

He found himself glad *this* girl didn't do that, and then noticed she wore only one earring. "I fear you've lost your left earring. Perhaps it slipped off in the pond?"

She touched the bit of tin and colored glass hanging from her right ear. "This is the only one I've got. I don't wear it all the time, though. If I do, it turns my earlobe green. Y'see, one time I read that Indians pierce their ears. I'm not an Indian, but I kinda liked the idea of piercin' my ear. Heaven must have read my thoughts because I soon found this earring. I pierced this ear all by myself. Used a needle and a potato. See, you gotta put somethin' behind your earlobe when you stick the needle through or else the needle might shoot into your brain, and then you wouldn't be able to think anymore. Bertie Snide told me that. I was real brave when I pierced my ear."

Saber nodded in all seriousness. "Bertie Snide sounds like quite the intellect. And please allow me to commend you on your courage in the face of such a delicate opera-tion."

"You're allowed. Go ahead."

"But I just did."

"You did?"

"I—Yes. I said—Well, no matter," Saber stammered, amusement continuing to rise. "And what of your other ear? It's not pierced?"

"Why would I have pierced both ears when I only had one earring?"

"I—" He broke off. He'd been going to argue, but her

question made perfect sense. "What are you doing here?" he asked instead. "Leighwood is private property, and by the looks of that dead rabbit over there, you've been hunting here. Did you know that's against the law?"

"Leighwood?"

"That's what this estate is called."

Goldie glanced at the rabbit and realized Big had been successful in finding their supper. "And that's a Leighwood rabbit?"

"I'm quite sure it is."

She paused to think about that. "So you're sayin' that if Big had chased it off Leighwood, it wouldn't have been a Leighwood rabbit? Or does this law of yours say that once a Leighwood rabbit, always a Leighwood rabbit?"

Saber automatically opened his mouth to answer her, but no explanation came forth. Her question made him smile instead. It was a moment before he realized he was grinning, and he wondered what he thought was so funny. "You're hungry, aren't you?" he asked, noticing how she kept looking over at the fat rabbit.

Goldie nodded. "A little tired too. Big and I have been travelin' for days lookin' for my duke. Two days ago, I gave all our food to Itchie Bon, my new dog. Big hasn't said a word to me since. You still mad at me, Big?"

Big grunted a swear word. "Goldie, I think it's time we were on our way. Get your sword, call Dammit, and let's go."

"Dammit?" Saber asked.

"He's my horse, and he's about a thousand years old," Goldie informed him. "I reckon he's piddlin' around somewhere with Big's mule, Smiley Jones. Big calls his mule that because the dumb thing likes to eat briars. When he eats 'em it looks like he's smilin'. I don't where Big got the 'Jones' part from, though. Where'd you get the 'Jones' part from, Big?"

"I just liked it," Big answered, and gave the giant another well-aimed glare.

"And I call my horse Dammit because I say 'dammit' a lot when I'm ridin' him," Goldie continued. "See, since he's so old it takes him a long time to get goin'. I don't mean to cuss at him though. It just sorta slips out. So I named him Dammit. That way, he thinks I'm sayin' his name instead of cussin' at him. I wouldn't want to hurt his feelin's. I've only had him for a few weeks. Found him wanderin' near my village. Smiley Jones was with him, and Big and I took 'em in. Dammit and Smiley Jones are best friends. Do you know what *pusillanimous* means?''

"Pusillanimous?" Saber's mind spun as he tried to keep up with her. "Uh . . . lacking courage. Without resolution. Why do you ask?''

She gaped at him. "It's my new word for the day. I find a new one every day in my dictionary. You're the first person I ever met who already knew my new word for the day. Where'd you learn it?''

Saber smiled again. "I don't know, really. I guess I just heard it somewhere.'' God, she was an amusing bit of female, he thought. But try as he might, he couldn't quite put his finger on what it was about her that he found so funny.

"Did y'know that Itchie Bon means 'Number One' in Japanese?'' Goldie asked. "I knew a Japanese man once. Met him in South Carolina, but I can't remember which town. I can't remember his name either. It was a funny name, as I recall. He was tryin' to make a livin' by sellin' fish. He didn't do well though because he didn't cook it. Served it up raw as raw could be, and folks thought he was crazy. He's the one who told me what Itchie Bon means. I thought it was a good name for my dog. Big and I didn't mean to break any laws, mister. You think we should find the owner of this Leighwood estate and apologize for killin' his rabbit? I could offer him half of it as a peace offerin'. 'Course then there wouldn't be much left for Big and me.''

Still smiling, Saber shook his head. "I don't think he'll miss one little rabbit, but I caution you against hunting anywhere else. You can get yourself into very serious trouble.''

"These English estate owners must be a selfish bunch. I wonder if Mildred Fickle knows that?'' she mused aloud, then looked at Big. "Go on and skin it, Big. I'd help you, but y'know how guts make me sick. There's a knife in my saddlebag, but you'll have to find Dammit to get it.''

"But this son of a bitch—"

"Big," Goldie intervened, "I told you he's not a dreaded English highwayman-ravisher, and I don't think he's a son of a bitch either." She looked Saber straight in the eye. "You're not a son of a bitch, are you, mister?"

Saber threw back his shoulders. "I should say not!"

Goldie frowned. "You should say not? Just what the hell does that mean? Are you sayin' you aren't sure you should admit you're a son of a bitch? You may as well tell the truth right now, mister, because we'll find out whether or not you're lyin'. Sons of bitches can't hide their true natures for long, y'know."

Saber felt irritation and amusement at the same time. "I am not a man you need to fear."

Goldie nodded. "I'll be safe with him, Big. Daddy's honor, I will. Go on and skin supper."

Mumbling more profanities, Big walked out of the clearing, the rabbit swinging in his hands.

Goldie dug her bare toes into the cool sand. "I just can't take the skinnin' part of huntin'. I can't do the killin' either. All I can take is the eatin' part. I can catch fish though. I don't know why, but catchin' fish isn't as bad as shootin' runnin' animals or flyin' birds. Maybe it's because fish don't bleed and scream. 'Course I don't reckon it feels too good to have a hook stuck up in the roof of your mouth. You ever go fishin'?"

Saber picked up a twig and began flicking sand around with the point of it. After a moment, he tossed the stick into the pond. As he watched it splash into the water, he recalled that the last time he'd fished was when his father was still alive. A forgotten memory came to him. He remembered catching a really big fish. His father had been so proud. Della had cooked it that night. What a wonderful evening that had been, sharing his catch with his mother and father. He hadn't thought of that night in many years. "I haven't fished in a very long time," he said quietly.

Goldie saw the wistful look on his face and thought he would have liked to go fishing. "It's a damn shame we don't have any poles, huh? I'm a good fisherwoman. The secret is the bait, y'see. Most people use worms, but not me. I use cheese. You wouldn't believe how much fish love cheese."

"How fascinating," Saber said, thinking about all the many things she'd told him in the ten minutes she'd been talking. "You mentioned a duke. *Your* duke, to be specific. Who is this duke?"

Goldie sighed again. "Duke Marion. I thought it was gonna be so easy, but we haven't found anyone who looks like him. They all had something that wasn't right. My Duke Marion's gotta be tall and strong like you. His eyes have to be green . . . like yours. His hair . . . black. Strong jaw, high cheekbones . . . long, straight nose . . ." Her voice trailed off as she studied him more intently. On her hands and knees, she crawled toward him, stopping only when her face was a mere inch away from his. "Great day Miss Agnes!"

Before Saber could react, she'd thrown her arms around him and planted a kiss right on his mouth.

Instantly, Goldie drew back. "I—I'm sorry. I didn't mean to kiss you like that. I—It's just that—" She took a moment to regard him, and when she saw that he didn't look angry, her excitement returned in full force. "I've never kissed a strange man before, but I reckon I kissed you because I'm so happy right now that I just couldn't help myself! The fact of the matter is that you're only the second man I've ever kissed. Fred Wattle was the first. You know anything about duke stuff? I'll swannee, I can't believe I've been talkin' to you for so long and didn't see how much you look like ole Duke Marion! You just can't believe how desperate I was to find you, and now here you are!"

"I—Did you say *Marion?*"

"Y'know anything about dukes?" she asked again. "Maybe you've been near one, one time? The more y'know about dukes, the easier it'll be on all of us, y'see. But if you don't know anything, don't worry. I'll teach you. I've got the diaries. Even though there's a bunch of water spilled all over 'em you can still read parts, and I guess at what I can't read. And I remember everything Mildred Fickle said. And everyone knows *some* stuff about dukish men. A lot of it's just plain common sense. For instance, y'know those canes dukish men carry? Not *all* dukish men are crippled, so y'want to know why they *all* carry canes?''

Saber couldn't keep up with her quicksilver chatter. "Why?" he asked absently.

"Well, if some common person dares to insult a dukish man, the duke man uses his cane to bash the commoner over the head. *That's* the kind of thing everyone knows about dukish folks. We'll get you a cane as soon as we can. And when Big gets that rabbit ready, the first thing I want to see you do is sniff each bite of it. It's not really poisoned, but you have to get a good whiff of it anyway. Think you can remember to smell your food every time you eat?''

Saber frowned. "Whiff of it? Poison? Uh, did you say *Marion?*"

She nodded, her curls bouncing every which way. "Mister, my name's Goldie. I don't know what your name is, but from now on, you're His Royal Highness Lordship Duke Marion Tremayne. I know it's a ridiculously long name, but you need to learn to respond to it. See, my Uncle Asa got drunk and told the villagers that we know the duke personally. If I don't cover up his lies and bring back Duke Marion, the villagers are gonna throw Uncle Asa out of town. They said they didn't want any lyin', troublemakin' drunks around. I haven't had a real home since my mama and daddy died, and I'm hell-bent on stayin' at the one I've got now, so no matter what ole Dora Mashburn says is gonna happen, I've got to make this work. Big says Dora's just jealous, but Big's all the time sayin' dumb stuff like that. Dora. Sometimes I call her Dora Squash-scorch. Get it? Mashburn—Squash-scorch.''

"Squash-scorch," Saber mumbled. "Yes, I . . . uh, *get it.*"

Goldie closed her eyes for a moment, picturing Hallensham. "It's so purty there in the village. So green, so open. There's a bed of dandelions growin' right by my front door. But I can't stay there without Uncle Asa though,'' she explained and opened her eyes. "He's . . . the only real family I have left in this whole wide world, and I—He's got a good heart inside. Once he gave me a new dress. He's only testy when he's drunk, and since he's almost always drunk—'' She broke off, swallowing painful emotions. ''I—Well, anyway, I've been searchin' all over for a man who looks like Duke Marion, and you match his description.''

Saber could hardly believe what he was hearing, however mangled it all was. ''Goldie—''

''I wish your skin was whiter though. I kinda get the feelin' that dukish folks are pasty-white. You're tanned. But you'll do, I reckon. You'll be the duke, and if you stay out of the sun, maybe your tan will fade some. I'll pay you. The only things you have to do are learn duke stuff and come to Hallensham for a few hours. After that, I'll give you the money, and you can be on your way.'' She drew away from him and looked into his wide, green eyes. ''Say yes?''

Saber stared back at her. He remained silent and incredulous as her words reverberated in his mind. Bash people over the heads, she'd said. Sniff each bite of food. Learn duke stuff and go to Hallensham. She had a lot of big ideas, this little person called Goldie. And the most outrageous of them all was that she was willing to pay him to impersonate *himself!*

The thought made his lips twitch. The corners of his eyes crinkled. A great burst of something he'd forgotten he could feel exploded inside him.

Quite unable to help himself, Lord Marion Westbrook Saberfield Tremayne, eleventh Duke of Ravenhurst, threw back his head and laughed.

# Chapter 4

A soft breeze mussed Winston Alders' thick brown hair. "I wonder where Saber has gotten off to?" he asked, slowing his horse as they entered the woods.

David Clarkston leaned sideways in his saddle and peered into the underbrush. "He's hiding, no doubt. He knows very well that he's to clean our tack and polish our boots after we finish our ride, and he's trying to escape the chore."

Kenneth Lynnly pushed a lock of red hair out of his eyes, and chuckled. "Just as he's tried avoiding everything else we've commanded him to do. It's really a good thing he was born into the aristocracy. He'd starve if forced to be someone's servant."

"He *has* been rather stroppy since our arrival yesterday, hasn't he?" Addison agreed with a smile. "And there's really no earthly reason for such irritation. I didn't think asking him to prepare us for bed last night was anything out of the ordinary for a slave. Why, you'd have thought I was asking for the world when I ordered him to fluff my pillow."

"And what of him shaving us this morning?" Kenneth reminded his friends. "I must admit I was a bit on the nervous side when he came at me with that gleam in his eyes and that razor in his hands."

"He nicked my chin," David said. "And you know, although he denied it, I believe he did it on purpose."

"He refused to butter my toast this morning," Winston added, swatting at a branch with his riding crop. "I was forced to remind him about a certain trip to Paris before

53

I could induce him to obey my instructions. And then he smashed a great blob of butter on my bread, but refused to spread it. I asked him what I was supposed to do with such an ill-prepared piece of toast. His answer does not bear repeating.''

Addison grinned. "Yes, I believe it is safe to say that the Duke of Ravenhurst is being well and truly ruffled. And his resentment will more than likely rise with each day we are here. Why, even now, he's probably sulking in some hiding place and—''

"What was that noise?'' Kenneth asked abruptly, sitting straighter in the saddle as he listened. "Do you hear it?''

"It sounds like someone talking,'' David said.

Addison listened intently. "That's Saber's voice.''

"Who do you suppose he's speaking to out here in the middle of the woods?'' David asked.

"I think a bit of spying is in order,'' Kenneth said, smiling.

Winston nodded. "But let's go afoot so our presence won't be noticed.''

The men dismounted and secured their horses. Tiptoeing through the woods, they soon came upon a pond and hid behind the scraggly hedgerow surrounding it.

"There he is,'' Addison whispered. "My God, look how dirty and wet he is!''

"Who's that girl?'' David asked, parting the branches of the shrubbery so he could see better. "My, but she's a dainty bit, isn't she?''

"Be quiet,'' Addison ordered. "Let's listen.''

"His shirtsleeve is torn,'' Kenneth commented. "It appears as though he's been fighting.''

"Shhh!'' Addison begged for silence.

"Good heavens, she's kissing him!'' Winston exclaimed.

"What's that about bashing people over the heads with canes?'' David asked.

"Quiet!'' Addison whispered loudly.

"She wants him to be Duke Marion,'' Kenneth mused quietly. *"Duke Marion.* Good God. Only an American would use such a term.''

Impatiently, Addison glared at his friends, waving his

hand to quiet them. Turning back to the pond, he continued to listen. Soon, rich, deep laughter hit his ears, a sound so foreign, he almost didn't recognize it for what it was. He was astonished. It was a moment before he could speak. "Saber," he whispered. "Good heavens, our Saber is *laughing!*"

"He is at that," Kenneth concurred. "And if I wasn't hearing it with my own ears, I'd never—"

"I wonder who that girl is?" Addison asked softly, more to himself than his friends. Whoever she was, he mused, Saber was enjoying her company. Addison decided then and there she couldn't be allowed to get away.

Winston wiped tears of merriment from his eyes. "Can you believe it?" he whispered. "The little chit wants Saber to impersonate *himself!*"

Kenneth chuckled. "And she offered to pay him!"

David held his belly, silent laughter shaking him. "Imagine putting the Duke of Ravenhurst—one of England's wealthiest men—on *salary!*"

Winston peered through the bushes again. "I wonder what the little American would do if she learned she'd just offered duke lessons to the one and only . . . uh, *Duke Marion?* Shall we tell her?"

"Wait," Addison whispered when his friends prepared to emerge from behind the hedgerow. He stared at Saber and the girl again, his mind spinning with a newborn scheme. "Boys, when we show ourselves, let me do all the talking. However strange it is, agree with everything I say."

"What are you going to do?" Winston asked.

Addison only grinned in answer. The men shrugged and followed him into the clearing. "What have we here?" Addison cried.

Goldie scrambled to her feet, reaching for her claymore.

Addison smiled at her. "You've no need to fear me. I only came to see what happened to . . . to my cousin. Saber, what are you doing here with this girl?"

Goldie looked down at Saber, who was pulling on his boots. "Your name's *Saber?* What the hell kind of name is that?"

Swiping sand from his wet breeches, Saber rose. He frowned at Addison. "My real name is—"

Addison thought fast. "He's Saber West," he blurted, borrowing the "West" from Saber's second name, "Westbrook." "I'm Addison Gage, and Saber is my fourth and misfortunate cousin. He and I— Uh . . . Although he and I are of the same age, I don't believe it would be erroneous to say I'm something of a guardian to him. You see, it recently came to my attention that he was in dire straits. When I met Saber I believed it my duty to assist him financially and otherwise. As his blood-cousin I could do no less."

Saber rolled his eyes. "Addison, that's ridic—"

"And these men are Winston Alders, Kenneth Lynnly, and David Clarkston," Addison broke in smoothly, pointing to the three men standing beside him.

Goldie nodded and smiled at each of them. "Does one of you own this estate? Y'see, we got a rabbit, and even though Saber says it's all right, I still want to say I'm sorry. I don't want anybody to get mad at me."

Saber laid his hand on her shoulder, deciding the charade had gone on long enough. "Goldie, I—"

Winston coughed loudly. "Another friend of ours owns Leighwood."

"Winston," Saber said, a note of warning in his voice.

"Quite right," David agreed with Winston. "But he's a dreadfully boring man."

"Positively the dullest man in all of England," Addison added, removing his gloves and slapping his palm with them. "He rarely ventures out of London. With his permission we are enjoying his estate for as long as it pleases us to stay."

Goldie stared at him. His mannerisms were kind of fancy to her way of thinking. "Are you some sort of dukish man?" she asked anxiously.

"No," Addison hurried to say. "I am only a mister." He realized he couldn't tell her he and his friends were earls. If she knew, she'd have a more correct idea of aristocratic behavior. And *her* plans for Saber were much more amusing. "Mr. Addison Gage, at your service."

Groaning, Saber glanced at the treetops. "Goldie, allow me to introduce myself properly. I'm—"

"He's Saber West," Addison said again, glaring hard at his old friend. "Saber, have you given any more thought to that trip to Paris? The last time I spoke to you about it, you were unwilling to go. Have you changed your mind?"

Remembering that his defiance would send him to France with the aunties and their friends, Saber returned Addison's glare. "No, I have not," he snapped. He suddenly understood that Addison was adamant that he not reveal his true identity. Why, Saber didn't know. But he had the uneasy feeling Addison was hatching some obnoxious scheme. And since he had no idea what that scheme entailed, he couldn't very well thwart it. He became silent and wary.

"While the boys and I neared this pond," Addison addressed Goldie, "we couldn't help but overhear you talking about your problem. You say our Saber resembles Lord Tremayne?"

"Spittin' image," Goldie replied. "At least I'm almost sure he is. You ever seen the real Duke Marion?"

Addison closed his eyes as if in deep thought. "You know, I believe I have. It was many years ago. And if my memory serves me correctly, Saber here does indeed resemble him. The real duke, though, is much more handsome."

Saber exhaled angrily. "Addison, I don't know what you think you're doing, but—"

"It doesn't matter that the real Duke Marion's betterlookin' than you, Saber," Goldie cooed. "Folks in Hallensham won't know that, and it'll be our secret." She looked up at him. Was it possible the real duke was more handsome than Saber West? She found that hard to believe. Saber's looks weren't bad at all.

Saber saw the sympathy in her eyes and watched her gaze touch his every feature. He felt caressed, like she was really touching him. It was a moment before the feeling passed. "Goldie," he said softly, "I don't recall agreeing to accept your proposal."

At the downcast expression on Goldie's face, Addison took her hand. "Saber, you are without a doubt the most coldhearted man walking this earth. How could you let this sweet girl down? She's obviously in dire need of your help. Her Uncle Asa is in a spot of trouble, she's trying to get him out of it, and you refuse to cooperate with what could possibly be the answer to her prayers. Have you no shame? Have you no compassion? Have you some desire to see Paris?''

"With a group of fascinating women?" Kenneth added.

"Alone with them," Winston reminded him.

"At their mercy," David speculated.

"Well?" Addison asked. "Will you be Lord Tremayne, or won't you? It wouldn't hurt you to learn what Goldie is proposing to teach you, you know. I realize you're ignorant of the social graces because of the lowly, wretched existence you led before I so graciously offered to assist you, cousin. But now you have a splendid opportunity to acquire knowledge of them. Do you not wish to better yourself? Have you no dream of becoming a . . . a *dukish man?* You may most certainly borrow my cane. After all, you never know when some commoner might dare to insult you.''

Saber saw his friends were all on the verge of hysterical laughter. It pleased them enormously to see him so thoroughly caught in such an absurd state of affairs. He looked at the ground and rubbed the back of his neck.

God, how he would relish getting back at them for this.

The thought made him snap up his head. They obviously believed that practicing to be Goldie's duke would aggravate him to no end. That it would be the worst predicament they'd ever gotten him into, and that it would be a hilarious thing to watch.

So why not turn the tables on them? Not only would he agree to be Goldie's duke, he would give the impression that he was having the time of his life doing it! While Addison and the boys waited for him to become maddened, he would love every minute of it. At least he would *pretend* he did.

It would only be for thirteen days anyway, he reminded himself. And if he acted the part of Goldie's duke, he would be spending all his time with her and have none left for playing servant to Addison and his three cohorts. Then the time at Leighwood would be over, and he could return to London.

"Saber?" Goldie prompted. "I really need to know your answer. I don't have much time, y'see. I'll swannee, there's no tellin' what sorta trouble Uncle Asa's gonna get into while I'm gone, so I gotta get back to Hallensham as soon as I have my Duke Marion."

He looked down at her. She was staring up at him, a mixture of anxiety and hope pouring from her golden eyes. He felt a pang of guilt. Her plans were ludicrous to him and the boys, but they were very important to her.

He remembered she'd traveled for days to find her Duke Marion. Her Uncle Asa was a drunk. Her horse was a thousand years old. A midget and an ugly gray mongrel were her only companions. By the looks of her dress, she was destitute. She'd never had a home. Now that she had finally found one in Hallensham, she was willing to do anything to be able to stay.

"Saber?" she pressed.

"Well . . ." he began lamely, his guilt worsening when he saw the desperation in her amber eyes again.

It wouldn't be right to humor her and then cast her away when the game was over, he realized. But if he saw her plans for him all the way to the end, he'd have to go to Hallensham, which was situated on Ravenhurst—and nothing, no one, would get him back to that godforsaken place.

Perhaps he could write a letter to the villagers of Hallensham, he mused. She could take it back with her as proof that she'd spoken to him. He could even give her some little trinket with the Tremayne coat of arms engraved upon it. She could show it to everyone there. And he could give her enough money to be able to finance a festival in the village. It would be a sign of his goodwill.

Yes, all that would work nicely, he decided. She'd achieve her goal, he'd achieve his, and everyone would be content.

"So what's your decision to be?" Addison asked, noticing Saber's deep contemplation.

Saber took Goldie's hand and tucked it into the crook of his arm. "I believe that's roast rabbit I smell," he said to her. "Shall we go see how long it will be before it's ready to eat? And I do solemnly swear to sniff each bite before I put it into my mouth. You can explain more . . . uh, *dukish stuff* to me while we dine.'' Smiling, he led her in the direction Big had taken.

"Never in my wildest dreams would I have guessed he'd accept his situation with such good grace,'' Winston murmured.

"He was quite willing, wasn't he?'' Kenneth remarked.

"Eager, I think, is a better word,'' David amended. "What do you think, Addison?''

Addison continued to watch Goldie and Saber until they disappeared. The forgotten melody of Saber's laughter came to him again. He folded his arms across his chest and grinned. "Do any of you believe in miracles?''

Dusk was beginning to fall when Saber urged his ebony stallion into the barn, Goldie and Big right behind him on Dammit and Smiley Jones. He dismounted and waited for the stable hands to see to the mounts. "Vincent?'' he called when no one appeared. "Alvin?'' Impatient, he demanded their presence again, this time more loudly.

"What are you carryin' on about, Saber?'' Goldie asked, jumping off Dammit.

"The stable lads,'' he said, peering into the dim stalls. "They're supposed to attend to our mounts. I can't imagine where they've gotten off to.''

"Well, who needs 'em?'' Goldie asked. Deftly, she removed Dammit's tack. "Don't you know how to take care of your own horse?''

Saber stared at her incredulously before he remembered he'd temporarily given up his title and therefore his right to servants also. "Of course I can see to Yardley.''

Goldie giggled. "Yardley? Saber, why'd you give that brute of a horse such a sissy name? Somethin' like Big Butch would fit him better. Or Giant Jack. Or Mammoth Max.''

"Or Colossal Clyde,'' Big added.

Saber frowned at them, then looked at his horse. "I don't think Yardley is sissy at all. It's a fine name.''

Goldie smiled and took hold of Dammit's forelock. She led him into an empty stall, Smiley Jones clip-clopping along behind. Itchie Bon came loping in too, happily settling himself in a soft bed of hay. "And what do you think about the name Marion for a man? Think that's a fine name too?"

Saber's eyes narrowed. "I most certainly do. A fine name indeed."

Goldie shook her head. "Yeah? Well, I don't. It's like Yardley. Too sissy. And you know, Saber, that gives us somethin' to think on. I figure this Duke Marion might be sorta girlish, y'know what I mean?"

Saber sucked in a breath of astonishment. "Are you implying that the duke likes . . . Goldie—I am *sure* the duke prefers women to men."

Goldie giggled again. "All I meant was that his mannerisms are probably . . . delicate. I know Duke Marion isn't one of *those* men. I know it because I found out he was gonna marry Angelica Sheridan. He loved her with his whole body and soul. She died though."

Saber felt sorrow come crashing down upon him. He gripped Yardley's reins as if he could crush the leather to powder.

"That's a sad, sad story, Saber," Goldie continued. "If I think on it too hard, it makes me cry."

When he heard the quiver in her voice, Saber looked at her from over Yardley's back. Her head was bent; she was staring at the straw on the floor of the stall. Was she crying? If so, why? The tragedy hadn't happened to *her*.

"Yeah, a sad story," she said again. "I'll tell it to you sometime."

"I already know it," he whispered too quietly for anyone to hear. He took a moment to get hold of his raw emotions, then quickly finished with Yardley before walking out of the barn. When Goldie and Big didn't follow him, he turned and saw them climbing into the hayloft. "What are you doing?"

Goldie looked down at him. "Beddin' down."

"In the hayloft?"

From his position on the ladder, Big stared at Saber. He still didn't trust the man. "Is it any of your damn business where we sleep?"

"Actually it *is* my business," Saber answered. "Leighwood is at our disposal, there are twelve bedrooms in it, and I assumed you and Goldie would be sleeping in two of them. However, if you prefer hay and dirt to downy feather mattresses, fluffy pillows, and clean silk sheets, by all means indulge yourself. Goldie, where would *you* like to stay?"

"Y'mean we're invited to stay in the house?"

The astonishment in her gold eyes and the long pieces of straw sticking out of her wild, wheat-colored ringlets made Saber smile. *"You* are, but I'm not sure about *him,"* he said, inclining his head toward Big.

Big scrambled down the ladder and stormed to where Saber stood. "You just want to get her alone, you—"

"I've heard quite enough out of you," Saber declared hotly.

"Oh, you have, have you?" Big blustered. "Just who the hell do you think you are? The King of England?"

Saber raised his chin. "The last I heard, we had no king."

The man's imperious manner infuriated Big. "Well, seeing as how you gave your horse such a sissy name, perhaps you think you're the *Queen* of England!"

Saber's hands curled into tight fists. It wasn't going to be easy getting along with the cantankerous midget. Big was intent on badgering him.

Goldie descended the ladder and joined the two men. "Big, what in the world's gotten into you?"

Big stuffed his hands into his pockets and saw her cast a glance at Saber. There was a sparkle in her eyes, and that worried him. "Nothing's wrong," he lied. "Nothing."

"Then shall we?" Saber asked, sweeping his hand toward the mansion.

As they strolled across the grounds, Goldie admired the luxurious garden that was profuse with colorful flowers of every kind. She picked dandelions.

"Saber! Goldie!" Addison called merrily, waving from the steps that led to the manor house. "Come in, come in," he said as they arrived. "And who might you be, sir?" he asked the small man beside Goldie.

Big grunted. "I might be Big Mann. I might be someone else, too. I might be Jeffry Roberts. I might be Sam Brown. I might be—''

''He's Big Mann,'' Goldie cut him off. ''And he's not in the greatest mood today. A regular ill-box is what he is.''

''Ill-box?'' Addison echoed.

''She uses that expression for a person who is crabby,'' Big explained gruffly. ''I, however, am no ill-box.''

''I'm sure you're not,'' Addison replied, and looked at Saber. ''Tell me, Saber. How was the rabbit? Did you sniff each bite of it?''

Saber assisted Goldie up the steps. ''I did.''

''And he held his pinky finger out while nibblin' the meat, too,'' Goldie added, presenting Addison with her bouquet of dandelions. ''I'll swannee, he looked just like a duke, eatin' that way.''

Addison had to look at the ground to keep from laughing. ''Yes, well, that's splendid, Goldie. You've gotten off to an excellent start teaching etiquette to my backward cousin.''

''Amusing, Addison,'' Saber muttered as he led Goldie into the spacious marble hall. ''Very amusing.'' He stopped as Goldie let go of his arm. ''What are the two of you doing?'' he queried when he saw her and Big on the floor struggling with their shoes.

Goldie peered up at him. ''Same thing you should be doin'. Take off your boots, Saber. A duke wouldn't ever track mud all over a house as beautiful as this one. It just isn't proper.'' She rose, placing her hands on her hips as she waited for him to obey her instructions.

He stared down at her. He knew if he got mud all over the house, the servants would clean it up. The thought made him look around. Where was Freeborn, the butler? And that little maid, Abigail, who was forever hovering around the foyer? ''Addison, where are all the—''

''Saber, did you hear what I said?'' Goldie demanded, wiggling her bare toes upon the polished marble floor. ''Take off your boots.''

''Yes, Saber,'' Addison agreed. ''How dare you get mud all over the house! My shoes,'' he said to Goldie, ''are clean. I changed them the very second I came in.''

She nodded approvingly, patted his arm, and then glared at Saber. "You gonna take your boots off, Your Royal Highness Lordship Duke Marion Tremayne?" she asked, emphasizing the name.

Bending, he snatched them off. Goldie noticed his irritation. "Saber, you can't be gettin' mad every time you have to do somethin' mannerly. You're just about as mulish and touchy as ole Roscoe Snood down in Sharksville, Tennessee."

"Sharksville?" Addison repeated. "How very interesting."

"Y'know, I never did understand why they named that town Sharksville," Goldie told him, glancing at the tremendous crystal chandelier twinkling from the high ceiling above her. "There wasn't a single shark anywhere nearby because the ocean was about sixty-five million miles away. Anyway, ole Roscoe—Remember I just told you he lived there? Well, you couldn't even *look* at the man without him takin' your head off for doin' it. I looked at him once, and he hollered, 'What the hell you lookin' at, girl?' Great day Miss Agnes, he near about scared me to death. Nobody's ever yelled at me just for lookin' at 'em before.

"Well, ole Roscoe, he got it into his head to build a house on Can't-Make-Up-My-Mind Hill. Folks tried to tell him the hill got its name for good reasons, but Roscoe was mulish just like I already told you. He built that house and strutted around like he was God's gift to the world. Well, a big rain came. The hill washed away and sprang up in another spot. Nobody could ever figure out how a hill could change places like that, but that one did. That's why it was called Can't-Make-Up-My-Mind Hill. It couldn't make up its mind where it wanted to be, y'see. Roscoe's house washed away too. Worst thing about it was that Roscoe was in it when it did. Nobody ever found him. Some folks said he's buried inside Can't-Make-Up-My-Mind Hill. They were gonna wait till the hill moved again, then look for him. But I don't know if they ever did that because Uncle Asa and I moved on. And there you have it, Saber."

Saber stared down at her again. Her story was so outlandish, it was a moment before he realized she was waiting for him to comment. "Poor Roscoe," was all he could think of to say.

Addison laughed until his sides ached. "I do believe you owe Goldie an apology for being so mulish and touchy, Roscoe . . . er, *Saber*. Oh, and I'm quite sure that *dukish folks* say they're sorry on bended knee," he informed Goldie.

When Saber saw Goldie point to the ground, his first thought was to refuse. The Duke of Ravenhurst bowed to no one but royalty, and that was that.

But the mulish and touchy Roscoe Snood came to mind, and it went against Saber's grain to be compared to the man buried in a traveling hill down in Sharksville, Tennessee. Too, he remembered he was supposed to be enjoying these blasted duke lessons. He sank to the floor on bended knee. Taking Goldie's hand, he pressed a light kiss to it.

Her eyes widened when she felt his lips upon her hand. His touch flowed up her arm and spread throughout her entire body. Her breath caught in her throat. Never had she felt anything so wonderful. So romantic.

Saber looked up and noticed the blush on her cheeks. He smiled. "I humbly apologize for balking, Goldie. For showing such blatant obstinacy. For making your job more difficult. For—"

"Saber!" Winston called as he, Kenneth, and David descended the staircase. "What are you doing? Proposing?"

Saber rose. "Apologizing." He watched as Goldie and Big began examining various pieces of furniture. "Addison," he whispered, "where are all the servants? There's no one in the barn or the house."

"Hence, there's no one to call you 'milord' or 'Your Grace.'"

"We told them we wouldn't be needing their services for the time being," David added.

Saber frowned. "But—"

"Who's the man with Goldie?" Kenneth asked.

"He's her friend, Big Mann," Addison answered.

"*Big Mann?*" David repeated, his lips twitching.

Addison nodded. "And take care not to ruffle him. He's an . . . ill-box."

"He's a what?" Winston asked.

"Saber," Goldie called, motioning for him to join her in front of a large, gilt-framed portrait. "Come look at the man in this picture." Absently, she caressed the hand he'd kissed.

In his stockinged feet, Saber advanced, glancing at the portrait of his mother's Uncle Radcliffe.

"Look at his hair," Goldie said, studying the picture carefully. "We need to get you one of those white wigs. This man is obviously a dukish person, Saber. His flarin' nostrils are a sure sign of that. Mildred Fickle said dukish people always flare their nostrils. Lemme see if you can do it." She looked up at him, her eyes focused on his nose. "Go on. Flare away."

Saber's lip curled when he heard his friends laughing. Drawing himself up to his full height, he inhaled through his nose, making sure his nostrils flared as wide and sharply as they would. "Was that satisfactory?"

She cocked her head, her ear almost touching her shoulder. "Could you make a small snortin' sound while you're flarin'? Mildred Fickle didn't say anything about snortin', but it sounds like it sorta goes with flarin', don't you think? I mean, you don't have to sound like a hog rootin' around for grub, but a soft little wheeze and sniff would go real good with the flare."

"Wheeze, Saber," Addison demanded, wiping a tear of laughter from the corner of his eye. "Wheeze and sniff."

Saber had to swallow his aggravation. Flaring his nostrils again, he attempted a wheeze, but all that came from him was a strangled sound. God, he felt ridiculous.

And yet Goldie was right, he mused. Many noblemen he knew *did* flare their nostrils and make wheezing sounds. They sniffed their noses at many things, and they did it to demonstrate their displeasure or condescension. He'd never paid much attention to it. But as he thought about it now, he realized what an arrogant mannerism it truly was.

"Goldie, I'm afraid I don't know how to wheeze," he

told her, feeling very glad that particular habit was not one of his own.

At the look of defeat in his eyes, Goldie reached up and caressed his cheek. "Don't worry about it right now. I don't expect you to learn everything in one day, Saber. We'll practice wheezin'. Before you know it, you'll be flarin' and wheezin' right along with the best of 'em."

"Great day Miss Agnes!" Goldie exclaimed when Saber lit several lamps in the room where she would sleep. She'd already explored the rest of the gorgeous house, each thing amazing her with its luxury and elegance, but this bedroom surpassed everything she'd seen so far. It was even nicer than the one in which she'd just left Big.

Decorated in pristine white, vivid pink, and apple-green, it was the most beautiful room she'd ever beheld. Gleaming brass was everywhere, providing a striking complement to the color scheme. Warm oak furniture served to soften the effect. Goldie couldn't suppress another soft squeal at the sight of the white lace canopy sweeping delicately to the floor. She knew it would be sheer heaven sleeping in the princess bed.

"Does that little squeal mean you like it or dislike it?" Saber asked. He ambled over to the glass doors that opened to the balcony and began to pull the pink silk drapes across them.

"No, don't close 'em!" Goldie cried, running to the doors. Flinging them open, she stepped out onto the balcony. The moonlit garden met her wide eyes; the fragrance of night-blooming flowers caressed her senses. A graceful tree branch swept lightly across one corner of the balcony, creating a pleasant and soothing sound. Absolute contentment floated through her. "Oh, Saber," she whispered, looking below. "I can't believe I'm stayin' here. It's like a—Well, like a dream," she said shyly. "This house is like a castle. If I were still a little girl, I'd pretend I was a princess."

Saber smiled, suspecting that once he left her alone in the room, she *would* pretend to be a princess. She'd been a mermaid in the pond, hadn't she? "How old are you, Goldie?"

"I'll be nineteen in five months and three days," she replied, still hanging over the balcony. "How old are you?"

"Thirty, and don't lean over so far." She was so little, her feet weren't even touching the ground as she balanced herself upon the rail. "You're going to fall into the shrubbery below."

He scowled suddenly, remembering the time when *he'd* fallen from that same balcony and into those same bushes. God, he hadn't thought of that in years. Quickly, he looked down at his right hand. There it was. The little scar from the injury caused by the fall. Lost in the memory, he ran his finger over the telltale white mark, trying to suppress the bittersweet nostalgia.

"When will you be thirty-one?" Goldie asked.

"I only recently celebrated my thirtieth birthday."

"Did you have a party?"

"No."

"Why?"

"I—Because I didn't want one." Saber's thoughts drifted again to a time when he had birthday parties every year. His mother and father filled the house with presents, and he was pronounced "King for the Day." He even got to wear a crown. He hadn't been "King for the Day" in twenty years. Potent emotion seized him once more, making him long for those days.

Those days that had been taken from him when he'd needed them the most.

"I never knew someone who didn't want a party," Goldie informed him. She got down from the railing, turned to face him, and lifted her balled hands beneath her chin. "Are you sure the owner of this Leighwood estate won't mind me stayin' in this room?"

Saber leaned against the door frame, folding his arms across his chest as he contemplated her. Her eyes were so wide, so full of gold sparkle. Her stance, the way she held her hands, and the unmitigated wonder in her soft, childlike voice . . . She was like a little girl who'd just wandered into the land of make-believe. This made him almost sure that she would be Princess Goldie very shortly. "Why would he mind?"

Slowly, she relaxed her fists, her fingers uncurling on her cheeks, their tips disappearing into the unruly curls framing her face. "I—Well, it's such a *fine* room, Saber," she tried to explain. "Finer even than Imogene Tully's tea parlor back in Bug Hill, Kentucky. The town had a lot of crickets, y'see. I always liked to hear 'em singin' at night. Ole Imogene used to have tea parties in her tea parlor every Wednesday at three o'clock. She near about wore herself into a frazzle puttin' the parlor together. She traveled all over the state huntin' out frilly things to put in it. I wasn't ever invited to her parties, but once she hired me to clean that parlor. It was the first and last time she ever let me in there."

"Bug Hill, Kentucky, and Imogene Tully," Saber mused aloud. He watched Goldie's arms fall to her sides. She clutched handfuls of her dress. The sight of her pale, slender fingers wrapped around the coarse brown fabric of her skirt disturbed him. He thought about how nice they would look lying upon folds of rich, crimson satin.

He brought his gaze upward. The kiss of moonlight upon her bright gold hair made those curly locks seem almost alive. "Why was that the last time you ever saw Imogene's magnificent tea parlor, Goldie?" he asked gently.

The tenderness she perceived in his rich, deep voice made her stomach flutter. "I like the way you say my name."

His brow rose; a slight smile touched his lips. Most women he knew liked the size of his wallet. The vast acreage of his lands. The centuries-old honor of his title.

Goldie liked the way he said her name. "Goldie," he said again for her.

"Goldie," she repeated in a whisper, mesmerized by the intensity of his eyes. "You ever seen seaweed? Not dried-up seaweed, but *wet* seaweed? The kind that washes up with the waves and lays all spread out over the sand? It's such a purty green. So fresh. The seawater makes it sparkle, and it looks real good against the warm, tanned shore. You have seaweed eyes, Saber."

Seaweed eyes. Saber pondered the sound of that. Jillian was fond of telling him his eyes reminded her of exquisite emeralds. Emeralds and seaweed. There was a drastic difference between the two, but how much more vivid was the image of fresh, wet seaweed against a warm, tanned shore. He smiled, thinking of it.

"It was Uncle Asa," Goldie said quietly.

Snatched from his pondering, Saber looked at her blankly. "What was Uncle Asa?"

"Well," she began, still fingering the material of her skirt, "he came to Imogene's lookin' for me. He'd been drinkin.' He—He always drinks," she squeaked. "I tried to keep him out, but Uncle Asa . . . well, he doesn't listen to anyone when he's been drinkin'. Close your eyes, Saber, and imagine a big, clumsy elephant tryin' to walk through a patch of buttercups without crushin' 'em, and you'll know what Uncle Asa looked like in Imogene's parlor.

"He'd barely set foot in it when a lamp crashed to the floor. It was the one with Chinese pagodas painted all over it. A vase broke next, and the water and flowers spilled all over Imogene's love seat. She said she had that little sofa special made by a French sofa-maker, and that she paid a hundred dollars for it. I never believed her. She didn't have a hundred dollars to spend on a sofa. Nobody in Bug Hill had that kind of money. 'Cept maybe old Hiram Winkler. He had a hairbrush that was made of pure gold."

Saber let out a long, slow whistle designed to show her how very impressed he was over Hiram's gold brush. Inwardly, he smiled.

"Hiram was so proud of that brush, he wore it around his neck on a chain. He said he did that so he'd always have his brush handy when his hair got messed up. But Saber, 'cept for about three hairs above each of his ears, the man was *bald*. He just wore the brush like that to show it off. I always wondered what it would be like to brush my hair with a pure gold brush. You think pure gold brushes work any better'n plain wooden ones?"

Saber's inward smile reached his lips. A low chuckle escaped. Goldie had maddened him several times today, but he decided she was quite the most entertaining person he'd ever met. "I really couldn't say. I've never had one."

He did have a sterling silver brush, he remembered, wondering if that counted.

"I don't even have a *wooden* one since I lost the one I had," she said wistfully. "Anyway, the harder Uncle Asa tried to keep from messin' things up in Imogene's parlor, the more he wrecked 'em. Imogene came in and clubbed him over the head with a statue of a chicken. She hollered that neither one of us was fit to be in her parlor and that she didn't know what in the world had possessed her to hire me to clean it. It really hurt my feelin's, Saber, because I hadn't broken anything before Uncle Asa came. I'd been as careful as I know how to be." She bit back tears, succeeding.

"And I want you to know right here and now that I'll be careful in *this* room too," she swore, crossing her heart. "Daddy's honor, I won't touch anything. I'll just sleep in the bed, and that's all. So if you or Addison ever talk to the owner, you can tell him that all I did was sleep here and that I didn't mess anything up while I was sleepin'. And I sleep in a tight little ball, Saber, so I probably won't even wrinkle the sheets all that much."

The promise radiating from her tawny gaze made Saber's throat constrict. *I probably won't even wrinkle the sheets all that much.* Jillian had been here many times and when she left, it most likely took the servants a month to clean things up.

Goldie's promise filled him with something tender. "This is not Imogene Tully's tea parlor, Goldie," he said softly. "And the owner of this estate *does* have a hundred . . . uh, *dollars* to buy a sofa. To buy anything. Wrinkled sheets are the last thing in the world that would upset him. He'd want you to feel comfortable and happy here. I'm sure of it."

"All the same, I'll be careful." She swept past him and back into the bedroom, stopping in front of a beautiful full-length mirror. With her fingers she began brushing her hair.

Saber strode to the door. His hand on the knob, he wished he could make himself invisible and watch her pretend to be a princess, for he still suspected that was exactly what she was going to do when he left. "Good night, Goldie."

Her fingers entangled in her tight curls, Goldie returned the sentiment and smiled.

As Saber left, he felt an odd desire to buy her a brush. A *gold* one. Upon further deliberation, he discovered he wanted to buy her a tiara too. A princess just wasn't a princess without one.

# Chapter 5

**D**ane Hutchins pressed a scented handkerchief to his nose, but could still smell the fetid odor of the cold, dark London alleyway. Sidestepping a pile of rotting offal someone had dumped from the cracked window above, he waited for an old woman to finish picking up the bones littering the muddy ground, then read the name he'd written on a scrap of paper. He stared at the man before him. "It wasn't easy finding you, Ferris, and I would appreciate your undivided attention. I am terribly offended by the stench of this place and wish to conclude this unpleasant business as soon as possible."

Diggory Ferris looked up from the knife he was sharpening. "If ya got 'alf the brains ya pretends ter got, ya'd call me *Mister* Ferris. You bleedin' toffs is all the same. All wind an' piss, ya is. Ya needs a job done an' think ya can waltz out 'ere where all the *filth* lives an' order us around like ya does the blinkin' servants y'got in yer fancy 'ouses. Go git buggered, is wot I say. I ain't no grotty cod's 'ead, I ain't, an' I don't follows no friggin' orders from nobody, 'ear? I *own* the part o' London-town where ya is, see? Yer on *me* grounds, and ya follows *me* lead. I earned me nickname, 'the Butcher,' an' I'd be more'n obliged ter show ya why, guv." With one swift motion, he threw his knife, impaling a large rat.

Dane brushed his coat sleeve. "I'm afraid I really must insist that you address me as 'milord.' " He pulled out a wad of bills.

Diggory's eyes widened at the sight of the huge sum of money. "Milord!"

Dane smiled. "I'll give you three times this much when the job is done. Now repeat what I've told you about her."

"She's little," Diggory recounted. "Curly yellow 'air wot touches 'er shoulders. American, an' talks like one. She's got a bleedin' blastie with 'er. I'll finds 'er an' the dwarf, milord. If she's anywhere in this stinkin' 'ell-'ole, I'll finds 'er. London-town's big, it is, but I got me army ter 'elp me cover it. Best band o' cutthroats wot live, they are, an' I trained 'em meself. Nobody comes or goes without us 'earin' about it. Every street in the friggin' city 'as eyes an' ears." He snatched the money and pocketed it quickly.

Dane nodded, taking a step away from the ruffian. Being in the midst of such repugnant surroundings was highly distasteful to him, but after some inquiring, he'd learned that Diggory Ferris was the most feared assassin in the East End. Dane had spent several days and a veritable fortune tracking the criminal down. For future reference, he pocketed the scrap of paper that had Diggory's name written on it. "I'll be back as soon as I'm able. But you must understand that I have to be careful about leaving my home. I don't want to be connected to this." He slid a gloved finger across the rim of his hat, then looked to see if any grime had come off on it.

"O' course ya don't," Diggory agreed, caressing the bulge of money in his pocket.

"When I do get back, I want to see her body with my own eyes. Hers and the midget's."

"Ye'll see 'em. I'll saves the bodies even if they rots on me."

Dane smiled again. Thinking back, he recalled how furious he'd been when he'd learned Goldie and Big were gone. He'd set out for London immediately, determined to find the American girl before she made contact with Marion Tremayne. He needn't have worried, he mused now, his smile broadening. Lord Tremayne wasn't even in London. The man was on holiday. It hadn't taken Dane long to learn that satisfactory bit of information.

"I'll be going now, Ferris. Back to my home." He reached up, his hand closing around his jeweled stickpin. He shut his eyes. "My home. I am master there, you know," he whispered. "And it is right and good that all is mine because I have deserved it for many years. *He* was once the illustrious prince there. While *I* was the one who labored, *he* ran, danced, and played. He wallowed in luxury while I had to be content with a measly salary and a home fit only for a peasant. It wasn't fair. I knew that from the very beginning."

He opened his eyes, staring blankly into the dark. "He left it long ago. It was his own choice. He cannot have it back. It is my dominion now, and I will do whatever is necessary to keep it." With that, Dane turned and hurried out of the alley.

"Wotever ya say, milord!" Diggory called after him. "Wot a bleedin' looby," he murmured. Shrugging, he went to retrieve his knife. After wiping the rat's blood on his shirt, he continued to sharpen the dagger.

Saber couldn't believe it was only last night when he'd felt that odd desire to buy Goldie a gold brush and a tiara. What he wanted to buy her right now was a seat on the next coach departing for Hallensham. Or better yet, passage back to America!

He left her standing in the middle of the library and stormed to the bookcases. There, he snatched out a dusty volume, thumbing through it as if it were the most interesting book he'd ever had the luck to come across. "I'm not going to walk like that, Goldie," he snapped. "Dukes do *not* wiggle while strolling along."

Goldie fumed and blew a ringlet away from her eye. It flew upward and settled on her eye again, curling cozily upon her lashes. "Since when do you know so much about duke stuff? You're just makin' that up so you won't have to move your bottom a little bit when you walk. Saber, I'm tellin' you, dukes sway their—"

"They do not."

"Yes, they do."

"No, they don't."

"Yes, they do."

"No, they don't."

Goldie's brow rose. "No, they don't," she repeated mischievously.

"Yes, they do," Saber answered automatically.

She tapped her toes on the floor, waiting for him to realize what he'd said. It only took a second. She smiled at the anger in his eyes.

"You duped me!" he yelled at her.

"And tricked you too," she added with a giggle.

Saber slammed his book closed. The dust that rose from it made him sneeze several times. "Listen, Goldie—" He sniffled, his nose still itching. "—dukes do *not* move their—"

"You did it!" she squealed. "The sneeze made you *wheeze!* Oh, Saber, do it again!"

He closed his eyes; his shoulders slumped. "I did not *wheeze*, dukes do *not* move their bottoms while walking, and that is the *end* of this lesson."

"The end of what lesson?" Addison asked as he, Winston, Kenneth, and David ambled into the library.

"Saber isn't refusing to learn something, is he, Goldie?" Winston asked.

"She says dukes wiggle when they walk!" Saber exploded. "Tell her what a ridiculous notion that is!"

Addison took careful note of Saber's exasperation and liked what he saw. The starch was definitely crumbling. Calmly, he sat upon the blue velvet sofa, Winston, Kenneth, and David each taking a chair around it. "I'm sorry to say that I must agree with Goldie, Saber," he said, examining his nails. "I've seen dukes walk, and they *do* . . . uh . . . wiggle."

If Saber had a gun, he knew he'd use it to shoot Addison. "No, they—"

"French dukes do it too," Addison broke in. "You know—the kind who live in *Paris?*"

Saber remembered he had a gun in the next room. "I do not find this amusing. It's—"

"Y'see, y'all," Goldie began to explain, "some people inherit flat feet, bony knees, or crooked teeth. Lunk Milligan back in Spittin' Falls, North Carolina, inherited his mama's hairy ears. Everyone gets somethin' from their folks. Dukish people get a wiggly walk bred into 'em. Mildred Fickle said that even if you dressed a duke in tattered clothes, you'd still know he was a duke by watchin' him stroll. It's all in that blue blood of theirs.''

Saber rolled his eyes. He decided that he'd shoot Addison first, then go to America and shoot Mildred Fickle. ''Goldie—''

''Saber,'' Addison cut in, drumming his fingers upon his knee, ''it would seem to me that instead of balking, you should be thanking heaven that dukes inherit a wiggle walk instead of furry ears. If it were the other way around, I have no doubt Goldie would be trying to come up with a way to glue hair to your ears.''

''That's right,'' Goldie agreed, nodding vigorously. ''There's nothin' I wouldn't do to turn you into a duke, Saber.''

''Saber?'' Addison pressed. ''Kindly let us see that dukish wiggle.''

''Right now,'' David added, smirking.

Saber stormed across the room, his back straight, his shoulders thrown back, his bottom as still as he could keep it.

Addison began whistling a popular French tune. But he was smiling so broadly, he had reach up and squeeze his lips into a pucker in order to perform a proper whistle.

Saber decided a bullet was too merciful. Being drawn and quartered would hurt more.

Winston, Kenneth, and David, seeing Saber's adamant reluctance, joined Addison in whistling the French melody. They even managed to harmonize the tune, whistling louder with each passing moment.

Enraged, Saber spun and faced them, his jaw clenching rhythmically. There was simply no escaping. He took a deep breath, lifting his chin. He wiggled his way across the room, knowing he looked as foolish as he felt. His knowledge was verified by his friends' wild, though silent laughter.

Goldie clapped. ''Oh, Saber, that was just wonderful!'' She skipped to him and gave him a congratulatory hug.

He felt her small breasts caress his middle. The heat of his anger cooled as warmth of a different kind invaded his body. It caught him so quickly, he was unprepared for it and inhaled raggedly. Suddenly oblivious to his friends' presence, he stared down at the bright grin Goldie was giving him, his hands sliding up her arms to rest upon her slight shoulders.

Goldie's smile faded when she saw the smoldering look in his eyes. Those green orbs were afire with something she'd never seen before. Whatever it was, it was catching. She, too, began to feel warm.

Her senses were aroused. He smelled of sandalwood. Sandalwood and silk sheets and another scent akin to something heating slowly, something simmering. She remembered his voice. Deep, rich, full of promise. Sort of like the soft, distant rumble of thunder. Her arms were around the expanse of muscles in his back. She spread her fingers to feel them better. Pressing those muscles, she discovered that they were none too pliable, and his obvious strength pleased her. Her pulse quickened.

Saber could feel the rapid beat of her heart against his belly. "What are you thinking about, Goldie?" he whispered, besieged with the desire to know.

"I—" She closed her lips. She couldn't tell him how handsome she thought he was. How good he smelled or how nice it was to hold him this way. He'd think she wanted him to be her sweetheart, then he'd laugh just like Fred Wattle had.

Oh, if only she were taller, she sighed inwardly. Tall enough so that the top of her head reached his chin. That was the best height to be. And if only she had bigger breasts and could make her freckles go away. Men were drawn to clear flawless complexions, not ones that were splattered with little brown dots. And if only she could make her hair behave. It looked like a yellow bush sitting on top of her head. It was always so wild, as if it led its own separate life and had nothing at all to do with the girl who grew it.

And most of all, she thought wistfully, if only she could think of wonderful and witty things to say! Artful and flirtatious things that other women could think up right on the spot. She said only what was on her mind, and what was so wonderful and witty about that?

Yes, if Saber knew how she felt about him, he'd laugh. A man as handsome as he was looked for a woman who had everything *she* lacked. Sadness welled inside her. Her feelings of inadequacy were nothing new to her, but she wondered why she felt them so much more strongly with Saber.

"Goldie?" Saber urged, still wondering what was going on behind those huge golden eyes of hers. She looked a bit dismayed, and he couldn't think of a reason why.

She wet her lips and blinked. "Saber . . . Do you know what *frugivorous* means?"

Her question was so unrelated to the feelings floating between them, Saber had to think for a moment before he could answer her. "New word for the day?"

She nodded and forced herself to smile.

"Well, let's see," Saber stalled, pretending he had to do some hard contemplating. "Frugivorous. It sounds very much like *carnivorous*, which means to eat meat. Frugivorous. Frugivorous. Could it be, little scholar, that frugivorous means to eat fruit?"

She was amazed. "How did you—"

"What the hell do you think you're doing?" Big demanded, rushing into the room. "Goldie—You—I—Get your hands off her!" he commanded Saber. "I turn my back for one damn minute, and you—"

"Big, stop that," Goldie admonished, stepping from the circle of Saber's arms. "I was only congratulatin' him for walkin' like a real duke. You had no call to—"

"A simple 'Good job, Saber' would have been enough!" Big yelled. "You don't have to hug—"

"Her behavior has been nothing short of proper all morning," Saber intervened. "Like she said, she was only congrat—"

"And you were just eating it up, too, weren't you, you . . . you overgrown octopus!" With that, Big showed Saber his fists and began swinging.

Saber sidestepped Big's assault, then reached out and laid his hand on Big's head. Thus, he kept the ferocious little man at bay. Big continued jabbing, though at thin air. Goldie tried catching hold of his pudgy hands, but his rage made him too fast for her. Saber used his free hand to help her.

Though Addison was irritated that Big had interrupted

Saber and Goldie's embrace, the sight of the three of them grappling and grabbing at each other made him laugh so hard that he nearly fell off the sofa. His three cohorts were equally amused, each of them bent over their knees.

Many moments passed before Addison was able to get control of himself. "What Saber and Goldie say is true, Big," he chortled. "My companions and I have been here the whole time, and nothing indecent whatsoever went on between them. Their embrace was quite innocent."

"And why the hell should I believe *you?*" Big huffed, jerking himself away from Saber's restraining hand. "You're on the octopus' side! Why, it could be that all *four* of you are just waiting for a chance to—"

"Big!" Goldie hollered. "You—"

"Goldie, they—"

"Cease!" Saber bellowed, satisfied when his order was obeyed. He looked down at Big. "Sir, I have warned you before about your conduct. You—"

"And just who are *you* to warn me?" Big demanded. "I've had just about enough of your royal attitude! You—"

"Why don't we all sit down and have a pleasurable conversation?" Addison suggested merrily. "Saber, pour the tea."

Big watched Goldie take a place beside Addison. "I don't have time for sitting around drinking tea. I'm going fishing, and while I'm gone," he told Saber, "you better—"

"Big loves to fish," Goldie broke in. "He's gonna catch us supper. He uses cheese, same as I do. You gonna fry the fish, Big?"

Big took hold of his chin and thought for a moment. "You know, I think I'll stuff it, then bake it."

Saber sighed. If Big's stuffed fish turned out anything like the ham and biscuit breakfast he'd made, it would be inedible. Big had volunteered to do all the cooking, and Saber was positive they would all starve to death soon. God, how he missed the servants. "What do you plan to stuff it with, Big?" he asked suspiciously.

"Well now, I don't know. What do you think would be good—" He broke off, suddenly remembering he was supposed to be angry with the haughty giant. "You're trying to be nice to me to get on my good side, aren't you, you scheming devil! Look, I've decided I won't fight you right now, Saber West, but I'll be keeping my eye on you and Goldie, and if I see or hear one inappropriate gesture or word, I'll—"

"I'll keep that in mind and remember myself at all times," Saber swore.

"See that you do!" Big puffed out his chest and swaggered from the room, confident he'd set matters straight for the time being.

"Saber?" Addison said. "The tea, if you please."

Saber glanced at the huge silver tea set Big had brought into the library earlier. His aggravation rose. Storming to the tea cart, he sloshed tea into five cups, then passed them around.

Addison stared at his brew. "What about sugar?"

Saber stalked back to the tea cart, retrieving the sugar bowl. Frowning, he handed it to Addison.

"Two sugars, please," Addison instructed.

Saber realized he didn't have a spoon. Too irritated to care, he simply turned the sugar bowl over, dumping sugar into Addison's tea. "That was about two spoonfuls, don't you agree, Goldie?"

"Looked more like two *cups* to me," she replied. "Saber, you want me to help you?"

David shook his head. "How very kind of you to offer, Goldie, but Saber is the official tea-pourer here at Leighwood, and I'm sure he wouldn't like anyone taking over his duty."

"Oh," Goldie said. "But Saber, you really should be more careful, y'know. You aren't a good tea-pourer."

"Well, carry me out and bury me decently!" Saber quipped angrily.

"I'll have milk with mine, Saber," Winston informed him. "But just a tad, mind you," he added when Saber brought the small pitcher of milk.

Brow raised, Saber poured one, very tiny drop of milk into Winston's tea.

"Well, a bit more than that," Winston said.

"And I take sugar *and* milk with mine," Kenneth said.

"Same for me," David agreed.

Saber's fingers whitened around the pitcher. "Perhaps I could *drink* the tea for the four of you as well? Heaven forbid that you should strain your throats while swallowing."

"I think we can manage the swallowing, but you failed to bring us napkins," Addison answered, laughing. "I cannot drink my tea without a napkin."

"Oh, really?" Saber asked sardonically. "Then I fear you won't be drinking your tea, Addison, because I'm not going to—"

"You know, the *French* don't drink as much tea as the English," Winston informed Goldie. "Isn't that right, Saber?"

Saber threw Winston a terrible look and fetched the napkins. He laid them over his lower arm, bowing as each man took one. "Just leave them on your laps," he instructed them. "If I should see a drop of tea on any of your mouths, you may be sure I'll rush to pat it off for you."

Goldie saw Saber's irritation. "If it'll make you feel any better, Saber, I'll drink mine just like it is. Y'all are makin' too much of a fancy fuss over tea drinkin' anyway. Y'got that big ole silver service sittin' on the rollin' table over there, cloth napkins, and cups so fragile they'll break in your mouth if you set your lips on 'em too hard. Great day Miss Agnes, you pay so much attention to *that* stuff, it's a wonder you even enjoy the tea when you get around to drinkin' it."

Saber glanced at the tea service and the gleaming tea table upon which it sat. He looked at the fine linen napkins and studied the delicate china cups and saucers. He'd never given a second thought to the elegance of teatime. But now that he dwelled on it, it *was* rather ostentatious.

Goldie took a sip of her tea, grimacing. "This stuff tastes like dirt!"

Saber couldn't suppress a grin. "And when was the last time you feasted upon dirt?"

"Well, never. But I'm sure it tastes like this tea."

Addison took a sip of his also. "Mine tastes like *sweet* dirt. It would seem that Big doesn't know how to prepare tea properly."

"Ah, Big," Kenneth said. "He was truly an . . . *ill-box* today, wasn't he?"

Winston looked at Goldie. "But he cares for *you* very much."

"Only breathing comes before his duty to defend you," Saber added, stabbing his fingers through his hair.

She smiled. "He and I have been together for about four years. I was fourteen when I met him. I saw him with some big men, and they were makin' fun of him. They were callin' him a dwarf, and Big hates that word. He prefers to think of himself as a small piece of humanity in a very large world. Anyway, I wasn't all that much taller than he was, so when I saw those men ridiculin' him, I figured it was my obligation to step in and help him cuss 'em out. Big didn't really have anywhere to go after that, and since I liked him right off, I invited him to come along with me and Uncle Asa. Uncle Asa didn't like it much, but when Big started helpin' out with the chores and stuff, he quit gripin' about it."

"And you care for him, too, don't you, Goldie?" David asked.

She nodded. "Big . . . well, he's the best friend a person could have."

Saber felt a rush of envy over Goldie's love for Big. He didn't take the time to understand why he felt the way he did. He only knew Goldie's affection was something he wouldn't mind having in the least.

"Big's an ill-box sometimes, but there's nothin' in the world he wouldn't do for someone who really needed him," Goldie explained. "You just gotta look under that grouchy outer part of him and find the softy. Uncle Asa—He—I think he's like that too. Hard on the outside, but tender underneath. Lots of people are like that, don't you think?"

Addison gave Saber a meaningful look. "Yes," he agreed quietly. "I know someone who's exactly like that."

"Then there's some who are mean through and through," Goldie continued, twirling a curl around her finger. "Ole Raleigh Purvis down in Pee Dee, Georgia, is one of 'em. Raleigh used to pull the wings off butterflies, then watch 'em crawl away. It was the saddest thing I ever saw. Those poor butterflies, they—''

When she broke off, Saber saw a suspicious glitter in her eyes. *She cries for butterflies.* For some reason he couldn't fathom, he was touched by her tears.

''Ole Raleigh was punished though,'' Goldie went on. ''He got a horse mad at him. The horse threw him, then reared over and over again, poundin' down all over Raleigh. Raleigh lost both his arms.''

''Poetic justice,'' Saber mused aloud, noticing how quickly her tears disappeared.

''Yeah, well, anyway,'' Goldie said, ''Raleigh wanted to die after he lost his arms. I know he had it bad, but y'know, I think dyin's easy. I've never been dead, but it doesn't seem like there's much to it. All you have to do is lie in your grave. It's livin' that's so damn hard sometimes. Some days come and it takes every bit of patience and courage you've got to make it to nighttime. Big and I talk about that sometimes. Y'all ever feel like that?''

She drew her legs up, rested her chin on her knees, and waited for someone to answer her. But the five men only stared at her. She wondered why and decided to stare back.

She saw something similar to admiration in the gazes of Winston, Kenneth, and David, and couldn't understand what they were so impressed about. Addison's eyes were smiling with what looked to be expectation, and hope, and even excitement. She couldn't understand what he was thinking either.

And Saber . . . Goldie cocked her head to her shoulder, studying him. He had a faraway look in his seaweed gaze. A bit of sadness. There was a hint of longing in it too, as if he were dwelling on something he used to have, missed, but could never have again.

Saber watched Goldie skip along the garden path. Her hair, bouncing and shimmering upon her slight shoulders, looked like a soft cloud filled with gold dust. The sight reminded him of the gold brush. If he was going to get it for her, he had to do it soon. Though she was unaware that he and the boys had planned to stay at Leighwood for only a fortnight, *he* knew there was only a week left to that time.

He'd be revealing his identity to her then. He wondered what she would do when she learned he was the Duke of Ravenhurst. She was so capricious with her emotions and thoughts, it was hard to say what her reaction would be.

"Why do you pick dandelions when there are so many *beautiful* flowers to choose from?" he asked as she added several more to the tremendous yellow mass she already held.

She stopped and looked down at the brilliant flowers. "But dandelions *are* beautiful, Saber. And you can weave 'em into crowns, too."

*Who would want a crown of weeds?* he wondered. Taking her elbow, he led her to a group of shade trees. There, he helped her onto a tall wrought-iron bench, smiling when he saw the foot of space between her feet and the ground.

"Good spot, Saber," she said. "Real *umbrageous.*"

He glanced up at the tall trees and nodded.

Goldie frowned. "Did you understand what I said?"

"What?" He looked down at her, smiling at the astonishment in her eyes. *Umbrageous* was her new word for the day, he realized suddenly, and she hadn't believed he'd know what it meant. "I—I'm fairly sure it means 'shady.' Of course I could be wrong."

"You're not," she whispered. "It *does* mean shady."

He clasped his hands behind his back. "Then this is indeed an umbrageous spot." He watched her swing her legs. She looked like a little girl, sitting there with her flowers in her lap. "I thought dandelions were weeds."

"Shows how much *you* know," she replied sassily.

His brow rose. He didn't think there was much to know about dandelions. But the secretive tinkle in her voice and the knowing gleam in her eyes made him wonder if there was a veritable wealth of valuable information within those bright yellow clusters she caressed so tenderly.

He sat beside her, watching as she lifted the flowers to her nose. He knew they were not sweetly perfumed, but the light in her golden eyes told him she was enjoying their fragrance. She was so simple, this little person called Goldie. A whole garden of breathtaking blossoms grew nearby, just waiting for someone to come and sample their heady scents, touch their velvet-soft petals. And Goldie had her dandelions. He smiled again when she brought them away from her face. She had pollen on her nose.

The sight of the yellow powder took him back some twenty-five years. He remembered gathering pollen in a small cup. He'd mixed water with it, trying to make yellow paint. He hadn't thought of that pollen paint in years, and tried to dismiss the memory now, too. What good did it do him to recollect times that had ended all too soon and would never come back again?

"Goldie, you have pollen on your nose."

She wrinkled up her nose, looking down at it. Cross-eyed, she saw two noses and two blotches of pollen. Her hands occupied with the flowers, she turned her head to the side, trying to wipe the pollen off on her shoulder. But she couldn't get her nose down quite low enough. "Can you get it off for me?"

"I rather like it there. It goes nicely with your yellow hair."

"Nicely with my yellow hair," she repeated slowly. A thrill spun through her at the compliment. "Oh, that sounds so purty. I'll leave it on then."

Saber chuckled. "I was jesting, Goldie. I'll remove it straightaway." He raised his hand toward her face.

She drew away. "Y'mean it *doesn't* look good with my hair?"

"What?"

"The pollen."

"Yes . . . yes, it matches your hair, but would you wear it simply because it does?"

"Yes."

"Why? It's *pollen.*"

"So? You said it looked good with my hair."

Saber sat back and crossed his arms. "I know, but people don't wear pollen."

"They can if they want to. I want to. It's not hurtin' anyone, is it?"

"It'll make you sneeze," he warned.

"I like to sneeze. Sometimes I sniff pepper just so I can sneeze. Y'know that little nose tickle that comes right before a sneeze? You feel it startin'. It builds and gets stronger, and you tingle all over waitin' for it to peak. When it comes it feels so-o-o good."

Saber thought of something else that was just like that. Something that started with a tickle, built, became stronger, and felt like heaven when it finally reached the crescendo. Funny. He'd never compared lovemaking to sneezing, but there were a lot of similarities. The thought made him smile. He felt his mirth rising.

When Saber burst out laughing, Goldie frowned. "Well, if it looks *that* ridiculous, I'll get it off." She leaned toward him and wiped the pollen off on his chest, leaving a bright yellow smudge on his snowy-white shirt. She caught his scent of sandalwood again and lingered near him for as long as she dared.

When he felt her nose wiggling and inching along his chest, Saber laughed harder. He couldn't remember the last time he'd felt such profound amusement.

Reluctantly, Goldie sat back in her place on the bench. "Great day Miss Agnes, Saber, you sure are silly today. What's gotten into you?"

He started to tell her, *she'd* gotten into him, but no sooner had the thought entered his mind than he realized the significance of it. His laughter ceased. His smile faded.

God, was he becoming well and truly attached to her? He couldn't let it happen. What good would come of a deeper relationship between them? He'd be leaving for London in a week, and she'd go back to Hallensham. They'd never see each other again.

He felt a sudden touch of sadness and couldn't understand why. After all, he'd only known her for five days. Certainly not enough time to develop any sort of feelings for her.

Certainly not, and he had no use for feelings anyway. No use, and that was the end of it. "Have you no duke lesson for me today?" he snapped.

His abrupt irritation wounded her. She tried to think of what she'd done to deserve it. She couldn't remember what it was, but was sure it was something. It always was. "I'm sorry," she whispered.

He realized he'd come close to shouting at her. The hurt

in her eyes stole his voice away. It was a moment before he found it. "Goldie—"

"Oh, *I* know why you're mad!" She reached out, brushing the pollen off his shirt. "It's all off now. Are you still mad at me?"

"Mad at you? I wasn't mad at you."

"You weren't? Then why'd you snarl out that question about the duke lessons? You almost bit me in two. Somethin' on your mind?"

He made a mental note to try and control his emotions. Her sensitivity was tender and deep, and she took everything very personally. He had no wish to hurt her. He had no wish to tell her what was on his mind either. "No," he replied.

There was *so* something on his mind, she argued silently. She searched his face carefully, seeking some sort of clue that would tell her what it was. He was frowning slightly. His lips weren't relaxed; they were sort of pinched up. His eyes were narrowed. His jaw was moving rhythmically. "What are you chewin'?"

"Chewing?" His frown deepened. What in heaven's name was she talking about? "I'm not chewing anything."

She didn't believe him. "Open your mouth and let me see." She got to her knees on the bench, leaning closer to his face. "Go on and open it. You're chewin' somethin', and I want to know what it is."

He clenched his teeth together, speaking between them. "If I'm chewing something, what business is it of yours?"

"It's my business because you have somethin' to eat, and you didn't share it with me."

"Oh, good God." Saber opened his mouth wide, watching her peer into it. He felt thoroughly absurd. No one had ever stared into his mouth before.

"I don't see anything but teeth and a tongue," Goldie informed him, her eyes a fraction of an inch from his lips. "You have good teeth, Saber. Real white, and real straight. Now, what were you chewin'?' Your cud, like a cow?"

She was comparing him to a bovine! "Goldie, I told you I wasn't chewing—" He broke off. This conversation was the most preposterous he could recall ever having. It made him laugh again.

"Your jaw was movin'. Why was it movin' if you weren't chewin'? I never saw anyone's jaw move like that when they weren't chewin'. That's a strange habit you have, Saber."

Her face was still very close to his. He looked at her lips, wondering how they would feel upon his. *You have a very kissable mouth, Goldie.* The thought both disturbed and excited him. He raised his gaze, looking at her speckled nose. Quickly, he performed the feat of counting those little brown dots. "You have seventeen freckles on the top of your nose."

Her bottom lip quivered. She caught it between her teeth so Saber wouldn't see it trembling. *Why, God,* she asked silently, *did You give me these ugly freckles?* Sitting back down, she buried her face in her dandelions. The flowers drew the tears from her lashes and the sadness from her heart.

"Actually, I have nineteen," she corrected him, speaking into the blossoms. "Nineteen on the tip of my nose, and seven between my eyes. Rudy Lumpkin down in Dilly Corner, Tennessee, said that sometimes freckles get wiped off on your pillowcase at night. None of mine do. I know, because I count 'em every mornin'. Rudy was such a liar."

She spoke so softly, Saber almost couldn't hear her. Earlier, however, he'd noted a suspicious, yet fleeting shake in her voice. "Goldie?"

She pretended to scratch her cheek, thus drying the last tears from them. "I've got a lesson for you," she said lightly. "It's not a duke lesson, it's a lesson about dandelions." She pulled one from her handful, holding it up to him.

He noticed it was a gray, furry one that had gone to seed. He noticed, too, a solitary droplet of water on Goldie's chin. Morning dew from her flowers? Or a tear?

"Dandelions are the most misunderstood flowers in all the world," she announced, raising the gray puff higher. "Most people, includin' a certain seaweed-eyed man I know, think they're weeds. But there's a lot to be learned from the humble dandelion."

"Ah, and what is that, pray tell?" He cast another glance at her chin. The droplet was gone.

"Watch." When she had his full attention, she blew on the dandelion. The breeze caught hundreds of furry seedlings, carrying them swiftly in many directions.

Saber wondered what she wanted him to say. "Am I supposed to clap?"

"No, you're supposed to *think*. Think about those little seeds, floatin' along. They're gonna land somewhere and more dandelions are gonna spring up."

As if in the deepest state of concentration a human being was capable of, Saber squeezed his eyes closed and pinched the bridge of his nose—an action he often performed when he really *was* in the throes of profound deliberation. "Amazing. Truly amazing."

She looked at him from the corner of her eye, realizing he was teasing her. She liked it when he did that. "People have the same power dandelions do, Saber. I've thought long and hard about it for many a year, and sometimes I think about people when I blow on dandelions. Wanna know why?"

She was so excited about telling him, he felt just as anxious to know. "Tell me."

"Well, take bad moods for example. When you're mad, your anger takes off in a great burst, blows along, and pounds down on other people. It takes root and grows, then those people are in bad moods right along with you, and sometimes they don't even know why. Now take happy moods. A nice smile, a cheerful hum, a good deed . . . they spring from you, drift along, and settle on people too. They root, grow, and then those people start feelin' inclined to smile, hum, or do a good deed. And the best thing about it all, is that you can actually *watch* it all happenin'. Just like with dandelions. Seeds from other flowers aren't as visible. But blow on a dandelion, and right before your eyes you see it give up its treasures. And . . . And don't forget that if you blow 'em *all* off, you get a wish," she added softly.

He heard the wistfulness in her voice. "And do all of your wishes come true, Goldie?" he asked gently.

She stared down at her bouquet, assaulted by memories

so painful, it was a long moment before she could forget them. "And you can't kill off dandelions either, Saber," she gushed nervously. "Pull 'em up, smash 'em down, and they come right back. You can't keep dandelions down for long, and that's the way people should be too, I think. So when you're feelin' low, spring back up. It's all in the dandelion, Saber. Now what other flower do you know of teaches those kinds of lessons and gives you a wish too?"

He knew of none. Nor had he ever been told something so meaningful in such a simple way. Her words touched a secret part of him. One he'd been unaware he possessed. He smiled.

She returned it instantly. He watched her smile. It was brilliant with joy. What she was so joyful about, he didn't know, but he felt it too. It was a tranquil and quiet sort of happiness that didn't stem from anything specific. It was just there.

It began to loosen the knots he'd tied around his memories. "I played with dandelions when I was little, too," he told her quietly, hesitantly. "I—There was a big iron pot in our yard. I used to fill it with water, dirt, and dandelions. It was a stew, you see, and I'd stir it with a long stick." God, he thought. That had been so much fun, making that stew. He almost wished he could turn time back and do it again.

But he couldn't. Those days were over. Dandelion stew, his parents, Angelica . . . everything he'd ever loved was lost to him, and he could never have it back again. Sadness, like smoke from a dying fire, curled through him.

"You made dandelion stew?" Goldie asked loudly. "Saber, I did that too! But I didn't have an iron pot. I had a bucket. Just think! We lived a million miles away from each other, but we both liked to make dandelion stew! Isn't that funny?"

Her amazement was contagious, and he felt his sadness fading. "That *is* rather amusing, isn't it?"

Her grin widened little by little. "Saber, you want to do it again? I haven't done it in *so* long."

He looked at her bouquet. As much as he'd enjoyed making dandelion stew as a boy, he wasn't likely to do it now. He was the thirty-year-old Duke of Ravenhurst, for heaven's sake! "Goldie, I don't think—"

"Aw, come on, Saber!" She hopped off the bench and began pulling at his hand. "Let's see if it's as much fun now as it used to be!"

"Goldie, we are both adults," he reminded her sternly. "As such—"

"Can't adults have fun?" she asked, cocking her head. "What harm can dandelion stew do anybody?"

"Well, none, but—"

"Please, Saber? Please?"

The enthusiasm pouring from her bright eyes was too much for him to resist. He could find no more will to deny her. Standing, he took a quick glance around, satisfied when he saw no one about. He'd never live it down if Addison and the boys saw him occupied with dandelion stew. "All right," he said quietly, his gaze still darting about, "but I'm only doing this because *you* want to do it. Myself, I find it utterly outlandish."

"But it'll be outlandishly fun."

"Perhaps it will be for *you*. I will more than likely dislike it completely." He looked around again, relieved when he still saw no one around. "There are feed buckets in the barn. You may use one of those."

Goldie nodded and laid her dandelions on the bench. "And you start diggin' up dirt."

Saber smiled as he watched her scurry to the barn. The wind lifted her skirts, providing him with a quick, but tantalizing view of her dainty legs. She wore no undergarments. The realization made him very warm.

"Dig the dirt, Saber!" she called, disappearing into the barn.

"Oh, yes," he mumbled. "The dirt. Quite right." He set about looking for a place where he could dig, soon finding a good spot in the garden. The flowers grew high, thus hiding him.

But he had no shovel. He imagined he could find one in the barn, but had no intention of taking the risk of being spotted with one. Shrugging, he bent to the ground and began clawing at the dirt with his fingers. "I cannot believe I'm doing this," he muttered to the red blossom touching his nose.

But the loosened earth felt cool and good to him, he realized, scooping up a great handful of it. He squeezed it, smiling when it formed a soft, moist ball in his hands. Bringing it toward his face, he sniffed it. The scent filled him with contentment. He'd loved dirt as a boy, and discovered it still held a certain fascination for him. Grinning, he dug up more, making a pile by his foot.

"Oh, Saber, that's good, soft dirt!" Goldie exclaimed, arriving with the tin bucket and dandelions. "There aren't any clods in it at all."

He dried his perspiring brow on his crisp shirtsleeve, noticing the dirt beneath his nails. He hadn't seen them look like that in twenty-five years. "I worked all the clods out."

"I never let any clods get into the stew, did you?"

He shook his head and wiped his dirty hands on his immaculate trousers. "Rocks either." Standing, he took the bucket from her. After filling it with water from the garden fountain, he brought it back and placed it on the ground. He handed Goldie a stick he'd found lying among the roses. "For stirring," he explained.

She nodded. "Now, you put in the dirt, and I'll add the dandelions."

He looked around again, still sure someone was going to catch him involved with this unseemly activity. "It's your stew. I dug the dirt, and I'll do no more. I'll merely watch."

"Watchin' isn't any fun."

"Nevertheless, it's all I'll do."

"Y'know what, Saber?" she asked, looking up into his narrowed eyes. "You're about as much fun as a hangnail."

"Indeed," was his only response.

Sighing, Goldie added the dirt and dandelions to the water, then began to stir the mixture with the stick Saber had provided.

Saber observed her quietly for a moment, deciding she was going about it all wrong. He kept his opinion to himself for as long as he could, but soon couldn't resist giving her a suggestion. "Goldie, you have to stir harder than that. If you don't, the dirt on the bottom won't get mixed in well. Here, let me show you." He tried to take the stick from her.

She held it tighter. "What are you? A professional dandelion stew maker? I made enough of these stews when I was little to know that stirring it—"

"Look, I made them too, and I'm telling you that you're stirring too—"

"Then get your own stick and stir the way you want."

For a split second that was exactly what he felt inclined to do. But no sooner had the urge hit him, than it faded. He remembered himself immediately. "I told you I was only going to watch."

"Yeah? Well for someone who's only watchin', you're sure interferin' a lot."

He raised his chin defiantly. "I was only offering suggestions. It's your stew, and if you want all the dirt to stay on the bottom then by all means let it. And I must tell you, Goldie, that I don't appreciate being compared to a hangnail."

Goldie grinned, feeling mischief overtake her. "Maybe you're right, Saber. Maybe I'm not doing this right. Show me how it's done." She snatched the stick from the stew and tossed it to him, her eyes widening in feigned horror when dark mud splattered the front of his stark-white shirt.

He glanced down at himself, unable to determine if he was angry or amused, to utter a word or decide what to do.

"Oh, Saber. Look how filthy you are."

He heard a naughty lilt in her voice and looked up from his shirt. The dare radiating from her huge amber eyes erased all thought of remaining genteel. "And you're a tad too *clean,* you little brat." With that, he reached into the bucket and got two handfuls of mud.

"Saber," Goldie squeaked, backing away, "don't."

Stalking her, he caught her and smeared the mud on her cheeks, adding a blob to the end of her nose for good measure.

"You're gonna get it now," she mumbled, watching the mud slide from her face to the front of her dress. Marching back to the bucket, she got some mud and spun to face him.

He refused to let the childish game continue. "Goldie, this has gone on far enough. You dirtied me, I dirtied you, and that's the end of it. Now drop that mud immediately and we'll go tidy up."

She paid him no mind. Quickly, she patted her mud into a pie. Drawing back her arm, she aimed carefully.

"Good God!" Saber yelled when the pie slapped into him. "Goldie!"

She screamed loud and long when she saw him racing toward her. She knew if she ran, she'd never escape him. Instead, she picked up the bucket, having every intention of sloping its contents all over Saber when he arrived.

But the bucket was heavy, and she dropped it. Mud sloshed all over the ground. Her eyes widened when Saber flew into the puddle. As he slipped, one foot caught hers, causing her to fall with him. He splashed down on his back; she landed directly on top of him.

They were nose to nose, chest to chest, almost mouth to mouth. Both were still for a very long moment.

Saber couldn't ignore the feeling of her breasts pressed against him. Nor was he impervious to the way the mound of her femininity burned into his belly. A special heat curled through him, and the cold mud in which he lay didn't seem so chilly anymore. "Goldie," he murmured.

The odd sound in his voice when he said her name gave her a deep sensation of something wonderful. She was well aware of the feel of him beneath her. He was so hard. Ridges and valleys of muscle covered him all over. Her breath quickened. "I—Saber—Isn't this fun?" she whispered, wondering where her voice had gone and why she couldn't think of anything else to say.

He read her emotions in her eyes and heard them in her whisper. Smiling, he reached out and pulled a soggy dandelion from one of her mud-caked ringlets. As he played with the curl he struggled with desire, and thought about his situation. The Duke of Ravenhurst was covered with mud. Not only that, he was lying in it as well. He contemplated many things at that moment. The smell of dirt. His black fingernails. The stew. The stirring stick. The mud fight. If not for Goldie and her dandelions, he'd never have remembered how much fun those things had been. There was nothing in his life to *cause* him to remember them.

"You know, Goldie," he said softly, watching that sparkle in her eyes, "you're right about dandelions. They aren't weeds at all. They're very special."

*Just like you,* he told her silently. *Just like you.*

# Chapter 6

F rom the threshold of the library, Saber watched her.
The little person called Goldie, he mused, liking that
description of her. She was sitting cross-legged on the
floor, leaning over the large book in her lap. Her hair fell
around her face, shielding her expression from him, but
he knew her eyes were bright with whatever it was she was
feeling at that moment. Delight, worry, excitement, anger,
sadness . . . she could hide nothing. He liked that, too.

Chuckling quietly, he reached up to his head, patting
the wig Addison had found in the closet of one of the
unused rooms. White powder floated all around him. He
slid a fine, pearl-handled cane through his fingers, absently thinking about the insulting commoners of the
world. Smiling, he wondered what his teacher would say
when she saw him. It occurred to him that he was anxious
for the sweet giggle and bright grin she'd probably give
him. Hers was a beautiful smile, and it never failed to
make him want to smile back at her. "Do I look like a
duke?" he asked.

Her head snapped up, her curls bobbing. "Oh, Saber,
*look* what I found!" She held up the book, scrambled to
her feet, and began running toward him.

Saber watched her coming. A footstool sat directly in
her path, and he could tell she didn't see it. He dropped
the cane and bolted out of the doorway, reaching her just
as she tripped over the stool.

She fell into his arms. "Put me down, Saber, and let
me show you what I found!" She tried to squirm her way
to the floor.

He grinned when she showed no gratitude for his heroic rescue. She hadn't noticed his wig either. She was simply too excited over her book. Chuckling, he set her down. "Don't I deserve some praise for saving your life the way I just did?"

"Savin' my life? Great day Miss Agnes, Saber, if I'd fallen, I'd only have gotten the breath knocked out of me. People don't die from that, y'know."

He pretended to be insulted, exaggerating a woebegone expression.

Goldie relented. "Thanks for catchin' me."

His expression became sadder.

"Thanks for keepin' me from gettin' the breath knocked out of me."

Saber hung his head.

"Oh, all right, I owe you my life." Goldie knelt and pressed her lips to the toes of each of his boots. "There," she said, rising. "I've kissed your feet. Satisfied now?"

He laughed loudly. "Goldie—"

"Saber!" Giggling, she reached up and touched his wig. "Oh, Saber, you look so *dukish!* And . . . and so *ridiculous!* Take that thing off."

There they were, he mused. That giggle and that smile. They made him feel so content. "I thought you *wanted* me to wear a wig."

"I do, but not until we get to Hallensham. Why, you look an old lady with it on! Oh, Saber, look what I found!" She picked up his hand and laid the book in it.

He looked down at it. It was Shakespeare's works. But before he could ask her what was so all-important about the volume, she snatched it out of his hands and flew to the settee.

"Saber, this guy, Shakespeare, really knew duke stuff. I was kinda worried about how dukes talk, but I'm not anymore."

"Oh?" Saber asked suspiciously. "And why is that?" He removed the wig, tossed it to a table, and joined her on the love-seat.

"Because Shakespeare wrote just like dukes talk. I'm sure of it. He uses words like 'thee,' 'thou,' 'dost,' 'hath'—"

"But Goldie, Shakespeare lived over two hundred years ago. People don't talk like that anymore."

"Dukes do. Saber, trust me," she begged, looking up at him. "I know more about this than you do."

Saber tried to look serious. With all his might, he succeeded in keeping more laughter at bay. That this little American was so sure she knew more about aristocrats than *he* did . . . well, it was quite the most amusing thing he could think of. "Very well, Goldie. You have my trust."

He spoke so softly, she thought dreamily. His velvet voice reached out, caressing her. She forgot about her book, and became lost in thought. Ever since they'd played in the mud, Saber had claimed nearly every notion that entered her mind.

And it was happening again, now. Her eyes fluttered closed. Warmth settled around her, hugging her. Images took shape in her head. Saber was near. He was coming closer to her. He held her tenderly, kissing her, whispering the sweetest things . . .

"Goldie?"

"Saber," she answered, her eyes still closed.

"Goldie, are you falling asleep?"

Her eyes flew open. Hands shaking, she opened the book in her lap, trying to concentrate on the words. But they were nothing but black blurs spread across the page. She could dwell on nothing but Saber's nearness, his wonderful scent, the tender way his voice touched her. Bittersweet longing seized her. Never had she been attracted to any man the way she was to Saber. "It's just never hit me this hard before," she whispered.

"What hasn't?"

Her gaze widened. *Great day Miss Agnes. I talked aloud!* "Uh, nothin'. I—Saber, Shakespeare added 'eth' and 'est' to the end of words. You don't *walk*, you *walketh*. *Think*, I reckon, is *thinketh* or *thinkest*. *Kiss* is *kisseth*. *Love* is—"

She broke off, horrified at what she'd inadvertently said. Now Saber was going to think she wanted to kiss him. That she was falling in love with him. He'd laugh at her

. . . or maybe, like Fred Wattle, he'd play her along first, *then* laugh.

Humiliation and dread smothered her. She didn't know what to do or say. Her fingers turned white around the black cover of the book.

Saber saw her distress instantly and was completely bewildered by it. One minute she was about to burst with excitement, and the next she was nervous. Almost afraid. "Goldie—"

"Yes, yes, yes, I'm sure dukes talk like this!" she blurted, pointing to the page. "I'll leave this with you. Read it, Saber. Learn how to put all those 'tweres,' 'hithers,' 'wilts,' and 'henceforths' into your vocabulary." She stood, pushing the book into his hands. "We'll practice together tonight after supper."

She knew she had to leave the room. She was on the verge of tears and had no wish for Saber to see them. Turning, she crossed to the door, but stopped when she reached the upside-down footstool. As she righted it, she spied a woven circle of dandelions lying nearby, and realized it must have fallen out of her pocket when she tripped. Picking it up, she returned to Saber and placed the wreath around his head. "It's a crown," she whispered. He was so handsome, she thought, a catch in her throat. So handsome, so sweet . . . so very wonderful. His eyes were full of softness. "I meant to give it to you earlier, but I forgot."

Saber watched openmouthed as she spun on her heel and fled from the room. There had been the glitter of unshed tears in her eyes. The memory awakened the desire to dry them for her. He felt an overwhelming longing to follow her, take her into his arms, and kiss away her odd melancholy. Kiss her. Deeply. A passionate kiss that would tell her how he felt about her.

How he felt about her?

Anger spiraled through him. This was the second time he'd wondered about his feelings for her. *No!* he raged. What in God's name had he been thinking of by imagining himself holding Goldie? By kissing her with all the emotions she evoked in him?

There were no emotions. She was a special person, yes,

but only because she was so different from anyone he'd known before. Unique. But that didn't mean he felt anything deeper than friendship for her. She was only a girl he knew, and that was the extent of it.

There was no time left for embraces, kisses, or feelings anyway, he reminded himself. The time at Leighwood was over. Tomorrow morning they would leave.

He stood, looking down at the book; noticing a wet spot that stained one word on the page. It was Goldie's tear. He knew it to be so, and touched his finger to it. His heart longed to know why she'd shed it. His mind dismissed it.

He looked at the page more closely. The tearstained word was *love*.

Love. The cause of every heartache he'd ever had.

He tossed he book to the settee and left the room.


"You've been crying," Big said. He left the doorway of Goldie's bedroom, ambling to her bed, where she was sitting. "Has Saber done something to upset you?"

Her gaze touched everything in the room but him. "He had on a white wig a little while ago. He looked just like a duke."

Big crossed his arms over his chest. "You're evading my question. What has he done? He . . . Goldie, he hasn't tried to touch you, has he?"

*If only he would,* she answered silently. "Big, Saber and I are just friends. Why would he touch me?"

Big saw her eyes were brimming with pain. "And that's the problem, isn't it?"

She slid off the bed, crossed to the mirror, and began brushing her hair with her fingers. "I don't know what you're talkin' about."

His eyes narrowed. "You're good at many things, Goldie Mae, but the one thing you can't do well at all is lie. Every single thing you feel or think shines from your eyes. Did you know that? You like Saber, and you want—"

"I told you we're just friends."

"But you're dreaming of it being more than that. I'm not blind, Goldie. I've seen the way you look at him. Why, yesterday you spilled tea all over your dress when he *smiled* at you! Imagine spilling your drink on account of some ridiculous grin.''

''His smile isn't ridiculous. It's beautiful. And I only spilled a few drops. It was just as well. I don't like tea.''

''Well, these English people can't live without it. Lord, I can't even count how many pots of the mess I've brewed since I took over the kitchen. Me, I like my coffee. Now, shall we get back to your tears? You were crying over that man, weren't you?''

She shook her head.

Big tapped his foot. ''Daddy's honor?''

She looked at the floor. She'd never been able to hide anything from Big, and she couldn't now either. ''He's so handsome, Big. So strong. Sometimes his grin is crooked. He looks like a bad little boy when he smiles like that. I never thought I'd meet a man I'd like better than Fred Wattle, but Saber . . . He teases me and makes me laugh. And he treats me so nice! He always gives me the softest chairs. In the parlor he helps me into 'em. In the dinin' room, he pulls 'em out for me. He does a lot of nice stuff with chairs. He's smart too. He's known all my new words for the day. He probably hears Addison say 'em. And there's somethin' about him. Something real special, Big. Like he knows exactly what he's gonna do next and has no doubt at all that it'll turn out right. He's real sure about things.''

''Conceit,'' Big huffed.

''Well, sorta, but not really. It's somethin' else. It's different from conceit. He does and says things real fast, like he doesn't even have to think about 'em. He just *knows.*''

''He has an air of authority.''

''Yes! Yes, an air of authority.''

''And no right to it. Goldie, the man was destitute before his cousin Addison began assisting him. We know that. And yet he acts as though he has all the power in the world right at his fingertips. He—''

''I like the way he acts. When he gets forceful about somethin', his chin raises a little bit. My stomach goes all fluttery when he does that. And y'know? I think that chin-raisin' of his is real dukish. And I didn't even have to teach it to him. He does it all by himself. Yeah, he's comin'

right along with bein' dukish. It won't be long before we'll
set out for London for the duke-spyin'.''

Big frowned, realizing she was trying to change the subject. He refused to let her. "You're attracted to his chin?"

She blew a curl out of her eye. "Big, I like *all* of him,
not just his chin. I like his everything."

Big stiffened. "His *everything*? And just what the hell
does that mean?"

"Nothin'," she replied flippantly. "But even if it did
mean somethin', you forget I'm eighteen. And I'll be
nineteen soon. Phyllis Crackle got *married* when she was
sixteen. Big, I'm not a little girl anymore."

Big felt a wave of sadness. "I know. But . . . It's hard
for me. Sometimes I think of you as my daughter. I try
to—You—I worry."

She softened immediately. "I'm sorry, Big. I didn't
mean to talk back to you like that. You know I love you."

He nodded. Her love was a precious gift, he thought.
He hoped to God that if she decided to offer it to Saber,
the man would see its worth. "Tell me why you were
crying."

"Oh, Big," she squeaked. "I'm so afraid to show him
how I feel. I say dumb things to him. When he looks at
me with that softness in his eyes, I don't know what to
do. I'm so scared I'll mess up, and then he'll laugh at
me."

Big decided then and there that if he ever saw Saber
taunting Goldie, he'd kill the blackguard with his bare
hands. "Be yourself," he advised sternly.

"But he won't like—"

"If the man doesn't like the real Goldie Mae, he's too
stupid to bother with in the first place."

"But—Big, the real Goldie Mae . . . I'm so . . ."

When her voice trailed away, he knew exactly what she
was thinking. "I've told you over and over again that the
things people say about you aren't true, Goldie," he said
as tenderly as he knew how. "I suffer ridicule too, and I
know how hard it is to ignore cruel remarks. But—"

He broke off. How many times had he tried to convince
her of her worth? He'd never been able to do it before,
and found he didn't have the right words now either. Nev-

ertheless, he'd try. "Many people criticize you because they're jealous, Goldie. They wish they could be more like you, and since they can't, they make themselves feel better by taunting you. Others tear into you because of Asa. And Asa himself—The things he says—You *aren't* worthless. You *aren't* ugly. You *aren't—*"

"Big, you say that because sometimes you think you need to be a father to me, and that's the sort of thing a father would say."

Her distress was almost tangible. "Goldie," he said, and heard his voice tremble, "that's not why I'm trying so hard to convince you of your merits. You—"

"Big," she cut him off, unwilling to hear more of what she just couldn't make herself believe, "you're always tellin' me—"

"I *know* I've told you all this before, but it just doesn't sink in! Your problem is that you've been put down so much and for so long and by so many people that you can't see anything of value about yourself. You've suffered so much anger and hatred from people that you're scared to death of making someone mad at you. So you're never sure how to act in certain situations. That makes you nervous and totally lacking in confidence.

"Oh, you're very good at hiding your secret pain and anxieties from others," he continued, "but do you know how many nights *I've* laid in bed worrying about you? Wondering if there is anyone in this entire world who can open your eyes and heart to the special person you are? It tears me up to see you trying so hard to do everything the way you think others want you to. To see you dreaming so hard for things, only to have those dreams vanish right before your eyes. I can't even count how many prayers I've said that someone would come along one day and make you feel like the beautiful princess you are."

"Oh, Big, I'm not a princess."

"You take everything so literally, Goldie. To me, a princess is a girl deserving of every wonderful and beautiful thing she desires. She's someone who deserves to be cherished and loved."

He shuffled to the door and turned to look at her. The longing on her face tugged at his heart; he knew very well she was yearning for Saber. His misgivings about her feelings for the man didn't lessen, but he knew at that moment there was nothing he wouldn't do to help her. "I have to go make supper now, but before I go I want you to know something, Goldie. I can't understand what it is you see in that big oaf, but whatever it is, I trust it's something good. Granted, you showed poor judgment over that half-witted Fred Wattle, but you were younger then. As you said, you're going on nineteen now, and I guess that's old enough to recognize good qualities in a man. So if there's any way that I can assist you with all this romantic nonsense, I'll try. Lord knows I'll probably regret it, but I'll try."

She shook her head. "Big—"

"I know, I know. It won't work, right? He won't respond. He'll laugh at you. You're not good enough for him. You don't deserve him. It'll all start out like a dream come true, and then it'll disappear. Right, Goldie? Isn't that what you're thinking? Isn't it?"

She didn't answer. He'd already said it all.

"Couldn't we just try?" Big suggested. "What harm is there in that?"

"I—Well . . ."

"Who knows what might happen? And now that I think of it, it's probably a damn good idea for you to be around the man as much as possible. Saber's got enough confidence in himself to share with the entire world, and you have none at all. It could be that some of his self-assurance might rub off on you. And I *don't* mean that literally, Goldie Mae. There will be no rubbing going on between the two of you."

She blushed. "What are you going to do for us?" she asked anxiously, wanting with all her heart to believe that a romance with Saber might very well be possible.

"Well, I might could make a special supper for the two of you one night. Maybe some nice pork ribs and—"

"Oh, no, Big. Ribs are too greasy, and if he smiled at me, I'd drop 'em on my dress."

"Right. Then I'll make a beef stew and—"

"But I might spill that too."

"Look, Goldie, you're going to have to calm yourself

when the man smiles at you. If you don't, you're going to starve to death. That or ruin all your clothes.''

She nodded obediently. "I could make sure not to look at him when I'm puttin' somethin' in my mouth.''

"Yes, do that. And the night I make the supper, I'll put fresh flowers on the table and maybe a candle or two.''

In an excited gesture, Goldie clapped her hands together. "And you could play your harmonica in a darkened corner! You know how good you play 'Amazin' Grace.' ''

"Yes, I could do that, couldn't I?'' He nodded, dwelling on his musical talent and feeling rather smug over it. Goldie's giggle brought him back to the moment. He cleared his throat. "Yes, well, I can't promise I'll ever like the man, but since you do, I'll try to be civil to him. I ask only one thing from you, and that is for you to be careful. Guard your heart well, Goldie. It's the only one God gave you, and I can't imagine Him giving you another.''

"Thanks, Big.''

Big started into the hall. "Oh, and one more thing. I don't know why you're brushing your hair with your fingers. There's a perfectly good brush lying right there on that table. You may as well use it while you're here.''

When Big was gone, Goldie hurried to the dressing table. There, gleaming up at her from a snow-white doily, was a gold brush. She picked it up, staring at it for a very long while before clasping it to her breast.

Only one person here at Leighwood knew of Hiram Winkler's solid gold brush, she realized. Only one person here knew of her secret desire to find out how well a gold brush worked.

A tear of pure joy slipped down her cheek.

Sitting at the massive desk in his room, Saber looked at the papered wall in front him. On the other side of it was Goldie's bedroom. She'd been in there since running from the library earlier that afternoon. He wondered what she was doing. Wondered if she'd found the brush, his farewell gift to her.

And he wondered why he felt so empty inside.

He turned up the lamp and reread the letter he'd written to the people in Hallensham. It said everything he wanted it to say, and he hoped it would convince the villagers that Goldie had, indeed, found him. He folded it, sealed it with the Tremayne crest, and placed it next to the packet of money he would instruct her to use for a village festival. Near the money lay the diamond stickpin he would give her also. It, too, bore the Tremayne coat of arms.

From across the room, Addison stared at Saber's back. "It wouldn't take very long to journey to Ravenhurst. A week. Probably less. You could stay for only a short while. Saber, it would do you good to see your lands, and—"

"No." Saber rose, but kept his back to his friend. "I'll never go back."

"Goldie lives there," Addison hinted. "If you never go back, you won't see her again."

Saber tensed. That empty feeling came to him again. Blast it! He had to get control of himself. "What has that to do with anything?"

"You like her. I can't say fairer than that."

"I like the tailor who makes my shirts too, but if I never saw him again it wouldn't be the end of my life." Comparing Goldie to his tailor was utterly ridiculous, but in light of his impatience for this conversation to end, it was the only thing he could think of to say. He had no desire to discuss Goldie. It was hard enough to keep from thinking about her.

"The end of your life," Addison repeated. "She's *brought* you to life again. Can you not see that?"

"Addison—"

"She makes you laugh."

"Lots of things make me laugh." God. Another utterly ridiculous statement. Goldie wasn't a thing. She was a person. A special little person. One who, after tomorrow morning, he would never see again. He looked at the wall, again wondering what she was doing on the other side of it.

"Lots of things make you laugh?" Addison asked. "Name one."

Saber tried and failed. He tried again. Nothing.

"Admit it," Addison pressed. "She's—"

"Leaving for Hallensham tomorrow," Saber finished for him. "Just as I am departing for London. Her world is in the village, mine is in the city. And that, Addison, is the end of this discussion."

Addison sighed. He felt extremely disappointed, for he'd been hoping with all his heart that Saber would want to see more of Goldie. But apparently the time they'd spent together simply hadn't been sufficient for Saber to become truly attached to her. If only something would happen to keep Saber here at Leighwood, he thought wistfully. Something important enough to make Saber want to stay.

But there was nothing Addison could think of that would successfully bring about those ends. "Very well, Saber." He rose and walked to the door. "Will you be joining us for the last charred meal we'll be forced to eat? The boys and I hunted ducks today. They were fresh and plump when we gave them to Big. I shudder to think about what they look like now."

Saber smiled. "I'll be there."

"Saber?"

"What now?"

"Your crown is crooked."

Saber reached up and felt the wreath of flowers he'd forgotten to take off. Removing it, he held it for a moment, then dropped it to the desk. It landed over the stickpin. From within the circle of bright yellow blossoms, diamonds glittered up at him.

Diamonds and dandelions. And dreams weaving through them. Dreams. His, all lost. Hers . . . He didn't know. He knew only she had them.

God, so many, many dreams, and all of them buried so deeply.

"Daydreaming, Saber?" Addison asked, noticing Saber's profound reflection.

"Addison, did I ever tell you about the time when *I* caught a duck? I was nine."

It was a moment before Addison could answer. This was the first time Saber had offered to share a memory of his childhood at Ravenhurst. "No," he said softly. "You never told me that."

Saber stuffed his hands into his pockets and walked to

the window. He stared out at the pink sky of dusk. "I told my parents that I would bring home the meat for supper that night. I was so anxious to provide it. I worked all afternoon on a trap of my own design. When I'd finished it, I set it near the pond, put a bit of corn inside it, then hid to wait and watch. About an hour later, a duck walked straight into it. The door snapped shut, and he was caught. Addison, I was so proud that the trap had worked.

"I brought the duck home, and my father instructed me to kill it. I couldn't do it. Instead, I freed it, even though I was afraid Father would be angry at me. I'd wanted so much for him to see how manly I was."

"Was he angry?"

Saber felt a rush of tender feelings. "No. He laughed, and so did Mother. We ate eggs that night. No one said a word to me about not being able to slaughter the duck. I remember those eggs being one of the most delicious meals I ever had."

It was difficult for Addison to imagine Saber catching a duck. Poignant emotion swept through him at the thought. "Eggs are good for supper," he said lightly, trying to talk past the lump in his throat.

Saber nodded, still staring at the rosy sky. "And I had a tree house," he mumbled, more to himself than to Addison. "The men in the village built it for me. I hung a painting of the Nativity in it. I've never been overly religious, but that particular painting was the only one my mother was willing to part with. And I really did like the picture. My favorite thing about it was Mary's donkey. It had the most gentle eyes, and it made me want a donkey of my own. I . . . wonder if my tree house is still there? I wonder—" He broke off, looked down at his boots, and cleared his throat. "Addison, I'll be downstairs directly."

Addison realized he was being dismissed. Ordinarily, he might have stayed to drag more information out of his friend. But Saber had revealed much already. More than he ever had before. He left quietly.

Saber heard the door close. But inside him, another opened. He stood at the window for a long while daydreaming, reliving memories he'd forgotten.

* * *

"I suppose it never occurred to you to *help* me, did it?" Big blasted. "I'm not a cook, dammit!"

Addison and his companions looked at Big, then at each other, and then at the charred meat on their plates.

"*We* provided the meat," Winston reminded him.

"*We* provided the meat," Big mimicked, achieving just the right degree of haughtiness in his tone. "So what! Anyone with a gun and a halfway steady arm can shoot ducks sitting on the water! *Cooking* them is an entirely different matter!"

"Big is right," Saber announced, strolling into the dining room. "If you boys think you can cook any better, why haven't you?"

"But he didn't even remove all the feathers," David said, picking up a wing and showing Saber the burned feathers still sticking out of it. "Isn't there anything else to eat, Big?"

"Yes, as a matter of fact, there is," Big assured him. Turning, he waddled to the sideboard, returning with two platters.

The men looked at a pile of black lumps on one dish, and a hunk of something even blacker on the other.

"What is that?" Kenneth asked.

Big slammed the platter covers onto the table. "Bread and potatoes!"

"Oh," Kenneth said. "How terribly stupid of me not to see that with my own eyes."

"Look," Big snapped, "I've been listening to the four of you gripe for almost two weeks, and I've had just about enough—"

"Big," Goldie called as she walked into the dining room, Itchie Bon loping beside her, "what's got you into such a huff?" She stopped when she saw Saber. Her breath escaped her on a ragged sigh. As if he might disappear in the next instant, she took her fill of him.

He wore snug buff trousers. They hugged his lower half, leaving very little to her imagination. The muscles in his thighs were evident. He had long legs. Thick. Full of strength. The thought made her feel weak.

She lowered her gaze. Shiny boots encased his calves. The black leather provided a striking contrast to the pale ivory rug. They were only boots, but they looked so elegant on him.

She looked up a bit. A bit more. When she realized where her gaze had stopped, she blushed. Great day Miss Agnes, she'd never stared at a man *there* before. She'd never even been tempted. But with Saber . . . Her gaze flew upward.

His white shirt was as well-fitting as his pants. It stretched tightly across his chest, and was opened slightly, creating a vee, giving her a glimpse of . . . more muscle, she mused, flustered.

His hair, dark and wavy, touched the top of his snowy white collar. Chandelier light shimmered through those midnight-black locks. It looked to Goldie as if he wore hundreds of tiny stars upon his head.

She saw he was watching her, too. Those eyes of his, she thought tenderly. So green. So beautiful. So filled with something she wished she could name. It was the same look he'd given her when she'd placed the dandelion crown on his head. It was that softness. She wished she could capture it and put it into her pocket to keep for always.

She reached up, touching her hair, hoping he would understand her silent gratitude for allowing her to borrow the brush. He didn't answer, but his eyes told her he understood. Her knees went shaky when he inclined his head toward her.

"Goldie, did you hear what I said?" Big demanded, stomping his foot.

"What?" She looked at Big. "What are you carryin' on about?"

"They're complaining about the dinner I slaved away cooking for them! Goldie, haven't you heard a word I've said?"

She stole one last glance at Saber before turning her attention to the black foodstuffs on the table. "It doesn't look any different than what you've been cookin' since we got here."

"And they've been whining since we got here!"

"Well now, Big, that reminds me of somethin' I've been meanin' to ask you. Do you cook these meals of yours in the kitchen or in the fires of hell?"

"Well!" he blustered. "If that's all the thanks I get for—"

"You won't make those pork ribs and that beef stew like you made these ducks, will you?" she hinted.

His anger faded at the sight of her gentle smile. "No. Of course not."

"Pork ribs and beef stew?" Saber repeated. "Can you make those dishes without burning them, Big?" he asked, unable to keep his hope from his voice.

Big nodded. "Yes. I can, and I will."

Saber's stomach growled. "Tonight?"

"No, not tonight! I—I'm sorry. I didn't mean to yell. No, I can't make them tonight."

"Saber and I will make another dinner tonight," Goldie announced. She removed Big's apron, tying it around her own waist. "I would have been cookin' all along, but what with Saber's duke lessons, I just haven't had time. Now, Big, go feed Dammit his mush. I already mixed it up, and it's waitin' in the barn. And take Itchie Bon with you. Y'all go keep Big company," she told Addison, Winston, Kenneth, and David. "I know you're all hungry, but it'll be a while before dinner's ready, and you'll just have to wait until it is."

Saber was amused when his four friends, who also happened to be four earls, jumped from their seats and followed Big out of the room. He wasn't surprised though. Goldie had a way about her that made people do what she wanted. She wasn't forceful; she was sweetly persuasive.

He himself, however, was capable of remaining immune to her compelling charms. He'd never cooked a meal in his life, and had no plans whatsoever of doing so tonight. If Goldie wanted to cook, fine. But he would merely watch.

Saber stirred the soup and looked at his hands. They were covered with flour. The Duke of Ravenhurst, he mused, had made a loaf of bread. Furthermore, His Grace was anxious to know how it would turn out. It smelled right; like bread was supposed to smell. "Goldie, are you sure my bread hasn't been in the oven too long?"

"I'll check it if you ask me in Shakespeareez."

"Shakespeareez?"

"The language of Shakespeare." Looking up from the pie dough she was rolling out, she blew a curl out of her eye. "I told you we'd be practicin' tonight."

He smiled. "Goldie, are thee sure my bread—"

"No, I think you should say *sureth.*"

"Are thee sureth my bread hasn't been—"

"No, Saber. Say, 'Are thee sureth my bread hast not beenest in the oven too longeth?'"

"*Beenest? Longeth?* Goldie, that sounds ludicrous."

"*Soundeths.* It *soundeths* ludicrous."

He bent over the pot of soup, laughing. "You *soundeth* like you have a lisp! Or should I say *lispeth?*"

She paid him no attention whatsoever. "And I've found several ugly names in those Shakespeare books, too. In case one of the Hallensham villagers dares to insult you, you—"

"I know. I bangeth him overest the head with my caneth."

"Well, yeah, but then you call him a *scullion.* Or a *rampallian.* Or a *fustilarian.* I don't know what those names mean, Saber, but I'm sure they're real bad. Saber?"

He was so amused that it was a moment before he could answer. "What?" he finally managed to reply between chuckles.

"I been meanin' to ask you somethin'. The villagers are always talkin' about blood. Why do English people talk like that?"

"They talk about blood?"

She filled the pie crust with apples, raisins, nuts, and sugar. "Yeah. They say things are either 'bloody' or 'bleedin'. The way they talk, you'd think the whole damn country was runnin' red with the stuff."

Saber let go of his stirring spoon, laughing so hard, his belly cramped. But pain or no pain, he could not control his laughter. He fairly choked with it.

When Goldie saw him doubled over, she raced toward him. "Great day Miss Agnes, Saber, what the hell's wrong with you? You swallow somethin' that went down the wrong pipe?" She pounded him on the back.

Saber grappled for a chair and sat down. "Goldie, don't say anything more for a few minutes." He looked up at her and couldn't resist adding, "I bloody well need to catch my bleedin' breath." His own joke sent him into another wild fit of mirth.

She stared at him, deciding he'd lost his mind. Maybe she'd been working him too hard. "Saber, you just sit there and rest a while. I'll finish supper." After patting his shoulder, she returned to the pie. "Yeah, English folks talk real strange," she continued, picking up the subject again. "For example, take the word *calf*. The way English people say it, it sorta sounds like *cough*. The day I got to Hallensham a farmer with a baby cow to sell came up to me and asked, 'Will you be wantin' a cough, miss?' I'll swannee, Saber, when he said that, I thought he was tryin' to warn me that I was fixin' to get sick. I kept tellin' him that I'd take care of myself so I wouldn't get a cough, but he only—"

Saber howled. Bent over the kitchen table, his shoulders shook as laughter rumbled through him.

Goldie stared at him. No doubt about it, Saber was on the brink of madness. He definitely needed a day off from the duke lessons. She strolled to the oven and removed the bread he'd made. "Turned out perfect, Saber." She took it to the table, then returned to the oven to slide in the pie.

"Addison says strange things too," she continued, taking Saber's place at the soup pot. "The other day, he commented on all the beggar's velvet under the chairs in the parlor? Well, I didn't know what the hell he was talkin' about. So he showed me. He knelt and picked up some lint. *Lint*. Addison calls it 'beggar's velvet.' Is that what you call lint too, Saber?" When he didn't answer, she turned and saw him slicing the bread. "Saber, it's not even cooled off yet!"

He didn't care. He held a piece of the steaming loaf, and stared at it.

Goldie left the stove to join him. Saber was examining the bread so intensely, she thought that maybe there was something wrong with it. But it looked all right to her. She brought her face closer to it. It still looked all right.

"I made this," Saber said quietly. "All by myself."

She tilted her head and looked up at him, noting awe in his eyes. Amazement so great, it bordered on reverence. Great day Miss Agnes, it looked like he was *worshipping* the bread.

"With my own hands," he added.

She wrinkled her forehead. "Well, how the hell else would you have made it? With your feet?"

"I . . . I've never made bread before."

She saw his pride. It was so great one might have thought he'd just performed some kind of miracle. The thought made her think of a Bible story. "Wonder what you could do if you had some fishes to go along with that bread of yours?"

He continued admiring his bread.

"You did a real good job, Saber," Goldie cooed, laughter edging her voice. "That's the purtiest bread I believe I've ever seen. I wonder how it tastes?"

As if he'd forgotten he could actually *eat* the results of his hard work, Saber's eyes widened. Quickly, he handed her a piece, then popped some into his mouth. He closed his eyes.

Goldie chewed her bread. It tasted like bread. But Saber was relishing it as if it were some kind of rare delicacy. "It's good," she told him.

He opened his eyes and cut another slice. "It's more than good," he corrected her.

She stepped away from him, watching him make quick work of his second slice. "All right, it's *real* good. Wonderful. Mouth-waterin'. It's—"

"Savory."

"Yeah, that too. Saber, you made such an absolutely luscious loaf of bread, that if I had a medal I'd pin it to your shirt."

He finally realized she was teasing him. He realized also that he was fawning over a simple loaf of bread. But he couldn't help it. He really *was* proud of himself. Whoever thought Marion Westbrook Saberfield Tremayne, eleventh Duke of Ravenhurst, had culinary skill?

And he realized he felt happy too. The evening with Goldie had been a cozy one. The fire in the corner was dancing merrily and crackling occasionally. The kitchen smelled of good things. He and Goldie had chopped onions and boiled a chicken together. Pared apples and made dough. They'd talked, teased, and laughed. They'd done a lot of simple things tonight. Things in which he rarely, if ever, indulged.

He felt a sudden rush of tenderness for her and did nothing to hold it back. They'd part tomorrow, so he decided to enjoy their last night together to the fullest. What harm could one embrace, one kiss cause, especially if they never happened again? In truth, he wanted both and could find no will to dismiss his desire.

His gaze drifted down her body, then back up again, his own body responding. God, she was so lovely. So irresistible to him. He could barely wait to touch her.

"Goldie," he whispered. "Come here."

# Chapter 7

She heard something odd in Saber's whisper. Something promising. She wanted whatever it was he offered, but hesitated to trust it was real.

He saw the wariness in her eyes and made the decision for her. One long step was all he needed to reach her.

He was so close, she could feel the warmth of his body. Looking up at him, she saw that softness in his eyes again. How it captivated her. Oh, if only it would last and not disappear like good things usually did. "Saber," she whispered.

"Your hair," he told her, reaching out to push his finger into the hollow of a ringlet. "You brushed it."

She was completely enchanted. "Yes. I—Thank you for letting me borrow the brush."

"But it's yours."

"Mine?" She could find no words to express her astonishment. She'd never owned anything so beautiful in her life. "But—I can't—"

"Does it work as well as a wooden one?"

She nodded. "It's a lot purtier, though. But I . . . it must have cost a lot of money, and I don't really—It's too nice—Well, you—Saber, you spent your allowance on it, and I don't think it's right for me to accept—"

"My allowance?"

"The money Addison gives you. He said he'd been helpin' you financially. You didn't have to spend it on the brush, Saber. What if you need it sometime?"

He smiled. The Duke of Ravenhurst on an allowance?

The thought was highly humorous. "Would you like me to return it and try to get my money back?"

Familiar disappointment swallowed her. "I—Yes, I guess maybe you should." She made a mental note to brush her hair at every opportunity she got before he returned it. It would be the last time she'd ever have the chance to hold and use something so lovely.

Saber reached for her shoulders, drawing her to him. He felt her tremble in his arms. Bending low, he smiled into the nest of silky curls on top of her head. "I want you to have it. It's my gift to you, Goldie. Goldie . . ." He straightened, looking down at her. He'd been going to call her by her whole name, and realized he didn't know what it was. "How very odd. We've been together for two weeks, and I've never thought to ask you your full name. How utterly strange. What *is* your name?"

"Mae," she whispered, still dwelling on the fact that he'd really and truly given her the brush. "Goldie Mae."

Saber's arms dropped from around her; he stared at her with wide eyes. "Mae." The name made him think of fresh gingerbread. Of a big, warm kitchen and the stout, merry woman who ran it. The same woman who'd made those delicious eggs when he'd failed to bring her the duck.

Della. Della Mae. He hadn't seen her in twenty years, but remembered her as if he'd seen her five minutes ago. How he'd loved her gingerbread. And her stomach. It was like a big, fat pillow, and he used to push his face into it, enjoying both its softness and the sweet smells of good food clinging to her apron. And he liked climbing into her lap. He'd lay his head on her ample bosom, and she'd tell him stories. Recollections of the things she'd done in her life. Tales about her ancestors and bits of what she knew about the few remaining relatives she still had.

Her family in America.

Della Mae. Goldie Mae. He sat back down, ran his fingers through his hair, and smiled disbelievingly. The world wasn't such a big place after all, he decided.

Goldie saw he was grinning at her as if he knew a secret. "Saber, you gonna share your secret, or make me guess?" she asked, tapping her chin with her finger.

He realized the time had come to tell Goldie who he

was. This was the perfect opportunity. He'd explain everything, then ask for news of Della. "Goldie, there's something I have to tell you. Sit down here with me."

His voice, like the light touch of a feather, brushed across each of her emotions, bringing them to life, making her shiver with sweet yearning. Her gaze never leaving his, she took a chair next to him.

Saber reached for her hand and held it between his own. He wondered how to begin and decided to be forthright. "Goldie," he said softly, "I . . ."

While waiting for him to finish, she detected the aroma of the baking pie. "Great day Miss Agnes, the pie!" She flew to the oven, grabbed a cloth, and snatched out the dessert. "Well, look at that. It's not even brown yet, and here I thought the thing was gonna come out lookin' like something Big and the devil made together. I guess I lost my sense of time. I do that sometimes, y'know." Smiling, she slid the pie back into the oven.

"Goldie, please let me tell—"

"One time Uncle Asa told me I was a good cook," she said proudly, sashaying back to the table. "I think it's one of those things people inherit. My Aunt Della was a cook. She worked up at that Ravenhurst mansion for years. I must have inherited her talent in the kitchen. 'Course, inherited talent can always be improved, Saber. It'll take me a long time to become as good a cook as Aunt Della probably was."

She sat back down, put her elbow on the table, and rested her head in her hand. "I was so excited about meetin' her, Saber. The whole way over here to England I thought about her. But when we got to Hallensham . . . she wasn't there. Her cottage was empty."

Saber's heart crashed into his ribs. "What? Where did she go?"

Goldie felt a tear slip down her cheek. "Heaven."

Saber scowled fiercely. "Heaven? What do you mean—*heaven?*" he yelled. "She *died?*" He rose, looming above her while waiting for her answer.

Goldie looked up at him. "Why are you hollerin' at me? I didn't kill her, y'know."

"She's dead?" he demanded again.

"Isn't that the only way she could have gotten to heaven? Saber, why—"

"How did she die? When?"

Goldie felt very confused at Saber's shouting. "Saber, why are you yellin' at me?"

Her question did nothing at all to dispel his shock, but it did make him realize how bewildered Goldie was over his unseemly behavior. Della. Gone. Grief clawed at his throat, strangling him. Turning, he walked slowly to the fireplace. While he stared into the flames, his heart summoned every image of Della it sheltered. He saw her clearly. He remembered. His little hand in her big one. Her moist kisses on his cheeks. Her soft arms around him. Aching, he made fists, watching them whiten and tremble.

Why hadn't he been informed of her death? Surely his estate manager knew of her passing. Why hadn't Hutchins sent word to him?

"Saber?"

Goldie's sweet voice flowed through his bitter thoughts. "I'm sorry," he managed to tell her.

At his words of condolence, another tear trickled down Goldie's cheek. Saber hadn't even known her aunt, and yet he felt sorrow over her death. His compassion touched her heart. She joined him at the hearth. "Thank you."

His fingers uncurled, slowly seeking hers. When they found them, he held her hand for a long moment before bringing it to his mouth and kissing it. He felt a special affinity with her. Goldie mourned because she'd never had the chance to love Della. He mourned because he had. "Tell me," he begged. "Tell me about Della."

She saw such sadness in his eyes. His sympathy was likewise echoed in his voice. He was asking her to share her sorrow with him. The thought warmed her far more than the blazes in the fireplace. "When I first got to Hallensham," she began quietly, "the only thing I could learn was that she'd died a month earlier and that the preacher was the one who found her. No one knew much more than that. Later, I discovered her diaries. They were hidden up in the rafters of the ceilin'. She—"

"Diaries? The diaries you've been talking about belonged to her?'' God, he thought. He'd been unaware that Della could read and write.

Goldie nodded and found comfort in his continued and genuine concern. ''I found a bunch of little books up in her ceilin'. Each one is full from cover to cover. They're small, and so is Aunt Della's handwritin', so it takes a long time to read 'em. And a lot of the pages are ruined by water, like I already told you one time. You can't read those pages at all. I've skimmed through some of 'em, but I haven't had time to get to 'em all.

''Anyway, Aunt Della wrote a lot about the folks and goings-on in Hallensham and at Ravenhurst. Everything's dated, so it's like readin' her life story. There's a whole lot about Duke Marion. She wrote of happy things until his parents died. Then her entries got sad. She wrote about havin' to sell some of her possessions. Her mama's lace shawl. Her daddy's watch. She sold her cow. Traded her little gold brooch for blankets. She sold some other stuff, too, but that part's messed up, and I can't read it. She started writin' about bein' hungry and cold. Things got worse as she got older. In her very last entry she wrote that she hadn't eaten in three days. She died the next day.''

''She had nothing to eat?'' Saber was astounded and appalled.

''That's what she wrote. She was old, Saber. And what with goin' for three days without food—She died of age and hunger. It's the only thing I can think of.''

Saber stepped away from her, staring at her without seeing her. Della . . . hungry? But *why?* He'd been having a substantial amount of money given to her ever since he left the estate as a boy!

His confusion and disbelief mounted. ''Goldie, what is your cottage in Hallensham like?''

She sighed. ''Same as all the others. I love the cottage and hope it can be my home forever and ever, but I'm tellin' you the truth, if Uncle Asa and I don't get enough money to fix it, it's gonna fall down on us while we're sleepin'. The roof leaks, and there are so many holes in the walls, I'm sure Aunt Della was cold clear down to her bones in the winter. I'm—I'm sorta used to livin' in places like that, but Aunt Della—I—As old as she was, it's . . .

not easy for me to think of her livin' like that. I wish I could have helped her in some way. But I was in America, and I didn't know. I just didn't know.''

Saber had been in England, and he hadn't known either. He felt sickened with regret and bewilderment. *Why* had Della been poverty-stricken? There was absolutely no reason for her destitution. With the money he'd provided her, she should have been living comfortably! She should have—

A sudden and terrible thought stabbed through his confusion. His eyes narrowed. The longer he dwelled on his suspicion, the more sense it made. Fury exploded inside him, and it was only with intense determination that he managed to keep it from his voice. "Goldie, I—I'm very sorry. About your Aunt Della. About the supper. But you see . . . I can't eat it. I've just remembered something I need to discuss with Addison. It won't wait. I'll send in Winston, Kenneth, David, and Big. Please enjoy supper without Addison and me. I'll see you in the morning.''

He stormed from the room, leaving her no time to question him. It took him only seconds to reach the front door. He took the steps leading to the courtyard three at a time and headed for the barn. He had to find Addison.

As he ran toward the stables, he thought of the one possible reason for Della's hunger, her poverty. If that reason turned out to be true, the man responsible was going to pay.

Pay dearly.

Saber tossed down another whiskey, pitched the glass into the fireplace, and charged to his office window. Snatching the drapes aside, he stared intently at the darkness outside. Out there somewhere was Dane Hutchins. Breathing the same air Della had. Walking on the same earth.

Was he now living on Della's money?

Hutchins was alive. Della was dead. Saber had never felt such anger. "Dane Hutchins," he growled. "What other answer is there? I swear to you, Addison, when I get my hands on him, I'm—''

"But you have no proof." Addison continued to pace

the floor. "It could very well be that Della *gave* the money away."

"Tell me in all truth that you believe that."

"No, I don't believe it at all. But the authorities will see it as a possibility; therefore you must see it that way, too. Without proof, you cannot—"

"I can do anything I damn well want to do!" Gulping in a ragged breath, Saber laid his hot forehead on the cool windowpane, closing his eyes. Images of Della filled his tortured mind.

If only he could see her one more time. Grief, fury, guilt . . . they all fought for a place inside him. He couldn't control them; and as they battled, he thought of their cause. It was love. Love was at fault for every agony he'd ever known. If he hadn't loved Della, her death would not be eating away at his heart right now.

"Don't you *ever* again suggest I go back to Ravenhurst," he commanded. "I lost three loved ones there, and tonight I have learned there is a fourth to add to the grisly list. Those lands . . . they run with blood, Addison, and nothing will *ever* induce me to set foot upon them again. No circumstance, no person."

Wisely, Addison remained silent, patiently waiting for Saber to speak again.

Saber took another deep, shuddering breath. "Goldie says that for the past twenty years, Della's diary entries are of nothing but sorrows. She didn't even have *blankets*, Addison!"

"Saber—"

"William Doyle," Saber seethed. "My man of business. He's been making periodic trips to Ravenhurst for years. When he returns to London, he gives me detailed accounts about everything happening on the estate. Why didn't he ever say anything about Della's situation?"

"Perhaps he didn't realize she was so important to you."

"But it's not just Della," Saber countered. "From what Goldie said, I gather all my tenants' houses are in sad condition. Doyle's not blind. He's *seen* that with his own eyes, and yet he never said a word about it to me."

"Are you suggesting Doyle and Hutchins could be partners?"

"I don't know what the hell to think!" Saber took another deep breath, struggling to control his frustration. "But the idea isn't ludicrous, Addison. If it's true, then it's more than likely that in exchange for Doyle's cooperation, Hutchins has been rewarding him well. Rewarding him with *my* money! If they're guilty of that—Damn those thieving bastards!"

Addison frowned. Saber rarely swore. The fact that he was doing so now spoke of his unmitigated rage. The last place on earth Addison wanted to be was in Dane Hutchins' or William Doyle's shoes—especially if the two men were guilty.

"All right, Saber. Let's presume your suspicions are true. If Della could write, why didn't she inform you about her circumstances? And why would Hutchins and Doyle have attempted what you suspect when Della could have written to you and told you about it?"

Saber stared at Addison for a moment, his mind working furiously. "They wouldn't have known Della could write either. And they'd never have given her the slightest clue that she was supposed to be receiving the funds, so there'd have been no reason for her to divulge anything. And as for her informing me of her dire straits, she was too proud. All suspicions aside, the one thing I know to be true is the extent of her pride. I may have been little the last time I saw her, but I remember it."

His shoulders slumped and his chin fell to his chest. "God, she preferred death over telling me about her deprivation. Or—Or maybe she believed I just wouldn't care. Perhaps that's what all the villagers believe. Perhaps—God. I don't know, Addison. I don't know what to think about any of this."

"Saber—"

"I recall the day I said good-bye to Della," Saber continued. He took a seat behind his desk, looking up at the moulded ceiling. "I was so worried about her. I begged her to come with me to London, but she said she couldn't leave her home. I tried to give her my pocket money. She refused it. I wondered how she would get along without a job, for there was no longer any need for a cook there.

"When my aunts and I arrived in London, I expressed my concern to them and asked if there was anything we could do. They arranged for Della to receive a generous sum of money each month. Hutchins was to deliver it to her personally. He was to tell her my father had bequeathed her the funds, and that if she refused them she'd be dishonoring her deceased lord's wishes."

"I gather no one suspected him of dishonesty."

Saber straightened in his chair, ramming his fingers through his hair. "Hutchins has been working as Ravenhurst's estate manager since I was a baby. The solicitors Aunt Clara and Aunt Lucy hired saw no reason to replace him. My father, apparently, never had a problem with him, or else he'd have discharged him."

Addison rubbed his chin. "But when your father was alive, Hutchins didn't have the opportunity to perform such treacherous deeds. That is, if he is, indeed, guilty of them," he amended.

Saber closed his eyes, sorrow and guilt fairly smothering him. "Addison," he whispered achingly. "However indirectly, I am responsible for Della's death. She died only a short time ago. If I had returned to Ravenhurst, I could have seen to her welfare myself. But I—"

"Saber, don't blame—"

"I was to have returned with Angelica," Saber went on, his heart throbbing. "Angelica. She wanted so badly to raise our son on the ducal lands that would one day be his. If she had lived, I would have gone back with her. But—"

"I know," Addison said quietly. "I know, Saber, but nothing that has happened is your fault."

"I can't understand," Saber murmured, "why Angelica didn't tell me about what was going on there. Surely she saw the state of the tenants' houses. She could have written—"

"I'm certain she would have," Addison tried to assure his distraught friend. "But—She didn't—Perhaps she didn't have enough time—Saber, she'd only been there for three days before . . . her accident. And it could have been that she was going to tell you everything in person once she returned to London.''

Clenching his jaw, Saber rose, drawing himself up to his full height. "I'll send a letter to Aunt Clara and Aunt Lucy, and in it I will tell them the truth," he said with no emotion whatsoever. "Two more reliable and understanding souls do not exist, and I know I can depend on their discretion. They must be told about what I'm doing, of course. Otherwise, they'd worry."

Addison realized Saber had formulated a plan. "Well, that's topping, Saber. But if it's not too much trouble, would you mind telling *me* what you're going to do, as well?''

"I would have thought you'd have figured it out."

Addison shrugged. "After all these years, the true shallowness of my intelligence is finally revealed. I'm not as quick-minded as you, and there you have it. Put me out of my misery."

"The diaries."

"The diaries," Addison echoed, frowning in complete confusion. "What about them?"

"Addison, there might be proof in them! Goldie said Della wrote about everything and everyone connected with Ravenhurst and Hallensham. And the diaries are all dated. If my suspicions concerning Hutchins and Doyle are true, it's possible I'll find evidence in those little books. Maybe Della saw something. Overheard something. Who knows? With any luck, I might find every scrap of information I need in them."

Addison nodded. "So you'll tell Goldie who you are, explain your suspicions, then ask to read the diaries."

"No to the first two, yes to the third."

"What?"

"No, I won't tell Goldie who I am, and no, I won't tell her what I think about Hutchins and Doyle. Yes, I'll ask to read the diaries. I'll explain I can learn more . . . uh, *dukish stuff* if she allows me to concentrate on what Della wrote. Addison, if she learns who I am, she or Big might be tempted to contact her drunken Uncle Asa. He, in turn, would announce the news around Hallensham, and Hutchins and Doyle would hear of it. If they're guilty, they'd have ample time to escape before I've attained the proof I need.''

''I see. But Saber, your time here at Leighwood is over. You were to return to London tomorrow, and Goldie was to return to—''

''She stays with me.''

Addison noted the emphatic nature of Saber's statement. *You're quite adamant about her staying with you, aren't you, old boy?* Pretending to smother a cough, he hid his smile. ''Very well, my friend. Goldie stays. You'll be spending the time here at Leighwood, I presume?''

''In London I'd have a difficult time keeping my real identity from her. You and the boys will return tomorrow and spread the word that I am out of the country. Say I went to Scotland and that you have no idea when I will return. Just make sure the aunties receive my letter before they hear the rumors about me. I don't want them upset.''

''You may depend on us.''

Saber didn't miss Addison's mischievous smile. ''Give over, Addison.''

''I hide nothing.''

Saber thought for a moment, realizing there was only one reason for Addison's secret delight. ''You're playing matchmaker again, and I warn you now that there is nothing at all romantic about my relationship with Goldie.''

''Of course.''

''If I find any evidence in the diaries, I'll be returning to London without her. I will, however, make sure Hallensham will be her home for as long as she wishes. And I will provide for her financially. She is Della's niece, and I can do no less.''

''Of course.''

''As you well know, she is a very entertaining person to be around. I admit to having enjoyed her company. But that is all.''

''Yes, yes, of course, Saber.''

''A relationship any deeper than mere friendship is out of the question.''

''Oh, yes. Completely out of the question.''

''She is an American.''

''She is at that.''

"I am an English aristocrat."

"With blood bluer than the sky."

"She lives in Hallensham, my home is London."

"Two totally different worlds."

Saber's thoughts drifted. *Diamonds. And dandelions.* He sat back down, folding his arms across his chest. "So I have made myself clear, Addison?"

"As crystal." Addison made a low bow and left the room.

Saber stared after him. Addison's eyes had been twinkling, and that familiar, telltale sparkle gave Saber two distinct thoughts: he'd either not made himself clear at all, or he'd made himself clearer than he'd meant to.

His mind continued filling with a myriad of reflections. Della. Hutchins and Doyle. Goldie. Ravenhurst, Hallensham. The diaries. Death and love and loss and pain and betrayal. So many thoughts writhed through him, he could concentrate on none of them. He felt suddenly stifled by them, and in only moments was outside. The cool night air ruffled his hair as he walked swiftly through the courtyard. He had no idea where he was going. He knew only that he had to get away.

He began to run, soon seeing moonlight splashing upon the maze of hedgerows. The maze! He sped into it, twisting and turning around its complex course, not stopping until he was sure he'd reached its center.

His chest heaving, he stared up at the sky. In his desperate loneliness and need, the stars looked to him like bright eyes. Millions of benevolent eyes peering down at him. "Gone," he whispered up to them. "Dead. Because of me. My fault. Angelica—Now Della. Ravenhurst. I tried to take care of you, Della. But you never knew that. You died thinking I'd forgotten you. I'm so sorry."

He fell to his knees. Guilt more horrible than he ever imagined could exist fell over him. Profound sorrow and regret burned from the very core of his soul. He wanted to shout out his anguish. Wanted to hear his own scream. Hot tears burned his eyes, but refused to fall.

Anger joined all the other emotions ravaging inside him. He raised a balled fist to the sky. "*You!* What else, dammit?

What other tragedies do You have planned for me to bear?
I can take no more!''

A brisk wind blew past him.

He thought he heard the sound of taunting laughter in
it.

Goldie slipped into her patched nightgown and stepped
out onto her balcony. She breathed deeply of the cool,
fragrant night air. It picked up her hair, sending curls flut-
tering across her forehead and cheeks.

"I wonder where Saber is?" she asked Itchie Bon. "He
left the kitchen in such a rush tonight, that I didn't—"

She broke off when she saw a man fleeing across the
courtyard. Squinting, she realized who it was. "Great day
Miss Agnes, there he is!"

With the aid of the moonlight, she watched him clear
the yard and enter a thick grove of bushes. What in the
world was he doing, running around at this time of night?
she wondered. Staring at the distant shrubbery, she chewed
her bottom lip, deliberating.

"Itchie Bon, I can either leave him in the bushes by
himself, or I can get in 'em with him." She concentrated
for many long moments, then turned to look down at the
dog. "Do you think I should meet him down there?"

Itchie Bon barked loudly. "That's just what *I* was
thinkin'!" Goldie exclaimed. Grinning, she raced out of
her bedroom, through the hall, and down the staircase.
Yanking the front door opened, she skipped down the steps
and rushed across the yard, soon coming to the tall hedges.
She entered hesitantly. The bushes were much bigger than
she was, and she wasn't certain of which way to go. "Saber?"

When he didn't answer, she turned right and kept walking. The wall of shrubs seemed endless. And was it only
her imagination, or were they closing in on her? She felt
the beginnings of panic. "Saber!" Spinning around, she
hastened back toward the entrance, true terror coming to
her when she couldn't find it.

Clouds drifted across the moon, shrouding its light. The
maze grew darker. "Saber!" she yelled, running now.
Branches scratched her arms. Pebbles bruised her bare

feet. Something big flew close to her head. "Saber! A bat! Oh, Saber, *please* come find me!"

Everything was dark and scary and unfamiliar to her. She increased her pace, racing as quickly as she was able. Her fear rose steadily, and with it came her tears. But she continued to run. Blindly she dashed onward until she ran into a solid mass.

"Goldie."

She felt Saber's arms go around her, easing her trembling. His scent of sandalwood floated into her, calming her fear. His strength wrapped around her, blanketing her with warm security. "Saber," she whispered, watching the moonlight return. "I was lost."

She shivered in his arms. The action touched something inside him. Something that felt very much like his heart. "But you're not now."

"I was afraid, Saber."

"So it would seem."

"A bat was after me."

"A bat, you say? Didn't anyone inform you that Leighwood is the home of England's vampires? You probably disturbed one of them with all your shouting."

"You're teasin' me."

"Am I?"

She looked up at him. "Aren't you?"

He saw the uncertainty in her eyes. "Yes." He urged her head back to his chest, holding her more closely. She felt so good in his arms, and he needed to have her in them. He didn't question his motive. His emotions were too raw, too complex for him to understand. All he knew was that he had to hold her tonight.

Potent emotion seized Goldie. To be in his arms, to hear the rhythmic beat of his heart . . . Happiness caught her, holding her fast. Tentatively, she put her arms around him. Her own action sent a sweet ache spreading throughout her.

But anxiety came, too. What if he didn't want her to hold him like this? What if she was making him mad? Or worse, what if he *laughed* at her ignorant attempt at romance?

She let her arms drop back to her side, and felt empty. "What are you doin' out here, Saber?"

"I might ask you the same question."

"You might?"

Smiling, he amended himself. "All right, I'm asking."

She sniffled. "I was gettin' chased by a bat, that's what."

Saber withdrew a silk handkerchief from his pocket, pressing it into her hand. "You sound like a duke, what with all that wheezing and snorting you're doing. Now, tell me what you're really doing out here."

"I saw you from my balcony."

"And?"

"And came out here to be with you."

He tried to resist the pleasure her answer brought him, but failed miserably. "Didn't it cross your mind that I might have wanted to be alone?" he queried with a smile.

"Do you?"

He took the handkerchief from her, and dried a tear she'd missed. His arms curled around her again. "Whether or not I want to be alone doesn't matter anymore, now does it? You're here."

"But I can go back to the—"

"Do you forget you were lost?"

She pressed her cheek to his . . . chest. "You could show me the way out."

"I'm afraid I don't know either."

She gasped. "Oh, Saber—"

"I'm teasing you. You're very gullible. Has anyone ever told you that?" He bent toward her hair. Her curls tickled his nose and smelled of air, pure and sweet. His need for her rose.

"Big's all the time tellin' me I'm gullible," she answered, a thrill shooting through her as she felt him nuzzling her hair. "But I'd rather try to believe in everything than never believe in anything. Sometimes it's real hard to believe stuff, though," she added very quietly.

"And what," he whispered, his hands sliding slowly down her back, "do you believe in, Goldie Mae?"

"That's the strangest thing anybody ever asked me," she replied, thinking of how good his hands felt on her back. She wondered if he meant to do that to her, or if it was just one of those things people did without realizing it.

"Have you no answer then?" Saber questioned her. His arms arched with the need to bring her even closer to him. To crush her to him. He still couldn't understand his desire, but tonight it didn't matter. The need was there, real, strong, and growing.

"Well," Goldie began, sensing a slight tremor running through his arms. "I believe in God. Do you?"

"Yes." *But I've yet to see any evidence of the mercy He's so famous for,* he added silently, bitterly.

"I believe in good things," Goldie continued, pondering the dark look in Saber's eyes.

"Such as?"

She had to think of the right words. "Like honesty. I believe in laughter. And growin'. I love to see things grow. Plants, animals, and people."

"Children."

"And big people too. Even hundred-year-old oak trees send out new branches."

He'd never thought of that. "And what else—besides honesty, laughter, and oak branches—do you believe in?" How odd, he mused. He'd begun this conversation on a light vein, but now yearned to know what she thought.

"Um . . . Compassion. Understandin'. Sharin'. Fairness and imagination. Those things are real important."

"Why imagination?"

*Because,* she thought, looking up into his beautiful green eyes, *the very best things that have ever happened to me have happened in my imagination.*

"Goldie? Why imagination?" he repeated.

"Because imaginin' stuff is fun."

He tilted her chin up. "And what do you dream of?"

That softness was in his eyes again, she saw, and quivered. "If I told you, you'd laugh."

"Try me."

She didn't want to, but recalled she'd just told him her feelings about honesty. "Well . . . sometimes I imagine a man kissin' my wrist. Nobody ever kissed my wrist before, but I saw a man do that to a woman one time. I wondered what it felt like, so I kissed my own wrist. It felt all right, but I reckon it'd feel nicer if someone else did it.

"And sometimes," she continued, "I dream that I live in a big house that belongs to me, and no one has the right to tell me I have to move. There's a white picket fence surroundin' it, and inside, all the windows have ruffled curtains made of pink and white gingham. And the windows all have window boxes under 'em with flowers growin' in 'em. I have pink sofas in the house, and the little arm pillows on 'em are white with red strawberries stitched on 'em. And I have a rockin' chair with my name carved on the back of it. And kittens. I have lots of kittens who sleep all over the furniture, and I don't ever get mad at 'em for gettin' cat hair on everything. And I have twelve children. Twelve's a nice, even number, and I always wanted to have lots of family around me."

"What about a husband?" Saber asked, smiling at the delight dancing in her eyes. "Do you have one of those too?"

"I—Um . . ." A dismal feeling overcame her. She looked at the ground, digging her toes into the earth and struggling to find her happy feeling again. "And think of how many *grandchildren* I'd get after havin' twelve children! If each one of my kids had three children, I'd have . . . *thirty-six* grandchildren!"

"But think of how expensive it would be for you to buy them all gifts at Christmas."

She frowned. "Oh. I never thought of that. Well, some things don't cost much. I could paint 'em all a picture."

"Can you paint?"

"Well, no. But I'd learn if I had that many grandchildren to paint for. Or . . . I could 'em make little cotton stuffers for when it thunders. They could stick 'em in their ears when storms come. Kids are afraid of thunder. I used to hide under the covers when it thundered. I don't anymore though."

Saber closed his eyes, dwelling on a memory. "Once when I was little, I jumped into bed with my mother and father because of thunder. It was so loud, I remember the walls shaking. But as soon as I was lying between my parents, all my fear went away. After that first time, I was allowed to sleep with them during every storm. I so loved being with them, that I actually began praying for thunder.''

''You're so lucky. Uncle Asa never let me in bed with him when it thundered. Mama and Daddy used to, but when they died . . . my thunder nights with 'em died too.''

*Lucky,* Saber mused. He'd lost everything that meant something to him, and Goldie said he was lucky. No, there was nothing at all lucky about his life.

''Where are your mama and daddy, Saber?''

He tensed. ''With your Aunt Della.''

''Oh,'' she murmured, and felt his pain. ''I'm sorry. Have they been in heaven long?''

''Many years,'' he said softly. He stepped away from her and took her hand. ''Come. Let's walk.''

She looked down at her hand, seeing nothing at all of it. His covered hers completely. The sight sent pleasure shimmering through her. ''So you were little too when your parents died. Just like me. Who raised you?''

Saber smiled, remembering Aunt Clara and Aunt Lucy. ''My aunts.''

''And were they good to you?''

''They were. And it wasn't easy for them. I missed my parents terribly for many, many years. I . . . I'm afraid I wasn't the most well-behaved child during that time.''

''Well, I reckon that's all right, Saber. Kids don't know any better. 'Course, sometimes grown-ups don't either. My parents have been dead a long time too, but I still cry and carry on sometimes. It's real hard to stop doin' that for good. Do you ever do it?''

''I don't cry, but I do . . . uh, *carry on* at times.'' As the words left his lips, he couldn't believe he'd spoken them. He'd never admitted his weakness to anyone. On the contrary, he denied it vehemently. ''Rarely ever though,'' he added hastily.

''I cried in front of Jane Gluck once. That was down in Dix-Wix, South Carolina. She said I was a crybaby. I was the only one in Dix-Wix who called her 'Jane.' She had everybody else callin' her 'Juanita' because she thought it sounded fancier than Jane. I called her Jane right to her face just to aggravate her. I don't usually set out to aggravate people, but she was the most hateful thing walkin' this earth.''

She ran her free hand along the hedgerow beside her. "I didn't have to put up with Jane for long, though. Uncle Asa got thrown out of Dix-Wix about a month after we moved there. He threw away a lighted cigar and set Myron Horton's hair on fire. Even though Uncle Asa was drunk, it was only an accident, and Myron got the fire out before it burned his scalp. But folks in Dix-Wix weren't the forgivin' kind, Saber.''

Though she spoke with a note of lightheartedness in her voice, Saber was not amused by her story. She often mentioned being tossed out of towns, and he was beginning to sense an underlying sorrow in her tales. "Do you cry often?''

"Yeah, I'm a real weepy person. I cry over everything. I know I'm too old for that, but the tears just come, and I can't stop 'em. Uncle Asa—Well . . . he doesn't like it much, so I try not to cry for long. Usually only for a few seconds. Well, maybe sometimes for a full minute. Then I'm better. I think it's good to go on and cry when you're sad. Why would God have given us tears if it wasn't all right to cry? I think that if He didn't want us to cry, He'd dry up our tears about the same time as He does our baby fat. So I let the tears come, get 'em over with, and then go on with other things. It's like that dandelion story I told you. It doesn't do any good to stay smashed down forever.''

Saber pulled a leaf from the hedgerow, then flicked it away. "But what of things that are so terrible, you simply cannot stop dwelling on them? Things that bring you fury and anguish every time you think of them?'' He found himself straining to hear her answer.

She stopped walking and looked at the ground again. "Why—Why are you askin' me that?''

He lifted her chin, looking into her eyes, seeing suspicion in them. "Goldie—''

"I—Nothin' that bad has ever happened to me.''

Nothing that terrible had ever happened to her? he repeated silently. Many terrible things had and were happening to her. Try as he might, he couldn't understand.

She saw his confusion. "Saber—I—You—" she stammered, trying desperately to think of a nonchalant way to answer him. "Well—All right, if somethin' *really* awful happened to me, I reckon I'd cry and carry on like I always do, then I'd try to find somethin' good about the terrible thing. Once I'd found it, I'd hang onto it for all I was worth. Then, if I ever started gettin' sad or angry, I'd remember the good thing and probably feel better."

Saber stared down at her. She was talking fast, and he had the distinct feeling she was very uncomfortable with the subject of the conversation. "What good thing have you found about the deaths of your parents?" he asked gently. "About having had to move from town to town for so many years? About the very real possibility of losing your home in Hallensham? I realize I'm to be the duke, Goldie, but what if something goes wrong with your scheme? Have you given any thought to that?"

She wound a curl around her finger. "Well, I—The good that came from my mama and daddy dyin', is that Uncle Asa got me. He—He was real lonesome. Now he has me. The good that came from movin' around from place to place is that I got to know a lot of people. And I got to travel and see lots of things I wouldn't have seen if I'd had a permanent home. I saw a famous rock one time. It's the rock folks say George Washin'ton sat on. And the good thing about maybe losin' my cottage in Hallensham is . . ."

"You see?" Saber asked when her voice trailed off. "You can find no silver lining to that cloud."

He was so wrong, she mused. "The silver linin' is that I got to meet *you*. If I hadn't had the problem of needin' to bring back Duke Marion, I never would have known you."

Her answer took him completely off-guard. She had no idea who he was. Knew nothing of his title or his wealth. She was simply glad to know *him*, the common man beneath the nobleman. A surge of happiness swept through him. "And I," he began very softly, "got to meet you, too."

A warning bell sounded in his head, but he ignored it.

Just as he knew dawn would break tomorrow, he knew he was going to kiss her. "Come here, Goldie."

The gentleness in his velvet voice made her knees weak. She took a step forward, laying her hand in his palm when he reached out his arm. Mesmerized, she watched him bring her hand to his mouth. Her emotions spun when he turned it over and touched his lips to her inner wrist.

The ground vanished beneath her feet. She no longer saw the moon. The hedgerows disappeared. The night breeze ceased to exist. She forgot to breathe.

All that mattered was Saber's kiss. Upon her wrist. His lips. Smoothing across her skin, touching every nerve she possessed. "Saber," she whispered. "Oh . . ."

Saber felt her fingers quiver upon his throat; his lips spread into a smile. "Is a kiss on your wrist what you thought it would be, Goldie?"

His deep voice vibrated upon her skin. It tickled. And caressed. And make her feel dizzy with pleasure. "Yes," she whispered.

"And what about a kiss here?" Slowly, he pushed up the sleeve of her nightgown, his lips inching up her arm, and stopping at the crook of her elbow. There, his kisses resumed.

"Saber," she told him, her body afire with a need she had no idea how to satisfy.

"Goldie," he answered her, knowing exactly what she meant by calling his name.

Her entire arm trembled. Like hot liquid, exquisite sensation flowed through her. It burned, and yet it felt strangely wonderful. She couldn't understand how that could be. "Oh, Saber," she whispered when his kisses began the slow journey to her upper arm. That odd, but demanding longing was growing. Sensing that fulfillment would come from Saber, she took a step closer to him, daring this dreamy experience to last for just a little while longer.

Saber straightened, realizing his breath was coming in ragged heaves. He'd done nothing but kiss her wrist and arm, yet the slight contact had filled him with desire. He gazed down at her.

Bright moonlight spilled all over her. It painted her

gown, and the sheerness of her night rail became apparent to him. He could see little more than the outline of her tiny body, but the sight was enough. He burned with a longing so great, he could think of no remedy for it.

None but one.

Reaching for her, he pulled her into his arms again. Goldie felt his hands pushing at her lower back, urging her closer to him. She'd never been held this way before. Never experienced such intimacy. Nor had she ever sensed such desperation in any man. She longed to respond to it. Yearned to show him her emotions matched his.

But she didn't know the way. Had no idea even how to begin. "Saber," she entreated softly, nervously, "I—Tell me what to say to you. What to do to you."

He was struck. Not by confusion, or amusement. No, not even by the rising passion. It was tenderness that thrummed through him. How it filled him, seeking and finding buried emotion within him. Her plea was so dear to him, he wished he could find a way to capture and keep it about him for always. She thought not of what would please *her*, but what would please *him*.

It was the most unselfish thing anyone had ever said to him.

He knew she didn't know what she was offering him, yet she extended it freely, honestly, and perhaps most importantly, with all the innocence and trust in the world. And that precious gift was not to be abused, he realized.

The thought caused him to take a step away from her. "Goldie," he began, lifting a flaxen curl from the corner of her eye, "you've said much. Done much. I ask nothing more than what you've already given."

Picking up her hand again, he pressed a last kiss to her wrist, then swept her into his arms. Looking deeply into her amber eyes, he saw a bereft expression in them. "Smile for me, Goldie," he beseeched her, his voice little more than a whisper.

Her confusion and dismay faded when she saw the softness in his eyes. She had no clue to his thoughts, no hint of his reasons for concluding the encounter. But she no longer cared. The tender glow in his seaweed eyes was all that mattered. Placing her palm on his cheek, she smiled for him.

She knew she'd never experienced a night as wonderful as this one. Even if the time with Saber were to end tomorrow, she'd live on the wonderful memories for the rest of her life. One thought of them would wash away anything bad that might ever happen to her.

As Saber began the trek back to the mansion, she curled her arms around his neck, resting her cheek upon his chest. She felt safe, warm, and happy in his strong embrace.

And for the first time in many years, she allowed herself to feel cherished.

# Chapter 8

Absently, Dane stared at the ceiling of the elegant master bedroom, one hand fondling the plump mass of Dora Mashburn's breast, the other holding a letter from William Doyle. William would be coming to Ravenhurst soon. Dane was anxious to see him, for William was a good friend. William handled everything so that Dane had little to do but relax and enjoy the life of a gentleman. Yes, Dane mused, William understood things. He comprehended the fact that Dane deserved all the respect and wealth afforded to the nobility.

He smiled, glancing at the letter again. William was in Cornwall now, buying copper mines. Not for Tremayne, but with Tremayne money. Dane laughed, thinking of the fortune William was amassing for them.

"Wot's funny?" Dora asked, wishing she could read. Purring, she pushed her hips rhythmically against his bare leg.

"I beg your pardon?" Dane snapped.

"Wot's funny, *milord,*" Dora corrected herself.

Dane tossed the letter to the bedside table. "Many things are funny. Many things are sad, too." He sighed deeply, pondering a great sorrow. "She hurt me. I was going to allow her to share her charms with me. Yes, I was going to do her that honor. I would have made her my lady. But she did not realize who I am. Didn't recognize my supreme authority. Why didn't she? That's a very upsetting thing for me to think of."

Dora listened to him sigh again, knowing exactly how to alleviate his sadness. The cure was just as wonderful to her as it was to him. "Close yer eyes, milord," she urged. "Close 'em, an' I'll be yer lady."

Excited, Dane shut his eyes, bringing the image of a delicate face to mind. Concentrating on it, he reached for Dora, lifting her atop his own body. "Milady," he whispered, smoothing kisses on her neck.

Dora began touching him all over, until he was ready for her. She moaned when he slid into her. "Yes, milord," she cooed. "I'm yer lady. Lady Hutchins."

"More," Dane groaned. "Tell me more, my dearest lady."

Dora knew the words by heart. "I love ya. I'll spend the rest o' me life lovin' ya. I'm yers, milord. Now. Tomorrow. Ferever. I'm yer lady."

Dane exploded inside her. Many long moments passed before his pleasure subsided. When it did, he opened his eyes, frowning when he saw Dora's face. "Get off!"

She complied instantly. It was always like this, but she didn't care. She lived for the sweet moments when she could be his lady.

Peering at him through her stubby lashes, she renewed her vow to become his lady in reality. Nothing would spoil her chances of making that dream come true.

Goldie sat, kicking off her slippers. Like little green swords, thick, stiff grass stuck up between her toes. "Y'know, Saber," she began, scratching Itchie Bon's head, "it's gonna be kinda lonesome here without Addison, Winston, Kenneth, and David. I reckon I got kinda used to 'em bein' around."

Her gaze darted to him, then left him just as quickly. She'd been stealing glances at him all morning, each swift stare sending thrills rolling through her.

Memories of last night spun into her mind. The two of them hidden in that romantic, moonlit tangle of bushes . . . his lips on her wrist . . . his body pressing close, so close, to hers . . . And it hadn't been her imagination either, she reminded herself. The dream had been real. Another wave of happiness splashed over her.

"You gonna miss 'em too?" she asked absently, daring

just one more glance at him and enjoying the heady sensation it brought.

Stretched out beside her on the lawn, Saber twirled a blade of grass between his fingers. Goldie's voice, like the tender melody of a song, played through his mind. She really had a lovely voice, he mused. So sweet, so soft.

At the thought, he dragged his fingers through his hair. He'd dwelled on it all night, deciding that whatever strange pull existed between them, he had to find the strength to fight it. To hurt Goldie . . . God, the very idea made him ill. Furthermore, he cautioned himself, *he* had no need, no room, indeed, no desire for an emotional relationship in his life anyway.

He would read the diaries, look for evidence against Hutchins and Doyle, then do for Goldie what he'd tried to do for Della. The charade had to end. He would end it as quickly as possible and think no more about it. The diamond, he remembered bitterly, belonged in the city. With all its walls.

The dandelion needed her open fields. "Where her wishing seeds can drift without hindrance," he said softly.

"What's that about seeds, Saber?"

He looked up at her. The pure innocence radiating from her amber eyes told him he was doing the right thing. "I didn't say *seeds*. I said *leave*. The boys had to leave. They couldn't stay—"

"Yeah, I understand about jobs. Addison said they all had to get back to work."

Saber threw the blade of grass into the breeze. What a perfectly outlandish lie Addison had spun for Goldie, he mused. Jobs. The earls of Aurora Hills, Dryden, Barclay, and Meadsborough *working* for a living? Saber subdued the urge to roll his eyes at the absurdity. "Am I not sufficient company for you, poppet?" he asked, absently watching a glint of sunlight dance through her hair.

She looked down at him. "Poppet?"

"What?"

"Poppet. You called me a poppet. What is that?"

The endearment had escaped him inadvertently, and that angered him instantly. What had come over him, that he broke a vow only seconds after having renewed it? ''You didn't answer my question.''

''Yes, you're enough company for me. Now what's a poppet?''

Blast it all! Saber thought furiously. What a morning this had been thus far! First he'd dealt with his friends' jests, raised brows, and knowing glances before seeing them off. What did they think? That he would *marry* Goldie once they were gone? And that breakfast Big made . . . what a bit of diversion that had been. He'd never before eaten eggs that bounced off his plate when he tried to cut them.

And the diaries, he thought irritably. Goldie had made no mention of them this morning, and he couldn't think of a way to coerce her into showing them to him. They were, after all, *diaries,* and as such personal and private. Granted, they weren't Goldie's, but she might not be willing to allow him to read her aunt's secret thoughts.

And now he'd called her a poppet. A sweet name reserved for someone for whom one felt affection. There was only one girl he'd ever called that before, and she'd been lost to him for five years.

''Poppet is just a name, Goldie. A name for . . . a small girl . . . or a little doll, or the like.''

Goldie's contentment vanished. *A small girl,* she repeated silently. *A little doll.* Oh, how she hated being so tiny! So flat-chested! Saber was right. She *did* look like a doll. A childish doll.

When she hung her head and began twiddling her thumbs, Saber realized she was dismayed. Could it be that she thought the name 'poppet' was derisive? ''Goldie, dolls are . . . Don't you think dolls are nice?''

She forced herself to nod, but continued to look at her lap. ''I have a doll,'' she told him, trying her very best to sound nonchalant. ''Uncle Asa gave it to me.''

Saber seized the opportunity to change the subject. He decided he'd listen to her tales about her uncle, then gradually lead the conversation to the diaries. ''Tell me about him.''

She sighed heavily, a reaction not lost on Saber. ''Well, Uncle Asa's my daddy's brother. But Daddy didn't drink or get into trouble. Daddy was the most honest soul in all the world. That's why when I swear to somethin', I say 'Daddy's honor.' "

Her earlier contentment returned. Thoughts of her parents often performed the feat of changing her gloom into cheerfulness. "Lightnin' will strike me if I ever lie against Daddy's honor. Not that I would though, Saber," she informed him, grinning.

Saber noted the rapid change of her mood. Her tears dried with the arrival of her smile; her smile disappeared upon the trickle of her tears. It wasn't easy keeping up with her. "Ah, I see. Daddy's honor." What a charming oath, he mused.

She sat up straight, curling her arms around herself. "I didn't know Mama or Daddy for very long, but I remember 'em both. Mama was from Georgia, and Daddy was from Alabama. I was born in both states. I bet you don't know anybody else who can say somethin' like that, do you?"

There was laughter in her eyes, and he wondered if she was teasing him. "How could you have been born in two states?"

Her grin broadened. "Well, when Mama and Daddy got married, they both wanted to live in their home states. Instead of havin' a fight over it, Daddy built our house right on the state line. When I was born, Mama's birthin' bed laid right over that boundary. The left side of me was born in Georgia, and my right came out in Alabama. My birth papers say I was born in Georgia though. Daddy let Mama have her way on that since she was the one who did all the work gettin' me into the world."

Saber looked at the ground and chuckled. The story of her birth was quite feasible, but it was outrageous at the same time. And that described Goldie herself too, he decided. There were some things about her that were common and familiar. And yet she was unique. He couldn't understand how it was possible to be ordinary and unique at once, but could think of no other way to describe her. "The little person called Goldie," he murmured, bringing his gaze back up to hers. "You're right. I don't know anyone but you who can say they were born in two places.

And it sounds as though your parents were special people to have come to such a fair agreement concerning your delivery.''

She wiggled her toes into the grass again. "Yeah, they were real special. One of the things I remember best about 'em was how they always talked about their troubles together. There wasn't a problem in the world that they couldn't solve when they shared ideas with each other. It was real nice when they were alive, Saber. They hardly ever got mad at me about anything. Well, one time Mama had to scold me when I got too near to Daddy when he was sick. He never got well. Died two days later. Mama went purty soon after that. Uncle Asa was there visitin', and I've been with him ever since. He—''

She looked up at the sky. "There's good in him," she said softly. "I've seen it and felt it. He always says he's sorry. So when he's in one of his mean, hollerin' moods, I try—It's only when he's drunk. He says he's sorry, Saber.''

He felt as though she was trying to convince herself as well as him. Compassion for her blossomed inside him. No one had ever mistreated him, and he couldn't understand what it was like to have to deal with that. "What kinds of things does he say to you when he's in one of his mean moods?''

"He doesn't know what he's sayin'.''

"Still, what does he say?''

"Well, you know. Mean stuff.''

"Goldie, you're staring at the sky. Will you please look at me?''

She gave him her attention. "Are you mad at me?''

"Mad?'' This wasn't the first time she'd worried about him being angry at her. It baffled him. "Goldie, why would I be mad at you?''

She ran her hand over a dandelion bed before answering. "For starin' at the sky.''

"For staring at . . . Why would that anger me?''

"I—Because I wasn't givin' you my full attention," she tried to explain. "Actually though, I *was* givin' you my full attention, Saber. I was just starin' at the sky at the same time.''

He took a moment to think about that. "And would your uncle have been angered at you for staring at the sky?" he asked gently. At her hesitant nod, something tender swept through him. "Goldie, what does your uncle say to you when he's angry?"

Pain clutched her heart. "Do you know what *stertor* means?"

His eyes narrowed. "I'm well aware of the fact that you are changing the subject."

"You don't know what it means, do you?"

"It's the act of making a snoring sound."

"And do you do any stertorin' when you're sleepin'?"

He stared at her for a long while. "Since you're so intent on playing your word game, allow me to ask *you* a word. What is *vituperation?*"

She breathed a sigh of relief that he'd apparently forgotten what they'd been discussing. "Vituperation? Well, I don't have my dictionary out here with me, but it sorta sounds like a spittin' word. Does it mean to spit?"

"No, Goldie," he said gently. "Vituperation is constant and bitter scolding and denunciation. When you vituperate someone, you are berating that person in an abusive manner. You would probably yell and use harsh words."

Goldie tried to smile nonchalantly, but didn't manage to succeed. He knew, she realized. He knew what she herself was always trying to forget. Lord, he was smart. So smart that he'd backed her into a corner without her ever suspecting.

"Goldie, I see no need to explain the word any further," Saber said. "I can see by that weak smile of yours that you understand exactly what I'm hinting at. I'm asking you to confide in me. Is that so terrible?"

*Yes,* she answered silently. She wanted no one's pity, especially not Saber's. "Saber, we need to get on with the duke lessons. I brought one of Aunt Della's diaries out here with me, and we'll read what she says about dukish people." She withdrew a small book from her dress pocket.

Saber felt a surge of excitement at the sight of the diary. But it faded immediately when he saw Goldie run her fingers over the cover of the book. Her hand was trembling. Though he was desperate to read Della's journals, he couldn't dismiss the significance of those pale, quivering fingers.

"We can read the diary in just a moment, Goldie. But right now, I want to discuss the *mean stuff—*"

"Uncle Asa's only mean when he's been drinkin'. I ignore what he says."

"If you ignore him, then why do the memories of his words cause such distressing reactions in you?" he fenced, his concern growing. "Tell me this, Goldie. Does your uncle strike you?"

"No! He's never hit me. Not ever. He . . . Uncle Asa loves me. Deep down inside, he loves me. I know he does. Really."

Saber was unconvinced. "How can you be so sure?"

"Because when he's sober he tries to make up for the things he says. I told you that, Saber."

He watched her carefully. She was winding a gold curl around her little finger, pulling the hair so tight that the tip of her finger turned white. It was obvious to him that though this Asa character acted remorseful when sober, his treatment of Goldie while drunk had left deep scars. Her very reluctance to discuss it tended to prove that fact.

"Why won't you talk about it, Goldie?"

"It's not important. Besides, other people have been meaner to me than Uncle Asa, and they weren't even drunk. Ole Burnell Firt, down in—I can't remember where. But ole Burnell once told me that my freckles made me look like I had a disease. And Naomi Gumm down in Gumm, Kentucky, said I had devil eyes. Said only devil people had yellow eyes. Naomi's daddy owned the town, so she could be as mean as she wanted, and nobody ever told her to stop. And Mathilda Snodgrass, who was Naomi's best friend, and whose mama was somehow related to one of the gardeners at the White House, said my hair looked like somethin' a dog had been shakin' around all day. Mathilda was a snooty sort. Probably because she had connections in the White House. So y'see? Uncle Asa's not as mean as all that."

Saber saw all right. He saw her attempt at lightheartedness. He saw her fail at it, too. She was trying to make him believe that none of those insults bothered her. But didn't she realize he could see the pain sweep into her eyes? It seemed to him her eyes would sting with it.

He wondered what kind of silver lining she found in shouldering such pain, but chose not to ask her. She was nervous enough right now.

"I do try to tame my hair," Goldie assured him, reaching up to smooth back the springy curls. "But it won't mind me. I used to wear a hat, but it blew off one day and slid down the street. By the time I caught up with it, it was the raggediest-lookin' thing you ever saw. I asked Uncle Asa if I could have another one, but he—"

She broke off abruptly, and Saber reached for her hand without realizing he had. When he saw her slender fingers lying within his palm, he had a thought to release them. But they were trembling again, and that decided it for him. Not only did he keep holding her hand, he grasped it more firmly.

"Your uncle refused to buy you another hat, didn't he, Goldie?"

She nodded, struck mute for a moment by the gentleness she perceived in his deep and velvety voice. How it touched her. How tenderly it caressed her senses. And how desperately she longed to respond to it! *Say somethin' witty,* she told herself. *Somethin' wonderfully clever like other girls do.*

"I—Your voice—You have such a nice voice. When I hear it, it kinda makes me think of chocolate. I've only had hot chocolate once, but I never forgot the way it tastes. It's thick and sweet . . . and rich. It's the kind of flavor that makes you want to close your eyes while you're tastin' it. You have a chocolate voice, Saber."

Her sentiment made him smile. It was a simple compliment, but she'd spoken it with such sincerity and sweetness, he decided it was quite the nicest thing anyone had ever said to him. And it was amusing, too. He had seaweed eyes and a chocolate voice. A low chuckle rose in his throat.

Goldie heard his quiet laughter, and felt her cheeks redden. She'd told him he had a chocolate voice. A chocolate voice? Whoever heard of such a thing? That wasn't wonderfully witty, it was *dumb!* Embarrassed, she began to turn away.

Saber reached up, catching her dainty chin. Mesmerized by the golden splendor of her eyes and the delightful way her beautiful hair glistened about her tiny face, he could not take his gaze away from her. She was so delicate, this little person called Goldie. So petite that he felt certain she'd never keep her feet on the ground should she be caught in a strong wind. The thought made him want to hold her, shelter her within the circle of his arms. That something tender inside him swelled again. Without warning, the desire to kiss her seized him. Her full, pink lips looked so soft to him.

He thought of Fred Wattle. Fred had kissed those soft lips, then laughed. "Fred Wattle was an imbecile."

His abrupt and unrelated statement made Goldie frown. She took a moment to try and understand what had prompted Saber to say such a thing. "You don't even know him."

Was she defending the blackguard? Saber wondered. Jealousy stung him. He scowled when he recognized it. He hadn't felt it in years, but hadn't forgotten the way it began in the pit of his belly, spread, and soon coursed through him. He clenched his jaw against it. He had no reason whatsoever to be jealous. Like Goldie had said, he didn't even know the brainless Fred Wattle. And what did it matter that the man had kissed Goldie anyway?

Furious at himself and his damnable emotions, he pulled his hand away from Goldie's and stood. Gazing down at her, he realized he still felt the desire to take her into his arms. His anger at himself had done nothing to change that. God, he had to get away from her. If he didn't . . . "I'm taking Yardley out for a while," he informed her curtly.

She rose, swiping bits of grass from her brown skirt. "And I'll take out Dammit."

"No."

His immediate refusal to allow her to come made her ache. Only with extreme effort did she keep her voice even and normal. "Yes, of course, you're right," she agreed quickly. "I can't go ridin' now. I—Big needs help changin' the bed sheets."

She turned toward the mansion and ran as fast as her legs could take her, Itchie Bon close behind. Tears blinded her, and she stumbled on a rock. She didn't fall, but her near-spill mortified her, for she knew Saber had seen it.

*I'm so clumsy! Just like Uncle Asa says!* Her cheeks burning with shame, she flew up the steps that led to the front door. Throwing it open, she raced up the winding staircase. She missed a step and fell to her knees, clutching the railing so she wouldn't fall further. "Chocolate voice," she moaned, her fist at her mouth. "How could I have said somethin' so stupid?" Choking on a sob, she fled to her bedroom. Itchie Bon barely made it into the room before the door closed with a resounding slam. Her nose pressed against it, Goldie stood there for many moments before turning around. The first thing she saw was the mirror.

Hesitantly, she approached the big, gilt-framed looking glass. It wasn't just a face mirror. It was nearly as tall as the wall, reflecting her full length. Full length, she thought. Full, nothing. She looked like an eleven-year-old child. Twelve, if she stood on her tiptoes. Staring at her image, she saw herself as Saber probably did.

Her dress, patched in many places, was four years old. Or was it five? "Four, five, what difference does it make, Itchie Bon?" she said in a broken whisper. "It's ugly. Brown. Plain, ugly brown. Stitched up and mended all over. I know it's the ugliest thing he's ever laid his beautiful eyes on."

She tore the hateful garment off, ripping it in the process. It landed on her foot; she kicked it across the room and looked back into the mirror. The sight of her nakedness made her eyes widen. Never having had such a big mirror before, she'd never seen her entire body at one time. And since arriving at Leighwood, it hadn't occurred to her to use *this* one for that specific purpose. She didn't like what she saw.

Sniffling, she remembered her Uncle Asa once saying that Melba Potts, down in Sugar Meadows, Alabama, had breasts like ripe melons. She hadn't understood what he meant then, but she did now. Melons were full. Round. Big. She brought her hands up to her own breasts.

"Figs," she murmured. "Little, unripened figs."

Her hands fell to her sides. She looked at her flat stomach. Her slight hips, slim legs, tiny ankles, and little feet. Turning a bit, she studied her small bottom. "Oh, Itchie Bon, there's just nothin' at all to me. No curves. No softness. Just skin-covered littleness. No wonder he called me a doll."

She walked closer to the mirror, examined her face, and decided her eyes were too big, her nose too small. She thought she had good eyebrows, though. They arched gently above her eyes and were darker than her hair. "But men don't fall in love with a pair of eyebrows, Itchie Bon. And they don't like yellow eyes either."

Yellow eyes. Whoever heard of such a thing? And yet they *were* yellow. Not bright yellow like dandelions, but they were yellow. "Big says they're gold with flecks of warm brown, but whoever heard of brown-speckled gold eyes either? Oh, why couldn't I have blue eyes? Not plain blue, but sky-blue. The kind Ruthie Applegate, down in Smallville, North Carolina, had? And Ruthie knew just how to use those robin's-egg eyes of hers, too, Itchie Bon. She batted 'em, and flitted 'em from spot to spot. She could even make 'em change color. Dependin' on her mood, they'd go from pale and shimmery to dark and smoky. Boys loved Ruthie's eyes.

"They made fun of mine," she squeaked. "One boy even made up a chant about 'em. It went, 'Yellow eyes, yellow eyes, Goldie's ugly no matter what she tries.' "

More tears welled, blurring her mirrored image. She rubbed them away, then stared at her hair. It had grass in it. A small leaf, too. Her hair was like a net. It caught everything flying around in the air, and those things stayed there until she found and pulled them out. Now, if something flew into *normal* hair—the long, smooth, and silky kind—it slipped out right away.

"Once a bee got into mine," she informed her mongrel, who sat wagging his tail at her. "It was buzzin' all around, tryin' to get free, but it was trapped. I knew it would sting me if I pulled it out, so I put my head in a bucket of water and tried to drown it first. But I couldn't do it. I just couldn't kill it, Itchie Bon, and it *did* sting me when I finally pulled it out. All the kids . . . they thought it was so funny.''

She pulled on a ringlet. When she let it go, it sprang right back into a tight little coil. ''If Saber were to try and run his fingers through this wild mess, his hand would get stuck for sure,'' she mumbled.

Angrily, she made two braids, each beginning directly above her ears. But her hair was so thick, so untameable, the braids wouldn't lay down. They stuck straight out on either side, as if she'd been shot through the head with a gold arrow. If Saber saw her like this, she knew he'd have every right to laugh, just as all other boys she'd ever known had done.

''But Saber,'' she whispered achingly, still staring at her reflection, ''isn't a boy, Itchie Bon. He's a *man.* He's big and . . . and real solid with muscles. Y'know, I bet one of his legs weighs more than my whole body. And he probably likes girls who come up to his chin. The way Velma Wiggins' came up to Fred's. I barely come up to Saber's chest. Hell, if I were just a tad shorter than I already am, my nose would just about fit into his belly button.''

She loosened her braids and felt suddenly weary, her despondency weighing her down. Her chin on her chest, she turned and shuffled to the bed, dragging her toes across the carpet as she walked. Set on a dais, the bed was so high, she could hardly get her knee on the mattress. Grabbing hold of the bedpost, she began to pull herself up, a feat she had to perform every time she got into this big princess bed. But she didn't realize she also had hold of the lace canopy. It loosened from its attachments on the four posts.

Like a thick, languid snowfall, it floated down just as she'd settled herself in the middle of the bed. Dismayed, Goldie watched it gently wafting toward her. ''Great day Miss Agnes, Itchie Bon, I broke the bed.''

Well, there was little she could do about it, she sighed. She wasn't tall enough to reach the tops of the posts and therefore could not reattach the canopy. Wondering if Sa-

ber was going to get even angrier at her than he already
was, she closed her eyes against both her distress and the
sight of the pearly material drifting downward. When the
delicate fabric settled over her, she realized she should get
up and fold it so it wouldn't wrinkle. But she couldn't
make herself do it. The lace felt so lovely upon her bare
skin. It touched her all over, yet barely at all. She'd never
felt anything so sheer and fragile against her body.

And she never would again, she remembered. Lace and
princess beds, gold-framed mirrors . . . and tall, dark-
haired, handsome men . . . they were the stuff of dreams.
And like dreams, she could have and enjoy them for a
while, but then she'd wake up and they'd be gone. It'd had
been like that with every dream she'd ever had.

She sighed, her puff of breath moving the lace that covered her mouth. "Self-pity doesn't do much but make you
feel worse, and I don't usually feel so sorry for myself,
Itchie Bon," she informed the gray mongrel, who was still
wagging his tail for her. "But then, I've never met anyone
like Saber. Not even Fred Wattle made me feel the way I
do with him. When he gets that softness in his eyes—Itchie
Bon, it makes me feel all wobbly. My stomach sorta sinks.
I can't swallow. No, ole Fred Wattle, as handsome as he
was, *never* took my swallowin' away from me."

She curled into a tight ball, the lace still covering her.
"It's no use, Itchie Bon. Even though Big's gonna help
me with the romance, there *is* no romance. I'm foolin'
myself, dreamin' of Saber. I'm settin' myself up for heartache, just like I did with Fred. I'm likin' him more and
more every day. I try to see him just as the man who's
gonna help me get out of the mess Uncle Asa got us into,
but y'see, my heart and my mind, they aren't workin' together on this. I know from experience nothin's gonna happen between us, but deep down I keep hopin' that maybe
this time it'll be different. That maybe this time . . .

"He held me last night," she remembered aloud. "And
kissed my wrist. Oh, Itchie Bon, you just can't know what
that felt like. His body's so big, so warm, so strong. He
smells so good. His lips were like dandelion puffs on my
wrists. They touched me, but hardly at all. I couldn't decide whether to laugh from the tickle, or faint dead away

from the pleasure. And today he held my hand. But then—
Then he didn't want to go ridin' with me. He even acted
sorta mad.''

Staring through the lace at the beautiful room, she tried
to think of what good thing was coming from her heartache. It was a very long time before she thought of one.
"A warnin'," she mumbled, her voice edged with sorrow.
"A warnin' that nice things—They just aren't for me. I
better guard my heart before it breaks, just like Big said,
Itchie Bon.''

She swallowed hard. "I gotta hurry up with all these
duke lessons, boy. Then I'll get him to London. We'll—
Lord, I still haven't told him about goin' to London, so
he thinks we're leavin' for Hallensham from here. I wonder if he'll mind spyin' on dukes? He didn't want to
wheeze or do the wiggle walk, so he probably won't want
to do any duke-spyin' either. Wonder how I should bring
up the idea without him gettin' mad about it?''

She could come up with no ready answer, but felt sure
she would soon. "And then from London," she continued
softly, "we'll hurry on to Hallensham. The sooner he's
done playin' Duke Marion in the village, the sooner he'll
be gone, and . . . the sooner my heart will be safe from
breakin'.''

She lapsed into deep thought. Yawning, she closed her
eyes again. "I wonder what he's thinkin' about," she
whispered groggily. "Wonder if he's still mad at me. Saber. Saber.''

When slumber claimed her, his name still lingered on
her lips, and his image drifted into her dreams.

Saber stormed into the house. His three-hour ride
through the country had done nothing at all to keep his
mind off Goldie. On the contrary, he'd thought of nothing
but her since galloping out of the barn.

He'd hurt her feelings, and that fact made him feel sick.
"Goldie!" he called, frustrated when she didn't answer
immediately. Blast it all, why didn't she come when he
called her? "Goldie!''

Big emerged from the parlor. "What are you yelling—''
"Have you seen Goldie?''

Big snorted. "No, and I think you can change your own sheets from now on. I'm not a slave, you know."

"So she didn't help you change them." He'd suspected as much.

"No, she didn't, and she's not a slave either."

Saber frowned, throwing back his shoulders. He was in no mood to fence with the churlish little man. "Big, I'm well aware that you have taken it upon yourself to do all the cleaning and cooking, but I do not find it necessary. There are many women in the nearby village who could—"

"Goldie said you didn't have any money. Without money, you can't even buy food! The only reasons we won't starve soon are because the pantry is well-stocked and I'm a good aim with a gun. Now, how could you pay those women to come up here and work?"

"I—" Saber broke off. He was supposed to be Addison's needy cousin, he recalled. Too, he remembered that the villagers knew who he was.

At the dismay in Saber's eyes, Big softened. "Saber, being poor isn't anything to be ashamed of. You ought to count your blessings. Your cousin Addison is a generous man. He's the one who had the pantry filled this morning. He went to that little village and had all the food brought up here. I appreciate your offer about having the women come, but I'll do the cooking and the cleaning. You and Goldie have a lot of work to do, and you must complete it quickly. Goldie and I have to get back to Hallensham. Asa—Lord, there's no telling what that man has done in our absence. Anyway, you and Goldie have no time for anything but the duke lessons," he added firmly, "but I'll do it. I'll even change your sheets."

Saber felt suddenly humbled, realizing that beneath Big's surly exterior, there existed a kind and understanding man. "Thank you," he said, thinking about how odd that sounded. He'd never before thanked anyone for serving him. It wasn't necessary. Servants did their duties, received their wages, and that was that.

But Big was gaining nothing at all in reward for his servitude. He was doing it out of love for Goldie. The thought made Saber realize that Big could very well be the key to understanding more about her. "Big," he began cautiously, searching for just the right words, "I—I've noticed Goldie's penchant for sudden sadness. She—"

"What have you done to upset her?" Big demanded, his anger returning in full force. "Did you say something mean to her? Did you yell at her? Did you—Look, Mr. Saber West, I've warned you before about this. You do one thing to hurt that girl, and I'll—"

"Big—"

"You so much as *look* at her wrong, and I'll—"

"I'm sure you would, but before you do, would you mind telling me about—"

"Why do you want to know?" Big asked suspiciously.

Saber felt sudden anger. How *dare* Big question him! "Because I just do!"

"Well, I'm not telling you a damn thing! If she wanted you to know about her feelings, she'd tell you herself! The fact that she hasn't proves—"

"Look," Saber interjected, summoning patience. "I'm concerned about her. Do you find some evil intent in that?"

Big searched Saber's face for evidence of dishonesty, but found none. "Do you care for her?"

*Yes.* Saber replied mentally. *No. I don't know.* "I think perhaps that that is something that concerns Goldie and myself."

"Anything to do with Goldie concerns me too," Big argued hotly. "I'm the only friend she has, and—"

"No, sir, you are not. I, too, am her friend."

Big raised a brow. "Then as such you shouldn't have to come to me for information," he said slyly. "If you were a *real* friend, she'd trust you, and then you could find out anything you wanted to know from her."

"Very well!" Saber roared, totally fed up with the man. The devil take him! "We will never discuss Goldie again." He turned and crossed to the staircase.

"We'll discuss her when I say so!" Big hollered. "You may be bigger than I am, but I'm *older!* I don't know about here, but in America folks are supposed to respect their elders, and *you* . . . you hotheaded young buck . . . you have shown absolutely no—"

"I'll thank you to think carefully before calling me a name," Saber admonished. "Good day." Swiftly, he ascended the staircase. Big might be kind and caring at times, he thought as he stepped into the long hallway, but it when it came to defending Goldie, the man was about as cordial as a rabid dog.

No, he'd get no help at all from the huffy midget. If he wanted to know more about the sorrows Goldie felt, he would have to discover them for himself.

*If you were a real friend, she'd trust you . . .*

Big's statement burst into Saber's mind as he approached Goldie's room. He stopped, staring at the floor. Could it be that Goldie didn't trust him? The thought disturbed him, and he couldn't understand why. What difference did it make whether or not she trusted him, for heaven's sake?

"It makes *no* difference," he murmured to a painting of one of his ancestors. "None at all. She has to go home. *I* have to go home. She—I—We—It makes no difference whatsoever. The only thing I want from her are those diaries. Tonight I'll *demand* she allow me to see them, and that's that." Squaring his shoulders, he turned around, advancing toward his own room.

But when he reached it, he looked down the hall again. His mind painted Goldie's image for him. Suddenly she stood before him in the corridor. Her hands were outstretched, a solitary tear gleaming at the corner of one of her golden eyes. He could have sworn the vision was real and that she was begging for his help.

Her plea tore at him. The thought of the diaries vanished, and he could think of nothing but that tear he'd imagined by her eye. Before he realized it, he was at her door again. His image of her was gone, but within the room was the real Goldie. The warm one who smiled and teased and made him laugh and made him want to hold her.

The Goldie who had found the common man beneath the nobleman.

"Goldie," he whispered, and knocked softly.

She didn't answer. Could it be that she was out on her balcony and couldn't hear him knocking? He stared at the doorknob, knowing full well it was highly improper for him to open the door, but knowing also that that was precisely what he was going to do.

He opened it only slightly, his in-bred manners forbidding him to go any further before announcing his presence. "Goldie," he called through the crack. "Goldie, may I come in?"

No answer. Yes, she was on the balcony, and he was sure she was decent. People didn't stand out on their balconies in a state of undress. Bolstered by his hypothesis, he swung the door open wide and stepped inside.

What he saw stole his breath away.

Goldie lay sleeping. She wore nothing but diaphanous white lace. The Duke of Ravenhurst realized he should leave the room immediately.

Saber Tremayne stayed.

# Chapter 9

H e stared at her, his fascination so great it rendered him motionless. He saw how the late-afternoon sun, streaming in from the open glass doors, bathed her in its golden light. A soft, sweetly scented breeze whispered across the delicate fabric covering her. The gently rustling lace created shadows that played and danced upon her milky skin.

Delicate gold. Gentle lace. Sweet dance. Soft play. Sun and shadow. Such words came into Saber's mind as his gaze rested tenderly upon her. "Upon this little person called Goldie," he whispered, so quietly he could not hear his own words.

Slowly, she unfolded a petite ivory leg. Saber felt as though he were watching a fragile blossom spreading its petals. She sighed in her sleep. A small, contented bit of breath that held a hint of her voice within its airy resonance. Whatever slumberous images flowed through her mind, Saber realized they were obviously pleasing to her. He experienced an intense yearning to know what they were.

He took a few steps toward the bed. And saw her closer. And wanted to touch her. And almost did.

But didn't.

God, she was lovely. Swathed in sunbeams, lace, and tranquility . . . she looked like an angel. Her luxurious mass of golden curls lay upon her pearl-white pillow, and there was nothing Saber could think of that he desired more than to lose sight of his hands within them. Hers was no ordinary hair. Those curls would capture his fingers, he knew. Like satin tentacles, they would coil around his hands, refusing him release, and he would savor his imprisonment.

He looked at the gentle mound of her breast. The fine lace veiled it artfully, giving him only a hint of the treasure that lay beneath it. He'd seen her breasts clearly once. Now he could not. Now he could only imagine what he could not see.

He envisioned peaches, soft, subtly touched with pale pastel hues, perfect, and kissed warm by the sun. He could picture her breasts in his hands. They weren't heavy. They laid lightly upon his palms, blushing prettily for him. They tempted. Enticed. Saber's fantasy was so real, he could almost feel his lips upon them. Silken and supple, they filled his mouth with sweetness.

"Goldie." His lips formed her name, yet no sound escaped them. His gaze caressed her face.

Warm, rich cream with flecks of cinnamon on top, he thought, then studied its shape. A heart came to mind. A little one, perfectly and softly formed.

Her lashes. Surely they were spun of burnished gold, he decided. They fanned out beneath her eyes, long, lush, and sweeping across the finely sculpted crests of her cheeks. And her brows. How gently they arched above her eyes, like a pair of tawny, upside-down smiles.

Her lips twitched suddenly, as if reminding him that he hadn't yet looked at them. In truth, he'd been saving them for last, and now he allowed his hungry gaze to take its fill of them. Their pink tinge was not hidden by the alabaster fabric. Indeed, the opaline lace deepened the color of her mouth. He imagined a scarlet flower with intricate snowflakes lying upon its crimson velvet. He would pluck the blossom and raise it slowly to his mouth, his eyes never leaving it. He would smooth his lips across it, relishing its rich texture and savoring its precious scent. The thought made him tremble with desire. He fairly ached with the need to have her close to him.

At that moment, he felt all reserve melt away, like frost upon a warm windowpane. He sensed it slipping from him, tried to hold onto it, but couldn't. It was gone, and he knew then that the man standing before this sleeping girl was a vulnerable one. He felt as naked as she was, yet felt no shame.

No fear.

*What do you do to me, Goldie?* he wondered. She lay there silently, doing none of the things that so delighted him. He saw nothing at all of her captivating smile, nor did he hear the music of her voice. Yet he felt mesmerized and enchanted by the sweet sight of her sleeping beneath her lace blanket. And it wasn't that the whole of her beauty was revealed to him; that she lay there in a state that would make any man wild with desire. *Ah, golden angel, if only it were that simple. But it's more. More, but I don't know what.*

As he stood there gazing down at her, he realized just how much he wanted her. How much he longed to feel her tiny body cuddled next to his big one. How deeply he yearned to hear her tell him everything she knew; all the things that made her so special.

"How is it that when I am with you, I forget to be the man I am supposed to be?" he whispered, too softly for her to hear. "I am a duke, Goldie." And yet with her, he thought tenderly, he was a child watching dandelion seeds float in the breeze. With her he dug in the dirt and played in the mud. She made him remember things he had no desire to remember, yet when those memories came he found them pleasurable instead of painful.

A part of him wanted her to awaken and see him standing there. He became bolder and took another step toward her bed, his knees brushing her mattress. "Five years ago, little Goldie, I swore never to care for a woman again," he continued to whisper. "I kept my oath." Until he met her, he amended.

And now he found himself angered at the thought of anyone mistreating her, and admonished himself again for whatever hurt he inflicted on her. He'd bought her a gold brush because she lacked even a wooden one. He was filled with the compulsion to get her a hat since her uncle had refused to buy her one.

"And last night, while lying abed, I even thought of Imogene's tea parlor and how she threw you out of it," he admitted quietly. "The thought enraged me. I would *give* you a tea parlor, Goldie. A grand tea parlor. And then I would watch while you decorated it to your heart's content.

"Goldie," he murmured. One glint of pain in her eyes, a slight tremble of her lips, a single tear on her cheek sent concern shooting through him, and he could think of nothing but how to soothe her sorrow. And how was it that his determination to read the diaries kept fading? How was it that her problems and struggles were becoming so important to him?

He bent, and with one finger caressed her lace-covered cheek. "Only hours ago, I renewed my vow yet another time, and already I have broken it. I thought I rode alone, yet there you were. In the sky. In the breeze. In the fields. Everywhere, all around me, there you were. Tell me—does it do me any good to continue swearing an oath that I cannot seem to keep?"

He drew his hand away from her cheek, feeling the separation from her instantly. "What will become of this, poppet? Of this tenderness that grows between us? I am powerless to stop it. Morever, golden angel, I've no further strength to try."

He watched her sigh sleepily. Her eyelids fluttered. She stretched langorously, and he realized she was trying to awaken. With all his heart, he longed to stay. But he knew his presence would startle her.

He left the room, closing the door quietly behind him. As he stood in the hall staring at her door, he thought of the thing he'd just done. He felt like a little boy who'd just gotten away with mischief without having been caught. The thought made him grin. "Goldie?" he called loudly, and knocked. "Goldie?"

"Goldie," she repeated, her eyes still closed, sleep holding her for as long as it could. *Saber.* she dreamed. He was calling her; she would answer. "Saber." she whispered to him.

"Goldie?" He knocked again.

Her eyes opened. She saw the room. *Pearls,* she thought. *It's rainin' pearls in here.*

"Goldie, are you awake?"

"Saber?" She sat up, looking down at the pool of lace in her lap. "It's not rainin' pearls. This is lace."

"Pearls?" Saber asked. "Goldie—"

"Saber?" Great day Miss Agnes, it *hadn't* been a dream! Saber was out there calling her!

"May I come in, Goldie?"

"I—Wait!" She scrambled out from beneath the lace and jumped off the bed. Finding her dress, she discovered it was ruined and remembered she was the one who ripped it. "Saber, I'm not dressed. My clothes . . . I tore 'em up."

"You tore them up? Why did you do that?"

Goldie bit her bottom lip. *Because they're ugly, and I wish I could be pretty for you.*

"Goldie?"

"I didn't mean to tear 'em up," she explained. "But—"

"Don't you have anything else to put on?"

"Big's washin' the rest of my things." The rest of her things, she lamented. Those "things" consisted of a dress just as ugly as this one.

"Well, look in the closet," Saber suggested, his lips touching the door. "Maybe there's something in there you could wear until Big is finished with your other clothes. At the very least, you might find an old robe." He smiled, knowing full well what Goldie would find in the closet. Jillian always left gowns behind at Leighwood, and many of them were hanging in Goldie's closet.

Goldie stared at the big closet doors. How many times since she'd arrived at Leighwood had she resisted the temptation to open those doors and see what was inside? She'd never gone through with the urge, her conscience telling her it wasn't right to go through another person's things. Even now she hesitated. "But Saber, what if nothin' fits me?" she asked, her eyes trained on the brass closet handles.

He frowned. Jillian was tall and generously endowed. Goldie had a point. The clothes would swallow her. But Saber felt impatient. He *had* to talk to her! "Well, you could put something on for the time being, couldn't you? At least it would cover you up until Big returns your other clothes."

Goldie took a step closer to the closet. "The things in this closet don't belong to me," she reminded him, her voice betraying her anxiousness to open those doors. "And what if they're man clothes?"

"You'll never know until you look. And as far as wearing someone else's things . . . Goldie, who's going to know? Big won't tell, and I won't either." Saber almost laughed. If Jillian knew someone else was wearing her finery, her smooth, porcelain skin would mottle with rage. For some reason, the thought pleased Saber enormously.

"Saber, if I put somethin' on from this closet, Daddy's honor you won't tell?"

Saber chuckled. "Daddy's honor."

Goldie needed no further urging. She flung open the doors. "Oh!" she squealed in pure delight. "Oh, Saber!"

He smiled. "Are there any clothes in there?"

"Any clothes? Oh, Saber!" She walked into the closet, her fingers caressing silk, satin, velvet, and brocade. Every kind of fabric known to man. And the colors! *Dozens* of colors! "Oh, Saber!"

"You've said that three times," he informed her with another chuckle. "Goldie, get something on so I can come in. I want to talk to you."

Her pleasure grew as she touched each gown in the closet. She sighed repeatedly over each of them. They were gowns too beautiful to be real. Gowns fit for a queen.

Her smile vanished at the thought. What if she ruined these expensive dresses? What if, in her clumsiness, she fell and tore one of them? Tears sprang into her eyes. Viciously, she wiped them away and walked out of the closet. She closed the doors, shutting away the gowns, her delight with them, and her impossible dream of actually wearing one.

Her brown dress lay wadded up on the floor. She slipped into it, noticing it wasn't that badly ripped. Only the shoulder seam was torn. A few stitches, and it would be as good as new. "It wasn't even good then," she mumbled. "You can come in now, Saber."

His hand on the knob, Saber wondered which dress she'd chosen. He swung open the door, expecting to see her drenched in flowing silk or encased in shimmering satin.

She stood before him in her multi-patched, mud-colored

frock, her hand clasping the shoulder seam. "Goldie, why—"

"Because I might tear 'em. Saber, I know you wouldn't tell, and neither would Big. But what if I spilled something on one of those gowns? What if I stepped on the hem and ripped it all to pieces?"

She turned toward the balcony, but not before Saber saw the tears shining on her lashes. She was doing it again, he realized. Happy one second, crying the next. Blast it all, he was going to get to the bottom of this, and right now!

"Goldie, come here."

His command hit her ears harshly. That air of authority was in it. It dared her to disobey him. She turned but did not advance. "Are you mad at—"

"No, I'm not mad at you!"

"Then why are you yellin' at me?"

His jaw clenched. Instantly, he relaxed it, knowing she was going to ask him what he was eating. "Goldie, I don't mean to shout at you, but your sudden tears baffle me, and I become impatient with them. Explain them to me."

"I . . . Saber—"

"Tell me, Goldie. What it is that so upsets you?"

She didn't answer.

"All right," Saber said, closing the door. "Let's talk about the gowns. Why did you weep over them? And don't tell me you didn't, because I saw your tears."

"I already told you. I might mess 'em up."

It was on the tip of his tongue to tell her that if she ruined them, he would replace them with a thousand more. "All right," he said instead, "but you cried because you *do* want to put one on. Isn't that right?"

She nodded.

"If you soil one, couldn't we wash it? If you rip one, couldn't we mend it? As long as you don't set one on fire, I don't see why we couldn't repair whatever damage you might inflict. Do you?"

Her gaze drifted back to the closet. "But what if I *do* set it on fire? Gertrude Micklewhite set her cape on fire once. And she had it tied in such a tight knot, she couldn't get it off before it burned the tips of her ninnies. They didn't burn so badly that they melted or anything like that, but they got seared some.''

The unseemly thought of ''seared ninnies'' struck Saber's sense of humor. It occurred to him that breasts aflame were no laughing matter, but after all, they hadn't melted or anything like that, he remembered with a smile. ''Goldie, why don't I watch you at all times while you're wearing the gown? I'll warn you if you get close to a flame of any sort.''

''Well . . .''

Saber returned to the hall. ''I'm giving you exactly one minute to put one of them on. After that, I'm coming back into this room.''

She jumped when he shut the door. Slowly, hesitantly, she removed her dress, stepping out of the muddy puddle it made at her feet. She rummaged through the gowns once more, choosing one of warm coral silk. It rustled as she held it, the delicate sound making her shiver with anticipation.

''The minute is almost over, Goldie!''

''Oh, great day Miss Agnes, he's gonna see me naked!'' With one smooth motion, she lifted the gown over her head, feeling it caress the length of her entire body as it fell into place. Lost in the wonderful sensation, she closed her eyes and allowed herself to enjoy it. ''I'm wearin' silk. Pure silk, and I'm really and truly wearin' it.''

''And does it feel as nice as it looks?'' Saber asked.

Her eyes flew open. He was standing in the threshold of the closet. ''You—''

''I told you I'd give you one minute. The minute ended, and here I am.''

''Well, it's a damn good thing I got the thing on in time, isn't it?''

He was fully aware that his sudden return into her room was thoroughly improper. He tried to summon shame over his action, but instead grinned rakishly.

''You look like Smiley Jones, standing there grinnin' like that, Saber,'' Goldie told him, unable to keep from smiling back at him.

''I don't recall ever being compared to a mule.'' How odd, he thought. Only two weeks ago being likened to a mule would have annoyed him greatly. Now he found it amusing.

"You should be flattered," Goldie informed him. "Smiley Jones has a nice smile. Here, would you do me up?"

When she turned, the shoulders of the gown fell away, sliding down to her upper arms. Saber saw the creamy expanse of her back, and wondered what that skin would feel like beneath his palms. He decided he would discover the answer for himself.

He stepped closer to her. So close, Goldie felt his warm breath wafting down to the top of her bare shoulder. That ache . . . that strange, sweet ache began its slow-winding dance within her.

*Guard your heart, Goldie,* she remembered suddenly, struggling to heed the warning. "Saber, do me up," she told him, trying to sound impatient.

Saber raised his hands, placing them upon the ivory flesh of her shoulders. Her skin was so warm. So soft. God, he wanted to taste it. "Goldie," he whispered, his fingers smoothing down her arms.

"Do me up," she told him again, every fiber of her being tingling with that yearning she always experienced when he was near. *Breathe, Goldie,* she told herself when her lungs began to burn with lack of air. *Breathe and calm yourself!* "Saber, are you gonna do me up, or you want me to get Big to do it?"

"I," he said, bending toward her shoulders, "will do it."

Having had no idea, no forewarning of what he was going to do, Goldie gasped when she felt his lips touch her shoulder. Her knees buckled, but even before she knew she was falling, she was in Saber's arms.

And they were descending, she realized. Slowly. He was kneeling, taking her with him. On the floor, he sat and laid her across his lap, allowing her head to rest within the crook of his elbow.

She looked up and saw his gaze overflowing with that softness. It swept over her face. Smoothed down her neck.

And stopped at her breasts.

With a trembling hand, she touched her chest. It was bare. Her breasts were revealed to him. *Figs. Little, un-*

*ripened figs!* Embarrassment coursed through her. She tried to cover herself with her arm.

"No, Goldie," he told her, staying her arm. Slowly, he raised his other hand.

She saw he lifted it to right above her chest, then watched as he brought it closer to her. Nearer to her breasts. Part of her screamed for her to get up and run. The other part couldn't bear the thought.

*Yes, touch me,* her heart begged. "No," she said out loud. "Don't. Please don't." Her heart pounded as she waited to see what he would do.

His palm was only a fraction of an inch above the treasures he longed to hold. To taste. "Goldie—"

"Saber, please. You don't understand." *I'm so afraid, Saber,* she continued silently. *So afraid to trust this.*

The expression in her eyes told Saber what words could not. As much as he wanted to touch her, know the feel and taste of her, he would not take what was not offered. "Very well," he whispered. "As you say." He moved his hand to her shoulder. There, his fingers caressed her bare skin.

Goldie realized she should get up. Every instinct in her body told her to do just that. But the feeling of lying in his arms . . . on the floor . . . in the dim sanctuary of the closet . . . made her unable to do what she knew she ought. Wetting her lips, she glanced at her breasts. "You're seein' me," she said nervously.

He took note of the blush on her cheeks. "I've seen you before," he reminded her.

She missed a breath. "But it was different then."

"Yes."

*Get up, Goldie,* she told herself. "Did you want to touch me then, too?"

"Yes." He moved his hand from her shoulder, let it trail across her neck, then slid it up to her mouth. There, he traced the outline of her lips. "But I was afraid you would run me through with your claymore."

She smiled. *I'm lyin' in his arms, practically naked, and I can still smile at him.* The realization baffled her. "I need to get up. I have to get dressed."

"But do you *want* to get up? Do you *want* to get dressed?"

"Yes."

"Daddy's honor?"

Her smile disappeared. "That's not fair."

"And why not?"

"Because you know I can't lie against my oath."

His fingers journeyed into her hair. As if alive, her curls captured them, winding around them. He pushed his hand deeper into the flaxen cloud, knowing he'd never felt anything so wonderful. "Ah, then you admit to speaking a falsehood."

She didn't answer. She couldn't. Her voice wouldn't come. Instead, she looked up into his eyes. The softness was still there, but it was dark now. A smoldering softness, like he was on fire inside. The sight of it caused a great need to rise within her. It was more than the ache his nearness always brought. It was almost pain. Her body throbbed with it.

"Saber, somethin's happenin' to me. I'm almost naked. I'm in your lap, and you're seein' what no other man has ever seen. It's makin' somethin' happen inside me."

Her innocent admission made his chest tighten. "And what is it that's happening to you, Goldie?"

The slight tilt of his lips made her realize he already knew the answer to his question. "Saber . . ."

"Goldie . . ."

"I'm embarrassed."

"You've no need to be."

"I'm scared."

"I'm doing nothing to you."

"I—Yes, you are."

"Really? What?"

"You're makin' me feel things. Things I don't understand."

He never took his gaze from her face. "And these things . . . are they unpleasant?"

She saw a knowing twinkle in his eyes. "You know they aren't."

Her answer deepened his desire, and he longed to show

her everything he did, indeed, know. "So what would you suggest we do with these pleasant things you're feeling?"

She frowned slightly. "What's to do with 'em? Don't they just come and go like all other kinds of feelin's?"

He smiled gently. "Yes, I suppose they do, but there are many ways to enjoy them while they last. In fact, there are many ways to heighten them and make them last longer."

"And you know those ways, don't you, Saber?"

He wasn't sure how to answer her, and wondered if it would anger her to know he had experience with lovemaking. "I might. Tell me, Goldie, do *you* know anything about them? Anything at all?"

His question sent worry shooting through her. She knew next to nothing about the intimate things that could happen between a man and a woman. And if Saber knew that, he would laugh at her, she knew. Or maybe he'd get mad at her. A man as handsome as he . . . he'd want a woman who knew how to respond to him. Who knew how to give him what he wanted. She felt her own ignorance keenly.

"Saber, please—I don't know . . . I can't—We—If you laughed, of course I'd get over it. In time, I would. But it wouldn't be easy. And it'd be even harder if you got mad. I hate to make people mad, Saber."

He couldn't understand her fragmented explanation, but detected a suspicious squeak in her voice. God, how that sad sound tore at him. Helping her into a sitting position upon his lap, he smoothed the curls from her eyes. "Goldie—"

"I'd try to find that silver linin' you talked about. Try to find the good thing about bein' laughed at or havin' you angry at me, but—"

"But I'm not angry at you. Nor am I laughing. Why would you think—"

"Well, for one thing, because of Melba Potts!" she blurted, and felt her cheeks heat again. Quickly, she pulled up her gaping bodice, feeling familiar inadequacies spin through her. "Figs," she mumbled, tears spilling down her cheeks. "I've heard about melons, all round and full. But to have figs! *Unripened* ones! Oh, Saber, you're a man, and you just can't imagine how hard it is to see *figs* instead of melons. Not watermelons. I guess those would be *too* big. But cantaloupes would be nice. They're not all *that* big, but they're big enough. Well, think how you'd feel if instead of seeing *ropes* of muscles, you saw *threads!*''

"Muscle threads? Goldie, what are you talking about?" Completely bewildered, Saber pulled out his handkerchief, pressing it to each of her wet cheeks. "Who is Melba Potts? And what is this about figs and cantaloupes? Why is the thought of fruit making you cry? Goldie, what—"

"And your hands got trapped just like I knew they would. Just like the bee did. But I can't help it. I didn't *ask* for this yellow bush, y'know. And given a choice, I wouldn't have picked yellow eyes either. No one likes to go around with devil eyes, Saber, so don't think for one minute that *I* do."

"Goldie—"

"Saber, you just can't know how nice this has been," she sniffled. "Lyin' here in the closet with you, with all this silk and satin hangin' all around us, and you lookin' down at me with all that dark softness in your eyes. These feelins are just too wonderful to describe. But Saber, I'm not—You're the kind of man—We aren't—Together, we just don't . . . Even though you make me lose my swallowin'—Dreams never last, y'see. I—It's about my heart. It's the only one I have. I have to guard it. If it breaks, God won't give me another one."

His hands fell from her shoulders. *She has to guard her heart,* he repeated silently. *From me. Yes, from me. How right she is.*

"Then guard it well, Goldie." With deft motions, he turned her slightly, fastening the back of her dress.

Goldie stood and watched him rise. She'd have given anything to know what he was thinking. But all she knew was that the softness was gone from his eyes. "Saber—"

"I will await you in the library," he told her, already leaving the closet and heading for the door. "Bring the diaries."

"Why?"

He opened the door. "I'm going to read them. Do they

not contain stories of noblemen? Would you keep such information from me? And do you forget that time is passing? You said yourself that you were afraid of what your uncle would do in your absence, and Big echoed that sentiment earlier. You've been here for two weeks already. I would think you'd want to hurry things along."

That authority was in his voice again, she heard. So was a tinge of anger. And a bit of impatience, too. "I'm sorry. For whatever I've done, I'm sorry."

Her apology tore at him. It was all he could do not to take her back into his arms. "You've nothing to apologize for, Goldie. On the contrary, *I'm* the one who—"

"No! Saber, you haven't done anything wrong at all!"

"Goldie, we will forget this afternoon ever happened," he told her firmly, his insides coiling at the idea of never being able to touch her again. "It was a mistake, and we both know that. I'm sure you feel the same as I do in that you never want it to happen again. Now, put yourself right, gather up the diaries, and meet me in the library."

He shut the door quietly, but Goldie jumped anyway. Every nerve in her body pulsed with hurt. Her tears ran freely until she noticed they were dripping onto the silk gown. Horrified, she removed the beautiful dress and hung it back in the closet before slipping into her brown frock.

She stood in the middle of the room, holding the shoulder of the dress together. *It was a mistake,* he'd said. *We will forget this afternoon ever happened.*

"Forget," she murmured, tasting the salt of her tears. "How can I forget the way you touched me? The way you looked at me? How—"

"Goldie?" Big called from the hallway. "I've got your clothes. May I come in?"

She wiped her eyes on her dress sleeve. "Yes."

Big waddled in, her extra gown lying over his arm. He stopped when he saw her. "Your dress is torn."

She took her other one from him and slipped behind the big mirror to dress. "Big, we have to hurry up. We gotta make Saber into a duke as soon as we can. Before Uncle Asa does somethin' awful. Before Dane Hutchins kicks us all out." *Before my heart gets shattered all to bits.*

When she stepped out from behind the mirror, Big saw

how red her eyes were. He bent his head and stared at the floor. "You're falling in love with him, aren't you, Goldie Mae?"

She made herself busy gathering all the diaries into the burlap sack in which she carried them. "He told me to meet him in the library. Said he was gonna read all the stuff about noblemen that Aunt Della wrote down. With a little luck, we should be back in Hallensham in a little over a month. We'll just have to rush the duke-spyin' in London."

"And I have to admit he's concerned about you," Big muttered to himself. "He stopped me earlier, wanting to know about the things that make you sad."

"Big, you're mumblin'. I can't understand what—"

"Could be that he cares," Big continued incoherently. "Maybe the oaf isn't an oaf after all."

Goldie threw him a baffled look, then slipped the last diary into the bag. "Well, I guess that's all of 'em," she said, slinging the sack over her shoulder. "If you need me, I'll be in the library. We have to hurry, Big. I'm gettin' more and more worried about what Uncle Asa's doin', and we don't have time to dilly with this. I've decided we'll leave for London tomorrow. We can keep on readin' the diaries there. Lord, I hope I can talk Saber into spyin' on dukes. I still haven't told him about that part of the lessons, y'know."

"Stop right there," he ordered her when she crossed to the door. "I mean it, Goldie."

She obeyed, but stomped her foot to show him she wasn't pleased at being detained.

"What's going on between you and Saber?"

"Nothin'. Everything's fine."

"And you're crying over how fine it all is." He joined her at the door and took the sack of diaries from her. "You go feed Dammit, Smiley Jones, and Yardley. I'll take the diaries to Saber."

"But—"

"You're in no shape to face him right now. Besides, he'll be reading for quite a while, and probably won't appreciate any interruptions. Go on now, Goldie."

She knew he wasn't going to back down. Too, she realized he was right. She *wasn't* ready to see Saber again right now. Nodding, she left to do his bidding.

Big watched as she walked down the hall. After a while, he left her bedroom, heading for the library. His pace was slow, and he stopped many times to dwell on all the thoughts running through his mind.

When he finally reached the library, he knew what he would do.

"I believe you wanted these brought to you?" Big laid the bag of diaries on Saber's desk.

Saber leaned forward in his chair. "I did. But I believe I asked Goldie to bring them."

"Well, as you can plainly see, she didn't. I did."

Saber pulled the sack closer. "Thank you." When Big made no move to leave, he asked, "Is there something I can do for you?"

"As a matter of fact there is."

"Then please be seated."

Big climbed into a huge leather chair and tapped his fingers on the arm. "Answer some questions for me, Saber."

"If I can."

"What has Goldie told you about herself?"

Saber studied Big carefully, searching for some sort of devious expression on the man's face. But Big's features registered nothing. "Goldie talks about many things, but rarely does she speak about herself. Surely you know that."

"Then she has revealed nothing at all to you."

"I didn't say that."

"Then?"

Saber rose, clasped his hands behind his back, and began a slow journey around the room. "What are your reasons for this inquiry, Big?" He stopped in front of a collection of miniature paintings, his back to Big.

"I have an important decision to make, Saber, and what I decide depends on your answers. I'm trusting you to be honest with me."

Saber turned, his curiosity aroused. "Very well. Goldie has told me very little about herself. It's what she *doesn't* say that has significance. If I reveal to you what I know about her, will you do me the favor of telling me whether or not my conclusions are correct?''

Big nodded.

Saber raised his chin. "I've decided that Goldie has been mistreated since her parents died. I'm well aware her relationship with you is a good one, but what concerns me is the one she has with her uncle. I've learned that when he has been drinking, the man abuses her verbally. That persecution has left its scars. Too, other people have criticized and ridiculed her. Unjustly, I believe. She has a deep-seated fear of making people angry at her, and fairly shakes when she believes someone is cross with her. She has been tossed out of every place in which she's lived, and though she tries to act as though it doesn't bother her, I believe it hurts her very much.

"In conclusion, Big, I believe Goldie is crying out for the acceptance she never receives. There's a great sadness inside her, and although I don't know the extent of what has caused it, I am reasonably certain that it stems from the fact that her years with Asa have been a series of broken dreams. Am I correct in my observations?''

Big managed to conceal his tremendous satisfaction. He slid off the chair and walked to the door. "I'm leaving Leighwood, Saber. I came in here to tell you that. Goldie has expressed concern about what Asa is doing, and I think that if I go back to Hallensham and keep an eye on him for her, she'll feel less anxious about staying with you and completing her plans. She will, of course, still worry some, but not as much.''

When Big began to leave, Saver scowled. "You didn't tell me if I'm right or wrong about—''

"Nor will I.''

"You said you would.''

"Ah, but I didn't say 'Daddy's honor.' ''

Saber struggled to contain his ire. "Big—''

"I'm trusting you to take care of her, Saber, and I'm sure you'll do everything you can to see that no harm comes to her. I must admit that when I first met you, I had many misgivings about you. I apologize for thinking ill of you. Now, if you will excuse me, I'm going to find Goldie and tell her of my decision.''

''If I may ask,'' Saber said quickly, ''what have I done to earn your trust?''

''It's quite simple. You care about her.''

''We are *friends*. Beyond that—''

''There's nothing wrong with friendship to my way of thinking. Do you disagree?'' Big smiled.

Saber decided he didn't like Big's knowing grin. ''No. Of course not.'' He thrust his fingers through his hair.

''Then I'll let you get to the diaries. I wish you better luck than I had with them. So many are ruined by water that trying to guess at the obliterated parts drove me crazy.'' He began to leave, wanting to get away before Saber could continue questioning him. He had no intention of allowing Saber to know about his scheme.

''Big, wait!'' Saber called. ''You—''

''Saber, I must pack my things,'' Big hurried to argue.

''I understand that, but I—''

''And I've yet to speak to Goldie.''

''Of course, you must talk to her, but Big, I—''

''Would you delay me?'' Big fenced.

''Well, no, but—''

''Good day then.'' With that, Big rushed out of the library and into the courtyard. Itchie Bon joined him, and together they looked at the distant barn, watching Goldie lead Dammit into the paddock.

''Saber cares about her, boy,'' Big informed the dog. ''I had to know for sure, and now I do. Because he cares, he has succeeded in understanding the things she won't tell him. A man who didn't care would never have wasted the time or energy to do that.''

He swallowed down the huge lump in his throat. ''It's *time* she needs with Saber, Itchie Bon. And what with her worry about Asa, she's trying to rush things along so she can get back to Hallensham. I'm soothing that worry, and I hope to God I'm doing the right thing. Because you see, boy, I'm leaving her with the man who is either going to break her heart or make her feel like the true princess she is.''

# Chapter 10

~~~~~~~~~~~~~~~~~~~~~~~~~~~~~~~~~~~~~~~~~~~

**W**illiam Doyle entered his room in the Cornwall Inn,
locking the door behind him. He lit several lamps,
then examined the deeds to the copper mines. A feeling
of tremendous power seized him. He threw his shoulders
back and swaggered across the room, stopping in front of
a small mirror hanging on the wall. He felt extraordinarily
pleased over his appearance and his accomplishments.

"No one can stop you now," he complimented himself,
running a finger over his thick gray mustache. Not only
did he own copper mines in Cornwall, he mused content-
edly, but he also had iron mines in Norfolk and Stafford,
shipyards in Essex and Devon, and a salt mine in Chester.
Why, he even owned highly productive orchards in Here-
ford! And the most satisfactory part of it all, he thought
with utter glee, was that he'd never used his own money
to buy a thing.

"Why should I?" he asked his reflection. "I have the
Tremayne fortune at my disposal!"

He crossed to the bed, removed his clothes, and lay
down. His hands under his head, he stared at the ceiling
and began to laugh. Surely there wasn't a man in England
as clever as he, he decided, still chuckling. Everyone
trusted him; no one doubted he was on their side, looking
after their best interests. Starting with Marion Tremayne's
father, he'd gained the confidence of everyone he'd ever
needed.

All the years of hard work and planning had been difficult, but he'd seen them through successfully. And now
the time had finally come to bring his scheme to a fitting

end. He had everything he required: ready cash, land, and highly profitable investments. After getting rid of the people who stood in his way, he'd sell his town house in London, buy a rambling country estate somewhere, and live the life of a wealthy gentleman.

The thought brought Dane to mind. "Dane," he murmured. How simple it was to manipulate the man! "You sincerely believe I've done everything for *you*, don't you, Dane? There's not a doubt in your mind that I've worked all these years so you could live in a mansion, enjoying the luxury you think is your due. You, a *gentleman?* Lord of an estate? For God's sake, Dane! How idiotic can a man be? You were merely an instrument in my hands." William roared with more laughter, the mattress shaking beneath his tremendous frame.

Wiping a tear of merriment from the corner of his eye, he caressed his mustache again, and deliberated on the two people who had the means to expose him. Unfortunately for them, they'd never have the chance to do that.

As soon as he tied up all the loose ends concerning the copper mines and investigated a few more business opportunities in Cornwall, he'd leave for Ravenhurst. Once there, he'd dispose of Dane.

Then he'd hurry to London and deal with Marion Tremayne. He'd cause some kind of accident to befall His Grace, perhaps. Yes, an accident, he decided firmly.

He knew how to make accidents happen.

Goldie paced in front of the library. Glancing at the huge grandfather clock down the corridor, she saw it was half past midnight. "How long are you gonna stay shut up in there, Saber?" she muttered to the library door.

Ambling to the big velvet-draped window at the end of the hall, she peered out and saw the moonlit road Big had taken yesterday. "Yesterday. It seems like weeks, Big. Lord, how I miss you." How afraid she felt without his reassuring presence! And what with Saber locked away in the library since Big had left, she'd had no one to talk to. She was beginning to feel as though she were the only person in the entire world.

The thought made her angry. She *wasn't* the only person

in the world, and it was ridiculous for her to feel that way. She was well aware that Saber was avoiding her, but what did he think she was going to do? Throw herself into his arms and command him to fall in love with her?

She marched away from the window and stared at the library door. "Enough's enough. There's not gonna be anything romantic between us, but that doesn't mean you can treat me like I don't exist. And great day Miss Agnes, if I keep lettin' you hide away from me, we'll never get to London to start the duke research!" Her ire rising, she flung the door open.

"You've been locked away in here long enough, Sab—"

She broke off when she saw him. His face was shadowed with stubble. His eyes were red and bleary, black circles beneath them. His hair was mussed, his clothes rumpled.

She'd never seen him so unkempt. Her heart turned over when she saw the pile of diaries in front of him. He'd done this to himself for her sake. Just so he could learn to be a duke. "Saber, you haven't eaten," she said softly. "Your hair, your clothes . . ."

He looked up at her, saw the dismay in her eyes, and pushed his fingers through his hair. He was well aware of how he probably looked to her, but the many hours he'd spent poring over the diaries had proven successful. He'd learned a wealth of information already, and there were still many diaries he hadn't touched yet. Of course there were also those with pages that were too badly stained to read. He now understood what Big had meant when he'd said trying to decipher them had driven him crazy.

He ran his thumb over the one he held. "Goldie, do you know how your aunt learned to read and write?"

"How?"

"She wrote that she eavesdropped on Little Marion's lessons. After her day's work, she scurried home and practiced everything Marion had learned."

"She must have really wanted to learn, huh?"

He nodded, his newly gained knowledge too much for him to contain. "And do you know why she never wrote to the duke to inform him about the pitiful wages his workers were receiving or of the sad shape of his tenants' houses?''

''Why?''

He tossed the diary back to the pile. ''Because Hutchins has made everyone in Hallensham believe Lord Tremayne doesn't give a damn about what happens to them.''

Goldie's eyes widened. She'd never heard Saber curse before.

''He's been able to convince the villagers of this because he's had help,'' Saber continued, his voice deceptively calm. ''Uh . . . I gather from what your aunt wrote that Marion Tremayne employs a man of business, William Doyle, who makes periodic trips from London to Ravenhurst. Your aunt wrote that this Doyle character backs up everything Hutchins tells the villagers. That is, that the duke has fairly washed his hands of them. That he is entirely too busy to cater to a bunch of complaining peasants. Because Doyle and Hutchins both worked for Lord Tremayne's father, the villagers in Hallensham saw no reason to doubt their word. They still don't.''

Goldie ambled to his desk and sat on top of it. ''But even if Aunt Della believed Duke Ravenhurst forgot her, she forgave him. 'Course I haven't read all those diaries yet, but so far I haven't found anything mean about him. She went right on lovin' him just like she did when he was little.''

That was true, Saber reflected, but it still tore at him to know that Della had believed he'd forgotten about her. He thought about the many letters he'd written to her in care of Dane. ''I—You know, Goldie, it's possible Lord Tremayne *did* try and write to your aunt. If that's so, Dane never forwarded the letters. That would explain why Della didn't correspond with His Grace. She thought he wasn't interested.''

''I bet you a zillion dollars that's what happened.''

A lump formed in his throat at her statement. ''Is that really what you think, Goldie?'' he asked, wanting desperately to know her feelings. ''You don't really believe Lord Tremayne turned his back on the villagers?''

''No,'' she answered unhesitatingly. ''His Dukeship was a good boy when he was little. His parents were good, too. I think Dane just took advantage of Duke Marion's promise to never come back to Ravenhurst.''

Saber felt like pulling her off the desk and kissing her breathless. Her faith in the man she didn't think she'd ever met warmed him all over. He managed to subdue the urge to take her into his arms, but couldn't quite ignore the heat curling through his loins. It remained, a silent, but powerful reminder of his attraction to her. "I'm sure the duke would be touched to know how you feel about him.''

Realizing his emotions were spilling from his eyes, he skimmed another diary, smiling at the lines he read. Not only had the books opened his eyes to some of Hutchins' and Doyle's activities, they'd opened the door to his childhood as well. He'd been taken back to those years. He'd been with Della again, reliving all the wonderful things he'd done as a boy that were recorded in the precious little books.

*Marion rescued a baby bird this morning,* he read. *He climbed the tree and put the bird back into its nest.* Saber remembered that day clearly. After he'd returned the bird to its mother, he'd fallen out of the tree and twisted his ankle. Della had baked him a cake as reward for his bravery.

"Saber, I didn't mean for you to read every one of the diaries without stoppin'," Goldie told him.

*Little Dora Mashburn stole half of Marion's apple this afternoon.* Saber read on. *He came home and—*The words were water-stained after that, but Saber had no need to guess at them. He remembered exactly what he'd done after Dora had stolen his apple. He'd gone home and drawn a picture of her, complete with horns and a pitchfork.

Goldie pushed herself closer to Saber and gave his hand a little nudge. "I need to talk to you." She tried to suppress the warm feeling his nearness brought to her, but failed miserably. His fragrant, masculine scent made her tremble, the sight of his muscles, straining against his snug shirt, sent that sweet ache seeping through her. She longed to reach out and touch the disorderly mass of black curls on his head.

"Saber?"

He closed the diary. "I've been reading these at random," he told her, hopelessly lost in a valley of memories. "There are so many, I didn't know which one to read first. And your aunt's handwriting is so small, it takes almost an hour to get through a few pages. I'm reading bits from the ones that aren't too badly stained." He picked up another one and began reading again. *The harvest was bountiful. It's the best Ravenhurst has had in years.* Absently, Saber glanced at the year recorded in the top left-hand corner of the page.

Last year, he mused. And last year, Dane had reported an extensive *loss*. Doyle, too, had described a dismal situation. It was yet more proof.

"Y'see," Goldie continued, "we're goin' to London, Saber. I meant to tell you about my London plans earlier, but—Well, you turn into such an ill-box over the duke lessons sometimes, that I was sorta afraid to tell you that I wanted us to go to London for duke research. There's really no reason why we should stay here at Leighwood any longer. I've shown you how to walk and talk. We've practiced eatin', wheezin', and snortin'. We have the wig and the cane. In London we'll find out more stuff about dukes. Dukes are *crawlin'* all over London, y'know. We'll spy on 'em and pick up a few more things we need to practice. And we can keep on readin' the diaries in the city."

Vaguely, Saber heard her rambling. He tore his gaze from the diary and looked at her again. "This Hutchins and Doyle should be punished for what they've done." *And how I will relish meting out that punishment,* he added silently.

Goldie realized he hadn't heard a word she'd said, nor did he even really see her. She gave his hand another nudge. "I said we're goin' to London. We'll spy on dukes there. It'll take about a month or so, I reckon."

Saber nodded absently and deliberated. He decided he needed to review the accounting books Hutchins sent to him. Too, he would review Doyle's reports. And he would hire Tyler Escott, the best detective in England, to assist him with the task. Perhaps Tyler could even figure out a few of the illegible words in the diaries. And Tyler would probably make a trip to Ravenhurst to observe the situation for himself. After that, Saber was sure there would be enough evidence to put Doyle and Hutchins behind bars for the rest of their lives.

"How long do you think it'll take us to get to London, Saber?" Goldie asked. "Is it far away from here? And do you think the owner of this here estate would mind if we borrowed that fancy carriage he's got out there in that coach house? I've never ridden in one before, y'know. And I saw the villagers down yonder takin' care of some horses in a pasture. Maybe we could borrow the horses too. We could tie Dammit and Yardley to the back of the coach. Say yes?"

Saber looked back down at the diary, remembering that Hutchins' account books were in London. Every book from the past twenty years was in the city. So were Doyle's reports. For that matter, so was Tyler Escott. "I'm sorry," he mumbled. "What did you say, Goldie?"

She watched him pick up another diary. He opened it and began reading. With a heavy sigh, she did likewise. " 'Miss Angelica,' " she read. "Oh, I've never read this one before," she told Saber, her eyes still skimming the page. "Too bad it's so stained. There's only a few words left that I can read."

Saber's head snapped up. "What was that about Angelica?" he asked, his heart pounding.

She glanced back down at the page. "The only understandable words are 'Angelica,' and somethin' that looks like 'ring.' "

"Let me see it." He took the book from her, a mixture of frustration and anguish rolling through him when he saw how impossible the entry was to make out. He turned a few pages, reading more single words. " 'Angelica,' " he read again. " 'Roses.' "

"Roses?" Goldie echoed. "Angelica planted a whole garden of roses for Duke Marion, y'know. They don't bloom though. Legend has it they won't flower until the duke finds true love again. Sad story, that one."

Saber continued to read. " 'Miss Angelica and I laughed at—' " He could read the obliterated passage no further.

"Wonder what they were laughin' at?" Goldie mused aloud. "Let's see. Angelica. Ring. Roses. She and Aunt

Della laughin' at somethin'. Maybe Angelica planted the
roses in a ring, and it looked so dumb that she and Aunt
Della laughed at it,'' she suggested.

Saber turned a few pages. " 'Dora,' '' he read.

Goldie cocked her head. ''All right. Angelica planted
the roses in a dumb-lookin' ring. She and Aunt Della
laughed at it. Dora came along, and she laughed too.''

''But these words occur on separate pages, Goldie.
There are several damaged pages between them. We cannot connect the words as if they were all a part of the
same sentence or even the same paragraph.''

''Well, that's what *I've* been doin','' she argued sassily.
''In one really ruined diary, Aunt Della wrote the word
'marquis.' Two pages later I made out the word 'gold.'
The next page was 'sapphire.' The last words I could read
were 'lambs' and 'shoes.' Put two and two together, Saber. It's perfectly obvious to me that Aunt Della saw some
marquis who wore gold shoes. And on the gold shoes were
lambs made with sapphires.''

Saber heard her chatter, but continued to stare at the
diary. He remembered that Angelica had not been wearing
her ruby engagement ring when her body had been returned to London. He'd always wondered what had happened to it, and now suspected that maybe Della had
known. But it wasn't only the ring, he realized suddenly.
It was Della and Angelica's laughter. What had they found
funny? How had they spent their time together, and what
had they discussed? And why had Dora been with them?

An eerie feeling began to nag at him, and he felt a
profound need to solve these mysteries. But piecing together the information in the water-stained diaries and
making sense of it was like trying to connect ''one'' to
''one hundred'' with no numbers in between.

Still, he had to know. Had to understand. His heart, his
soul, his memories demanded it, and if it took years, he'd
study each diary carefully. For surely there was more, he
realized. More, much more, but what?

Like a slight, but steady drip of water, the strange feeling he had continued to bother him. His suspicions and
frustration rose until a sudden thought soothed them. He'd
hand over everything—the books, the reports, and the di-

aries—to Tyler Escott. And he'd pay the man a veritable fortune to uncover every hidden truth.

His decision made, he shoved suspicion from his mind. It would do him no good to dwell on it now. Dropping the diaries back into their sack, he realized that if he was going to take them to the city, Goldie would have to come along too. She wouldn't part with her aunt's treasures. "We're leaving Leighwood," he announced abruptly. "We're going to London."

She frowned at him. "But that's what I've been tryin' to tell—"

"I realize London wasn't in your plans, but I—"

"Saber, I just told you that we—"

"You see, Goldie, it's not proper for us to take advantage of our host's generosity. He offered us his country home, but surely he didn't mean we could stay here indefinitely. It's time to leave."

"Saber, I—"

"You'll like London. We can continue with the duke lessons in the city as well as we can here. And Big has rejoined your uncle, so I really see no reason why you would balk at the idea of going."

"But—"

"Addison . . . uh, gave me my allowance before he left, so you needn't worry about finances. We have enough money for the trip. We'll borrow our host's coach and horses for the journey. I have a house in London, and you'll stay there, of course. The house . . . was a present from Addison. So you see? There is no earthly reason why you should refuse to go. Now what is your decision?"

Goldie couldn't for the life of her understand what had gotten into him, but she decided not to argue any further. Saber was asking her to go to London, and that's exactly what she wanted to do anyway. She'd tell him about spyin' on dukes as they traveled to the city. The journey would give her the perfect opportunity to talk him into it should he resist the idea.

Nodding at him, she looked at the bag he was holding so tightly. "Did you learn some good duke stuff while readin' the diaries?" she asked. "Did you read the part about that marquis who wore purple satin pants? Do you think we should try and get you some like that? And did you get to the part about that earl who smelled like a woman? Aunt Della wrote that he wore more perfume than Duke Marion's mama. I like perfume, but I've never had any. I tried to make some one time though. I boiled some apple peel and vanilla beans together, then crushed it all up. But the vanilla turned my neck brown, and Big said I smelled like a pie. I would have used flowers, but it was almost winter, and there weren't any more growin'.

"Harriet Orabel Gordon down in Beetle's Elbow, Alabama, had her a bottle of perfume," she continued. "I used to think her name was so funny. Her initials spell 'Hog,' y'see. But I didn't ever call her Hog. She was as fat as one, though. Anyway, she was so scared to use all her perfume up that she hardly ever wore it. Then it was Wendell Snitch's birthday, and Harriet was sweet on Wendell. So she put on some of her perfume to go to his birthday party. But the thing is she'd let that perfume sit for so long without ever usin' it that it went rancid. I mean to tell you, the girl was *ripe* when she got to that party. Wendell's mama made her go home and take a bath. Saber, do beetles really have elbows?"

Saber sat back down, feeling some of his tension leave him. Goldie's soft chatter had such a soothing effect on him. Looking up at her, he was reminded of his promise to Big that he would take care of her. The thought wasn't unpleasant in the least. In truth, he needed her as much as she needed him. Especially now. God, especially tonight.

"Goldie, I will not wear purple satin trousers, nor will I drown myself in sweet-smelling perfume," he informed her firmly, but couldn't help a slight grin when she looked at him with a you-will-if-I-say-you-will expression on her face.

With a toss of her head, Goldie threw her curls off her shoulders, then examined her nails. "Did you happen to notice that Aunt Della didn't write in the *uncial* way?" she queried offhandedly.

At the impish ascent of her brow, Saber's grin widened. "Well, now that you mention it, yes, I did notice that."

Goldie glared at him. "You don't know what *uncial*

means, Saber. Nobody knows that word 'cept for the fella who wrote the dictionary. You're just actin' like you know it, aren't you?''

More of his tension evaporated. He leaned back in his chair, folded his hands in his lap, and regarded her. She was in a sassy mood tonight. He liked it. "I think that perhaps it has something to do with making spelling errors."

She smiled smugly. "Ha! *Wrong.*"

"Then is it a word for improper grammar?"

"Nope."

"Poorly formed letters?"

"You're way off, Saber."

He loved her smug smile. "Then perhaps *uncial* is a handwriting employed in Greek and Latin manuscripts? Maybe one that was used from the fourth to the eighth centuries A.D.? Could it be, Miss Dictionary, that this handwriting of which you speak is made with rounded capital letters and cursive-like lower-case ones?"

Her face fell before she stuck her tongue out at him. "I always wondered what it would be like to be a genius. Now I know it'd be borin'. What's the fun of knowin' everything in the world? I think it's more fun havin' to *look* for answers. So what do you think about that, Mr. Fountain of Knowledge?"

"What do I think? I think we're having a *logamachy.*"

She scowled. "You're such a show-off. All right, tell me what *logamachy* means. I know you're dyin' to do it."

He chuckled. "It's a dispute about words."

She wanted to remain miffed at him, but his crooked grin softened her. She giggled, reaching out to tweak his nose. "That little Marion was a happy little boy before his parents died, wasn't he, Saber? Did you read the part that Aunt Della wrote about him singin' all the time? She said he always had a song whenever anyone wanted one. I bet he doesn't sing and hum anymore though."

*He doesn't,* Saber answered silently. Suddenly he began to wonder if he should tell her the truth about who he was. It would certainly make things a lot easier in London. And surely he could make her understand the need for discretion. If he could convince her of the importance of keeping his discoveries about Hutchins and Doyle a secret, she wouldn't send word to Hallensham about having found him. After all, the bastards had stolen money from her aunt.

"Goldie," he began, pausing for a long moment. "There's something I have to tell you, poppet."

He frowned when he saw pain deepen the color of her eyes, and realized he'd hurt her feelings. A fragment of comprehension came to him. "Poppet," he told her. "I've called you that twice, and both times you've reacted as if I'd called you an offensive name. I told you the name means a small girl or a little doll. Do you find something insulting in that?"

She turned away, sliding off his desk. "I went fishin' today and left you some fried fish in the kitchen. Whipped up some cornbread too. Well, I reckon I'll go to bed now. We'll probably leave for London real early. 'Night, Saber."

When she crossed to the door, he came out from behind his desk and strode toward her. "Not so fast, Goldie. You will not escape me tonight. I've asked you a question, and you're going to answer it."

"You're mad at me, aren't you?"

He felt like lying and telling her he wasn't angry, but realized the truth was better in this situation. "Yes. I'm mad because you refuse to talk to me. Every time I come close to a subject that upsets you, you withdraw from me."

She felt a tear trickle down her cheek and wished Big hadn't left. She felt so alone without him. Especially now, with Saber mad at her.

That droplet on her cheek was sufficient water to drown Saber with remorse. God, what was the right way to get through to her? "Goldie—"

"I was so lonely when I came in here, Saber," she told him, sniffling. "I paced the hallway for hours. You've been shut up in here since Big left."

"Goldie, you're trying to change the subject. Now tell me why—"

"This is the first time since I met Big that I've been away from him. Oh, Saber, I've been with him every single day for so long that I don't know how to act without him. I wouldn't have come in here to bother you, but I . . . I felt lonesome. I miss Big. He's my best friend.''

Saber felt guilt slide through him. He *had* been in the library a long time. He should have considered how sad Goldie would be all alone without Big to keep her company.

He thought about the day when he, too, would be parting from her. As hard as he tried, he couldn't help wondering if she would miss *him* like that too. "You're lonesome for Big, but you're not alone, Goldie,'' he reminded her.

He placed his hand on her dainty shoulder. Friends could put their hands on friends' shoulders, he told himself. It was only a simple gesture of affection.

But if that were so, why did the feel of her shoulder beneath his palm fill him with the desire to hold her and never let her go? Dear God, what special something was it she had that he craved so desperately? "You're not alone,'' he told her again, his voice as soft as he could make it.

His sentiment and touch sent Goldie straight into his arms. "Saber, I know dreams always go away, and I'm supposed to guard my heart, and we're supposed to forget what's happened between us, and we're supposed to understand that it was all a mistake, but—''

"Goldie—''

"But this doesn't have anything to do with figs, yellow bushes, or not bein' able to swallow,'' she continued, her eyes tightly closed as she slipped her arms around his waist. "This is about Big. Without him, it's like a part of me is missin'. He's always been there for me, and no matter what other people did to me, he helped me through it. And now he's gone, and I'm so nervous without him, and what if somethin' happens in London and I need him to help me? What will I do? And anyway, Saber, I can't see why you would get mad at me or laugh at me. You can make it as light and short as you want. 'Course I'll understand if you don't want to, but—Saber, please . . . please do it for me. Please—''

"Goldie, slow down,'' he interrupted, trying desperately to understand her. "What is it you want me to do for you?''

Slowly, she raised her face to his. What she saw there set her heart aflutter. His eyes were glowing with that special softness. The wonderful sight gave her the courage to answer him. "Hug me," she whispered. "Just one small hug."

Her plea was for precisely the same thing he longed to do. He was filled with such tender emotions that he could not get hold of them before they consumed him. "Oh, Goldie," he groaned. He pulled her closer to him, urged her face to his chest, and embraced her with all the concern and growing affection he felt for her.

If the sun had arms, Goldie mused, they wouldn't be any warmer than Saber's. Oh, how she loved being so close to him. "Thank you. Saber, thank you so much for this. You just can't know what a hug does for me. I think it's one of the nicest things in the whole wide world."

The tenderness inside him grew to something stronger. She was grateful for a simple *hug*. A hug was free, and yet to Goldie it was priceless. Her simplicity, her humble pleasures . . . God, how he loved what they did to him! He buried his face in the wild mass atop her head, breathing in the sweet scent of those golden curls. Their pure fragrance reached his very soul.

"Goldie," he whispered down to her, his voice refusing to come, "will you trust me to take Big's place? If someone should do something to you—If you should need help in any way, will you put your faith in me?"

When she didn't answer him, when she stiffened in his arms, Saber felt deep disappointment. He knew then he would have to earn her trust. He would have to deserve it.

Suddenly, her confidence in him was a treasure he wanted beyond all others. He'd wanted it yesterday, and he still wanted it today. Tonight, he decided, he would begin trying to earn it. "While you're with me," he told her softly, his lips still nuzzling her hair, "I'll let no harm come to you. If anyone should dare to insult you, laugh at you, or become cross with you, I'll rise to your defense just as Big did. While we're together, I'll take care of you, poppet."

The name stung her again. She dropped her arms from around him.

At her action, Saber was reminded anew of her aversion to the word. He took her shoulders and gazed deeply into her eyes. "Tell me what you feel when I call you a poppet. We'll stand here all night if necessary, but Goldie, you *are* going to tell me."

She could tell by the tone of his voice and the expression on his face that he wanted a straight answer and that he wanted it right now. "No," she told him, so quietly she could barely hear herself.

"Buy why?" Saber demanded, his frustration mounting steadily.

She felt dread slither through her. "Are you mad at—"

"No! Yes! I don't know!" He saw her eyes widen at his shout and felt completely overwhelmed with confusion. "Goldie, I didn't mean to raise my voice. I'm sorry. But I'm—You—Goldie, please tell me why the name poppet upsets you. Whatever your answer, I promise I won't laugh or become angry."

His eyes now looked even softer and gentler than before. She felt caution slipping slowly away.

"Tell me, Goldie." His fingers smoothed across her shoulders.

She heard the concern in his chocolate voice, and wanted desperately to trust it. "You said—" she began quietly, blinking several times. "You said that poppet was a name for a small girl. A little doll."

He watched pain flit across her face. "Is there something wrong with being likened to a small girl or a little doll?" He cupped her chin, lifting her face higher. "Tell me, Goldie. Tell me so I'll understand."

She dropped her gaze. More tears welled in her eyes; she watched them wet the back of Saber's hand. "I hate being so little," she whispered, her shoulders beginning to shake.

Comprehension flooded Saber. So many of her sad secrets became clear to him. "People make fun of your small stature, don't they, Goldie?" He stared at the top of her head, trying to remember every single thing she'd ever said to him since he first met her. "Yes. You commented once that Velma Somebody was tall and that that was the reason why Fred Wattle loved her. You said you didn't deserve Fred. And your eyes. Yes, your eyes. That girl . . . somewhere in Kentucky. Her father owned the town. She said you had devil eyes. You think your gold eyes are ugly.''

''Saber—''

''Yellow bush. Your hair. You've been ridiculed about your curly hair, too. Someone said it looked like something a dog had been shaking around. And what else?'' he mumbled, his mind hard at work summoning memories. ''Freckles. The day I said you had seventeen freckles on your nose, you cried. I thought it was dew, but it was a tear, wasn't it? You think your freckles are unattractive.''

She tried to break away from him, but he held her shoulders tighter. ''And the day we first met,'' he continued. ''By the pond. I told you that if your performance in the water was any indication of your fighting abilities, you couldn't pay me to ravish you. You thought I was telling you that you were too ugly to ravish. You—''

''Saber, I really have to go—''

''And figs,'' he murmured. ''Yesterday you said something about having unripened figs.'' He drew her intimately close to him. ''Figs, Goldie. And melons. Watermelons would be too big, but cantaloupes would be nice. You wept over fruit. Goldie, what were you talking about when you told me I couldn't imagine what it was like to have figs instead of melons? What—''

''Saber, let me go,'' she insisted, struggling in vain to step away from him. I—''

''You said something about how I would feel if instead of having muscle ropes, I had threads. You said—''

''Saber, please—''

He silenced her by pressing her face to his chest. His hands held her head captive. ''Oh, Goldie. Figs. Breasts. Breasts like ripe melons. I've heard the expression. Goldie, you were speaking about your breasts, weren't you?''

''Saber, I can't talk about this!'' she shouted, her voice muffled in his chest. ''You—''

''You really and truly believe you're ugly, don't you?'' he continued, his heart thrashing. ''You think that everything about you is homely and undesirable. This sorrow I've noticed in you . . . Goldie, how can I make you see how very wrong you are?''

"You've got my face pressed so hard against you, I can't see *anything*, dammit!''

He relaxed his hold on her, deciding then and there to tell her the truth about who he was. He'd tell her that as the Duke of Ravenhurst, he could have his pick among the most beautiful women in England, but that no other woman he knew attracted him the way she did. He took a breath and prepared to enlighten her.

But his breath remained trapped inside him. If she knew he was Lord Marion Tremayne, would she still feel comfortable with him? Would she still tease him, tell him outrageous tales, giggle and smile for him? Would she continue treating him like the ordinary man she thought him to be? Or would his title intimidate her?

He had to know.

"Goldie," he began, pausing, "If you were to ever meet the real Duke of Ravenhurst, how would you act with him?''

She felt relieved that he'd changed the subject. But his question was so unrelated to what they'd been talking about that she had to think a moment before she could answer him. "Well, I don't know. He's purty close to royalty, y'know, and Mildred Fickle said you're supposed to bow to royal people. So I reckon I'd bow to him. But I'd be a little afraid to be around him. Mildred Fickle said royal people can have folks' heads chopped off if they want to. I'd try not to do anything bad enough to make Duke Ravenhurst have my head chopped off for it, but you just never know what might happen. And than—'' She closed her mouth, sliding her finger across her throat.

At that moment, Saber knew with certainly he would not tell her who he was until he absolutely had to. The thought of her feeling she should bow to him irritated him greatly. He would prove to her how beautiful she was, yes, but without admitting who he was. "Goldie, I seriously doubt you could do something so wrong as to be beheaded for it.''

She saw that softness in his gaze again. It sent her senses reeling. "Saber."

He knew exactly what she was feeling. He felt it too. "Goldie," he started, desire coiling through him. "What happened between us yesterday in the closet . . ."

"I know. We're supposed to forget it happened," she replied, trying to ignore her disappointment.

"And have you forgotten it?"

"No," she answered honestly. "Have you?"

"I tried."

"But you didn't?"

"No." He placed his hands on her cheeks. "Goldie."

"Saber."

He bent closer to her, his eyes only a fraction of an inch away from hers.

"Are you gonna kiss me, Saber?" she asked, her voice trembling.

"Is the thought so terrible?"

"No, but . . ."

"But what?"

"I—Saber, I don't know how to kiss."

"Then let me teach you."

"But what if you laugh? What if—" She never finished her questions.

Saber's lips were suddenly upon hers.

# Chapter 11

He kissed her as softly as he knew how, only touching his lips to hers. Smoothing them across hers, he relished the satiny texture of her mouth. Desire exploded inside him, but he felt profound yearning to go slowly with her, to woo her gently, allowing all his tender feelings for her to come forth. This in mind, he lifted his head and smiled down at her.

Goldie's fingers trembled as she touched her mouth. She traced her lips, remembering the kiss Saber had just placed upon them. A myriad of intense emotions swirled through her. She felt warm. Elated. She felt a tremendous want for something she instinctively knew Saber could give her.

But she didn't know how to ask for it. Didn't even know if it was right for her to do so. She knew only that his kiss had meant more to her than anything anyone had ever done for her. "You didn't laugh," she whispered. "You don't look mad either. And you really did kiss me. I didn't dream it."

The expression of pure wonder in her huge tawny eyes set Saber afire. God, she was so innocent. So fresh and unspoiled. "You think your ignorance to be an undesirable thing, don't you, Goldie?" he asked, his understanding steadily deepening. "You're ashamed that you know so little about the things that can happen between a man and a woman. Ah, golden angel, if only you knew what your sweet inexperience means to me."

She blinked, wanting with all her heart to believe the wonderful things he was telling her. "I—You could show me. Show me what it means to you."

Her poignant offer touched the deepest part of him. She stood before him, vulnerable. He could almost read her thoughts. She knew very well she stood the chance of being hurt by him, and yet she was hoping he wouldn't do that to her.

It was the beginning of trust, and she was giving him the chance to prove himself worthy of it. His heart soared. "Yes, Goldie," he whispered, kissing her cheek, "I could show you. Put your arms around my neck and let me."

She did and caught the faint scent of sandalwood when he bent down to her. The fragrance beckoned to her. Hesitantly, she pressed her face into the warm hollow of his throat. Her lips parted, and she felt a strange, but intense desire to taste the warm skin beneath them. Before she even realized what she was doing, she was fulfilling her own wish.

Saber groaned when he felt her tongue darting so lightly upon his throat. "Goldie. Goldie. God, what do you do to me?" he asked huskily.

She lifted her face from him immediately, her arms falling to her sides. "I—I'm sorry. I didn't mean to do anything."

"I think," he started, swallowing, "that that is precisely why you succeed in doing it to me."

She gasped when he swept her into his arms. "Saber—"

"Goldie, let me show you. Let me show you."

She looked into his beautiful seaweed eyes, finding nothing in them to distrust. She nodded and felt anticipation rise.

He carried her to the window, something inside him wanting to see the pale silver of the moonlight mingle with the burnished gold of her hair. There, he sank to the floor, carrying her with him. "I have a confession to make," he said, his voice as soft as the tawny stars he saw in her eyes. "Yesterday as you slept beneath the lace . . . I watched you, Goldie."

Her eyes widened; she felt her cheeks heat. Profound embarrassment coursed through her. That he'd seen her—naked. With all of her defects. "Oh, Saber," she squeaked, covering her face with her hands.

Gently, he removed her hands, holding them captive in

his own. "I stood there mesmerized, Goldie. I thought you were so beautiful, I couldn't even move while gazing at you. Light touched you all over, as did the lace. You were white and gold, and shadow. So delicate, gentle, and soft."

"Saber, you shouldn't have—"

"I know. I know, Goldie. It was wrong. But I couldn't make myself leave. Your golden curls were spread all over your little white pillow, and you looked like an angel. I stared at those incorrigible ringlets and knew a deep yearning to slide my fingers through them. Like this, Goldie. Like this."

Her eyes fluttered closed when he slowly pushed his fingers into her hair. Humiliation seized her when his hand stopped suddenly. She knew very well he could get his fingers no further. Her curls were simply too thick, too wild for him to get through them. She took hold of his hand, having every intention of removing it.

"It knew it would be like this," he murmured down to her, resisting her efforts to pull at his hand. "I knew your curls would capture my fingers. It's as if they're alive. They twist and coil around my hand. As if they're embracing me. Soft. God, they're so soft, Goldie. The softest things I've ever touched."

She opened her eyes. "Saber . . . really?"

He smiled, removed his hand from her hair, and touched his thumb to each of her eyelids, "Devil eyes, Goldie? No. Of course I've never seen Lucifer, but I can't imagine that he has beautiful eyes. Only an angel could have eyes like yours. Gold eyes. And have you never given a thought to how costly gold is? How valuable? Yet real gold, as precious as it is, is lifeless, isn't it? It doesn't move, does it? And it's cold, too. But your eyes . . . so warm. They're like huge gold coins that dance in tune to your thoughts. Gold brought to life. How enchanting."

She blinked several times, sure this was a dream and that she would wake up soon. "Gold brought to life," she repeated quietly, loving the way those words sounded.

His hands moved along the sides of her face "A heart. Your face is the shape of a heart. A dainty one, perfectly formed. And your lips. God, how lovely they are. Little, but full. Pink, lush. Do you know, Goldie Mae, that when I look at them I always think about how kissable they are?''

His question stole her breath. Her throat tightened, her body quivered. Saber. Her mouth formed the name, but no sound came.

He raised an ebony brow. ''And about those freckles of yours . . .'' he began, deliberately letting his voice trail away. ''I must be honest with you, Goldie. I don't know a single woman who has any.''

Her growing pleasure disappeared, replaced with sorrow so great it made her ache. ''Saber, please don't—''

''And all those women I know,'' he continued, a smile tugging at the corners of his mouth, ''are the same. Their complexions look like they all came out of the same bottle. So flawless, so utterly without blemish that they're really quite boring. But *your* complexion—As I watched you sleeping yesterday, I thought of warm, rich cream with flecks of cinnamon on top.''

Confusion seized her. She didn't know whether to feel flattered or hurt. She floated somewhere between both, ready to go toward one or the other as soon as he elaborated.

''If I look close,'' he told her, bending nearer, ''I can see pictures on your face. Here,'' he said, touching her left cheekbone, ''your freckles form a little star. And here,'' he said, caressing her chin, ''is a diamond. Next to it is a flower. How fascinating. A girl with stars and diamonds and flowers on her face. What a good time heaven must have had designing your complexion. Close your eyes and think of all those little cherubs, each with a bucket of freckles. Each one arranging the freckles to form pretty pictures. How special that makes you, Goldie.''

She did as bade, closing her eyes and smiling when she imagined the chubby angels with their buckets of freckles. Her pleasure came back to her. *How special that makes you, Goldie.* The words sang through her.

''Open your eyes now, Goldie.'' When she did, he saw her happiness. It shone, danced, and flickered prettily for him. The sight filled him with warm contentment, and he realized he was truly enjoying coercing her to see herself as he saw her. It was a challenge, yes, but oh, how sweet the reward!

Slowly, he moved his gaze from her eyes to her breasts. Her brown frock covered them. He would remedy that problem.

Goldie felt a surge of panic when his fingers began tugging at the shoulder of her dress. He slid it down to her upper arm. "Saber—"

"Peaches," he informed her on a long, heavy breath, and moved his hand to her other arm to slide the dress down that one, too. "How can you think of figs, Goldie? Unripened ones! Don't you know they're hard? Your breasts . . . figs? No, Goldie. Peaches. Peaches," he whispered huskily, "are soft."

Goldie gasped when he slid his hand inside her dress. His warm palm cupped her breast. Starting at her nipple, the feelings he evoked radiated throughout her entire body, leaving quivers in their wake. A strange, flowing pleasure writhed within her.

"Soft," he told her again, his voice deep and mellow as he pulled the dress down to her waist. "Think of peaches. A swirl of pastel colors. Round, warm. Feel how nicely they fit into my hand, Goldie. They're neither too big, nor too small. They're perfect."

"Peaches?" she asked, so thrilled with his description she could think of no more words to tell him.

His other hand moved to cup her other one. He held them both, and felt rising excitement. But he summoned patience, renewing his vow to go slowly with the golden treasure lying in his lap. "And see how prettily they blush. Ah, Goldie, see how beautiful they are next to my hands."

Her gaze left his eyes, sweeping to her breasts. Her cheeks warmed again at the sight. No one had ever touched her so intimately. So gently. And her breasts *did* fit into his palms. They fit as though they had been made for his hands.

His alone. The thought was so beautiful to her.

As leisurely as possible, Saber slid his thumbs back and forth upon the stiffening peaks of her breasts. He became lost both in the pleasure shimmering from her golden eyes and the low mewling sounds escaping from her slightly parted lips. "Goldie," he told her, wanting her to understand every emotion he put into the sound of her name. "You are so delicate. Yes, Goldie, you *are* a poppet. Small, precious, and irresistible. Your daintiness is not a thing to ridicule. It's a thing to prize. I often imagine you being swept away in a strong wind, and the thought makes me yearn to hold you close to me. In my arms. Where you'll be safe, and no wind can steal you from me.

"And when I call you a poppet," he continued silkily, "that is the picture I have in my mind. You. In my arms. Me. Holding you like this, Goldie. God, just like this."

He pulled her from his lap, holding her as he would a fine and precious doll, and let forth a low moan when her bare breasts touched his chest. His hand plundered the golden mass of curls lying on his arm. His other hand held her tightly to him.

And he kissed her. It was a kiss of passion, longing, and a tenderness so deep it almost hurt as it flowed through him. "Goldie," he told her, his lips still pressed to hers. "Open for me."

His voice seemed to be coming from a hundred miles away. But somehow it found its way through the haze of pleasure he'd brought. *Open for me*, he'd told her.

Saber groaned when her lips parted for him. He'd never known such sweetness existed. Desire such as he'd never felt for any other woman took hold of him. He touched her breast again. He held it. Savored the way it felt.

And wanted to taste it.

"Peaches," he whispered, lifting his face from hers. His lips at her chin, he began the slow, delicious journey to her breasts.

"Saber." She tensed at this new thing he was doing to her.

His lips found and loved her. "Peaches," he murmured, his mouth full of her. "Sweet. So sweet."

Goldie felt wave after wave of longing rock through her. How she yearned for . . . for something that would satisfy her! That would put an end to this glorious agony Saber brought to her. "Saber, your mouth—Your lips—"

"And hands," he added, and slid his hand down the

smooth, flat expanse of her ivory belly. Lower he went. Still lower until his hand disappeared beneath her skirt. The sensual blazes grew higher within him when he found no undergarments to delay his quest. "God, Goldie. You wear nothing—Nothing under your dress."

"Oh, Saber. Not there. You can't . . . I—Please."

His fingers stopped. He let them rest unmoving upon the silken nest at the apex of her thighs. He waited in silence for her to give him some clue as to what she wanted him to do. "Tell me," he whispered, his tongue circling her breast. "Tell me, Goldie."

She couldn't. She couldn't speak, or breathe, or even think. Spiraling through her was a desire so great it stole every thought she had. Every thought but the one of Saber and what he was doing to her. Instinctively, she arched into his hand.

It was all the hint he needed. Lifting his face from her breast, he brought it down to hers. "What I am about to do," he began pressing kisses to her cheeks, temples, and brow, "will bring you pleasure, Goldie. The kind of pleasure a man desires to give to a beautiful woman."

She felt a shred of fear at this unknown pleasure he was going to give her. "I don't know what you're sayin', Saber. I've never . . ."

"I know you haven't," he told her, his lips at her ear. "But tonight you will. For the first time, tonight you will."

She felt his hand dip lower. His fingers found her most secret place. She knew she blushed, but she was beyond caring. The pleasure he'd spoken of, the one he'd already begun, sharpened. His hand, his warm palm made moist by her, circled rhythmically upon her. And then he was inside her. First one finger, then two. He moved them in, out, deep, deep, deeper.

"Give yourself up to it, Goldie. Let it happen. Let me make it happen to you."

She clutched his shoulders, closing her eyes. It was beginning. Something strong. Something she felt she had no control over. It was a thing of power, and Saber mastered it. It was a beautiful wave, and Saber directed it onto her. It drowned her with feelings too wonderful to contain. She felt as though she were awash upon a sea of exquisite sensation.

"Saber." She moaned his name over and over again. And the pleasure seemed never to end. Saber's hand seemed never to stop moving.

"Goldie," he answered, and knew she'd found the bliss he'd promised her. She pulsed around his fingers, her ecstasy filling him with such wild desire, he could barely subdue it.

But suppress it he did. Tonight was not his. It belonged only to her. He wanted this night to remain branded in her memory until the next night came. The night they would share.

"Goldie, you're beautiful. So delightful to me. Your stories, your smile, your giggle . . . you've no idea what they do to me. Your simplicity touches something inside me that I'd forgotten I had. Everything, Goldie. Everything about you . . . there is no part of you that doesn't charm me. Enchant me."

His words and the feelings he'd given her brought tears to her eyes. She looked up at him, seeing his concern. "I'm not cryin' because I'm sad. I'm cryin' because I'm happy. You've made me happier than I've ever been. You've told me things I didn't think I'd ever hear. Dreams . . . you've made dreams come true for me tonight, Saber. And no matter what happens, no matter where we go or how far apart we might be one day, I'll never forget this night."

He winced at the thought of being separated from her. It was becoming harder and harder to think about the day they'd say good-bye. Gathering her into his arms, he stood and carried her from the library. Up the staircase he took her, stopping only when he reached her bedroom. Gently, he laid her upon her princess bed, kissing her cheek before he straightened and smiled down at her.

He willed her to tell him how she felt. God, how he wanted her to tell him he was as special to her as she was to him. He waited a long moment to hear the words. But she only stared up at him. He felt stabbing disappointment but reminded himself that her years of abuse had left deep scars. Such profound wariness couldn't be erased in one night. It would take time to make it fade.

He wondered how much time he had left with her.

"Good night, Goldie."

"Saber?" she called when he turned to leave the room.

"Yes?"

"Do you think it's all right to have two best friends?"

He rubbed his chin while trying to think of an answer. "How can there be two bests? Don't you think there can only be one?"

"I think there can be two."

"Very well," he said, thinking her quite lovely lying there on her huge white bed, moonlight pouring down on her.

"Big's already my best friend," she told him. "And now . . . so are you. You're my other best friend, Saber."

Though he couldn't understand how that could be, her declaration filled with him contentment. Friendship. It was the beginning of the kind of relationship he wanted to have with her. It was the foundation upon which he could build.

" 'Night, Saber."

"Good night."

"Saber?"

"Yes?"

"It was like a sneeze, only better."

He laughed out loud. "Yes. Like a sneeze, poppet."

He left then, but just as he shut the door behind him, he heard her repeat the name he'd called her. He tensed, waiting to hear her cry. But she giggled merrily. He looked at the portrait of his ancestor hanging in the hallway. "I think I did it," he told the bewigged man. "Yes, I think I got through to her."

He smiled when he realized he was talking to a painting. This was the second time he'd done it. He spoke to inanimate objects now. He, the Duke of Ravenhurst. "And all because of Goldie."

Still staring at his deceased relative, he dwelled on all the whimsical things he'd said to her tonight. Things he never would have thought of before meeting her. The buckets of freckles. The fat cherubs who painted stars, diamonds, and flowers on faces. The huge gold coins that danced. The curls that hugged his fingers. He'd chosen those descriptions deliberately. "Because of you, Goldie," he told his mental image of her. "Because they were words I knew you would take to heart."

Unable to stop himself, he laughed loud and long. He felt tremendous happiness.

All because of Goldie.

# Chapter 12

From the coach window, Saber looked at the London sky. Whatever pure light the moon shed on the city was shrouded by thick black flakes of soot and oily smoke. He slid his gaze away from the depressing sight, allowing it to rest upon the slight girl nestled against his shoulder. The coach's rhythmic rocking had finally put her to sleep. That and the fact that she'd chattered incessantly since they'd left Leighwood at dawn. No doubt she'd worn herself out, he decided, and suspected, too, that she would sleep through the night without waking.

He smiled when he thought of her reasons for wanting him to come to London. To spy on dukes, she'd said. To do duke research. She'd even suggested they find the real Duke Marion and stare at him. "But when we arrive, poppet," he whispered down to her, "I think perhaps we will learn that His Grace is in Scotland with no immediate plans to return."

Tracing her cheekbone with the tip of his finger, he dwelled on what it was he felt for Goldie. Affection. Yes. But how deep it went, he didn't know. He knew only that during what little time they had left together, he wanted her to feel it for him too.

The thought made him sigh. "Goldie, what's to become of us? You, a free-spirited American, and I . . . I've had the proper mode of aristocratic decorum preached to me since the day I came into this world."

He picked up the gold ringlet shimmering up at him from his arm. By its own volition, it twisted around his finger. He stared at the curl, thinking about how much

205

like its owner it was. Goldie, too, had wrapped herself around him so thoroughly that he could not imagine what it would be like not to have her with him.

He closed his eyes. "The diamond, the dandelion," he murmured, his heart twisting at the comparison. "Try as I have, I cannot find the common link between the two."

Opening his eyes, he urged her closer to him, the thought of being without her making him want to hold her while he still had the time to do so. Pulling a thick quilt up over her shoulders, he peered out the window again, absently watching London's sordid nightlife pass by. His arm tightened around Goldie as he watched a drunken costermonger kick an old woman's pile of baked potatoes out of his way. The hag screeched a torrent of profanities at the man, then tried in vain to keep the hungry street urchins from stealing the rolling potatoes.

He saw a public house, illuminated by the greasy light of yellow street lamps. Whores, some old, some too young to even understand what they were doing, loitered around the building. Shouting came from within, and Saber guessed that a brawl was taking place inside. His guess was confirmed when men came shooting through the door and windows like fragments from an explosion, their fight continuing on the filthy sidewalk.

Saber noticed the elegant carriage was beginning to draw attention. In the past he'd always had his driver fairly fly through this area, but he couldn't give that order now. Goldie's mount, Dammit, was tied to the back of the conveyance, and Saber knew the old horse wouldn't be able to keep up with a quicker pace. "Blast it," he muttered, withdrawing one of the pistols strapped to his side. He had a thought to close the satin draperies, but decided against it. Yardley followed beside Dammit. Saber felt reasonably certain that not even the most desperate thief in London would resort to stealing Dammit, but Yardley, blooded steed that he was, was worth a king's ransom.

" 'Ave a 'eart, guv!" one woman shouted at his window, her hands outstretched in readiness to catch any coin.

"Potato, milord?" a boy yelled, and Saber knew the lad offered him a potato filched from the woman down the street.

"Buy me tarts!" a buxom lass begged, holding up the fruit pies for him to see. "Buy me tarts, sir!"

"Steamin' elder wine!"

"Sponges!"

"Buy me nutmeg, guvner! Best in all o' London-town!"

"Chestnuts! 'Ot chestnuts!"

Most of the vendors were harmless, Saber knew. They followed the coach only because they were desperate to make one last sale before returning home to the slums in which they lived. But one character in particular seemed intent on mischief. He was loping alongside the coach, his gaze darting from Saber to the horses following behind. "Steal my horse, will you?" Saber murmured, raising his pistol.

At the sight of the gun, the man slowed, but in the next instant, he charged out of Saber's line of vision. "Damn," Saber cursed quietly. As gently as he could, he maneuvered himself away from Goldie, settling her beside Itchie Bon. After signaling for the driver to stop, he opened the door. By the time his feet hit the squalid ground, both of his pistols were in his hands.

The vendors backed away. Saber ignored them and concentrated on the beefy man who had hold of Yardley's halter. "Are you stealing my horse, or simply admiring his silken coat? Cates, get down here," he ordered the Leighwood coachman. "Keep your back to the door."

Cates bolted down, his own gun ready in hand. "Yes, sir," he replied, proud that he'd remembered not to use his lord's title.

Saber's eyes never left the horse-stealing lout in front of him. "Are you deaf as well as stupid?" he asked the ruffian. "Answer my question."

The man snatched out his own gun, but never even had the chance to curl his finger around the trigger. Instantly, and quite neatly, Saber's bullet grazed his knuckles. The shot seemed to quiet all of London. Only the man's surprised moan of pain broke the heavy silence.

When the man spun and fled into the dense night mist, Saber was careful not to let his relief show. The only way to leave this area safely was to show no fear. Slowly, he swept the barrel of his pistol toward the crowd. "Would anyone else care to feel my horse's coat?"

No one said a word. They simply stared. "Cates, get us out of here." When the driver moved away from the door, Saber opened it and stepped inside. But just as he began to close it, another man neared. Saber felt rising anger when he saw how intently the pockmarked scoundrel looked at Goldie.

"She ain't no bigger'n a bee's knee, she ain't. An' Gorblimey, look at 'er 'air! Canary yellow an' curlier'n pigs' tails!"

Saber's anger grew to pulsing fury. With one firm kick, he knocked the brute away and slammed the door. The coach jolted forward, but not before several curious costers peered into the window, too. Saber blocked their view of Goldie with his own body, and kept his pistol at the window. He maintained his guard until Cates turned onto a quieter street. Only then did Saber relax.

Here, rows of shops came into view. They were neat, organized, and Saber knew the coach was approaching the more civilized side of London. But the odor of the section they'd just left had permeated the small compartment. The thought of Goldie breathing such a disgusting smell angered Saber anew. He'd promised to protect her, and to his way of thinking, that included shielding her from stench as well. He signaled Cates to stop, and purchased a bunch of wilted violets from a woman trudging her way home. Sliding Goldie into his lap, he tucked the sweet flowers beneath her chin. Thus, he held her until the coach finally came to a stop.

"Goldie, we're here, poppet. Can you wake up, or shall I carry you?"

Her eyes fluttered, but remained closed. "Here," she mumbled. "Everything all right?"

He realized she was half-asleep. "Well," he began, and took a moment to kiss her nose, "we were accosted a while back. Someone tried to steal Yardley, and I had to shoot the brute. I only nicked his knuckles though."

"That's nice," she answered, still drugged with slumber.

Saber smiled, wondering what it would take to awaken

her. He decided to find out. "And London is on fire. We rode right through the torrid blazes."

"Fire," she murmured into his chest, snuggling closer to him. "Warm."

"And after we rode through the fire, a man shot me," Saber continued merrily. "He put a hole through my heart. I'm a ghost now, Goldie. You're being held by a phantom."

"Ghost," she repeated softly.

"And as much as I regret having to tell you this, you were shot also, poppet. We're both spirits. We're together in the spirit world for all of eternity."

"Together," she whispered. "Eternity."

He was well aware she had no idea what she was saying. "Together," he repeated wistfully. "You and I."

That thought in mind, he alighted from the coach, and carried her up the steps that led to Addison's house.

Addison watched how tenderly Saber put Goldie to bed, and recalled how long it had taken his friend to decide which bedroom was the best for her. It was as if Saber was seeing to a newborn baby, he mused. And Saber had expressly refused any aid from Mrs. Stubbs, the housekeeper. "Are you certain you want her to stay here?" he whispered as Saber pulled the silk sheets under Goldie's chin. "It was one thing for her to be alone with us at Leighwood, where there was no one to speculate. But Saber, here—Someone will see her here in the morning. It would be bad form to—"

"I'll hear no more of it tonight, Addison."

Addison raised his chin. "I'm only thinking of her reputation. Surely you know that."

"I do. But she had little sleep last night, and has traveled far today. My mind is made up on the matter."

"Then perhaps we could send for your aunties? They could chaperone, and—"

"I wouldn't think of disturbing the aunties. They're most likely abed. That's why I came here instead of going home. Here Goldie is, Addison, and here she will stay until I say otherwise."

Addison took careful note of Saber's possessiveness. He

smiled. "How is it, old boy, that you know how well
Goldie slept last night?"

Saber ignored the question and motioned for Itchie Bon
to lie down on the plush throw rug beside the bed. Instead,
the dog trotted toward the bed, leaping gracefully upon it.
His paws sinking deeply into the soft mattress, he lay down
beside Goldie, his head on her pillow, his snout a mere
inch from her cheek. He sighed with unashamed delight,
rolling his eyes up at Saber. "How Goldie can sleep with
this mongrel night after night is beyond me," Saber said,
ruffling the dog's ear before turning down the lamp.

Addison's brow rose. "And do you sleep with Itchie
Bon as well?"

Saber heard the unspoken insinuation. "Don't give me
any of your codswallop tonight, Addison. I daresay it will
get you nowhere. Besides, when was the last time you
knew of me sleeping with an animal?"

Addison thought of Jillian Somerset, but refrained from
commenting. He followed Saber out of the room, noticing
how long his friend watched Goldie before finally shutting
the door. "An evasive answer, Saber, I must say."

"Nevertheless, the only one you're getting." Saber descended the staircase, heading straight for the bottle of
brandy Addison kept in the office. There, he poured himself a generous amount, swallowing it in one gulp.

Addison accepted the snifter of brandy Saber handed
him. "So you're indulging tonight," he said, watching
Saber pour a second brandy. "That can only mean one
thing. What's got your wind up? And you *do* owe me an
explanation, Saber. You are, after all, in *my* house, enjoying *my* brandy, and will no doubt sleep in one of *my* beds."

"You forgot that I am also suffering *your* infernal curiosity."

"That too. Now why have you brought Goldie to London? And where is that little ill-box?"

Saber set his glass down and lowered himself into a
damask-covered chair. "Where Goldie goes, the diaries
go. Addison, I've begun reading them. Although many of
them are illegible, I've learned a great deal about Hutchins' and Doyle's activities. But there's probably more. I'm
going to hire Tyler Escott to investigate. I'll have him read

all the diaries, and I'll show him Hutchins' books and Doyle's reports, too. I want those two punished for *every-thing* they've done, not just part.''

"I hear Escott's the best detective in London. Some say in all of Europe."

Saber nodded. ''It's not only Hutchins and Doyle I want him to investigate. It's more. I—Della—She also wrote about Angelica. There's something about a ring, and I suspect it's her engagement ring. I always wondered what happened to it. There are other passages too. Fragments that leave me with a vague, uncomfortable feeling. I'm hoping Escott will comprehend more than I could. I want to know everything Della wrote about Angelica. It might amount to naught, but—I—For my own peace of mind, I must know.''

Addison stared at Saber, waiting for his friend's familiar display of grief. It didn't come. Saber simply sat there, wait-ing for Addison to comment. A full minute passed before Addison could form a reply. ''Saber, please forgive me, but you don't—That is, you aren't acting like you usually do when Angelica is the subject of the conversation.''

"It still hurts," Saber murmured. "But she's been gone for five whole years, Addison. Besides, it doesn't do any good to stay smashed down forever.''

"Smashed down? What—"

"Dandelions," Saber explained, running his fingers through his tumbled black curls. "You know. Smash them down, and they come right back. Grief, anger—They won't bring Angelica to life again. I loved her. I'll never forget her. But she's lost to me, and . . . and I have to go on without her.''

"Dandelions? Uh, yes. Yes, of course." Addison took a seat across from Saber, studying his friend carefully. ''It's Goldie, isn't it?'' he guessed. ''Somehow, she's made you realize that you *do* have a life to live. It's got to be her. She's the only new thing in your life. She's—''

"I can't love her."

Saber's abruptness gave Addison pause. ''Why are you so defensive? I don't recall having mentioned love. I merely commented upon—''

"I care about Goldie, Addison, but I'm reasonably certain that I don't love—I can't love her. But she's different, you see. She—Addison, if your office was stuffy and hot, what would you do about it?''

"What? I—Uh, well, I suppose I would open a window."
"Yes."

"But what does a window have to do with—"

"It's the breeze. It would blow through the window."

Addison deliberated. "Goldie," he began, sipping at his brandy. "She's the breeze. And you . . . stuffy and hot. Is that what you're trying to say?''

Saber let his head drop back and stared at the ceiling. "I tried to ignore it. How she made me feel. But her stories made me laugh time after time."

"I see."

"I knew you would do this, Addison. I knew full well that you would start interrogating me the second I—"

"But I've asked you little! You've not given me the chance! You're sitting there *volunteering* all the information!"

Saber raised his head, glaring at Addison. "There's no way around it, I suppose. I either tell you everything you want to know, or you will become a perishing nuisance, won't you, Addison?''

Addison pretended to wipe a drop of brandy off his mouth, and hid his grin behind his hand. Saber was about to explode with all the thoughts running through his muddled mind, and Addison realized he had but to sit quietly to hear everything. The thought of His Grace in such a state of confusion tickled him thoroughly. And all because of a freckle-faced imp from America!

Saber stood, stuffed his hands into his pockets, and ambled to the window. "When she talks about such subjects as Beetle's Elbow, wrist-kissing, freckles coming off on pillows, farmers selling calves, the blood that runs all over England, and breasts aflame . . . I never know from one moment to the next what she will say, what she will do. She keeps me in a constant state of amusement and anticipation. Well, what man *could* resist such an intriguing girl, Addison?''

"Well, I—Breasts aflame?"

"Goldie and I are together here in London because I need the diaries, and she wants to spy on dukes. Big has returned to Hallensham to take care of Asa. That is the extent of it, and it has nothing whatsoever to do with love. Now, is there anything else I can clear up for you?''

"I—"

"She's a sad girl,'' Saber murmured, staring out at the night. ''She's been abused for nearly her entire life.''

Saber spoke in such a fragmented fashion, Addison was forced to take a moment to put his thoughts together. ''Abused?''

"Not physically, I don't believe, but . . . God, I don't really know. Attaining information from her is like trying to milk a bull.''

Addison took another sip of brandy, watching Saber over the rim of the snifter. ''And you've milked so many bulls in your life,'' he said sarcastically.

"I don't know what to do.'' Saber stiffened, clenched his jaw, and tightened his fists. ''Addison, I don't know what to do.''

Addison couldn't believe what he was hearing. He knew full well what it had taken for Saber to admit to such a thing. ''About what?''

"Her. Goldie. She—I—I don't know what to do. Perhaps nothing. Nothing at all. Diamonds, dandelions. There's no common link, you see. I can't love her. I can't. She'll be returning to Hallensham, and I'll stay here. Loving her—Allowing myself—It simply wouldn't do. Maybe there's not a speck of sense in even wondering about it.''

"But perhaps there's every reason in the world to give it your unmitigated concentration.''

"I wish I knew how she felt.''

"Ask her.''

"No.''

"Afraid of her answer?''

Saber spun away from the window. ''No. Yes. I—What did she do, Addison? How did she do it? Do you know I actually stopped the carriage and bought violets because the thought of her breathing such foul air infuriated me?''

"No, I didn't know that. How chivalrous of you, Saber.''

"I've got my own blasted problems. Hutchins, Doyle, the situation at Ravenhurst, unraveling the mystery about

Angelica . . . So why do I think about tea parlors? It enrages me that Imogene Tully threw Goldie out of hers.''

Addison crossed his legs, fully prepared to allow Saber to ramble on to his heart's delight. "A pox on Imogene Tully." *Whoever she is,* he added silently.

"And hats. I think about hats too."

"Hats are nice." Addison grinned.

"And so help me God, if I hear one person say anything about her that I deem insulting, I will—"

"I didn't notice the pistols at your sides. It would seem that you've become quite violent since last I saw you. Don't get me wrong though. I rather like it. It's topping to see the starch curtain has fallen."

"Curtains," Saber repeated quietly, staring at empty space, at nothing. "Pink and white gingham. All those kittens she wants would probably climb those curtains, shredding them to pieces. And do you know she's never had any perfume? She actually tried to make her own once. It made her smell like a pie. Imagine a girl as beautiful as she never having had a bottle of scent."

Addison's grin split his face. "I have a sneaking suspicion she'll soon have more than she could possibly wear in a lifetime."

Saber pulled down the cuffs of his sleeves and straightened. "I'll be gone when she awakens in the morning, Addison. The first thing I want you to tell her is that you've learned Lord Tremayne is in Scotland. I've much to do on the morrow, and will see to her when I return."

"Where are you for?"

"I'll call on Tyler Escott, then visit Aunt Lucy and Aunt Clara."

"The aunties will enjoy having Goldie stay with them for a while. They like having someone to fuss over. I remember how sad they were when you stopped letting them mother you."

Deep in thought, Saber rubbed his chin. "Tell me, Addison, is your grandfather's town house still in your possession? The one he used for . . ."

"His mistresses," Addison supplied with a grin. "Yes, it's still mine. Why?"

Saber folded his arms across his chest. "I'll be living

there for a while. If I recall, the house is situated well away from the fashionable parts of town, is it not?''

''Grandfather had no wish to flaunt his affairs in front of his peers. The house is on the corner of Pickering and Landon. That's not a slum, of course, but the area isn't as desirable as this one. I've heard of several robberies around there recently. Are you sure—''

''I am.''

''Then you are welcome to it for as long as you have use for it. But may I ask why you want it? To the best of my knowledge your own house hasn't burned to the ground. In fact, your aunts are in it, waiting for your return.''

Saber shook his head. ''But every member of the ton knows where Lord Tremayne lives. In your grandfather's house, no one of significance will see me. Goldie and I will be staying there. I've already told her you bought it for me.''

''I never knew how truly generous I was until I became your distant cousin,'' Addison teased. ''But Saber, you cannot mean to continue with this masquerade. This is *London*. When Goldie begins spying on the aristocracy, she'll most likely want to drag you along with her. Someone will see you. You will not be able to hide your identity for long. Tell her the truth.''

''No.''

Addison frowned. ''But—''

''No. I will not tell her.''

''Why?''

*Because I don't want her to bow to me,* Saber answered silently. ''Addison, we discussed this at Leighwood. I refuse to risk the chance that Goldie might send word to Hallensham of having found me.''

''If you told her what you know about Hutchins, I'm certain she would understand the need for discretion.''

Saber secretly agreed. But he couldn't make himself be honest with her. Not yet. It was too soon. He continued to crave that special something she gave, and once she knew who he was she'd be in awe of him. Just like every other unmarried woman in England. ''I won't tell her, and that is the end of it.''

Addison sighed. "And if you do meet someone you know? What then?"

"That won't happen. Neither of us will be seen."

"You will if she insists on spying on dukes. To do that, she must be near the aristocracy. Someone will see—"

"I am going to take her to all the places where *dukish people* may be seen. The theaters. The park. The opera houses. White's. We will drive by those places in the carriage, and she may spy from the window."

"It won't work."

"It will."

"What are you going to do? Lie down in the floor of the coach? Someone is going to see—"

"Addison, it's the only way around this outrageous plan of hers. I will not go gallivanting around London with her. Good God! Imagine my spying on my own fellow aristocrats! Knowing her, she'd have me peeking into their windows at night to see what sort of nightclothes they wear!"

Addison laughed. "You forget that I know Goldie too, Saber. I cannot believe she will be content with spying from a coach window. She's going to want to get close enough to—"

"I'm afraid she will not have her way on that account. Good night."

Saber left the room so quickly, Addison didn't have the chance to return the sentiment. He poured himself another brandy, absently picking up Saber's empty snifter. "What are your *real* reasons for not telling her who you are, old boy?" he murmured. "Tea parlors. Violets. Hats. Bull-milking. Dandelions and breezes . . ."

Addison smiled broadly. "You can't love her, eh, Saber?" Completely unable to help himself, he fell back into his chair and laughed.

Seated in a huge leather chair, Saber looked around Tyler Escott's office, then watched the investigator thumb through one of the diaries. He'd already told the detective the entire story from beginning to end, and now waited to hear what the man thought. "Do you think it's possible to somehow read the stained words? I realize many of them are completely obliterated, but some are merely smeared."

Tyler leaned over his desk. "I'll do my best. Maybe by the time you get Dane Hutchins' account books and William Doyle's records to me, I'll have deciphered some of these diary passages. I've met William Doyle, by the way. He and I attended the same dinner party about a year ago. He spoke highly of you and told me how much he enjoyed working for both you and your father."

Saber smirked at that.

"Yes, well, at any rate, Lord Tremayne, continue with your masquerade, and by all means take up residence in your friend's house. I think it's a superb idea for all of London to believe you are in Scotland. I've no doubt that the fact Miss Mae is looking for you hasn't set well with Hutchins. If he should come to London or contact Doyle, both men will be . . . uh, *relieved* to know you are not in the city. That, of course, is a measure of safety for Miss Mae, too."

"So you believe Hutchins and Doyle have committed the crimes."

"Of that there is no doubt in my mind. But I must find irrefutable evidence. Otherwise you cannot press charges."

"Of course." Saber stared at the detective, needing to ask a question, but hesitant to hear its answer. "Tyler," he began, then paused. "Goldie's in danger, isn't she?"

Tyler saw his client's extreme anxiety and sought to soothe it as best he could. "I wouldn't be overly concerned at this point. There is cause for suspecting many things, but I don't like discussing mere conjecture. As I said, continue with the masquerade, and stay in your friend's house. After all, if no one can find *you*, it will be next to impossible to find Miss Mae either. And let us not forget that Hutchins is obviously not a stupid man. He'll think twice before leaving Ravenhurst in search of Miss Mae. Many people would see him leave the estate."

"And he'd be without an alibi," Saber speculated.

"Exactly."

Saber stood and shook Tyler's hand. He realized many things had been left unsaid between them, but understood that that was the way the detective worked. Until the time came to discuss them, all suspicions would remain unmentioned. "I'll be on the corner of Pickering and Landon should you need to contact me."

"Fine. But please do not think you can never leave the house. That wouldn't be feasible at all, and from what you've told me about Miss Mae, I doubt very seriously that you could keep her locked up anyway. I only caution you against going to places where your acquaintances might see you. Places where members of nobility might be found. Stay away from those locations, and the fact that you are in London will most likely remain unknown."

Saber thought about Goldie's determination to seek out dukes, and gave a great sigh. "I'll try. Good day."

When his client was gone, Tyler returned to his desk, thinking about everything they had and hadn't discussed. He glanced at the sack of diaries. Somehow, he had to force those little books to give up their secrets. The case went much deeper than uncovering Hutchins' and Doyle's theft. It was also a matter of Angelica Sheridan's accidental fall down the staircase, and Tyler knew Marion Tremayne understood this too.

That thought in mind, Tyler picked up a diary.

"Lucille, my dear," Clara scolded gently, "you are twisting your bracelet again. If you do not stop, you are going to wrench your arm." Primly, she touched her salt-and-pepper hair and smoothed her skirts with a wrinkled but very soft hand. Her twinkling blue eyes never leaving her sister, she patted her reticule, which was lying beside her.

Lucille gave Clara an impatient look and let go of her bracelet. "I may twist my bracelet, Clara, but at least I don't carry my reticule wherever I go. I only have mine when I'm leaving the house. You take yours from room to room. Why, it wouldn't surprise me to learn that you sleep with it under your pillow!"

Clara raised a brow and removed her hand from her bag.

Smiling smugly, Lucille pushed her round, silver-rimmed spectacles back to the bridge of her nose, never noticing when they promptly slipped back down to her plump and rosy cheeks. "Besides," she began, fingering her bracelet again, "I cannot help feeling anxious. Our boy is back in London! And with the girl no less! Oh, why isn't Marion here yet? It isn't that far from Addison's house."

"We only just received his message. Do you think he has wings?" Clara slipped her reticule strings around her wrist, rose from the padded couch, and set to rights the arrangement of peacock feathers Margaret had knocked over. "Margaret, you naughty girl," she said to the blond spaniel. "A lady takes care when she walks about a room. Where are your manners?"

Margaret affected a soft whimper, earning a loving pat from Clara.

"Do you think he'll bring the girl with him?" Lucille asked excitedly, giving her bracelet a firm twist. "Addison said she's really quite beautiful. Oh, Clara, do you think it presumptuous of me to wonder if our boy feels anything similar to affection for her? And why didn't he bring her here last night? This *is* his home, after all. Do you suppose—"

"I think, sister, that as soon as our boy arrives, he will deliver the answers to all our questions. But have a care not to overwhelm him the second he steps into the room, Lucille. He's likely to be tired from his journey yesterday, and not inclined to—"

"Good morning, aunties," Saber greeted them from the doorway of the drawing room. "I see you received my message. How beautiful you both look. But you didn't have to put on such finery for my sake. I've seen you both at your worst, and have continued loving you in spite of it."

Clara shook her head disapprovingly. "Marion, that's positively an indecent thing to say."

Lucille patted her bright silver hair, then rose slowly from her tapestry chair. "And these gowns cannot be considered finery, Marion. Why, these are morning gowns, and only of sprigged muslin. But do you remember my blue velvet? That is finery, my boy. I wonder where that dress is? I haven't worn it in so long."

"Lucille, you gave that gown to charity eight years ago," Clara informed her sister. "Now do sit down, stop playing with your bracelet, and let's hear what Marion has to say, shall we? Marion, where is the girl? I must tell you that it is quite distressing to me that you and Addison slept in the same house with her without proper chaperone."

"But Mrs. Stubbs—"

"Is Addison's housekeeper," Clara finished for him.

Saber smiled sheepishly and made himself comfortable on the padded satin sofa. "I'm sorry," he said, feeling no remorse whatsoever. "Now, aunties, I need your help."

"And you shall have it," Lucille promised. "Is it help with the girl you need?" She leaned forward, presenting her good ear to him. "Why didn't you bring her with you this morning? Addison informed us she is pleasing to the eye and kindhearted as well. Because of that I suppose we can forgive her for being American. The girl can't very well help being from that country, now can she? One certainly cannot choose one's birthplace, and—"

"Lucille," Clara admonished. "You are chattering."

"You'll like Goldie, Aunt Lucy," Saber told her. "She chatters too."

"Well, that is all we need." Clara threw up her hands, her reticule swinging from her wrist. "Two chatterboxes in the house. We've prepared the pink room for her, Marion. It is the room furthest away from yours," she added, her meaning thinly veiled.

"Does she like pink?" Lucille asked.

He thought of the pink and white curtains. "Yes, I believe she does, but she won't be staying in the pink room. She and I will be residing in Addison's town house across the city."

"His *grandfather's?*" Clara exclaimed. "Why, Marion, that will never do. You simply cannot be seen in that section of—" She broke off, her eyes widening, her hand clutching the bodice of her gown. "Did you say that you and Goldie would be residing there? Alone? Marion!"

"Aunt Clara—"

"You may be His Grace, the Duke of Ravenhurst, but in my eyes you are first and foremost *my boy*. And if you think—"

"He's *my* boy, too, Clara," Lucille interjected.

Clara took a deep breath, gathering patience. "Marion, you will not live with the girl alone. I forbid it."

Frowning, Saber stood and ambled around the room. "Aunties, I know that Addison has already enlightened you as to Goldie's predicament, so I see no need to go into that. However—"

"Is her uncle here too?" Lucille asked. "We can allow no drunkards in this house, Marion. It simply isn't—"

"Asa Mae remains in Hallensham to the best of my knowledge," Saber answered.

"And what of the little man who guards her?" Lucille queried. "That Huge."

"*Big*, Auntie," Saber corrected. "Big Mann. He has returned to Hallensham to see to Asa. Now, what I need for the two of you to do is . . . Well, to put it very simply, I need you to lie."

"Lie!" Clara exclaimed.

"Lord Tremayne is in Scotland," Saber continued. "Addison has already begun spreading the news that His Grace is out of the country, and I want you to further it. I don't want anyone to know I'm back in London."

Lucille frowned. "My boy, you are not in Scotland. You are standing right here in this room."

"I am in Scotland," Saber insisted. "Goldie is bound and determined to seek out Lord Tremayne to spy on him. To prevent her from embarking upon such a vain task, Addison—probably at this very moment—is telling her that His Grace is in Scotland with no immediate plans to return. The nobility will be led to believe the same, and—"

"Marion, are you saying the poor girl still doesn't know who you are?" Clara asked.

Saber crossed to the piano and ran his finger over the violet satin that covered it. "She knows the common man beneath the nobleman." At the thought, a tender flame warmed his soul.

"The common man . . ." Clara began, baffled. "Marion, you are making no sense. Perhaps you should leave the room, come in again, and we can make a fresh start with this conversation."

Saber shook his head, clearing it of all thoughts but the information he had to give his aunts. He'd already decided to tell them just enough to satisfy them, but would not reveal anything that might upset their delicate sensibilities. "Listen carefully, aunties. In the letter I had Addison bring to you from Leighwood, I told you about Della's diaries. You will be glad to know that in the matter concerning Hutchins' and Doyle's thievery, those books have, indeed, been informative. There is a problem with them, though. Many of them are badly stained and next to impossible to read. This upset me, for I've found other passages in them that are a great deal of interest to me. Entries concerning Angelica. I—I need to know what Della wrote about Angelica. Surely you can understand how important it is to me to know what she thought about the girl I was going to marry."

"Well, of course we do, my boy," Clara murmured. She watched Saber carefully, waiting for his blank expression to crack with pain. His eyes reflected anxiety, but not the profound agony she was accustomed to seeing when Angelica's name was mentioned. She frowned in total confusion.

Saber left the piano and sat down beside his Aunt Lucy. "I have just concluded a visit with Tyler Escott. He's a well-known detective, and is going to study the diaries carefully. Not only that, but he is going to build an iron-clad case against Hutchins and Doyle. He agrees that it's better that no one knows I am in London. Every precaution must be taken to keep Hutchins and Doyle from learning Goldie has found me. If they knew, they'd have time to escape before I can bring them to justice. So you see? The fewer people who know she and I are together, the better. I can't very well live in my own home right now. Addison's other house will be my place of residence until Hutchins and Doyle are arrested." Looking at Clara, he raised his chin.

She recognized the unshakable defiance in his gesture, and lifted a gray eyebrow. "Very well."

Saber saw the arched brow and knew exactly what it meant. "Aunt Clara, whatever scheme it is you are planning right now, I can assure you I won't—"

"Marion, my boy," Lucille interrupted, "after Mr. Hutchins and Mr. Doyle are imprisoned, will you return to Ravenhurst with Goldie? Addison told us she is in danger of losing her home if she doesn't bring you back, and I must say I'm thrilled with the possibility of your return to your ducal lands.''

Saber shook his head. ''No, but Goldie will not lose her home. Ravenhurst will soon be in the hands of a new manager, who will see to her every need. And when she returns it will be with ample evidence that she has found me. I will not allow anything to happen to her. I'm going to take care of her, just as I tried to take care of Della.''

Clara studied her nephew. There was a soft glow in his eyes when he spoke of Goldie. But there was a crease of dismay on his brow, too. Clara's curiosity about the girl who caused such conflicting emotions grew. ''Where is she, Marion?''

''Addison will be bringing her shortly.'' He suddenly remembered the butler. ''You did instruct Tamworth to have a care when addressing me?''

''We did,'' Clara assured him. ''But I want you to know, Marion, that asking the servants to lie . . . that pulling them into this masquerade of yours is highly improper.''

Saber feigned a guilty expression, then promptly continued with his instructions. ''When Goldie arrives, do not call me Marion. I am Saber West. And pray, don't forget that Addison is our distant relative. He has given you this house and has furnished it for you as well. He—''

''Having to remember all of that is going to drive us quite mad,'' Clara predicted curtly. ''And I must say, Marion, that quite a change has come over you since last we saw you. Your morals have disappeared. You think nothing of telling falsehoods, and are you aware that your neckcloth has come untied? I have never seen it like that.''

Saber reached up and felt the cloth. With a firm tug, he removed it. ''No matter. These blasted things—''

''Marion!'' Clara exclaimed. ''Where in heaven's name is your sense of propriety?''

''I—'' He broke off when the butler arrived at the door. ''Are they here, Tamworth?''

Tamworth inclined his head. ''Lord Gage has arrived, Your Grace.''

Saber scowled. "Tamworth, you mustn't address me or Lord Gage thus. I thought my aunts explained that to you."

"They did, milord. And you may rest assured that I will call you *sir* in the presence of Miss Mae."

"Very well. Show them in."

"Miss Mae did not accompany Lord Gage, Your Grace."

"Saber!" Addison shouted, running into the room. "She's *gone!* Goldie's *gone!*"

Saber bolted from his seat. "Gone? Where—"

"We breakfasted together, and then she went upstairs to do whatever it is women do after breakfast!" Addison explained hysterically. "I went into my office to await her, but when she didn't come down I sent Mrs. Stubbs to check on her, and—She—We couldn't *find* her! We looked everywhere!"

Saber felt dread pump through him. "Addison, didn't you tell her you were going to bring her here to meet my aunts? Didn't you—"

"I told her Lord Tremayne was in Scotland, but that's all I had the chance to say! She began a stream of chatter that had no end! Went on and on about some chap named Duncan Gilmore who wore a skirt, had naked knees, and told everyone he was Scottish! I tried to talk, but she—"

"Addison! Goldie is wandering around London! *Alone!*"

"Saber, we'll—"

"I've got to look for her! She—"

"You take your coach, I'll take mine. We'll—"

Saber never heard the rest of what Addison suggested. He raced from the house, slamming the front door behind him as he left in search of the girl whose welfare depended on his finding her.

Before someone else did.

# Chapter 13

⁓⁓⁓

"**I**tchie Bon," Goldie murmured down to the dog, "I think we've found the street that leads to hell. I don't know how we got to this place, but we sure did take a wrong turn somewhere."

Revulsion snaked through her as she stared at her surroundings. Here the streets were not clean, as they were near Addison's house. *Filthy* didn't even describe them. Rotting garbage was piled everywhere, and Goldie noticed no one cared about having to step around it. Some people trudged right through it, and one woman was even huddled in it for warmth against the chilled morning mist. The air was filled with a cacophony of human voices, animal screeches, and rolling wheels. All around her were tall buildings, painted black by the greasy smoke she could see, smell, and taste. It seemed to her that the sunshine couldn't find a way past it. She decided her conjecture was correct when she saw no living plant growing anywhere.

Carefully making her way around a heap of fish heads, she tapped a young girl on the shoulder. "Can you tell me where I am?"

The girl frowned, then smiled. "Ya ain't from 'ere, are ya, miss?"

"I'm from America."

"I knew it. Yer speech ain't the same. Some says I'm dumb, but I ain't. Me name's Rosie Tetter, miss. I has sixteen years in me, an' I gots all me teeth."

Goldie returned the girl's smile, looking dutifully into Rosie's open mouth. "And what have you got in your basket, Rosie? Are you sellin' flowers?"

225

Rosie laughed. "Farthest thing from it, miss," she answered, lifting the rag that covered the basket.

Goldie's eyes widened; she took a step back. "Great day Miss Agnes, that's dog mess!"

The girl nodded and adjusted her black leather glove. "Been collectin' it since dawn. It takes a long time ter find this much pure. Ya'd think with all the dogs 'ere in London-town it'd be easy, but it ain't."

Goldie frowned, tightening her hold on Itchie Bon's leash when he began barking at a stray cat. "Pure?"

"I 'ear tell it purifies. The tanners in Bermondsey buy it an' use it ter make leather soft."

Goldie glanced at the full basket again. "I'll swannee, that's the strangest thing I ever heard in my whole life."

Rosie nodded in agreement. "I didn't used ter be the pure finder in me family, I didn't. Me grandfather was. But 'e passed away a few months ago, an' now I'm on me own in the world. I got two jobs, I do. See?" She pulled open her apron pocket so Goldie could see inside.

Goldie peered into the pocket, seeing what looked to be about fifty or sixty cigar ends. "Do you smoke those?"

Rosie laughed and swiped at a lock of limp brown hair. "No, I sells 'em. I got lucky last night, I did. Spent hours on Regent Street, an' found all these. There's a bloke in Rosemary Lane wot buys 'em. 'E sells 'em ter the cigar fac'try, an' they're made inter more cigars. Wot a joke on the toffs wot buy an' smoke 'em! Every time they lights one up, it might be the same one they smoked last month!"

Rosie's enthusiasm made Goldie smile. She felt herself warming to the friendly girl. "Do you live around here?" she asked, praying Rosie would say no.

"I live about a block away. Weren't ya watchin' where ya was goin', miss? Ya ain't the sort wot lives around 'ere."

Looking around, Goldie sighed. "I was watchin' where I was goin', but I got lost. I just kept walkin', and I ended up here. This is the first time I've ever been in London. And the worst thing about it is that no one knows where I am. They don't even know where to look for me."

"Don't be afeared, miss. Ya found me, Rosie Tetter,

an' I'll sees ter ya, I will. 'Ere," she said, digging into her blouse, " 'ave a bite."

Goldie looked at the moldy piece of bread. Compassion for Rosie bloomed. "No, thank you, Rosie. I've already eaten."

Shrugging, Rosie popped the bread into her mouth. "Why ya 'ere, miss?"

"I came to London to watch dukes, but I don't reckon I'll find any around here. Do y'know where I can find a group of 'em all together? I don't have time to hunt 'em out one by one, y'see. I figure if I can find a place where they make a herd, I'll get a lot more done."

"A 'erd o' dukes?" Rosie murmured, scowling. "I ain't never 'eard of 'em makin' a 'erd, but I've seen groups o' maybe five or six rich blokes before. Will that do ya, miss?"

"My name's Goldie. And yes, a flock of five or six would be—"

"Coo, Rosie!" a man exclaimed as he approached. "Who's yer friend? Fine skirt, she is. Dainty chicka-biddy."

Rosie spat at the man's feet. "She ain't *yer* bleedin' chickabiddy, Og, so don't ya go gettin' no itches ter put yer flamin' bunch o' fives no place on 'er! Ya got that, dicky dido?"

"Who ya callin' clay-brained, Rosie?" Og demanded, his fleshy face purpling. "I ain't the one 'avin' ter pick up pure, am I? Ya won't find me, Og Drit, workin' at some-thin' like—"

"Get knotted! Ya dress like a 'ardworkin' coster, ya do, but ain't nobody'll find ya workin', Og. When ya ain't doin' the Butcher's biddin', yer a bleedin' scuffle-'unter, ya are! Always 'angin' 'round the docks, actin' like yer lookin' fer work, but wot ya do is *steal* wotever ya can get yer—"

"Watch yer friggin' mouth, Rosie, or I'll—"

"An' sometimes 'e's a flamin' meat-monger," Rosie enlightened Goldie. " 'E's the sort wot no woman's safe with. 'E filled me friend Milly's belly last year, 'e did, an' now Milly—"

"Bloody 'ell," Og muttered, stuffing his hands into the

deep pockets of his long corduroy coat. "Wot a cake-'ole ya got on ya, Rosie. I'll warn ya ter 'ave a care with it, o' I might jest close it fer ya ferever one o' these days."

"Try touchin' me, Og, an' I'll cut yer friggin' bald-'eaded 'ermit in 'alf!"

"Rosie," Goldie said, "let's leave." She gave Itchie Bon more leash, allowing the snarling dog to get closer to Og.

When Goldie spoke, Og's eyes lit up. He took a step away, his gaze taking in each inch of her. Smiling suddenly, he spun and charged into an alley.

Goldie felt relief flood her. "What's a cake-hole, Rosie? And a meat-monger? And . . . a bald-headed hermit?"

Rosie continued to watch Og until he disappeared. "A cake-'ole's yer mouth. A meat-monger's a man wot can't resist wot's 'twixt a girl's legs. Og Drit's 'otter'n a flamin' chimney, an' 'is bald-'eaded 'ermit's wot 'e uses when 'e's wenchin'. It's 'is *cock,* Goldie. Do ya know wot a cock is?"

Goldie's eyes widened.

Rosie smiled and patted Goldie's shoulder. "Listen, Goldie, I ain't usually worried 'bout nobody but meself, but yer the sort wot gets inter bad trouble 'round 'ere. Yer clothes ain't much ter look at, but yer clean, an' ya got that look about ya wot the meat-mongers like. Og ain't the only one, ya know. 'Ell, there's even a business fer it. Blokes like Og, they nab young girls like you, Goldie. Some nobs pay ter 'ave virgins, see, an'—"

"Nobs? Rosie—"

"Rich people. Goldie, I can tell ya ain't never laid with a man afore. Iffen ya've got a mind ter keep it that way, ya got ter get out o' 'ere. Come on, luv. I'll shows ya the way."

Saber bolted out of the coach when it stopped in front of Addison's house. He'd been looking for Goldie for hours without success. He prayed Addison had found her. "Addison!" he shouted as he tore through the front door of his friend's house. "Is she here? Addison!"

Mrs. Stubbs scurried into the entryway and curtsied. "Lord—*Mr.* Gage is in the drawing room, Your Grace—

*Sir,''* she informed him, wringing her fat hands in her apron. "Miss Mae and her . . . friend are with him. The girl Miss Mae brought—She—Well . . ."

At her stammering, Saber stormed to the parlor, stopping short at the doorway. There sat Goldie, safe and comfortable on the enormous satin sofa. How dare she be safe and comfortable when he'd been searching for hours for her! he raged. Why, she didn't even have the decency to look tired! God, what he'd been through trying to find her, all the while believing the worst, knowing she was lost to him forever.

"There you sit, Goldie Mae, warm and happy as can be!" he thundered. "Do you have any idea what you put me through? I've been—"

"Saber!" She jumped off the sofa and ran to him. Once before him, she did a little leap and threw her arms around his neck, her feet dangling in thin air. "Saber, while I was walkin' home with Rosie, I came up with the most brilliant plan! You and I are—"

"Goldie, why—"

"Y'see, Saber, the real Duke Marion's in Scotland, so I decided that what we can do is—"

"Goldie, who is this girl?" Saber asked, looking at the bedraggled person perched on the edge of the love seat. "Where have you been? Why—"

"Oh, this is Rosie Tetter," Goldie explained, sliding back down to the thick carpet. "She's a pure and cigarfinder. Saber, do y'know what the tanners do with pure? Do y'know—"

"Yes, I know," he growled. "Goldie, tell me you haven't been in the East End! Tell me—"

"Well, I wish I could tell you I haven't been there, Saber, but y'see—"

"You've been in the East End—*alone*—and you can stand there rambling merrily on? Good God, Goldie, you should be scared to—"

"Are you mad at—"

*"Mad* does not begin to describe how I feel! *Wandering!* All morning! As if you knew London as well as your little towns in America! And here you are, none the worse! Not a scratch on you! Not as much as a slight tremble in

your hands! Why did you leave the house by yourself this morning?''

At his bellowing, hurt spiraled through her. But so did anger. Dammit, he wouldn't even listen to her explanations! Wouldn't even try to understand how important her plan was! "Don't you yell at me!" she hollered in a rare show of defiance.

Her shout took him aback. He'd never seen her truly angry at him before. "You shouted at me," he said, amazed.

Ire continued to weave through Goldie. "Well, you yelled at me first! Y'want me to be upset over what happened to me today, Saber? Do you? All right, fine!" She wrung her hands. Her chin on her chest, she began to shake as forcefully as she could get her body to do it. "Oh!" she wailed. "Oh, Saber, it was *awful!* All those fish heads! That black air! Those screechin' animals! And no growin' plants anywhere! The scare I got was so terrible, I just know that if I keep on thinkin' about it, I'll be dead by tonight!''

Despite his anger, his lips twitched at her dramatic performance. "All right, Goldie, you have made your point. Now tell me what happened.''

"Rosie helped Goldie find this neighborhood, Saber,'' Addison explained instead. "Then Goldie recognized my house. I'd been out all morning looking for her. When I didn't find her, I came home. Not ten minutes later, she arrived with Rosie.''

"It ain't none o' me business,'' Rosie told Saber, "but iffen ya've got a mind ter 'old onter Goldie, ya'd best not let 'er go back ter where I found 'er. She was like a lamb surrounded by a bleedin' pack o' 'ungry wolfs, she was.''

Saber glared at Goldie. "Do you know how dangerous the East—''

"Rosie got rid of Og Drit for me,'' Goldie said, casting a bright smile at her new friend. "He's a meat-monger, Saber. I learned what that is. And I learned what a bald-headed hermit is too. We don't say that word in America, y'know.''

"Goldie!''

She looked up at him, grinning. "Well, we don't. And it's not in my dictionary either."

Rosie smiled. "Then there's some who call it the best o' three legs, too," she added naughtily.

Goldie giggled. "Saber, do *you* know what those words—"

"I know *exactly* what they mean!" he exploded, more anger bursting inside him at the thought of her at the mercy of East End whoremongers. "Goldie, did anyone touch you while you were there? Did any harm at all come—"

"She's fine, Saber," Addison intervened. "Settle down, old boy."

Saber placed his hand on Goldie's shoulder. "I don't know whether to hug you because you're safe, or shake you because you left in the first place. What could you have been thinking? What—"

"I was lookin' for dukes."

"In the *slums?* Granted, I know little about the nobility, but I'm reasonably certain you won't find the aristocracy milling about in—"

"Saber—"

"Goldie," Rosie cut in, "I got ter go now, luv." She turned to Addison, smiling at him. "Obliged fer the meal, sir. Iffen there's anything I can ever do ter repay yer kindness, ya knows where ter finds me."

Saber looked at Rosie. Dear God, he thought. If not for the kindhearted urchin, Goldie might have been lost to him forever. "On the contrary, Rosie. We owe *you* a great debt of gratitude. If it weren't for you, our Goldie might still be wandering around lost. Or . . . or worse." He pulled a wad of bills from his pocket and held it out to her.

Rosie's eyes welled with tears. She looked up at Saber. "But Goldie told me ya ain't got no money of yer own, sir. I can't take—"

"You can and you will," Saber insisted, taking her hand and pressing the thick roll into it. "And if you should ever need help in any way, you may contact me through Mr. Gage. Do not hesitate to do so."

"Gawblimey," Rosie muttered, staring down at the money. She looked up at Saber and Addison. "Black as

Newgate's knocker, I am, an' ya let me inter yer warm, clean 'ome, feedin' an' treatin' me like I was somebody special. Then ya give me money fer doin' a simple kindness. The Lord bless ya both.''

Goldie embraced her friend and led her to the front door. "I'll come see you as soon as I can, Rosie."

Rosie shook her head. "Goldie, wot can ya be thinkin', luv? Don't ya never go back there again, 'ear? I might not be around next time, an' then . . .'' She broke off, and patted Goldie's shoulder. " 'Ang onter that Saber, Goldie. An' count yer blessins. 'E ain't only the nicest-lookin' man I ever seed, but 'e's generous, an' 'e cares about ya. Wot more could any girl want in this bloomin' world?''

"I—Rosie, do you really think he cares about me?''

Rosie laughed. "An' 'ang onter yer sweetness, too, Goldie. It's wot yer Saber's tryin' ter protect, y'know. 'E knows wot London-town can do to a girl innocent as you. I'll come see ya soon. Cheerio, now.''

Goldie nodded, and waved until Rosie was out of sight. She stood at the door for a moment thinking about what her friend had said before remembering the exciting news she had to tell Saber. Spinning around, she raced back to the parlor.

Saber was just leaving it when she got there. Her sudden and speedy arrival caught him off-guard, and he had no time at all to sidestep her. She ran straight into him. While she clung to his neck, he staggered backward, immediately toppling over a footstool. He landed, with a dull thud, flat on his back, his spill made worse by Goldie, who fell directly on top of him. "Goldie!"

She settled herself more comfortably upon his broad chest, grabbing his shirt collar so he couldn't get away before she was ready to let him. "Saber, you just aren't gonna believe what I decided to do! I was comin' home with Rosie, and all of a sudden I had the greatest idea I've ever had in my whole life! Duke Marion's in Scotland, and he's not comin' back any time soon. So I thought we could—''

"Goldie, could we discuss this in a more proper manner? We're on the floor, you're on top of me, and perhaps more importantly, your knees are . . . well, suffice it to say, the location of your knees is making me quite nervous.''

She frowned, then smiled when comprehension came to her. She tried to maneuver herself away from the spot he was so terribly afraid for.

"Good God!" Saber shouted when her knees dug into the exact part of his body he'd tried to protect. "Goldie—"

"I'm sorry! I didn't mean to—"

"Just get off so I can—"

"But Saber, I didn't get to finish tellin' you my plan!"

"I—"

"Y'see, we already know you look a lot like Duke Marion. You can eat, walk, and talk like a duke. And you know a lot about Duke Marion from what you've read in Aunt Della's diaries, so what I decided we'd do is—"

"Goldie—"

"We'll go to the dukish parties, and—"

"Allow me to assist you, Goldie," Addison broke in, offering her his hand and helping her rise.

Saber struggled to his feet, glared at Goldie, and straightened his rumpled clothes.

"Are you all right, Saber?" Addison asked, feeling genuine sympathy for his friend.

"I suspect I'll live, but I have serious doubts about the possibility of ever enjoying the pleasures of fatherhood."

Addison chuckled. "Your voice *does* sound several octaves higher."

Goldie blew a curl out of her eye. "Saber—"

"Goldie, I'm taking you to my own house." He looked at Addison. "I trust all is well there?" Addison's nod told him that Mrs. Stubbs had been successful at speedily gathering a full staff of trustworthy servants for him. Too, he knew those servants had not been told who he was. "Splendid."

"Saber, *listen!*" Goldie entreated loudly. "Somehow, we're gonna get us some fancy clothes, then we're gonna just waltz right into all those duke get-togethers! Nobody'll say anything to us because you're gonna tell 'em all that you're—"

"Goldie, we will discuss this in the carriage," he lied, his plans for the ride having nothing at all to do with talking about her harebrained scheme. "We're off, Addison. Many thanks for your hospitality."

Addison waved away his friend's gratitude. "If you will excuse me?" he begged off, anxious to give Saber and Goldie time alone.

When Addison was gone, Saber swept his hand toward the foyer. "All right, Goldie, shall we leave for—"

Goldie stomped her foot, then took hold of Saber's collar again. Pulling him down to her level, she speared him with a narrow-eyed stare. "You're gonna be Duke Marion while we're here, got that? We're gonna go to the dukish parties, and you're gonna tell everybody you're the duke. Talk about Ravenhurst, and Dane Hutchins, and Angelica, and all those Tremayne family things. Tell everybody Scotland was full of Scottish stuff just like it always is. Maybe you could even do one of those Scottish jigs for everybody as proof you've been there. Saber, once you start talkin' about stuff only the real duke could know, no one's gonna suspect you aren't who you say you are!"

"Goldie—"

"We'll be so close to all those dukish folks that we'll be able to see everything there is to see about 'em. Hell, we'll even be able to interrogate 'em. I'm gonna be posin' as a writer from America, y'see. I've got it all planned, Saber. I'll tell everybody I'm writin' a book about dukish folks, and that you're takin' me around so I can do all my studyin'. I'm sure when they learn that, they'll be more than happy to—"

"That," Saber began, his lips a whisper away from hers, "is the most ridiculous thing I've ever heard. We are not going to—"

"Yes, we are." She tightened her hold on his collar, keeping his face in front of her own. "It's too good of an opportunity to pass up."

"You *will,* however, pass it up."

"Wanna bet?"

"How much?"

"A whole pound."

Saber whistled. "I don't know if I can afford that, Goldie. A pound is—"

"All right, then we'll make it an ounce. Can you afford that?"

"An ounce? What in heaven's name are you talking about?"

"An *ounce!* An ounce of money! Great day Miss Agnes, Saber, have you been poor for so long that you don't know how much an ounce is?"

Still bent over, Saber frowned and thought hard. "An ounce. A pound," he murmured. "Goldie, do you think a pound is literally a pound of money?"

She saw the twinkle in his seaweed eyes and let go of his collar. It dawned on her then that a pound wasn't what she thought it was. She knew, too, that she must have misunderstood her Uncle Asa's explanation about English money.

Saber's slight grin reinforced her realization. "Of course I don't think that," she lied, smoothing her skirts as if it were the most important thing in the world to do.

He understood her chagrin immediately, and sought to soothe it. "Ah, then you were teasing me. For a second there, I believed you didn't know that the pound is the basic monetary unit of England."

"Well, of course I know that," she agreed, staring at her shoes. Reminding herself that Saber thought she was teasing him, she took a moment to get hold of her embarrassment, thankful beyond belief that he hadn't had the chance to make fun of her ignorance. "Now, gettin' back to the dukish fiestas—I met a Mexican once," she informed him sassily. "He told me a fiesta is a party."

Saber regarded her with amusement. "A dukish fiesta," he repeated, grinning. "I don't believe I've ever thought of the aristocracy's gatherings in such a way. I don't believe I will be attending one either."

She arched her brow. "Saber—"

"The carriage awaits us, Goldie," he told her, taking her by the elbow and leading her to the front door. He accepted his hat from Addison's butler, then wrapped his own coat around Goldie's shoulders. "Itchie Bon, you too," he told the dog, opening the door.

"Saber, why can't you give my plan a try?" Goldie asked as he helped her into the closed coach. Miffed at him, she sat in the seat opposite from him. "What do we have to lose? We—"

"Goldie—"

"You—"

"Come here, poppet," he instructed, reaching for her.

"No," she argued, resisting his efforts to bring her closer to him.

"Very well, I'll come to you." He changed seats, holding her tightly when she tried to move to the side he'd vacated.

"Don't touch me, Saber."

"Why not?"

"Because when you do, I feel like bein' nice to you. And I don't want to be nice to you right now."

He ignored her demands and lifted her into his lap. "You may do all the duke-spying you want from the coach window," he told her. "I'll take you past all the locations where the nobility gathers, and you can—"

"That's the dumbest thing I ever heard! Why—"

"Because I say so."

"Well, who the hell died and made you king?"

Her insulting question tickled him so thoroughly, he exploded with laughter. He thought about the time, not so very long ago, when such an unseemly query would have infuriated him. The notion made him laugh harder.

"Go on and laugh, Saber, but you're just about as arrogant as ole E.B. back in Hazel's Holler, Kentucky."

Still in the throes of laughter, Saber asked, "E.B.?"

"Well, his whole name was Earl Burl, but as you can plainly hear, that doesn't sound right. We all called him E.B. so we wouldn't have to say his whole name. Anyhow, ole E.B. was an arrogant thing. 'Course he had some right to his arrogance, Saber. He had this cat? Well, that cat was a direct descendent of Johnny Appleseed's cat. Most folks only think about Johnny Appleseed's ox, but he had a cat too. E.B. even had papers that proved his cat's bloodlines. Now, what right to arrogance do *you* have, Saber West?"

Many moments passed before Saber could control his laughter. Wiping the tears from his eyes, he looked at Goldie, hoping his expression looked serious. "What right? Madam, did I fail to inform you that *my* ancestor was responsible for naming one of the four cardinal directions? His name was Enoch West. He set out with his three friends, Samuel East, Jeremiah South, and Zachary North. The four of them—''

Goldie's laughter cut him short. Instantly, her anger at him disappeared. "Saber, that's the stupidest thing I've ever—''

"Nevertheless, it's my right to arrogance.''

She reached for his hand, holding it in her lap. "Saber, I'm sorry for yellin' at you a while ago. I didn't mean—''

"I liked it.''

"You liked me gettin' mad at you?'' she asked, amazed.

He nodded. "I've seen you do many things since I first met you, but today is the first time I've seen you defy me.''

"And that's . . . that's not bad?''

"I admit to being taken aback at first, but I rather enjoyed seeing you stand up for yourself. It proves that with all the sugar there is inside you, there is also a bit of spice.'' He drew her closer.

She watched his face come nearer, knowing in her heart it was the most handsome face God ever gave to a man. "Saber, are you gonna—''

"Yes,'' he murmured. "Yes, I am.''

Her eyes fluttered closed when his mouth touched hers. She parted her lips for him, as he'd taught her to, experiencing that sweet, hot ache when he accepted her invitation. Trembling, she reached up and slid her fingers through his ebony hair, its softness bringing to life every nerve in her palm.

"Goldie,'' he whispered thickly, his kisses trailing over her chin and down to her neck. He pulled the coat from her shoulders, tossing it to the floor before pressing more feathery kisses to the creamy expanse of her upper chest.

Mindless with the desire she was only just beginning to understand, Goldie dropped her hands from his hair and ran them down to his shoulders. Tentatively, she pulled him closer to her, moaning with pure pleasure when he responded the way she wanted him to.

With swift motions, he closed the satin curtains and

gently laid Goldie down on the velvet seat. His lips still nuzzling her neck and chest, he settled himself upon her, and, adjusting himself as well as he could within the cramped space, he covered her body with his own.

She felt his need for her. It was hard. Hot. It seemed to sear through her dress, branding her belly. It frightened her, but held her spellbound. Her breath caught in her throat as she concentrated on the heady sensation the feel of his masculinity brought to her.

And then he pushed himself lower, his hands tugging at her bodice. She moaned when he took her breast into his mouth. Need swirled through her, and she knew now what it was her body craved. "Yes," she told him. "Saber, yes."

He needed no further encouragement. Slowly, he inched his hand up her silken calf, across her thigh, his breathing becoming labored when she opened her legs and offered freely the treasure he sought. Desire throbbed forcefully through him when he realized again that she wore no undergarments. He decided then that he would never buy her any.

Goldie's delight began the second she felt his sensual invasion. She arched into his hand, bliss rolling through her as his fingers drove more deeply into her. The pleasure seemed never to end, but went on and on, the ecstasy so intense, she could barely breathe as it shimmered inside her.

"Again," he urged her, his voice rich as velvet, his hands still working their magic on her. "Again, Goldie."

Her mind couldn't grasp his meaning, but her body responded to his sensual command instantly. Once more the pleasure began, building steadily, taking her by surprise, filling her with a rapture too powerful to control. She rocked beneath him, clutched at his arms, wrapped her legs around him, and felt an eternity pass before the rising sensations began their slow winding spiral downward.

Before she opened her eyes, Saber moved above her again, allowing her to become accustomed to his weight gradually. He was halfway upon her, and halfway beside her, but no matter what position he attempted, he couldn't manage to get his long frame exactly where he wanted it.

Silently, he cursed the small compartment of the carriage and made a firm vow to have a huge one custom-made.

"Saber," Goldie whispered, opening her eyes to peer up at him.

At her whisper, he felt the arrogance she'd accused him of earlier. He'd brought her to climax twice, the ecstasy he'd given her almost more than she could bear. It had been so profound that it had stolen her voice, he mused smugly. Still smiling, he waited to hear her tell him what the glorious experience had meant to her. "Tell me, poppet."

"You're smashin' me."

Goldie pushed back the damask draperies and stared out the window of the bedroom she'd chosen as her own. The gray day suited her mood. "It's not fair, Itchie Bon," she fumed aloud. "He said he'd take me to all those places where dukes get together, and what does he do instead? He stays gone! It's bad enough that he's makin' me do all my duke research from a damn carriage, but what's worse is that he hasn't even let me do *that!*"

Whirling away from the window, she stormed to her bed and flopped onto it. "Where the hell do you suppose he's been goin' for the past two days? I haven't seen him long enough to do anything but kiss him good-bye and hello before he's up and gone again!"

She punched her pillow. "And where the hell does he get off tellin' me I better not go through that front door while he's gone? Oh, what I'm gonna tell him when he gets home! He said himself he liked it when I got mad at him, so I'll be more'n happy to oblige him! I'll knock him right off that high horse he's gallopin' around on! Dammit, by the way he orders everybody around, you'd think *he* was a duke himself!"

Antsy, she jumped off the bed, paced in a circle for a few moments, then returned to the window. A disturbance was happening in the street below. She saw a disabled carriage, one of its wheels lying broken on the pavement. A well-dressed man stood away from the coach, waiting patiently for two men to repair the vehicle.

She squinted to see the elegant man better, her eyes

widening suddenly. "That's a dukish man, Itchie Bon! Great day Miss Agnes, I can see his flarin' nostrils from all the way up here!" Excitement rushing through her, she ran to the door, having every intention of flying downstairs to meet the man in the street. But as her hand turned the knob, she stopped. "I promised Saber," she mumbled to her dog, "that I wouldn't go through that front door."

Her shoulders slumped, and she kicked a potted plant as she ambled back to the window. "Damn you, Saber! Damn this prison I'm in, and damn that stupid promise I made to you!"

Leaning against the sill, she placed her chin in her cupped hands and studied the fancy man below. "You could probably tell me everything I want to know," she told him, her breath fogging the pane. "But there you are, down in the street, and here I am, up here lookin' at you from the damn window.

"The window," she repeated, lifting her head from her hands. "The window." Swiftly, she opened it. A brisk breeze rushed through it, blowing her curls into wild disarray. "Oh, Itchie Bon, guess what I'm gonna do!"

Tearing back to the bed, she ripped the sheets off it, and quickly tied them together before attaching them to the leg of the heavy dresser near the window. She pulled on her homemade rope, satisfied it was strong enough to hold her weight, then dropped it down the side of the house.

As she prepared to descend, she threw a sheepish look at her dog. "Well, he said I couldn't go through the front door, Itchie Bon. He didn't say a damn word about the window. It's his own fault. He should have given his royal orders in a clearer way."

It took but a minute to scale down the side of the house. When her feet hit the ground, she turned and saw the elegant man staring at her. Smiling and waving to him, she skipped across the street and stopped before him.

"I saw you from my window up there," she informed him, reaching for his hand and pumping it vigorously.

The man frowned at her window, at her, and the hand she was shaking. Pulling it away from her, he gave her his back.

Calmly, Goldie pulled a scrap of paper and a pencil

from her pocket. "Dukish folks are rude," she said, reading each word as she wrote it. She walked around him, facing him again. "Do somethin' else. I'm takin' notes, y'know."

He lifted his chin. "Are you being punished, little girl? Is that why you escaped your house by way of the window?"

Goldie stiffened. "I'm almost nineteen," she enlightened him, standing as tall and straight as she was able. "And I left the house from the window because . . . because the door's locked, and I can't find the key."

He regarded her intently. "I see," he said, rubbing his chin. "You are an American."

She lifted her paper and pencil again. "Dukish folks don't *ask* people about their heritage, they *tell* 'em," she read while scribbling. Looking back up at him, she gave him a wide smile. "Y'say I'm American, huh? Well, I reckon I am, but there's other ways of lookin' at it, y'know. On my daddy's side I'm English and Scottish. On Mama's side I'm Polish and Switzerlandian."

"Switzerlandian?" He frowned again. "I believe the word is *Swiss.*"

"All right, *Swiss.* And Mama said her family always suspected that an Oriental slipped in somewhere along the line. If that's true, I wish I could have inherited his or her slanted eyes. Don't you think slanted eyes are purty? If I had slanted eyes, I wouldn't be so upset with my gold ones. I'm kinda gettin' used to 'em though. Saber says they're like dancin' coins. Anyway, I'm part English, like I already told you. So in a way you and I are countrymen."

The man stared down at her for a long moment before clearing his throat. "Yes, well, how may I help you? You climbed out of a second-story window to be with me. Considering your effort, I assume there is a reason why you wanted to see me?"

"Are you a dukish man?" she blurted, holding her breath while waiting for his answer.

"I beg your pardon?"

"A dukish man. You know—somebody like a duke. Maybe an earl? A baron? A knight? Does Queen Vicky really knight folks by puttin' a sword on their shoulders? Mildred Fickle said she did. I always wondered what would happen if Queen Vicky tripped and accidentally stabbed the man instead of knightin' him. What would happen if she—''

''Young lady, it is highly improper to call Her Majesty by such an indecent name. I realize you are an American, and as such you do not know any better. But you would do well to remember in the future.''

''Sorry,'' she mumbled, making a mental note to remember not to nickname royal people. ''Do you know Majesty Victoria?''

''Her Majesty the Queen,'' he corrected her.

Goldie wrinkled her nose. ''Well, do you know her?''

''As a matter of fact, I have the Queen's ear.''

Goldie's eyes widened. She took a step backward. ''Do you have it with you?'' she asked incredulously. ''I've never seen an ear off somebody's head before. How'd she lose it? Did she fall on her sword while knightin' somebody? Why do you have it? Did she give it—''

''My word, miss! That is not what I meant at all! And for you to suggest that Her Majesty cut off her ear—Why, I don't believe I've ever heard anything as preposterous in all my life!''

''But you said—''

''I merely meant that Her Majesty attaches great importance to my opinion. To have the Queen's ear is not an expression to be taken literally. Now, if you will excuse me, I have had quite enough of this witter, thank you very much.''

''Witter?'' Goldie lifted her pencil again. ''What's that?''

''Wittering, miss, is what you have a great talent for. It is pointless chatter.''

''Witter,'' Goldie murmured, writing the word. ''Do all dukish folks say that, or just you?''

He began to walk away.

''Wait!'' she called, running after him. ''Just answer a few more questions for me, and I'll—''

''What exactly is it you want from me? During the past ten minutes, you have spoken to me about lineage, slanted eyes, Mildred Fickle, and accidental stabbings. Now I ask you, miss, what do those things have to do with me?''

"I don't reckon they have anything to do with you. I just got off on those subjects. It's fun to go off on tangents and see where you end up. Haven't you ever done that?''

"I believe I have done so today, have I not? Really, miss, I must be going—''

"What did you have for breakfast this mornin'? One of the things I don't know too much about is what dukish folks like to eat.''

He sighed deeply, but complied. "Kidneys in cream sauce, a bit of mutton, bread, almond pudding, and tea.''

She grimaced. "Saber's all the time eatin' kidneys too. He's always tryin' to get me to eat 'em with him, but me, I don't eat guts. Can't see 'em, can't eat 'em. I like eggs and grits for breakfast.''

He sniffed haughtily, his nostrils flaring. "Young lady, I have never thought of kidneys as . . . *guts*. The very idea is revolting.''

"Then why do you eat 'em?''

"I assure you I will think twice before eating them again. You have spoiled for me what I once considered a fine meal.''

"Grits are better anyway. Eat those instead. If you could have anything you wanted to eat, what would it be?''

The man glanced at his carriage, saw that it would be a few more minutes before he could escape inside it, and decided to make the best of his absurd situation. He looked back down at Goldie. "Without a doubt, it would be eel pie. I confess to having a terrible weakness for it, and often overindulge.''

Goldie shuddered visibly. "Great day Miss Agnes.''

"Is there something wrong with eel pie? Surely you don't consider eels to be . . . *guts*, do you?''

"Well, no, but—Look, mister, I already spoiled kidneys for you. I don't want to spoil your pleasure with eels too.''

"Nothing you say could spoil eel pie for me.''

She took his statement as a dare. "They're slimy. May as well eat worms. Y'know, mister, I'm purty sure you're dukish. You flare and wheeze better'n I ever saw anybody do it before. And you've got a real nice wiggle to your walk. But you could be even more dukish if you could manage to talk like Shakespeare. A cane and a white wig wouldn't hurt either. Didn't anybody ever tell you about those things?''

''A wiggle?'' He closed his eyes for a moment, struggling for composure. When he opened them again, he saw his coach was ready, the footman waiting beside the door. ''Miss, it has been a . . . an experience meeting you. The best of luck to you in all your endeavors—whatever they may be.''

''Just one more question. What's your name?''

He took her paper and pencil from her and jotted down his name. ''Good day.'' With that, he walked to his carriage.

Goldie waved as it rumbled down the street.

Saber's mind was still on his meeting with Tyler Escott when the coach halted in front of the house. Looking out, he saw a streamer of knotted sheets hanging from Goldie's bedroom window. His first notion was that she'd washed them and hung them out to dry. But upon remembering that the house was full of servants, he discarded that assumption and became immediately angered when a second conclusion came to mind. He jumped out of the carriage and raced up the steps of the house. In the few seconds it took him to reach the front door, his anger had catapulted to fury.

''Saber!'' Goldie called from across the street. She raced to the house, her curls flopping as she bounded up the steps. ''See that carriage goin' down the street?'' she asked, pointing to it. ''There's a dukish man inside it, and I met and talked to him! He—''

Saber took her by her shoulders. ''What in heaven's name is that?'' he demanded, motioning toward the sheets.

She waited to feel the hurt his anger would surely cause. It didn't come. Instead, she felt flippancy. ''It looks like a homemade rope to me.''

''And what, may I ask, is it doing there?'' He clenched his jaw.

''Hangin' out the window and flutterin' in the breeze.'' She noticed his jaw moving. ''Saber, are you eatin'—''

"Goldie—" He broke off when Bennett, the butler, opened the door.

"Mr. West—Miss Mae!" Bennett exclaimed, his brow creased in confusion. "How did you—"

Goldie tossed him a bright grin. "I bet you're wonderin' what I'm doin' out here, aren't you, Bennett?"

"Bennett is not the only one," Saber muttered, urging her inside. For the sake of the servants, several of whom were spying from various corners, he smiled and led Goldie upstairs. Once in her room, he marched straight to her window and pulled in the rope. "Explain this, Goldie."

"I think you already know everything you're askin'," she replied, tossing her hair off her shoulders.

"You left the house. After I *told* you to—"

"You said I couldn't go through the front door. You didn't say a damn word about leavin' through the window."

He threw the sheets down and rammed his fingers through his hair. "Where did you go? You didn't, God forbid, return to the East End, did you?"

"No, but if I'd wanted to, I would have."

He stared at her. This was another glimpse of the new Goldie, he realized. One who not only stood up to him and bore his anger, but dared to disobey him as well. And as much as he wanted to stay mad at her, he couldn't. She was wonderful this way, he decided. He loved seeing her look at him with such stubborn confidence in her beautiful eyes.

Still, he could not allow her to come and go as she pleased. It was simply too dangerous. He crossed to her, enfolding her in his arms. "The East End is a dangerous place, Goldie. All of London is full of perils. I'm only worried about your safety. If something happened to you while you're in my care . . . God, poppet, I can't even think about it."

His gentle voice and sweet words touched her deeply. A tender feeling swept through her. She hugged him to her, inhaling the scent of sandalwood that clung to his clothes. "I'm sorry for leavin' the house, Saber. Really I am. I'm not usually this much trouble. But this duke stuff is so important to me that I just can't calm myself down over it. And when I saw the dukish man in the street, I just had to talk to him. I was only outside for about fifteen minutes before you got here. Daddy's honor, I'll try not to worry you like that again.''

He didn't miss the fact that she swore only to *try*. Smiling, he buried his face in her wind-blown curls, feeling them tickle his nose.

''You're right to eat kidneys, y'know,'' Goldie informed him. ''Lord only knows how you can choke 'em down, but dukish folks eat 'em, Saber. And you might try bein' a little rude every now and then too. The man I met today started out bein' an ill-box. He came around after a while, but he never did fall all over himself tryin' to be nice to me. Anyway, eat eel pie sometime too. And talk about the Queen's ear. The dukish fella has it, y'know. And in case you don't know, that isn't a literal expression. It only means that the Queen listens to his opinions and usually thinks they're right.''

''He has the Queen's ear?'' Saber's mouth fell open. Many moments passed before he could properly phrase the question that exploded into his mind. ''Goldie—Who— He—What was the man's name? Did you find out who he was?''

She dug into her pocket, withdrawing her paper. ''He wrote it down on here.''

Saber took it from her, examining it closely. His hand shook when he saw the name. ''Oh, God.'' He sat down upon the dressing-table stool and glanced at the name again. His only consolation was that the gentleman Goldie had met presented absolutely no danger to her.

He looked up at her, almost afraid to ask her what she'd said to the man. After all, he mused miserably, she could take the most innocent of subjects and turn them inside out before her listener had time to understand a word! ''What did you talk about with the man, Goldie?''

''Oh, lots of things. Grits, stabbings, guts—''

''Guts?'' Saber covered his face with his hands and looked at her through his fingers. ''You talked about guts with Lord John Russell.''

''So? Who the hell's Lord John Russell?''

''The Prime Minister of Britain.''

# Chapter 14

Asa looked up from the pile of dust on the stone floor of the cottage and saw Big was busy hanging curtains at the window by the door. Quietly, he lifted the small throw rug by the hearth, and swept the dirt under it.

"I know what you did, Asa," Big announced, without ever turning around. "Now you'll have to beat the rug as well as sweep the dust outside."

Asa cracked the broom over his knee. "I ain't no damn maid, Big!"

"Nevertheless, you cannot leave the dirt under the rug. You don't want Goldie to see it, do you?"

Asa shuddered with heartache, frustration, and his need for a whiskey. "No. No, I don't want her to see it."

"What do you think Goldie will say about the curtains we made?" Big asked, stepping back to examine them. "They cover the cracks in the panes nicely, don't you think? For two men who have never held needles, I don't think we did too badly. They—"

"My hands are shakin' again. Big—Big, I need a drink. You don't understand how hard it is."

Big turned immediately, his heart going out to the suffering man. "Asa, no. Don't. Think of how proud of you Goldie will be when she gets home. Think of how happy it'll make her to know you've given up drinking. And don't forget how much better a few of the villagers have been treating you since you've cleaned yourself up. Granted, they're still wary, but they're coming around. That will mean the world to Goldie."

Asa clenched his huge fists to keep them from trembling. Thoughts of Goldie tumbled through his mind. He ambled to her cot, picking up the rag doll he'd bought her years ago. Smoothing his quaking hand over the doll's stained face, he sighed deeply. "This is the only thing I've ever give her. Besides heartache. I've give her plenty of that."

Big joined Asa at the cot. "Asa, I couldn't believe it when I got here and saw the change in you. If your efforts to straighten yourself out don't prove your love for her, I don't know what does. How can you say you've never given her anything? One of her many dreams was for you to give up drinking. Well, you're giving it to her now."

Tears filled Asa's bleary eyes. "I chopped down her tree."

Big frowned in confusion. "You did a lot of things, Asa. The point is that you're trying to change and—"

"I ain't been without her since the day we laid her mama and daddy to rest. She's been taggin' along in my shadow for some twelve years, Big. I never paid much attention to—I—She—I didn't understand how much she meant to me until I stayed sober long enough to realize I didn't have her no more. God Almighty, Big, she had so many dreams. She'd tell 'em to me sometimes, but I never listened real good. I—I didn't make none of her dreams come true for her. I've given the girl nothin' but tears and problems. Now she's done grown up on me, and I ain't never gonna get another chance to be with the little girl she used to be."

"She's still that girl," Big assured him. "One minute she's an adult, and the next she's just as young as she always was. I've often thought she presents the best of both worlds. And believe you me, Asa, she still has her dreams."

Asa nodded and crossed the small room to stand in front of the fireplace. "It was her note that done it to me, Big. The day y'all left, I woke up and found it layin' by my whiskey bottle. She—She figured I'd find it there. She wrote that she'd gone to fetch the duke. Said for me not to worry. Said everything would work out. Said . . . said she loved me and that she'd miss me. She even left money for me and told me to use it for food. I—Big, I spent every damn coin on drink.

"Two nights later, I was layin' in my bed sober as all get-out, and hungrier'n hell. I started thinkin' about them nice things she wrote in her letter. I laid there, and it all of a sudden come to me that Goldie had laid in bed many a time with an empty belly, too. Sometimes, Big . . . sometimes I didn't feed her good. I was always gone, y'see. In the bars or wenchin'. Makin' trouble, fightin'. And Goldie? She was alone. In the darkness of whatever shack I stuck her in. Her only company was this doll. And I even laid into her for naggin' me to buy the damn thing for her.

"A doll," he groaned, leaning his head against the mantel. "Whatever love this doll give her, it was the only affection she got, Big. I don't think it was much because she used to cry into her pillow at night. It made me so damn mad! I'd yell at her to shut her mouth, but she only cried harder. Once . . . God Almighty, Big, once I kicked her out of the house for sobbin'. She slept on the porch step. When I got up in the mornin', there was snow all over her. She was seven then. Only seven years old. I picked her up from the step and said I was sorry. I was always apologizin' when I was sober, but it was too late by then. I held her in my arms, wiped the snow off her red cheeks, and I knew in my soul she was gonna hit me for doin' what I did. But she didn't. Big, she . . . she *hugged* me!"

He began to sob, his huge shoulders shaking. "I ain't never give her nothin'! All I ever done is holler at her and tell her how worthless she was! Over and over again! Not a day passed when I didn't tell her what a no-account bother she was to me! I even told her she was so bad that she didn't *deserve* better treatment'n what she got!"

"But Asa—"

"I never knew what to do with her! She needed so much, but I didn't know how to give it to her. I didn't know what little girls—It'd make me so damn frustrated that sometimes I'd yell at her just so I wouldn't have to figure out how to act with her. Then I'd start drinkin'. Once I was drunk, I didn't care.

"Goldie," he continued, tears still coming, "she cooked, cleaned, and mended for me. She saw to it that I was warm in the winter. She even prayed for me. She did. I heard her at it one night. And now she's gone. Maybe I won't ever see her purty little face again. Maybe—"

"Asa—"

"And I didn't ever even get her the damn curtains she wanted for so long! I—"

"But we did make her curtains!" Big exclaimed, rushing to the hearth to try and soothe the tortured man. "Asa, we worked for days on them! Goldie will love—"

"But they ain't her *dream* curtains, Big! They ain't pink and white gingham!" Asa wailed, his face still buried in the vee of his arm, his tears wetting his shirtsleeve. "And that white picket fence she wanted—I kept promisin' and promisin' I'd find us a house with a fence like that. I never did. I wouldn't even let her have the cats she kept tellin' me she wanted. And I let her bird go, too! I didn't make a single one of her dreams come true! And now . . . Now she needs me more'n ever, and I ain't with her. Maybe I won't ever be with her again!"

Big reached up, trying to put his little arm around Asa's thick waist. He considered telling him about Saber, but decided against it. If Asa should slip back into his old ways and begin drinking, all of Goldie's efforts would be for naught. "I told you I left her in a very nice boardinghouse," he lied. "She has plenty of money, and knows exactly what she has to do to find the duke. She's fine. Otherwise I never would have left her there alone. You'll see. She'll be along real soon, the duke in tow."

"Maybe I should go find her. Maybe she needs me to—"

"No, Asa. You have an honest job at the blacksmith's now. You'll lose it if you go to London. Surely you want Goldie to come home and see you working. And what if she should arrive and you aren't here?"

Asa's shoulders slumped. "You had to leave her because of me. Because you both knew I needed someone to see to me. Me, a grown man, needin' a guardian, and Goldie, a young girl, alone in London." He held Goldie's doll to his heart, huge tears still coursing down his cheeks. "Maybe she ain't in that boardin'house no more. Maybe she got throwed out. Maybe she's in the streets, hungry. Cold. Wet. Maybe she's scared, Big. God, I hope it ain't thunderin' in London. She used to be so afraid of thunder, and I—I never did let her sleep with me.''

"Asa—"

"Alone in that great big dangerous city,'' Asa sobbed. "With nobody to watch over her. Nobody to tell her how purty and good she is. God Almighty, Big, with nobody to care about her.''

Big remembered Saber and smiled. "With no one to care about her? Well now, Asa, I wouldn't say that. I wouldn't say that at all.''


Tyler Escott looked up from his notes, glancing around Marion Tremayne's study. He knew the time had come to reveal his discoveries. But he hesitated and stared at the gleaming surface of his client's desk. It was his experience that members of the aristocracy, high-strung as they were, did not accept bad news well. More often than not they turned hysterical.

Saber heard the clock strike half past midnight, and ran his fingers through his hair. "Tyler, we've been at this for hours already. You've shown me every bit of the evidence that Hutchins and Doyle have been stealing from me, and you've informed me that Doyle seems to have disappeared from the face of the earth. But there's much more you've yet to say, and I really must insist that you do so now. Have you been able to read the diaries, or haven't you?''

"I have. I dampened the diary pages slightly and carefully, held them up to a flame, and read them through a magnifying glass. I still couldn't make out everything, but many of the words that were difficult to read before became clearer. What I'm about to tell you is tangled at best, but it does give me something to go on.''

Saber nodded.

Tyler felt confused at his client's composure. The man was almost aloof. "Very well.'' Taking a deep breath, he looked down at the papers he held. "Dane Hutchins and Dora Mashburn are lovers, and have been for the past six years. Hutchins has been living in your manor house. When Angelica arrived at Ravenhurst, Hutchins remained

in the mansion with her. He treated her as though she were
a queen, going out of his way to please her in every way.
He procured rose bushes, thanked her profusely for planting them, and had Dora assist her. Dora ruined several of
them, causing Dane to fly into a rage. Angelica expressed
her desire to redecorate the master bedroom in green and
gold. Dora argued that crimson and white were more to
her liking. Della and Angelica laughed at Dora's impu-
dence. Angelica and Dora had a bitter quarrel concerning
the ring. Angelica forbade Dora to ever enter the mansion
again. Angelica purchased paper and writing utensils.
William Doyle arrived. The villagers held a birthday party.
The traveler drowned. Angelica fell down the staircase.''

When Tyler finished he looked up at his client, relieved
when he saw no evidence of hysteria. ''The mention of
the paper and writing utensils leads me to believe Angelica
might have tried to write to you. If she did, perhaps the
letter was intercepted. But as you can see, there are still
many unanswered questions, Your Grace. I can't understand what happened to the ring. The birthday party
baffles me, as does the traveler who drowned.''

Saber sat silently for many long moments. ''What questions *have* you answered?''

Reassured that his client was not going to lose his wits
over the matter, Tyler decided to give it to him straight.
He stood, placed his hands on the desk, and leaned forward. ''Bear in mind that many of the diary pages are lost
to us forever. But by going with what I have, I think
Hutchins believes he's the duke. He—''

''The duke? What leads you to conclude that?''

''He didn't move out of your house when Angelica arrived. And as if the grounds belonged to him, he *thanked*
her for planting the roses. I really don't believe I'm wrong
in saying he thinks he's lord of the estate. I won't say
he thinks he's Lord Tremayne, though. Instinct tells me he
considers himself Lord Hutchins. If that's true, then the
man is insane, and I don't think I have to tell you how
dangerous a madman is. Especially an enraged one, which
is what I believe Dane was when Angelica spurned his
attentions. In his twisted mind, I think he saw her as *his*
fiancée, though I am sure she showed him the utmost dis-

dain. She was in love with *you,* and I cannot see her responding to your middle-aged and overconfident estate manager in any way, shape, or form.

"Then there's Dora Mashburn," Tyler continued. "Quite a cheeky little thing to actually argue with Angelica, the future Duchess of Ravenhurst, about what colors to do the bedroom in. Don't you agree? Unless of course Dora herself wanted to be the duchess. She—"

"That's ridiculous. How could she have thought such a thing possible?"

"You must remember she was sleeping with Hutchins, who considers himself the duke. It's possible that since Dora shared his bed, she had high hopes that he would marry her. She's a naive, ignorant girl. Hutchins' position of authority at the estate would be bound to impress her. And when he began showing amorous interest in her, surely it flattered her beyond words. She was a mere maid from the village! So if Hutchins pretends to be a duke, why wouldn't she want to be his pretend duchess? Enter Angelica, who was to be the *real* duchess. Dora sees how attentive Hutchins is toward Angelica. Hutchins even became infuriated with Dora when she spoiled Angelica's roses. Dora was more than likely livid with both anger and jealousy. And a jealous woman is a dangerous one.

"And then there's Doyle," Tyler went on. "It's not clear exactly what day he arrived, but Della's writings concerning him fall close to the day Angelica died. So let us presume he got there the day of her death or very shortly before. He arrives at Ravenhurst, sees Angelica, and knows she will reveal his involvement with Hutchins to you as soon as she gets back to London. Knowing you as well as he does, he doesn't have to *wonder* what you will do to him upon learning of his betrayal. He *knows.* He is terrified. And—"

"A man terrified for his own welfare is a dangerous one," Saber finished for him. "You are suggesting that Angelica was murdered."

Tyler was again taken aback by his client's control. "Dora, Hutchins, and Doyle all had sufficient motive."

Resisting all emotion, Saber made a steeple of his fingers, his chin resting upon it. He sat still, silent, and numb.

Tyler cleared his throat. "Your Grace, there's something I don't understand about Angelica's trip to Ravenhurst. In one passage, Della wrote that a woman accompanied Angelica to the estate, and that the woman slept almost around the clock. There was no further mention of her. Who was Angelica's companion?"

Saber came out from behind the desk, shaking his head. "Mrs. Eliza Hatworth. Angelica's parents died when she was a little girl. She had no other family and was raised by her nanny, Mrs. Hatworth, who was already elderly when Angelica was born. When Angelica left for Ravenhurst, Mrs. Hatworth had to have been close to seventy years old. Due to her age, she slept constantly. I tried to induce Angelica to take a younger companion, but she refused. Angelica—She was very stubborn."

Tyler jotted down a few notes. "What did Mrs. Hatworth have to tell you when she arrived in London with Angelica's body?"

Saber rubbed the back of his neck. "She spoke highly of Hutchins, saying he'd taken full responsibility for handling the transportation of Angelica's body. I recall being more than satisfied with her glowing reports of him."

"She said nothing at all about Dora or William Doyle? Nothing about the condition of the estate?"

"Nothing. I doubt very seriously she saw or heard anything that would be of aid to us, Tyler. As you said, the woman was rarely awake."

"Perhaps I could speak to her."

"She died two years ago."

Sighing, Tyler rose. "I'm leaving for Ravenhurst tomorrow with a few of my men. We'll go disguised as itinerant workers. I'm hopeful that Hutchins will hire us. But even if he doesn't, we'll be staying in Hallensham, watching Hutchins and Dora, and questioning the villagers."

Saber nodded. "And Doyle?"

"The rest of my men will continue watching for his return to London. They know where they can find me and will inform me immediately if he arrives in my absence.

I've every detective I employ on this case, Your Grace, and I'm accepting no other clients until it is solved.''

Saber escorted the detective to the front door. Upon opening it, he saw rain pounding the porch, lightning crisscrossing the sky. "Thank you for coming by.''

Tyler studied him intently. "Lord Tremayne, are you all right? I must confess I was hesitant to tell you all the information I'd discovered. I thought you would—Forgive me, but I expected—''

"For me to become enraged?'' Saber took a gulp of the chilled, wet air. "She's been gone for five years already, Tyler. If indeed she was murdered, I want her killer brought to justice, of course. But rage on my part won't bring about those ends. Nor will it bring her back to life.''

Tyler nodded, feeling the utmost respect for Marion Tremayne. "Good night, Your Lordship.''

When the investigator was gone, Saber closed the door, pressed his forehead against it, and shut his eyes. Thoughts of Angelica filled his mind. "Angelica,'' he whispered, his lips moving upon the door. He waited for the familiar grief to seize him. He'd resisted it earlier, but now felt the need to release it. He knew exactly how it would feel when it came. It would start in the deepest part of him, sending pain shooting through his entire body. His chest would ache. His throat would constrict. His head would begin to pound. He waited in morbid apprehension for it all to begin.

But it didn't. Suddenly he remembered several other recent occasions when it hadn't come. Curious over this, he tried bringing Angelica's beautiful image to his mind, certain that would free his imprisoned agony. He recalled her thick chestnut hair and the way it fell in long waves down her back. He recollected her flawless ivory skin, her huge brandy eyes, her generous mouth, and her tall, curvaceous form.

But try as he did, he couldn't seem to put those memories together. They remained separate from each other, fragmented, refusing to merge into a whole likeness.

Determined to see her again, he concentrated with all the power he possessed. His eyes still tightly closed, a measure of relief came to him when a face drifted slowly to mind.

But the girl he pictured had freckles peppering her tiny, heart-shaped face. Her hair was not rich brown, but the color of sunshine. It didn't fall down her back in long waves. Instead, it was a chaotic mass of thick curls. Her mouth was small and pink, and her eyes were two golden orbs that dazzled him with the way they danced for him.

"Goldie." He opened his eyes, turned toward the staircase, and felt a profound need to be with her tonight. He'd been so involved with Tyler Escott lately that he couldn't even remember the last time he'd held Goldie in his arms.

Anticipation rolled through him. He knew well what the sight of her would do for him. Her smile was like a bright flame. When it flickered, all darkness went away. Her giggle was the sound of happiness, wafting through heavy, dismal silence, and her words, her stories . . . Their very outrageousness chased away gloom.

Just thinking about her lifted his spirits, and before he even realized what he was doing, he was bounding up the steps, heading for her bedroom.

He didn't bother to knock, but opened the door and stepped inside. His need changed to a powerful desire when he saw her.

Her only covering was the dim firelight that blanketed her with its warm, burnished glow. The sight reminded him of the day he'd found her swathed in lace. He was so enchanted with the beautiful vision before him, so completely taken with her bare loveliness, a long moment passed before he managed to make his legs work well enough to take him to her bed.

"Goldie," he whispered. Her nearness soothed him instantly. Bending, he smoothed kisses down her arm. He turned her hand over, pressing his lips gently to her inner wrist and savoring the feel of her silken skin. "My little person—No, my little *poppet* called Goldie."

She awoke with a start. Disoriented, she couldn't understand where she was, who the man above her was, or what he was doing to her. Thunder suddenly crashed through the room, bringing back little-girl fears. "Uncle

Asa!'' she screamed, tears appearing. ''Uncle Asa, let me sleep with you! Please! Uncle—''

''Goldie,'' Saber cooed, reaching for her, and enfolding her in his arms. He sat on her bed, holding her close to his chest. ''It's only thunder, poppet. You're safe. Safe with me.''

And she would remain safe for as long as she was with him, he vowed, smoothing her hair. He could do nothing at all for Angelica, and knew in his heart he'd finally accepted her death. Whether it had been accidental or plotted didn't matter. She was gone, and he'd buried her, just as he had his parents.

But Goldie was alive. She was here. In his arms. He looked down at her, almost groaning as he beheld the sight of her unveiled beauty. There was nothing but air between her bare splendor and his smoldering gaze. He burned for her with a fire so real to him, he felt he could touch the flames. ''Goldie, I—God, you're so beautiful.''

She blinked away her tears and saw him. ''Uncle . . . Saber?''

''I've been called many things, but never *Uncle Saber.*'' He grinned, marveling over the fact that a smile came so easily to his lips despite what he'd learned tonight. It was yet further proof that his mourning was indeed over.

''Saber, what—''

''You were frightened,'' he explained softly, brushing curls from her eyes. ''But it's only thunder.''

''Saber—'' Her words were drowned out by a second tremendous clap of thunder. The explosion was so powerful it shook the bed. ''Sleep with me, Saber,'' she begged, clutching his arms. ''I—The thunder. I thought I was over bein' afraid, but—It's so *loud!* Louder'n American thunder, and I—''

''Goldie—''

''Please sleep with—''

''I—''

''Saber—''

''Yes, Goldie,'' he murmured directly into her ear. ''Yes, poppet.'' Still holding her in his arms, he lay down with her, pulling her as close to his body as he could.

''I'm cold, Saber.'' She curled herself into a ball.

"You kicked all your covers off." He reached for the blankets, drawing them over both himself and her.

She caught his hand. "But—You still have all your clothes on. Even your shoes."

He raised an obsidian brow. "Yes. I do."

Taking the covers away from him, she pulled her gaze down the long length of him. His body was so big, she mused, the chill she'd felt earlier fading quickly. Her own body was so tiny next to his.

*Her own body,* she repeated silently, looking at herself. She waited for the familiar trepidation to fill her. She knew how it would begin. Her cheeks would warm, her hands would tremble. Shame over her imperfect form would flood her. She waited in tense apprehension for it to all begin.

But it didn't. She remembered the night in the coach when Saber had touched her so intimately. She'd felt no fear then either. Confused, she looked down at her body again, reminding herself how unfeminine, how lacking it was.

But try as she did, she could summon no embarrassment. Not even a hint of unease. Instead, she recalled sweet words. *Peaches, Goldie. See how perfectly they fit into my palms. You are so delicate. Your daintiness is not a thing to ridicule. It's a thing to prize.*

As Saber's words sang through her, a gentle peace settled over her. Smiling, she raised her eyes, her gaze caressing every part of his face. "I'm naked," she announced, as if he were unaware of that fact.

"So you are." He saw satisfaction in her smile, and was confused by it. He'd been waiting for her to become embarrassed. Instead, she seemed proud of herself. His heart skipped a beat when he understood the reason for her pride. "You're not ashamed for me to see your body anymore, are you, Goldie?"

She shook her head. "I'm—I'm little, but I'm not ugly."

Emotion filled his throat. It was a moment before his voice found a way past it. "You've no idea how glad it makes me to hear you say that."

"You taught it to me. You made me believe it."

He could think of no words to tell her, and remained silent as her sweet compliment eased through him.

"And I'm not afraid either."

"Of me, or the thunder?" he teased.

"Neither." Tentatively, she laid her hand on his cheek. "I've never been in bed naked with a man before."

"Surely you jest." He tugged on a flaxen ringlet.

"No. Daddy's honor."

His hand cupped the gentle swell of her smooth hip. "Why aren't you afraid?"

"I've had time to think it over. The thunder's not really all that loud."

His grin broadened. "Goldie," he said, a feigned note of warning in his voice.

She giggled. "Oh, y'mean why aren't I afraid of *you?*"

"Is there another man in this room to fear?"

"There's just you and the man I keep in the closet."

Before he could catch himself, Saber glared at the closet. When he realized what he was doing, he laughed out loud.

But his laughter faded instantly when he saw the expression in Goldie's eyes. They reflected the luster of unseasoned passion. Innocent desire.

She wanted him.

The knowledge made him wild with need for her. Every fiber of him yearned to make her his, and it was only with great effort that he managed not to rip off his clothes and ravish her.

Inhaling raggedly, he tore his gaze from her and studied the canopy. He had to get control of himself. Goldie wasn't some experienced courtesan. He refused to take her as though she were.

*Take her.* He hated the way that sounded. Like she was something to be grabbed and stolen. You didn't just *take* something so precious.

You *received* it, he decided. With great patience, you *waited* for it to come into your keeping. And when it did, you treated it with profound reverence.

"Saber, what are you thinkin' about? Why are you starin' at the canopy?"

He raised his brow again. "Are you mad at me?" he asked slyly.

"Mad?" she repeated, baffled. "Why would I be mad at you?"

He watched her tenderly, waiting for her to realize the significance of her own question. He knew she had when her face softened and a sheepish grin appeared on her mouth. "Now you understand why I was always confused when you asked me that same question, Goldie. There are situations when anger is appropriate. On other occasions mere irritation is quite sufficient. And then there are times when anything remotely related to ire is unjustifiable. As of late, I've been seeing signs that tell me you are beginning to comprehend that. I hope you never forget it."

"I won't," she whispered, mesmerized by the softness in his eyes.

He decided to take the conversation one step further. "I know how you've been criticized and ridiculed," he began, his hand still caressing her hip. "I've told you what I think about your 'devil eyes,' your 'yellow bush hair,' your 'unripened figs,' and your 'disease-like freckles.' Now Goldie, let me tell you what I think about the beauty *inside* you."

He turned to his side, so he was face-to-face with her. "Your courage impresses me beyond words. You've dealt with much heartache in your life. Much—"

"Saber," she said uneasily, not wanting to be reminded of things that made her ache. "Don't—"

"Please, Goldie." Before she could argue further, he touched his lips to hers, kissing her more gently than he ever had before.

Mellow pleasure drifted through her. His tender kiss drew all anxiety from her heart. "Tell me."

His lips still very close to hers, he put his arm around her shoulders, almost groaning when her breasts met his chest. "Your life with your uncle has been a chain of unfulfilled dreams. Because of that, you find trusting a difficult thing to do. You're wary. It's like you have an invisible shell, and when you feel threatened, you crawl inside it.

"But in spite of it all, you continue dreaming," he proceeded softly, his hand sweeping into her hair. "Even when you have little hope of attaining your dreams, you don't let them go. Take your home in Hallensham. Think of your extraordinary efforts to keep it! Surely you know—deep down—that the odds are against you. That—"

"But you're gonna be the duke, Saber."

Like the lightning splitting the sky outside, guilt stabbed into him. He shifted uncomfortably, wondering what she would think of him when he told her he would not be returning to Ravenhurst with her.

"Saber? You all of a sudden look sad. What's the matter?"

"I—Nothing. It's nothing, poppet." He kissed the tip of her nose, smiling at her. "Goldie, I'm speaking about the unshakable determination you have. It stands you in good stead. And through all the bad times in your life, you've retained an innocence that I find beautiful and unique. Goldie . . . sweet poppet, though you are tiny in stature, you are quite the biggest woman I've ever had the extreme good fortune to know."

"Big?" she asked, wondering what he meant by that.

"Your heart is huge. So tremendous, I cannot understand how it fits within your breast. I've heard the expression 'Good things come in small packages.' After knowing you, I realize the truth of it. How you manage to hold such an abundance of wonderful things inside you is quite beyond me."

Gazing up into his beautiful eyes, she felt contentment fill her. And the longer she concentrated on the sweet things he'd told her, the more her pleasure grew; soon it became joy so great it brought tears to her eyes. "Oh, Saber," she sniffled, her hands cupping his cheeks, "no one has *ever* said such nice, meanin'ful things to me. It doesn't even matter that they aren't true. It doesn't—"

"But they *are* true. Believe them, Goldie. Believe each and every one of them, and remember them always."

The look of pure awe in her eyes seized his heart. God, she needed so badly for someone to cherish her. Someone other than Big, whom she considered family. Someone who did not feel obligated to tell her loving things, as family members often did.

She needed a man to love her. A man who would treasure everything about her. A man who would devote his entire life to making all her many dreams come true.

His guilt grew, increasing to such an extent that he felt poisoned with it. He couldn't love her, and he had no intention of allowing their relationship to go that far. And yet he was courting her in every true sense of the word. Dammit, he was in *bed* with her!

He sat straight up. Staring at the wall, he rammed his fingers through his hair. It wasn't fair, he knew. Wasn't fair to either of them. But dammit, what was he to do? He couldn't resist her. Couldn't for the life of him figure out how to end what was between them, though he knew it would come to naught.

What was the way? he demanded silently. What in heaven's name was he to do?

"Goldie," he said, refusing to look at her, "I—I should never have come tonight. I woke you up. You were sleeping so soundly. I'm sorry. I'll leave you now so—"

"But I don't want you to leave, Saber. I want you to stay." She sat up beside him, turning his face to hers. "You said you'd sleep with me."

"But—"

"You don't *want* to stay with me, do you?"

He saw the glint of pain in her eyes, and remembered how profoundly sensitive she was. Considering how much of herself she'd freely given him tonight, it almost killed him to see the hurt he was causing her now. She was nigh to trusting him. He knew if he wounded her now, that trust would disappear.

But leaving her bedroom was the biggest favor he could ever do her! Dear God, what was the way? he asked himself again.

"Goldie, yes," he said, his voice strangled. "I *do* want to stay with you." *But I'm so afraid of hurting you.*

His answer filled her with happiness. She curled her arms around his waist, leaning into him. Timidly, she pressed light kisses to his shoulder, enjoying the feel of muscle beneath her mouth, the scent of sandalwood that floated around her. "Then stay. Because if you go, I'll be sad. Don't make me sad tonight, Saber. Stay the night, and hold me in your arms."

*Don't make me sad tonight.* Her plea echoed in his mind. Perhaps the sadness would come. Perhaps it was inevitable for them both. But tonight . . . it didn't have to happen tonight.

A moan escaped him as he pulled her into his arms. His lips met hers in a deep kiss so full of passion it made him shake. But it wasn't her physical surrender that he craved.

It was Goldie herself he wanted. From head to toe, inside and out . . . he wanted all of her, and he wanted it with a desperation he could find no will to fight.

As Saber laid her back down on the mattress, Goldie realized she yearned for whatever he would give her tonight. Whatever special thing he did to her, whatever wonderful words he told her . . . she wanted it all. All of *him*.

The thought brought her gaze to the bit of his chest she could see. With trembling fingers, she touched the top button of his shirt.

And undid it.

She continued until the shirt was opened completely, then slid her hand across the hard, warm expanse of his bare chest. The feel of his skin was so wonderful, her breath caught in her throat.

Saber began to chuckle. In spite of the sensuality of the moment, he simply could not keep from laughing. "Goldie, I'm terribly ticklish," he informed her, trying to roll away from her hand.

She smiled, feeling mischief take hold of her. Quickly, she reached toward him again, her fingers searching for his most vulnerable spots. She soon found they included his lower abdomen and the area around his collarbone. Deftly and delightedly, she concentrated her attentions there.

Saber howled, his laughter so great he couldn't breathe. Knowing he would soon die if he didn't get some air, he curled his body into a tight ball, shielding his tickle spots from her wiggling fingers. "Goldie!"

She found a shred of mercy and ceased her torture. But no sooner had she taken her hands from him than his came at her. "Saber, don't!" she begged, her own laughter even louder than his had been.

"I haven't even touched you yet!"

Her stomach heaved with laughter. "I know. But all you have to do is *think* about ticklin' me, and I laugh!"

"Well I'm going to do more than just *think* about tickling you, poppet." One hand began kneading her inner thigh, the other waltzed up and down her rib cage, before he discovered another good spot near her belly button.

"Great day Miss Agnes!" Goldie exclaimed, struggling to breathe through her laughter. "Saber, show mercy!"

"No."

"But I showed *you* mercy!" She tried removing his hands by force, but her laughter seemed to sap all her energy, and she could do nothing but hang onto him and continue laughing.

"So you're merciful, and I'm not." He tickled her for a moment longer, then stilled his hands upon her belly, his thumbs stroking her lightly. He thought about what they were doing, tickling each other. He hadn't been tickled since he was a boy, and had forgotten how much fun it was.

Goldie panted with relief. "You don't play fair. I couldn't tickle you well because you have all your clothes on."

Desire returned to him instantly. "Shall we remedy that?" His eyes never leaving hers, he removed his shirt altogether, kicked off his shoes, and pulled his stockings off. But when he touched the fastening of his breeches and Goldie's eyes widened at his action, he left them on.

She watched in wonder as he rose to his knees and began running his hands down the sides of her torso. The feelings his touch evoked made her every nerve pulse with heat, and need, and that sweet ache he always gave her.

Her eyes fluttered closed when he leaned down and took her breast into his mouth. She heard her own soft moan when his tongue began circling her slowly. "Saber, why do we groan and make noises when we do stuff like this?"

He smiled, his kisses meandering up to her mouth. "Because it feels good."

She thought about that. "Does it feel good to you too?"

He didn't answer, but only spread more kisses over her face.

"Well, of course it doesn't feel good to you," she decided out loud. "How could it? I've never touched you the way you've touched me."

His kisses ceased. His body went rigid. Would she touch him, he wondered? In the intimate way in which he touched her? "Goldie—"

"Saber . . ." Her voice trailed away, her hand found the fastening of his breeches.

Saber clenched his teeth. God, she hadn't even done anything to him yet, and he was already on the verge of losing control! "Goldie—"

"It's all right, Saber," she said huskily, succeeding at unfastening his pants. "I'm not afraid."

"*You're* not afraid?" he asked before he could stop himself.

She dropped her hand from him, certain she was going about this all wrong. "Are *you* afraid?"

"I—*Afraid* isn't exactly the word. Goldie, I've—I've wanted this for so long, that it's hard for me to—That is to say, it's not easy to hold back—You haven't even touched me yet, and I'm already—You see, it's like you laughing before I tickled you."

"Oh," she said, frowning. "Saber, *what's* like me laughin' before you tickled me?"

He laid back down beside her, realizing a bit of explanation was in order. Frightening her was the last thing in the world he wanted to do. He searched intently for the right words. "Goldie, remember how you said it was like a sneeze?"

"A sneeze?" She felt herself blush when his meaning became clear.

He saw the color tint her cheeks and knew she understood. "Men can have that 'sneeze' too. I—Goldie, you're so beautiful, so desirable, that it's hard for me to keep from sneezing—"

He broke off, feeling laughter rumble through him again. His explanation was so absurd! *Sneezing,* of all things! "Suffice it to say, poppet, that I'm so ready for you, that it's very difficult for me—"

"I'm ready for you too, Saber," she announced, wondering what it was she was so ready for.

Her declaration nearly rendered him senseless with desire. "No. No, you're not. Not yet. But I'm going to ready you, Goldie. I'm going to do it slowly. Gently, so you won't be afraid.''

"W-when?'' she stammered.

He smiled. "Now. Right now.''

# Chapter 15

"**I**'m not afraid, Saber."

He took her at her word. As smoothly as he could, he removed the rest of his clothes, his eyes watching hers. "If you're not afraid, Goldie, why won't you look at me?"

She knew exactly what he meant, but kept her gaze directly on his face. "I—It's just that . . . Well, you said I wasn't ready. And you said you'd ready me. You said—"

"I know what I said, and part of making you ready is having you look at me. Look at me, Goldie. Look so you'll understand."

She took a quick glance, then turned her eyes away again. "You have a birthmark on your upper left thigh. It's dark brown and shaped like a diamond."

"How very observant you are. Did you happen to see anything else?"

"No. That's all." She felt as though flames were flickering through her veins.

"But there's more, Goldie."

She could no longer resist the husky invitation in his rich voice. Inch by tiny inch, her gaze traveled down the firm length of his body. When it reached his manhood, her mouth dropped open. "Great day—"

"Miss Agnes has no place in our bed tonight," he teased, picking up her hand. "And don't bring Mildred Fickle into it either. Now touch me. You've seen me, now touch me."

"But—"

"It's doesn't bite."

His ridiculous declaration put her at ease. She didn't
resist when he urged her hand toward the thick black mat
of hair and the hard staff that lay upon it.

"Goldie."

She heard the unspoken plea in his voice. Biting her
lower lip, she quickly pressed the tip of her finger to him,
then jerked her hand away. "It's hot," she blurted, glancing at her finger as if he'd set it afire. "And you didn't
sneeze." She looked up at him. "Did you?"

Despite the tremendous desire that crashed through him,
her question made him chuckle. "No. I didn't."

She noticed his eyes were filled with a look of great
need. He wanted something from her. "I—Saber, am I
supposed to make you sneeze? Because if I am, I can't. I
don't know how. But even if I did, how would I know if
you were sneezin' or not? Since I have no experience with
this, I don't see how I—"

"You'll know, Goldie."

His velvet voice made her quiver. The ache returned.
"Show me what to do to you."

He couldn't remember ever having received such a sweet
request. "Touch me. Touch me, and let's see what happens."

She swallowed hard when he lay down beside her. But
her desire to please him in the way he'd pleased her overcame anxiety. She placed her hand palm-up upon his flat,
hard belly, smoothing it downward. When the soft hair
caressed the back of her hand, her fingers curled slowly
around him.

The ache inside her deepened at the feel of him. It
seemed to her she was holding the very essence of desire.
He was rigid, yet so soft. Hot, so hot, too. He was big,
but she could find no fear of him. Instead she knew tender
emotions. He looked and felt so vulnerable, yet he trusted
her to take care with him. The thought pleased her enormously.

Gently, she moved her hand, feeling more pleasure as
he slid between her fingers and palm. And then, with her
other hand, she held the velvety pouch that lay beneath
his staff. She moved her fingers lightly upon it, around it,
and under it, her other hand continuing to run up and

down the hard length of him. So involved was she with her own exploration, her own search for understanding, that she never saw the rapture her actions gave to the man she touched.

Saber resisted the rising bliss as long as he could, but when her hand began to move faster, he knew his end was just on the horizon. Raising to a sitting position, he took her hands and held them. "Goldie, wait."

"But you said for me to touch you, and I—"

"I know, but that's enough touching me for now."

"Y'mean I wasn't doin' it right?"

A pent-up breath rushed from him. "You were doing it right. If you'd done it any more correctly, I'd have—You—Goldie, it's my turn now. Now . . . now I'll touch you."

She was more than willing for him to do just that and lay back on the bed, waiting for him to begin. When he didn't, she frowned at him. "Saber—"

"There are other ways of readying you, Goldie," he told her, lowering his face toward her hips. "Others ways of bringing you the pleasure you await."

"What . . . are they?" she asked, every bit of her yearning for him to show her.

He smiled, and gently parted her legs. Beginning at her inner thigh, he began a trail of wispy kisses that soon led him exactly where he wanted to be.

"Saber! Oh, great day Miss—You—Oh, Saber!"

He paid her surprise no mind, but only continued pleasing her in the most intimate way he'd ever done to her before.

Goldie hadn't even gotten over her astonishment at what he was doing before the ecstasy started. It grew, rolled through her, peaked, then began again. The repeated, never-ending pleasure was almost too much to bear, but when it did begin to fade, she wished it back. "Again!" she begged him as it subsided. "Saber, again!"

He lifted his head, smiling. "Greedy little thing, aren't you?"

She had the grace to blush, but felt nothing at all related to shame. On the contrary, she was anxious for whatever else he planned to do. "Have you readied me enough, or do you still have some more readyin' to do?"

He knew she was dead serious, but her question made him grin again. "God, Goldie, how much readying do you need?"

She took a moment to think. "I don't know. Actually, I don't even know what I'm gettin' readied *for.*"

"The time has come for me to show you." His motions tightly controlled, he moved his body over her, lowering it gently. Careful not to put too much of his weight on her, he held himself up by his elbows. "Goldie," he began, settling his hips over hers and parting her legs with his own, "this is what you are ready for." Slowly, ever so slowly, he entered her slightly, then became very still.

Fear zigzagged through her when she comprehended exactly what he was going to do to her. "Saber, you aren't gonna—I—It's too *big!* It's gonna hurt—"

"Yes," he admitted, dreading giving her the pain she already suspected he would. "But it only hurts for a moment, Goldie. Only for a—"

"Saber, you're a *man,* not a woman! How do *you* know it only hurts for a minute?"

"Because I—I just know."

She deliberated, unsure whether to believe him. "Will you stop if I tell you to?"

"I'll try."

"What do y'mean *you'll try?*" she demanded. "If you don't swear to stop when I—"

"All right, yes. I'll stop." *God, give me the strength to stop,* he prayed. *Better yet, don't let her tell me to.*

"Just for a minute, Goldie," he told her again. "It only hurts for a minute." With that, he pushed more deeply into her. When he met her maidenhead, he took a breath and prepared to thrust through it.

"Wait!" Goldie yelled right in his ear. "Tell me again how you know it'll only hurt for a minute."

He grit his teeth. "Because—I—Well, I *don't* know. Not for sure. But—"

"So you were lyin' to me just so you could—"

"I was not. I was—I was only trying to soothe your worries. Goldie, listen to me. I—You—" Frustration gripped him. He gave a huge sigh and slid from atop her, deciding to wait a moment before he tried again.

Goldie looked at the disappointed expression on his face, then took her gaze down to the apex of his thighs. An idea came to her. Gently, she cupped her hand around the soft pouch beneath his manhood. "If I twist my wrist while holdin' onto you like this, how long do you think it'll hurt you, Saber? I'm not a man so I really don't know for sure. But I don't think it'd hurt for more than a minute. 'Course, there's only one way to find out, don't you agree?"

He didn't dare move a muscle. He suspected if he tried, she'd turn him into a eunuch. For a long moment, he simply laid there, staring at the twinkle in her eyes.

And then he began to see the humor of his situation. The destiny, the entire future of the Tremayne family lay in Goldie's palm. *Literally.* He could not contain his laughter.

"All right, Goldie, you've made your point," he sputtered merrily, carefully removing her hand. "And you made it very cleverly, I might add."

"You're not . . . irritated with me, are you?"

He smiled, pulling her into his arms again. "You're afraid, Goldie. I'd be an ogre if I couldn't understand that. But . . . perhaps we could try again?" he asked hopefully. "More slowly this time?"

She looked at him as if she couldn't decide what to do.

"Perhaps not," he amended.

She grinned at him, snuggling closer. "But perhaps yes. Tomorrow."

He glanced at the night-filled window, wondering how many hours there were left until dawn. Disappointment welled up in him, but the sight of Goldie's bright smile subdued it. There would be other nights, he reminded himself. Tomorrow would come. And besides, he mused, tonight had been wonderful. He'd had more fun tonight in bed than he could ever remember having before. "Tomorrow, eh? All right, but I want you to know that I don't think it's fair."

"What's not fair?"

"You got two sneezes, and I didn't even get one."

\* \* \*

A soft knock at the door awakened Saber the next morning. He opened his eyes, saw Goldie sleeping beside him, and smiled. "Who is it?" he called.

"Fern," the timid maid answered. "Mr. West, sir?"

"Yes, what is it, Fern?" Saber queried, watching Goldie open her eyes. He planted sweet, tiny kisses along the side of her face. "Good morning, poppet."

The slow, intimate smile he gave her brought back memories of the night. She felt herself blush. " 'Mornin'."

"Mr. West," Fern said from the hallway, "begging your pardon, sir, but you have visitors in the parlor."

Saber frowned. Casting a glance at the floor, he saw his breeches. He untangled Goldie's arms and legs from around him, got out of bed, and pulled his watch from his pants pocket. "It's seven o'clock, for heaven's sake! Who's come calling this early in the morning?"

"The ladies said they were your aunts, sir," Fern explained. "I told them you were still abed, but they insist on seeing you. I didn't know what to—"

"My *aunts!*" Saber exploded, yanking his breeches on. Good God! he thought, panicked. His aunts knew perfectly well he was staying here with Goldie. He wouldn't put it past the two women to come upstairs to see the sleeping arrangements with their own eyes! "Fern! Tell them—Give them tea! Do something with them until I get down there!"

"Yes, sir," Fern answered, and ran to do his bidding.

Goldie scampered out of the bed, rushing to the porcelain basin. She sloshed water into it, then splashed her face. "Hurry up, Saber! Hurry and let's go see your aunts! Oh, I'm so excited about meetin' 'em!"

Saber jerked his shirt on, his hands flying over the buttons. Stuffing his shirttail into his pants, he searched for his shoes, crammed his feet into them, then ran his fingers through his hair. "Goldie, do I look all right to you?"

She examined him, loving what she saw. Sleep still glazed his wonderful eyes, and his ebony hair curled naughtily all over his head. His ill-buttoned shirt parted to show her much of his smooth, broad chest. "You look real good," she assured him, her voice brimming with desire.

The luminous expression in her eyes didn't escape him. He took a step toward her, his gaze touching every part of her bare body, heat spreading through him.

"Your aunts," she reminded him, enchanted by the softness in his eyes.

"My aunts," he repeated absently. "My aunts!" He raced to the door. "Goldie, stay here. I'll—"

"I'm not stayin' here!" she argued, stepping into her dress. "I'm—"

"But I have to talk to my aunts first, and then—"

"I'm goin' too."

He had no time to argue. He left the room and bounded down the staircase. Taking a second to try to smooth his hair, he entered the parlor.

The look on his aunts' faces told him everything he needed to know about his appearance. "I—I was sleeping," he tried to explain. "I didn't want to keep you waiting, so I dressed with haste. I—"

"The tops of your feet are showing," Lucille remarked, twisting her bracelet.

Saber looked down and saw he'd forgotten to put on his stockings.

Clara held her reticule tightly. "And your shirt is not buttoned properly. You've missed two buttons, and the others are—"

"And your hair is mussed," Lucille continued, pushing her spectacles up.

"Your chest is showing," Clara added.

Saber threw back his shoulders. "It would have been good of you to give me notice of your impending arrival. Had you done so I would have had time to make myself more presentable."

"We thought to surprise you," Lucille told him.

"And it seems we succeeded," Clara said, her voice dripping with disapproval. "Moreover, this is not a social call. We are going to be—"

" 'Mornin'!" Goldie greeted gaily, sashaying into the elegant parlor. "Y'all must be Saber's aunts! Great day Miss Agnes, you just can't know what a pleasure it is to meet you! Since I don't have much family, I really like bein' with other folks' families. Someday I'm gonna have twelve kids, though, and then I'll have all the family I can handle.'' She gave one woman her right hand, and the other woman her left, shaking their hands firmly and quickly.

Goldie's brilliant grin brought a smile to Lucille's face. ''Addison has told us about you, my dear.''

''And did he buy y'all those purty dresses?''

Clara took a deep breath. ''We—''

''Yes,'' Saber broke in. ''Addison has also taken my aunts under his benevolent wing.''

Lucille smiled. ''Goldie, I am Miss Lucy, and this is my sister, Miss Clara. And this,'' she said bending to pat her panting spaniel, ''is Margaret.''

''Miss Mae, would you be seated?'' Clara asked, her words more of a command than an invitation.

''Call me Goldie.''

''Very well,'' Clara consented. ''Goldie, please be—''

''She can't,'' Saber blurted. ''She can't because . . . because she has to—She has to take her bath.'' As soon as the words were out, he wished he could retrieve them. Gentlemen did not discuss such things as a woman's toilette. He waited for his aunts' reaction.

Clara began to fan herself.

''It's all right, Miss Clara,'' Goldie said, noticing the woman's distress. ''I don't have to take my bath right now. I can take it later. I'm not all that dirty anyway. I'll sit down now just like you asked me to.'' She plopped into a huge velvet armchair, and began to swing her legs.

Clara saw Goldie's naked legs and bare feet and turned crimson. ''You—My dear girl, you are without shoes and—''

''I could only find one,'' Goldie explained, peering down at her feet. ''I figured it would be better to be all the way barefoot than to come down with only one shoe on. Did you happen to see my other shoe this mornin', Saber?''

Saber cleared his throat. ''Uh—''

''This is not a proper discussion at all,'' Clara snapped at him, her fan moving violently. ''Mar—''

''*Saber,*'' Lucille cut in quickly.

Clara struggled for composure. ''Sit down, *Saber.*''

He did. "Why—"

"Have we come?" Clara finished for him. "My dear boy, why *wouldn't* we come? We will be living with you. Goldie needs a proper chaperone, as I have already told you. Lucille and I are—"

"It isn't that we don't trust you, Saber, dear," Lucille said sweetly, "but for propriety's sake, we felt it was only right for us to stay with you. Surely you do not want anyone to speak ill of Goldie, do you?"

Saber's mind whirled. "I—No, of course not, but I—"

"Goldie," Clara said, "it is indecent for you to share a house with Saber. Have you not thought about this?"

"He hasn't ravished me," she assured the worried aunties. "When I first met him I thought he was the ravishin' kind, but he's not. I reckon I'm safe enough with him."

"The ravishing kind?" Clara nearly swooned. "Oh! Lucille!"

"There now, Clara, dear," Lucille cooed, patting Clara's hand. "He hasn't ravished her."

"I should say I haven't!" Saber thundered. "I—"

"Lucille, do you have my salts with you?" Clara asked shakily. "I feel quite faint."

"Miss Clara, you remind me a lot of Henrietta Smelt back in Spinny River, South Carolina," Goldie told the distraught woman. "She was the faintin' kind too. Everything sent her to the floor. I remember one time when she wandered into Searcy Hogg's barn lookin' for her lost cat? Well, Searcy was busy matin' his horses in that barn. The sight did Henrietta in. She fainted right into a pile of horse—"

"Goldie, have some tea!" Saber shouted, desperate to cut her off before she could say anything more.

Lucille waved smelling salts under Clara's nose. "Saber, my boy, I am going to go upstairs with Goldie for a while. Why don't you stay and talk with Clara? Come, Goldie," she said, rising and offering her hand to Goldie. "Let us become more well-acquainted, shall we?"

Goldie jumped out of her chair and took Lucille's hand, following the elderly woman out of the parlor.

When they were gone, Clara glared at Saber. "Marion, I find this whole situation utterly shocking!"

He raised his chin. "Nevertheless, it will continue until I choose to end it."

Regally, Clara rose, walking the length of the room, her reticule swinging from the crook of her elbow. "Do not blow that air of authority in my direction, Marion. It will not work."

He crossed his legs. He intimidated many people, but never his aunts, he mused. They knew and loved him too much to stand in awe of him. It was one of the things he adored about them. The thought softened his irritation. "Aunt Clara, I'm well aware of how all of this is upsetting you, but there is no help for it."

"Yes, there is. Lucille and I could remain here with Goldie, and you could rent another house."

"She stays with me."

His adamant declaration gave Clara pause. She watched him for a long while. "I wondered if this day would ever come," she said softly, poignant emotion sweeping through her. "You care for her very much, don't you, Marion?"

Saber shifted in his chair. He still had no name for what he felt for Goldie, and because of that he refused to discuss it.

"Fidgeting," Clara said. "When you were a boy you squirmed when faced with something that made you uncomfortable. You still do it. Explain to me why caring for her makes you so ill at ease."

"I don't care for—I mean, I *do* care for her. A lot. Some. As a friend. She—As a friend."

"Do you love her, Marion?"

"No! I mean, no," he said more quietly. "I just told you that she and I are friends. Really close friends, and nothing more." He clenched his jaw, wondering if his tangled explanation made any more sense to his aunt than it did to him. Dammit, *why* couldn't he understand what it was he felt for Goldie?

At the tortured look in her nephew's eyes, Clara almost laughed. "I see. The two of you are . . . *really close* friends. Then you shouldn't have any objections to our moving in with you. You don't have any, do you?"

"Would it matter if I did?"

Clara smiled lovingly. "No, I don't imagine it would."

"Ladies don't have legs," Lucille tried to explain.

Goldie stood in front of her bedroom mirror and lifted her dress. She looked at her legs, then cast a bewildered look at Rosie, who was watching the scene from the bed. "What do y'mean we don't have legs?"

"Nor do ladies speak of them," Clara added.

Goldie scowled and wrinkled her nose. "Is there somethin' nasty about legs?"

"And we cover them with underwear," Lucille said.

"We don't, however," Clara began, fingering her reticule, "speak about underwear either."

Goldie's frown deepened. "If we don't have legs, how can we cover 'em with underwear?"

"An' 'ow the 'ell can we walk without legs?" Rosie ventured, glancing at her own pair.

Lucille hid a smile from Clara, then twisted her bracelet.

"I won't talk about underwear, though," Goldie promised. "I don't have any to talk about."

Clara gasped. "Young lady, are you telling us that you wear nothing at all under your dress?"

Goldie felt embarrassed and wished Saber were with her. But ever since his aunts had arrived a week ago, they'd been intent on keeping her separated from him. "I—Can we call Saber up here, please? Just for a few minutes?"

"Into your bedroom?" Clara asked. "Certainly not!"

Goldie cast her gaze downward. "I'd wear underwear if I had any, but I've never had enough money to get any."

"Oh, you poor, dear child," Lucille clucked. "You may be sure that Clara and I will see to the matter straightaway."

"I ain't got none neither," Rosie chimed in hopefully.

Clara sighed, sat in a high-backed chair, and folded her hands in her lap. "And when a lady sits, she does not swing her feet as you have the habit of doing."

"When she enters the room, she will choose the straightest chair in it," Lucille elaborated. "She lowers herself into it slowly and gracefully. She does not sprawl in it, but keeps her back stiff, her shoulders back. She never crosses her legs. Her feet are together and flat on the floor.''

"But you said we didn't have legs," Goldie pointed out, baffled. "If we don't have legs, we don't have feet, either, right? Besides that, when I'm sittin' in a chair, my feet don't reach the floor."

"Maybe ya could jest sit right *on* the floor, Goldie," Rosie suggested. "Then yer feet could be flat on it."

Clara looked at the urchin and felt tender pity. Addison, having gotten permission from Saber, had given Goldie's address to the trustworthy girl, and now Rosie visited on a regular basis. She was company for Goldie, and every time she came, she brought along some small gift for Clara and Lucille. A bunch of wilted flowers, a package of needles, a few rolls . . . whatever she'd been able to procure. Clara could not find the heart to disapprove of her. Rosie, though hard on the outside, was a kind and gentle person inside, and that made all the difference to Clara.

She gave Rosie a benevolent smile, then turned back to Goldie. "And barnyard activities are not suitable for conversation," she continued. *"Modesty* is the word to remember, Goldie. Remember that, and all else will fall into place."

"Modesty," Goldie repeated, deliberating on the exact meaning of the word. "Before I met Saber I was modest as modest can be. So modest that I was ashamed of my own body. But Saber—"

"There is no need to explain further," Clara interrupted, rolling her eyes to the ceiling. "Lucille and I understand your meaning. But in the future, Goldie, please do not discuss your body. Most especially with Saber," she added, her brow rising.

Goldie felt very confused. Not only didn't she have legs, she didn't have the rest of her body either. Needing something of Saber near her for reassurance, she picked up her gold brush from the dressing table, holding it to her breast. "He gave this to me. He's given me a lot."

Lucille smiled at the luminous expression in Goldie's eyes. "What else, besides the brush, has he given you, my dear?"

Goldie looked at both women. "His company. He

makes me feel so special. When I'm with him, he treats me so nice. He hardly ever gets mad at me, but even when he does, it's always for a good reason. And he never stays mad for long. 'Course now I get mad at him too. I'm not afraid of him anymore, y'see. When I first met him, I didn't know how to act with him. But as time went on, he made me feel more comfortable. Now I can get madder'n hell at him, and I'm not afraid of what he'll do to me.''

"Goldie, ladies do not swear," Clara scolded. "But tell me, child. You don't fear his anger at all?" she asked, remembering the many people who did.

"Nope. Not anymore. Saber tries to act like a tornado, but he's really nothin' but a breeze. And he's a lot of fun too. At least he is when he's not in one of his arrogant moods."

"Fun?" Clara asked anxiously. "How is he fun?" She leaned forward in her chair.

"Well, he likes to play in the mud. He'd never admit it in a million years, but the day we had our mud fight he was havin' a good time. And he likes to cook. I mean to tell you he can make good bread. If you don't believe me, just ask him. He'll talk about his bread for hours if you let him. And sometimes he likes to talk about the things he did when he was a little boy. Things like makin' dandelion stew and sleepin' with his mama and daddy when it was thunderin'. But most of all, I reckon, he likes to laugh. I do too. That's why we get along. I'll swannee, we're always laughin' over somethin'."

"He spoke of his *parents* to you?" Clara asked, unable to believe what she was hearing.

"And his childhood?" Lucille asked.

"He played in the mud?" Clara queried, her hand over her heart.

"And made bread?" Lucille inquired, twisting her bracelet.

"And he laughs with you?" Clara continued. "My!"

"It seems that you and our boy have gotten along famously," Lucille speculated.

Clara stared at Goldie, a multitude of thoughts running through her shrewd mind. She smiled. "Goldie, my dear,

Addison has told us about your need to turn Saber into a duke. I wonder if you would like our assistance with that?''

"Do y'all know duke stuff?" Goldie asked anxiously.

"We know good manners," Lucille informed her, realizing what her sister was up to. "Manners befitting a duke. Ever since we came into Addison's care, we have had the good fortune to become acquainted with many elegant people. Our contact with them has taught us the proper mode of decorum."

Clara smiled at her sister's tales, deciding to elaborate on them. "Once, we even dined with the third cousin of the Duke of Brentford! And what a lovely woman she is."

"Great day Miss Agnes!"

"So would you like for us to teach you what we know, Goldie?" Lucille asked.

"Yes!" Goldie squealed.

"Lesson number one," Clara said, "is never squeal."

"Not even when I'm real excited?"

"When you are excited," Lucille began, "you may laugh with quiet delight."

While Goldie and Rosie practiced laughing with quiet delight, Clara rose, examining Goldie with a critical eye. It would take a lot of work, she realized. Many long, grueling hours of lessons. But it could be done, Clara decided, and was determined to do it. After all, the girl who could get Marion Tremayne to play in mud, bake bread, laugh, and speak of his parents was worth all the effort it would take.

And so, Clara mused, while Goldie turned Marion into a "duke," Clara and Lucille would turn Goldie into a lady.

From the bedroom window at Ravenhurst, Dane looked out over the estate, his gaze settling on the moonlit village. He could see the thatched roofs of the cottages, but could not make out the Maes'. "Everything is going wrong," he seethed.

Still glaring at the night-shrouded Hallensham, he thought of Big. The midget had returned. How was it possible? Dane raged. And the girl . . . was she dead?

Dora crept out of bed and sidled up next to him, pressing her bare breasts against his back. "Let me make it right fer ya, milord. Ye knows I can do it. Close yer eyes, an' I'll be yer Lady Hutchins."

Dane spun and glared at her. "I will not close my eyes! You don't understand! The midget's back, and the girl isn't! It could be that she actually found *him,* and now they're after me! It's possible I might lose everything that's mine!"

With that, Dane raced downstairs. Once in the drawing room, he proceeded to light every candle in it. He grabbed a bottle of brandy, pacing while he drank. "Something must be done," he told himself. "Yes, something . . ."

He passed the piano and set his brandy bottle down on it. Seating himself upon the velvet-covered piano seat, he smoothed his hair, then began to play a strain from a Beethoven concerto. "Remember when you showed me how to play this, my love?" he asked, his eyes closing as his mind filled with memories. "You didn't want to teach me. Why not? I had to make you. But weren't you proud of me when I learned to play your favorite melody?"

His fingers stilled upon the keys. "You did so many things wrong, my love. But I forgave you."

Softly, he began the concerto again, stopping at a certain section and playing it over and over. "William! You know nothing of what has happened, and you'll be arriving from Cornwall soon! You'll come here, and they might catch you, too! Maybe they're already on their way!"

Now he was banging on the keys, seized by hysteria, his chest heaving as he gulped in ragged breaths. "Oh, William, my friend, I can't let them catch us! I have to protect you so that you, in turn, can guard what's rightfully mine! I'll speak to Ferris. He hasn't killed the girl. I know he hasn't. I must go to London and do it myself. The girl. Goldie. Bitch! Try and outwit me, will you? Yes, yes, you must die!"

He jumped from the seat, his fists pumping. "Dora!"

Within moments Dora came scurrying into the room.

Dane closed his eyes. Taking her into his arms, he grew strangely calm and contained. "I am leaving for a while, my dear. I have some vitally important business to attend to. But if the villagers know I am gone, they will become lazy. Without me here to oversee them, they simply will not work. My dear, tomorrow I would like you to inform all of Hallensham that I have taken ill. Tell them I am in my bed, but that I will be recovering shortly. Will you do that for me, Lady Hutchins?''

Dora purred and removed her wrapper. "I will milord," she promised, rubbing herself against him.

"And when I return from my trip, my dear, we will have our house redecorated.''

"Oh, milord! Can we have our bedroom done in crimson an' white? Ya knows I always wanted it ter be like that.''

Dane kept his eyes closed, concentrating on the woman's image in his mind. "You've changed your decision then? I was under the impression you wanted it done in green and gold. Well, no matter. You are lady of the manor and may choose whatever your heart desires. I have also decided to open the closed bedrooms. All of them will be cleaned and refurbished. It only seems wise to get them ready for our children. I want children. I want an heir.''

Dora nearly fainted with pleasure. "I'll give ya as many as ya can fill me with, milord.''

"Yes,'' Dane whispered, lowering her to the floor and parting his robe. "And we will start now. Here. Tonight, I will do you the extreme honor of giving you my son.''

He pushed into her, burying himself deeply. "I love you, my dear,'' he grunted into her ear. "I will always love you, my beautiful Angelica.''

Diggory took another bite of the potato impaled on his dagger. "Yer not tellin' me nothin' I don't knows, Og. Three people 'ave already tole me they've seed a girl wot looked like 'er. She was in a coach a while back. Sleepin' on the seat, she was. Some bleedin' nob was with 'er.''

Og shuffled his feet on the filthy floor of Diggory's room, shivering with cold fear. "But I knows where she *lives*, Diggory,'' he repeated.

Diggory swallowed his potato. "Wot about the blastie she's supposed ter be with?''

Og bit his lower lip. "I ain't never seed the dwarf.''

Diggory wiped his mouth on his coat sleeve. "Tell me again. Everything from beginnin' to end.''

Og nodded. "I seed 'er with Rosie Tetter. She was little, jest like ya said she'd be. She 'ad yellow 'air, an' she talked strange, like she weren't from 'ere. Rosie made it all real easy, Diggory. 'Er an' the girl must be friends. See, I followed Rosie t'other day, an' she went to a big 'ouse wot's on the corner o' Pickerin' an' Landon. She walked up the steps jest as calm as ya please. When she knocked, the blonde chit opened a upstairs window, 'anged out of it, an' was wavin' ter Rosie. Then Rosie was let inside the 'ouse, she was. It was 'er, Diggory. The girl ya've been lookin' fer. I can takes ya ter where she is."

Diggory pulled his knife from the potato, wiping it on his filthy breeches. "Why should I do the job when ya can friggin' do it fer me, Og? It's a simple job, it is. Do it, an' bring me 'er body. An' if ya find the blastie, I want 'im too."

Og could barely contain his glee. "An' will ya pay me, Diggory?"

Diggory smiled and ran a finger across the flat side of his dagger. "I'll pay ya, Og. Ye'll get exactly wot ya deserve."

Saber leaned back against the carriage seat. Though he and Goldie were riding through an elegant part of London, he felt they were safe enough within the closed compartment of the rented coach.

He looked at Goldie, who sat across from him, and tried to remember the last time they'd shared anything remotely related to intimacy. What with the aunties always hovering about, private moments with her were few and far between.

But they were alone now, weren't they? he reminded himself with a grin. Devising a scheme of seduction, he watched Goldie pat her hair. His eyes narrowed at the sight. "Why do you have your hair like that?" he demanded suddenly.

She turned her face from the window, touching the knot of hair at the nape of her neck again. "It's called a chignon. You don't like it?"

"No. I like your curls bobbing all over your head."

"But this is a proper way for a lady to wear her hair."

"Who told you that?" he asked, as if he didn't already know.

"Your aunts. They're teachin' me stuff about customs and manners. Rosie's learnin' too." She leaned against the window.

"Goldie, don't press so hard against the window," Saber admonished. "I realize you don't want to miss a single detail about the dukish people out there, but if you continue pushing on the glass like that, it's going to break, and you're going to fall out into the street."

"But look at *that* one, Saber!" she cried, pointing out the window of the carriage as it rolled down the well-kept street. "Saber, he's got a pocket watch almost as big as a dinner plate! Great day Miss Agnes, where can we get one of those for you?"

"More importantly, where will we get the money to pay for it?" he teased. Taking great care not to let himself be seen, he leaned over Itchie Bon and got a glimpse of the man Goldie saw. It was Lord Wildon, the Earl of Drakethorne. "Yes, he certainly looks like a dukish man to me," he agreed, noting Percival Wildon's imperious swagger. How strange, he mused. He'd been with Percival on various occasions, but had never noticed the man's overconfident gait. "You've never seen *me* walk like that, have you, Goldie?" he asked uneasily.

"No, you walk normal. *Too* normal for a duke. I haven't seen you do the wiggle walk since we left Leighwood. You *do* hold your chin up like that man does though. And that's good. It's a real haughty thing to do. Real dukish, Saber."

Saber took another look at Percival Wildon. The man's nose was so high in the air, it nearly pointed to the sky. It irritated Saber to be compared to him, and he made a mental note to keep a firm grip on his own chin.

"There's another one!" Goldie exclaimed. "I'll swannee, *look* at his vest! It's got pink and purple *flowers* sewed on it! He looks like a walkin' garden!"

Saber strained to see the man. It was Lord Ivers, Earl of Wyeth. Geoffrey Ivers, Saber reflected, looked just as vain as Percival Wildon. "That is not a vest. It is called a waistcoat."

"You wouldn't ever wear a waistcoat like that one, would you, Saber? I mean, 'course y'would to be Duke Marion, but in real life would you?"

He remembered he had several elaborately embroidered waistcoats. True, he rarely wore them, but he *had* chosen to buy them. He'd thought them nice then, but now . . . "No," he announced. "I wouldn't wear anything like that." Sitting back into his seat, he made a vow to give his colorful waistcoats to charity.

"Saber, we learned a lot today. We saw six or seven dukish men." Goldie said, reviewing her notes. "Dukish folks are conceited," she read out loud. "They're God's gifts to the world, accordin' to them. They dress up like peacocks. They let their gold watches hang way down, probably to show off around poor people. They wear rings. Some even wear a ring on every finger. They—"

She broke off and looked up at him. "This stuff is all well and good, Saber, but y'know what? We still don't know what dukes talk about. I wonder what a typical duke conversation is? I mean, *normal* men talk about the cost of livin'. About the weather. About their friends. They talk about the best fishin' spot in the creek. But dukes probably don't talk about that stuff."

"*I* don't talk about the cost of living, the weather, friends, or fishing spots. Are you saying I'm not a normal man?" He sat up straighter, leaning forward while waiting to hear her answer.

She cocked her head. "You're right. You don't talk about those kinds of things. Why don't you?" She frowned, still staring at him. "Come to think about it, Saber, you don't hardly ever talk about yourself. Isn't there anything about you that you'd like to tell people?"

"I told you about my dandelion stews," he reminded her a bit defensively.

"Well, yeah, but that's not much. What other stuff is there to know about you?"

Determined to prove his normalcy to her, he tried to think of some common things he liked to do. "Well, I had a rock collection when I was little. And I could whistle with two fingers in my mouth."

"Do you still collect rocks? Can you still whistle like that?"

He sat back again. "No, I don't collect rocks anymore," he said softly, wondering if his old collection was still in his tree house. "But I can probably still whistle." Two fingers in his mouth, he blew hard.

Goldie giggled when no whistle came forth. "Well, I guess that answers that question. You can't do it anymore."

"Yes, I can." Again, he tried, and failed. "Goldie, I swear I used to be able to whistle like—"

"Forget about whistlin', Saber. What kinds of things do you like to do as a man?"

"Well . . . Lots of things. Things like . . ." Blast it all! he fumed. Besides investing his money, he couldn't think of a single thing he really enjoyed doing. And he couldn't very well tell Goldie about his investments. "I like to . . ."

"Sing?" she supplied.

"Sing? I don't know. I haven't sung in years."

"Why?"

"I—Because I don't know any songs."

Her smile faded. "Oh, how sad."

"I've never thought of it as *sad*. Why do you say that?"

"Well I never knew anybody who didn't know a single song. To me, that's sad. Want me to teach you one?" Without waiting for his answer, she burst into a stirring rendition of "Yankee Doodle."

Saber was enchanted. Her singing voice was much like her personality: sweet, happy, and completely lovely. He clapped loudly.

She finished her song and smiled. "You try it now."

He shifted in his seat. "Goldie, I really don't think—"

"Oh, all right, so you don't like to sing. Do you like to peel oranges?"

"I've never peeled one."

"Don't you like 'em?"

"Yes, I like them." *But the servants always performed the chore of peeling them*.

"It's a real challenge to get the peel off without breakin' it." Goldie enlightened him. "I even think the orange tastes better if you don't break the peel. I know that's silly, but there's just somethin' about holdin' an unbroken peel while you're eatin' the orange.''

A bittersweet emotion seized him. He realized he'd missed out on a great many things in life. Peeling an orange suddenly sounded like the most diverting activity known to man.

"I don't have legs," she informed him suddenly, pulling her skirt down.

"What? You have no legs?"

"Nope. And it's not very gentlemanly of you to say *legs* in front of me."

He frowned. "What on earth are you talking about?"

"Miss Lucy and Miss Clara said ladies don't have legs. Chairs, tables, pianos don't either. Nothin' has legs, Saber. And look at this." She lifted her skirt just a bit.

Saber saw lacy underwear covering the appendages she told him she didn't possess. He felt extreme disappointment at the sight. He'd loved her bare legs.

"And I'm sorry for squealin' when I saw those dukish men out there. I was supposed to laugh with quiet delight."

"I like your squeal."

"Well, it's not good manners to squeal. Do you like the way I'm sittin'?"

"You look like you have a board tied against your back."

"This is the way a lady sits."

"How wonderful, *Lady Goldie,*" he muttered.

"And I'm not supposed to let you take liberties with me ever again. Do you know what liberties are, Saber?"

"I have a vague idea," he snapped, anger coming.

"What are they?"

He realized she didn't know, and grinned rakishly. If she was unfamiliar with the word, she could look it up in her dictionary, he decided. But she would never get the definition from him.

"Itchie Bon, get down from there!" Goldie shouted when the dog began pawing and jumping at the door. She looked out and saw a stray mongrel, realizing Itchie Bon had seen it too. She reached for his collar the same time Saber did.

But before either of them had a firm grip on it, Itchie Bon made one last powerful leap at the door. It flew open, and he sprang out.

"Great day Miss Agnes, Saber, Itchie Bon—" She broke off and jumped from the slow-moving coach. Falling into the street, she rolled several times before managing to stagger to her feet. Once she was standing, she caught sight of Itchie Bon, who was running after the stray. She raced after him.

"Goldie!" Saber yelled at her. He, too, leaped from the coach, thankful the vehicle was going so slowly. Mindless of all the people staring at him, he tore after Goldie, reaching her quickly. "Stop!" he demanded, holding her arms when she twisted to get away. "Goldie—"

"But Itchie Bon's runnin' away!" she hollered, tears streaming. "Saber, I might not ever see him again!"

Saber saw the dog was about a block away. Reluctant to let Goldie go, he did the only thing he could think of to do. Two fingers in his mouth, he took a deep breath and blew hard.

The loud, shrill whistle that followed made several horses shy. Heads turned, people stopping to stare.

"Here he comes!" Goldie squealed. "Saber, you did it! You whistled, and here Itchie Bon comes!"

Acute mortification enveloped Saber when he realized how much attention his whistle had drawn. Desperately, he looked for the carriage, clenching his jaw when he saw it a great distance down the road. He knew then that his driver had no idea that the coach was without its passengers. Saber scanned the street for a cab, waving wildly when he saw one. "All right, let's go, Goldie," he said when the cab driver waved back.

God, he thought. If any of his acquaintances saw him, the masquerade would be over immediately. He surveyed his surrounding apprehensively, feeling tremendous relief when he saw no one he knew. He took Goldie by the elbow and grabbed Itchie Bon's collar, hurrying them both toward the approaching cab. Before the carriage had even reached a full stop, he was snatching the door open.

"I say! Marion!" a man's voice called loudly. "Marion, wait!"

At the sound of his name, dread pumped through Saber's every vein.

DIAMONDS AND DREAMS

(something) ped Chittingdon, he raced along, look
up (at) ...  It's been years since you've studied a
...ial gathering, Marion, I must say it will be splendid to
...ee you ... my wife, Caroline, and I are hosting an

# Chapter 16

❦

66 G et in," he told Goldie, lifting her into the coach
and dragging Itchie Bon in, too.

"Marion, I knew it was you!" the man exclaimed as he
arrived at the carriage. "I'd heard you were on holiday in
Scotland, my boy!"

Saber saw the man was none other than the elderly Lord
Chittingdon, Duke of Blexheath. "I—Good day," he
stammered. Casting a glance at Goldie, he saw a wild look
of excitement in her eyes, and he felt as if someone had
kicked him in the belly. Panic seized him, but he didn't
try to stop Goldie when she jumped out of the coach, for
he knew full well no power on earth could stop her.

"My name's Goldie Mae, sir," she told the man. "Are
you a duke?"

The man regarded her with a slight scowl. "I am Win-
throp Chittingdon, Duke of Blexheath. Who, may I ask,
are you?"

Saber swallowed. "She is—"

"I'm a writer from America!" Goldie blurted. "I'm
here in England to study dukish people. Folks in America
don't know much about y'all, so I'm gonna write a book
about you. Sab—*Marion* here is takin' me all around so's
I can do all my research. Do you think he and I could
come to some of y'all's get-togethers soon? It would really
help me to be with a whole herd of dukes all in one room,
y'know."

Lord Chittingdon stared at her. "Well . . ."

Saber shuffled his feet. "Goldie, I really don't think—"

"Any friend of Marion's will be a welcome addition to

290

our assemblies," Lord Chittingdon decided aloud, looking up at Saber. "It's been years since you've attended a social gathering, Marion. I must say it will be splendid to have you back. My wife, Caroline, and I are hosting an affair on the twenty-fifth, and I'm sure she will be pleased to have you and Miss Mae attend. There will be dinner and dancing."

"Set up a place," Goldie said, grinning. "Is it potluck? I went to a potluck supper once, and I took potato salad. Ole Olive Nookin only took stale soda crackers, but she sat down and ate enough food to bust her wide open. After I saw her do that, I swore on my daddy that I'd *always* bring a lot of food to any potluck suppers I ever got invited to. If you don't like potato salad, I could bring fried chicken. I don't really like to fry chicken because I get popped all the time. You know how grease flies all over when you fry chicken. But if you like fried chicken, I'll put up with bein' popped. Do you want me to bring fried—"

"Goldie," Saber cut her off, pulling at his shirt collar, "I doubt seriously that Lord Chittingdon's dinner will be . . . uh, *potluck."*

"Oh. Well, what time does the party start, Lord? I need to know, y'see, because Miss Lucy and Miss Clara said they don't agree with bein' fashionably late. I'll even get there about a half hour early to help your wife set the table and stuff like that. So what time's it start?"

Lord Chittingdon stared at her again. "I—I believe Caroline indicated half past six. But she—You—Miss Mae, there will be no need for you to assist with the table."

Goldie giggled softly. "Did you notice I laughed with quiet delight, Lord? I usually squeal, but Miss Lucy and Miss Clara say squealin's only for pigs. I have a pig. His name's Runt."

Saber rolled his eyes. "It has been a pleasure seeing you again, Lord Chittingdon," he told the bewildered man. "My fondest regards to Lady Chittingdon. Good day."

With that, he handed Goldie into the coach, got in behind her, and shut the door. He realized the rudeness of closing the door in Lord Chittingdon's face, but he knew if he didn't get Goldie away from the man, she would shock him into a coma. "We are *not* attending the Chittingdon—"

"Oh, yes, we are! Saber, there was no doubt in that man's mind that you were Marion Tremayne! I've really done my work well, haven't I? You acted so perfectly dukish that you fooled a *real duke!* You forgot to throw in a few thee's and thou's, though. Anyway, that duke said he hasn't seen the real Marion in a long time, so it's obvious he can't remember what ole Marion really looks like. If *he* doesn't remember, it makes sense that other folks won't either! Oh, this is just so perfect, Saber! Just *wait* till we get to that party! I'm gonna—"

"We are not going." He gave her a piercing glare.

"Saber—"

"I will hear no more about the matter." God, he thought dismally. By tonight everyone would know he was in the city. The only comfort he had was that no one would find him at his house. If they couldn't find him, they couldn't very well come calling on him. And no one would think to look for him at Addison's grandfather's house; therefore Goldie's location would remain a secret.

He heard Goldie muttering and assumed she was cursing him up and down. "Goldie—"

"You are so *mean!*" she yelled at him, tears of fury filling her eyes. "I bet you pulled the wings off butterflies when you were little just like that Raleigh Purvis I told you about!"

"I did no such thing. Goldie, listen to me. I—"

"No."

He realized the extent of her rage and frustration. "Very well, Goldie, later on we will discuss attending the affair. *Discuss* it, mind you. That does not mean we will definitely be attending. I will, however, think about it." He felt guilt nag at him. He had no intention whatsoever of accepting the invitation, but only said he would think about it so Goldie would calm down.

His answer thrilled her. She knew full well she could talk him into going. "Thank you, Saber."

He felt relief smooth through him. The subject of the dinner party would come up again, he knew, and by then he hoped to have a valid reason why he couldn't attend.

"Let's enjoy the rest of the afternoon, shall we?" He banged on the roof of the carriage with his cane, then opened the window slightly. "To the marketplace," he instructed the driver.

Goldie didn't think she'd ever seen so much food in her life. Saber refused to let her get out of the coach, but she had a wonderful view from the window. "So this is the London market," she said to him while he picked out the finest oranges he could find from the basket a coster-woman held up for him.

She saw stalls filled with fish, poultry, and meats. Fat cabbages were everywhere. Walnuts, apples, plums, onions, rhubarb, and potatoes. Piles of bright carrots, snowy cauliflower, deep-green broccoli, and purple turnips lay piled high upon the steps of a building, their brilliant colors soothing the shred of irritation she still felt toward Saber. There was coffee, tea, flour, sugar, salt, and all sorts of spices, too. Breads and sweets filled the air with a wholesome fragrance. Every kind of food she could think of had a place in the bustling marketplace.

And there were other items for sale also. Matches, shoe blacking, cutlery, razors, glassware, and hatchets. Caged birds squawked. Goldie saw metal trays and tin jewelry. Some stalls contained candlesticks, iron kettles, and music boxes. She'd never seen so many wares.

She looked far down the street, its pavement stained green by the leaves of vegetables that had been smashed into it over the years, and saw a long line of pony carts and donkey barrows. "Great day Miss Agnes, there's so much to see here!"

Saber added a last orange to the bag, taking care to stay well within the confines of the coach as he paid the woman for the fruit. "Tonight most of London will be eating the food you see now, poppet," he informed her as he began peeling an orange, its sharp, tangy aroma filling the carriage. "I think every cook in the city is here picking out dinner." He muttered a curse when his peel broke before he'd gotten it completely off the orange. Shrugging, he picked up another and tried again.

"And these flowers," Goldie said, fingering a bunch of

violets a young girl held out to her. "Will most of London have fresh flowers in their houses too?"

Saber nodded. "And you will be no exception." He purchased a thick bunch from the girl. Upon further reflection, he bought the entire basket of violets, handing the sweet-smelling gift to Goldie.

"All of 'em?"

The delight in her eyes warmed him all over. "All of them, poppet."

"I—Oh, Saber, nobody's ever given me flowers before." She buried her face into the fragrant mass of dark purple blossoms.

He digested that bit of information. "Indeed."

"You didn't have to buy *all* of 'em. You didn't have to buy *any.*"

"But you liked them."

She cocked her head to her shoulder. "Well, yeah, but I—This many flowers—Are you sure—"

"I'm quite sure." He felt confused. "Goldie, why is it so hard for you to believe I bought you a simple basket of flowers? You acted this same way when I gave you the brush. It's almost like you don't think you deserve to have pretty things. Why—"

"It's time to go home now, Saber. I promised Miss Lucy and Miss Clara that I wouldn't stay out all day long. It's not considered proper, y'know." She stuck her head out the door, yelling. "Let's go, Sir Carriage Driver!" With that, she slammed the door shut.

As the coach jolted forward, Saber's confusion grew to bewilderment. "Tell me about the violets, Goldie. Why—"

"They're very nice."

"That is not what I meant, and you know it. You couldn't believe I bought you a *bunch,* much less the entire basket. Now, I want to know why you—"

"I'm too tired to talk."

He felt angry. Dammit, *why* wouldn't she open up to him! *Why* did she continue refusing to share her feelings with him! "Goldie, I've been as patient with you as I know how to be. I've waited for weeks for you to tell me about the things you carry inside you. I even told you what I'd decided about you in the hopes that you would elabo-

rate! But you didn't. You say *I* don't talk about *myself*?
Neither do you!''

She said nothing. Forgetting she had no legs, she drew
them up beneath her, closing herself to him.

"Who told you you aren't good enough to have flowers?
To have anything? What happened to you that makes you
think good and pretty things aren't to be yours? Dammit,
crawl out of that shell, Goldie, and right now!''

Her only escape would be to jump out of the coach
again. She knew if she did, Saber would follow and catch
her. Anxiety twisted through her. "How long did it take
you to get used to havin' all the things Addison gives you,
Saber?'' she cried, struggling in vain to remain calm.
"You were poor before he found you! When he started
helpin' you so much, wasn't it a little hard for you to
believe it was really happenin'? And did you ever lay in
bed at night, wonderin' if when you woke up, it would all
be gone? And did it ever cross your mind that maybe your
good fortune was all a mistake?''

"A mistake?''

She tried to stem her flow of words, but failed. "You
don't understand, do you? Maybe you just don't remember
what it's like! I—Saber, I've never had anything! And
now—Since I met you, I've had almost everything I've
ever dreamed of havin'! I've never eaten such find food!
And off such fragile china! I've never lived in such fancy
houses or slept in such big, soft beds! I've never ridden in
these elegant coaches, or washed with such sweet soap,
or bathed in such huge, golden tubs!''

"But you are now! Can't you accept and enjoy them
while—''

"I *am* enjoyin' 'em! But don't you see, Saber? They're
gonna go away! Dreams, all of 'em! You know how dreams
are! You wake up, and they're over! Uncle Asa, he—''

When she broke off, he moved to her side of the carriage, taking her by her shoulders. "What *about* Uncle
Asa, Goldie? Tell me what the man did to you! Tell me
about the terrible things that—''

"No!''

"Tell me!''

"No!''

"I'll never stop asking you, Goldie. Day in and day out, I'll ask. Every second of every minute of every hour! I'll keep on—"

"You can't! You can't because you won't be with me that long! After you play the duke in Hallensham, you'll have to leave, and I'll never see you again!" Covering her face with her hands, she sobbed.

He held her in his arms, rocking her back and forth. "Oh, Goldie," he whispered, his heart pounding. "I—"

"It's *always* like this!" she cried, too upset to guard her words any longer. "Every time somethin' good wanders into my life, it goes away! Uncle Asa says it's because I don't really deserve it! He says that until I'm good enough to have my diamond dreams, the Dream Giver won't let 'em come true for me! He said—"

"Dream giver? Goldie, who—"

"God," she choked, tears burning her cheeks. "I think the Dream Giver is God."

"God? But Goldie, how can your uncle presume to know what God—"

"I've never been anything but a bother to Uncle Asa! Always trailin' along behind him! Always hungry or wantin' somethin'! Sometimes— Sometimes I wonder if he drinks just to find an escape from havin' to put up with me!"

"*He* puts up with *you?*" Saber roared. "What about what you've taken from him? The trouble he causes everywhere you go! The constant—"

"And all my cryin'! Oh, Saber, I wish I didn't cry so much! It makes him so furious! But I—Things are so—"

"Sad," he supplied. "So sad, Goldie, that you've every right to cry! Who *wouldn't* cry over such—"

"I know he loves me, but I wish . . ."

"You wish what, Goldie?" Saber asked, every fiber of him straining to hear her answer. "For the love of God, tell me what you wish!"

Clinging to his neck, she closed her eyes. "I wish lots of things."

"But what are they?"

Many long moments passed before she answered. "You aren't the Dream Giver, Saber," she whispered, exhaustion creeping through her. "And they're all diamond dreams anyway."

"Diamonds? Is that what you wish for, Goldie? Diamonds?"

"Diamonds," she murmured. "Diamond dreams."

He looked down and saw she'd fallen asleep. Settling himself in the corner of the seat, he pulled her into his arms, holding her as tenderly as he ever had before.

Her every word came back to him. "Years of being told you weren't good enough to have nice things, of being denied everything you wished you could have. And I know, Goldie," he whispered, gazing down at her soft features, "that you didn't ask for much. You probably wanted sweets every now and then. Maybe a dress with pretty lace on it. You wished for hair ribbons, a kitten, a small bottle of scent. You wished for all the simple things any young girl would want to have.

"But most of all," he continued, "you wished for love. You had every right to it, but it was denied you just like everything else."

He became silent and lifted Goldie higher, so her face was buried within the warm crook of his shoulder. So many emotions had hold of him, he was unable to concentrate on any of them. He knew only that all the tender things inside him, all the soul-touching feelings, were for Goldie.

An hour later, when the carriage stopped in front of his house and nighttime had fallen, he was still holding her next to his heart, his emotions still ebbing gently through him.

The driver opened the coach door; Itchie Bon bounded out. Saber handed the man cab fare, grabbed the basket of violets and the bag of oranges, and alighted, Goldie still cuddled in his arms. As the coach rolled away, he looked down at her again and saw her eyes were open. "We're home, poppet."

She smiled sleepily, squirmed from his arms, and smoothed her skirts. "We didn't get home before dark," she said worriedly. "Your aunts are—"

"They're visiting with friends tonight, remember? It's too early yet for them to be home. I imagine they'll be gone for several more hours. If you don't tell them you arrived after dark, they won't know. I assure you your secret is safe with me.''

He handed her her basket of violets and gave her his elbow. When she curled her hand around his arm, he covered it with his own. As he led her toward the steps, Itchie Bon began to growl. ''What is it, boy?'' Saber asked. ''What—'' A movement in the dark grove of trees beside the house made him break off his questions. Squinting, he saw a man emerge from the shadows. The man's small cloth cap, silk neckerchief, long, four-pocketed coat, and sturdy boots were typical of a costermonger, and Saber wondered what the street vendor was doing so close to the house. ''You there!'' he called loudly. ''What do you want?''

The man's response was to draw up his arm level to his shoulder. His odd action sent foreboding streaming through Saber. Reacting instinctively, he pushed Goldie to the steps, shielding her body with his own. Gunfire shattered the silence of the night. The basket of violets toppled down the steps, spilling to the pavement. ''Goldie!'' he shouted, terrified that she wouldn't answer. ''Goldie—''

''M-my violets,'' she whispered. ''My f-f-flowers.''

''Goldie, are you hurt? Are you—''

''My violets . . . gone. All gone. Just like everything nice.''

When she began shaking violently, Saber realized she was close to going into shock. ''Goldie, I'll buy you more flowers! I'll—'' He broke off, her strange concern about her flowers making him gasp. Dear God, maybe she'd been shot, and pain was clouding her mind! Frantically, he tried to examine her, but the tight curl of her body prevented him from doing so. He rose, looked at the grove and saw Itchie Bon sniffing the ground. Reassured that the assailant had fled, he lifted Goldie into his arms, and pounded on the door with his foot.

''Sir!'' Bennett exclaimed upon opening the door. ''I heard a shot! I—''

Saber tore past the man and raced toward the staircase.

''My violets,'' Goldie whispered. ''My flowers.''

Saber turned and saw Bennett still standing by the door. "Get the damn violets!" he commanded the butler.

Three steps at a time, he climbed the stairs, his heart banging in his chest, fear for Goldie throbbing wildly through his veins. Reaching her bedroom, he rushed inside, placed Goldie on her bed, and lit several candles.

"Don't be hurt, Goldie," he commanded, bending over her and fumbling with the fastenings on her dress. "Don't be hurt!" He saw his hands shake, cursed his terrible fear, and tried once again to remove her dress.

Goldie took his hands into her own. "Saber—"

"Goldie, I can't see! Is there blood? Dear God, are you bleeding? I can't get the dress—Goldie, tell me—"

"I'm not hurt."

"The buttons won't—"

"Saber, I'm not hurt."

He made fists of his quivering hands. "Are you sure?"

"I'm not hurt."

"Sir," Bennett panted from the doorway. "The violets." He lifted the basketful of ruined flowers. "There is a hole in this basket, sir. Is Miss Mae—"

"She's fine. Bring me the flowers."

Bennett obeyed. "I also collected the oranges, sir." He cast a look of tender concern at Goldie then left the room, shutting the door.

Goldie took the basket from Saber, and, one by one, she removed each bunch of violets, placing them on her stomach. When she'd taken them all out, she gathered the crushed blossoms in her arms, bringing them to her face.

"Goldie, I'll buy you more violets," Saber promised, confused by her preoccupation with the flowers. "Stay here, poppet. I've got to go see if that man is somewhere—"

"No!"

"Goldie, that man shot—"

"No!" The one word escaped on a long, loud sob. "Hold me, Saber! Don't leave me! Please, just hold me!"

Her tears almost killed Saber; they erased all thought of trying to find the assailant. He lay down beside Goldie, drawing her close to him. Violets fell all over him when she turned to him. Her tears wet his shirt, her soft cries burned his soul. He said nothing, but simply held her close like she'd asked him to do. And as he did, the thought of what had happened stabbed into him.

She'd almost been killed tonight, he raged. The bullet that might have ended her life had found the basket instead. But for that, she might be dead right now. Just like all the people he'd loved and lost.

Smoothing Goldie's hair, he concentrated on the fear that still rumbled through him. The thought of losing her, too, was unbearable to him. It filled him with horrible emptiness and anguish.

"Goldie," he choked.

Hearing the painful distress in his voice, she lifted her gaze to him. The sight of his sorrow-etched face touched something so deep inside her, she couldn't understand what it was. Taking shelter in his strong arms, every shred of fear left her, replaced by soothing tranquility. Slowly, she brought his head closer to her, kissing him with all the tender emotion flowing from her heart.

Saber tasted the salty tears on her mouth, and felt his own eyes begin to sting. Who was this girl who could bring him tears? he wondered. Who made him laugh? Whose simple wisdom affected him so deeply? Whose smile lit up his entire world, whose presence filled the aching void in his life?

And whose brush with death brought him such excruciating grief?

Goldie felt a tremor run through him. "Saber, everything's all right. We didn't get hurt."

"I know, but—The shot—The man—Judging by the way he was dressed, I think he was a coster." *A coster.* A coster, he deliberated, wouldn't be involved with Hutchins or Doyle. Had the man been intent on robbery? He made a mental note to notify Tyler Escott's men about the incident.

"A coster?" Goldie repeated.

"A street seller. I'm sure he intended to rob us, but you could have been hurt. Are you certain you're all right?"

"Yes," she tried to reassure him, but knew by the expression in his eyes that he was still doubtful. She wondered what to say to him that would convince him, but came up with nothing different from what she'd already said.

Actions were all she had left to her. The thought brought a warm, deep rush of anticipation. Languidly she removed her dress, her eyes never leaving Saber's face. Her underthings followed. Reaching up to the back of her neck, she removed the pins that held her hair and shook her head. Her curls sprang free, spilling to her breasts.

Instant desire twisted through Saber's loins. He wondered what she would do, when she would begin.

His heart slammed against his chest when she came closer.

The scorching expression in his gaze made Goldie sense the power she held over him. Excitement mounted as she contemplated the things she would to do him. Straddling his hips, she began to unbutton his shirt. As each button came undone, his shirt parted further, and she took time to touch her fingers to the smooth, hard chest so slowly revealed to her. Finally, she removed the garment altogether, bringing it slowly toward her face, and closing her eyes. The warm virile scent clinging to it surrounded her, drifting into her, heightening her anticipation.

Opening her eyes, she saw Saber regarding her intently, a slow, knowing smile slanting his lips. At the sight, an unexpected tremor shot through her. Her cheeks warming, she crawled to the end of the bed and removed his shoes and stockings before laying her palms on his upper thighs. Keeping her movements as leisurely as she could make them, she slid her hands toward the fastening of his breeches. The buttons there opened easily. She smiled when Saber accommodated her by arching his hips off the bed. Slowly, she rolled the breeches and his undergarments downward, pulling them off his legs, and smiling at the sight of the diamond birthmark on his left upper thigh.

She held the clothes, still warm from his body, in her lap, staring at them for a long moment before raising her eyes. The sight of Saber, of each perfect and wonderful part of sinewy form, set her heart aflutter and her body aflame.

A low moan escaping her, she buried herself in the arms

he held out to her. Desire curled inside her when he took her mouth in a kiss that was savage and tender at once. His hand brushed over the soft curls between her thighs; his fingers began to stroke her. Pleasure engulfed her, her desire building when she felt her own moistness, her own hot readiness. She knew Saber felt it too when his eyes darkened, and his body tensed as his fingers delved deeply inside her.

With those same fingers, he then parted her legs, and moved above her. She welcomed his weight when he settled himself upon her. His scent of sandalwood wafted about her as she felt his maleness probing between her thighs. Closing her eyes, she prepared herself for the pain. She knew it would come, but she didn't care. Only Saber mattered. Only Saber.

"Now," she whispered. "Please now."

Her desperate plea almost sent Saber over the brink. Struggling to leash his wild desire, he pushed into her only slightly, giving her as much time as she needed to adjust to him. To want more of him. To change her mind. His heavy arousal ached. Every nerve in his body throbbed, making control an impossible thing. But tenderness flowed inside him, too, soothing him, transcending his powerful need. He held himself motionless, waiting for her to show him what she wanted him to do.

"Saber."

He tried to decipher what it was he heard in her small voice, but the feel of her nipples stiffening against his chest, the pleading pressure of her fanned fingers upon the muscles in his back, and the way her silky legs curved around his own, stole every other thought from his mind.

"Saber, please."

"Goldie—"

She arched into him, gasping when she felt more of him slide into her. She opened further for him, spreading her legs wider, giving him complete, unhindered access to her.

Saber could feel the thin veil of her virginity. It was all that lay between him and the ecstasy he yearned to find in her body. Desire tightened each of his muscles; he felt them coil with readiness. The fire in his loins threatened to consume him. "Goldie," he said between clenched teeth, "I—I'm going to hurt you. I don't want to. God, Goldie, I don't want to."

His tender worry and heartfelt reluctance to cause her any pain were the sweetest things anyone had ever shown her. Determined to have all of the wonderful man gazing down at her with such gentle emotion spilling from his beautiful eyes, she lifted her legs, wrapping them around his broad back. Her heels pressed his firm bottom, urging his hips forward, coercing him toward the deepest part of her.

Saber could hold back no longer. He knew in his soul she wanted their sensual union every bit as much as he did. "Goldie," he whispered, his lips curved over her mouth, "come to me. Come to me, my golden angel." When she lifted herself to him again, he met her. With one bold thrust, he took her from her maiden's world and into one where he could be with her.

Her soft cry, the stiffening of her body, stilled him. "Goldie." Her name came from him on a tormented moan.

Goldie took his face between her hands. "Saber," she cooed, all pain melting away at the sound of his name, "It only hurt for a minute."

Her voice seemed to be wrapped in satin. Her words made him feel beyond wonderful. He began to move inside her, plunging, withdrawing, circling his hips upon hers, and loving each tiny, mewling sound that came from her.

Goldie was astonished by the odd, but completely beautiful way he felt buried so deeply within her. She felt her body move as if by its own accord. Indeed, she felt as though she had no control at all, and so, gave herself up to whatever desire led her to do. From side to side, she moved her hips, then circled them, lifted them, desperation taking her when he left her, rapture filling her when he came to her again. The pleasure he offered gathered slowly. It rose, then faded, built again, diminishing less each time, until finally it ebbed no longer, but instead burst, sending shimmering bits of bliss shooting through every part of her.

With a shuddering sigh, she peered up at him. The dark,

simmering look in his eyes told her he wasn't nearly finished with her. Her realization was confirmed when he drove deeply into her, seeking and finding the very center of her womanhood.

The muscles in his back knotted beneath her palms. There was no denying his strength. It was everywhere, exuding from his body, his groans of exertion, and the invisible aura of power that surrounded him. He was, she realized at that moment, a man different from the Saber she knew.

The man who held her so possessively in his arms, whose body demanded all she could give him, whose darkening eyes radiated such hunger, excited her. His scent of sandalwood was gone, replaced with the scorching fragrance of heat. Of something wildly afire. It made her burn for him again.

"Before now," he panted down to her, "you've found fulfillment alone. Now, Goldie, now find it with me. Stay with me, come into it with me, share it with me."

She flushed at the sultry sound of his voice, the unspoken promise that laced his sensual command. She met him halfway when he bent to kiss her, ribbons of returning desire streaming through her when his tongue began matching the same . . . deep . . . urgent . . . rhythm of his body. She felt swallowed by him, taken into him, and she gloried in the exquisite sensation his total possession of her brought.

"Goldie. Now. Goldie." With one, last all-seeking thrust, he gave her everything he had to give her.

She felt him grow harder inside her. He didn't withdraw from her this time, but stayed imbedded deeply within her, throbbing wildly. The pulsations, the ecstasy she felt pounding through him quickly brought her her own. Her cries joined his, their shared bliss lifting her so high, she wondered if she would ever come down.

"Goldie," Saber murmured, pleasure still seeping through him.

She clung to him, feeling the last, lingering bits of sensation slowly fade. Fulfillment pulsed through her veins; she felt drugged with tranquility. Surrendering to the quiet joy, she sighed, smiling into the soft curve of his shoulder, breathing deeply of his sensual male scent.

Saber pressed his face into the silken mass of her wild curls. He was loathe to withdraw from her, and so he stayed within her for as long as nature would allow. And when at last his body left hers, he slipped to the violet-scattered mattress, drawing her into his arms. "Goldie—"

"Saber, y'know what I'm thinkin' right now?" she asked, molding herself to the curve of his body.

The lush happiness he heard in her voice made him smile. "I cannot begin to imagine."

"I'm thinkin'," she began, her fingers tracing circles around his taut nipples, "that it's a damn shame you aren't the ravishin' kind. If you were, I'd have known what all this was about the very day you found me at the pond."

He chuckled both at what she told him and the tickle he felt as she caressed his chest. "Goldie, you wouldn't have liked it had I taken you by force. Rape has nothing at all to do with lovemaking, poppet. There's nothing but violence involved. What we just did—"

"Was the most beautiful thing that's ever happened to me. Saber, I— Thank you."

"No, Goldie. You owe me no gratitude. We *shared* everything that happened tonight."

She moved away from him a bit so she could see him better. As she did, she caught sight of herself and the bedsheets. "Saber," she whispered raggedly. Fear kicked inside her, a contained scream filled her throat.

"Goldie," he said in a rush of breath when he saw the reason for her horror, "you were a virgin. You bled. It doesn't mean you're hurt, and it won't happen again." Rising from the bed, he crossed to a small table upon which a soft towel and a pitcher of water sat. He dampened the cloth and returned to Goldie.

He held the wet cloth tightly in his hands for moment to warm it. "Lie still," he told her, sitting beside her. As if she were made of delicate crystal, he touched the cloth to her thighs and womanhood very lightly, smoothing it over her skin with whisper-soft strokes. He continued his tender ministrations until not a trace of her virginity was left.

"Saber."

He saw the fear had left her eyes, but a different emotion replaced it. It was something fragile. "Are you sorry, Goldie?" he asked brokenly. "Sorry you gave your virginity to me?"

She noted the haunted look on his face. "I wish I could have it back. So I could give it to you again."

Indescribable joy consumed him. His body rippling with the need for more of her, he crushed her to him, his hands skimming over each silken inch of her. "Maybe," he began, his lips whispering over hers, "it started the day you told me the story about dandelions. Maybe it started with our mud fight. Or the day you taught me how to bake bread. Or the night I found you wandering in the maze. Or maybe, my poppet," he decided, his lips moving from her mouth to her cheeks, to her temple, to her ear, "it began the day I first saw you. When you thought I was a highwayman. When you pointed your claymore at me, looking at me with such fear and fury in your eyes. Whatever the truth, from the moment I met you, Goldie, you have been a part of me. I'm lonesome for you when you're not with me, and I dream about you at night.

"For so long," he continued tenderly, his hand lost within the golden splendor of her hair, "I have wondered what it was I felt for you, tried to understand the joy your smile, your giggle bring to me. I have pondered the warm and quiet contentment the sight of you gives me. I—"

"Saber—"

"I lived behind a curtain before knowing you. Bit by bit, you lifted the veil, showing me the man who dwelled behind it. You reminded me about things I'd forgotten. Important things like the smell and feel of dirt. And flowers. Lazy days, moonlit walks, and holding hands. Your laughter pulls emotions from me that I never knew I had. You take the simplest things and paint them with profound significance. You're like sunshine, Goldie. You chase away the dark, warming everything you touch."

"Saber, you—"

"It's not infatuation. And it's not just that I enjoy your company. Goldie . . ." His words trailed away as he lifted his head and stared at her incredible beauty. With startling clarity, he realized exactly what it was he felt for the outrageously wonderful girl in his arms. There was no denying it any longer.

"Goldie," he told her softly, achingly, "I love you. Dear God, I love you. I—"

She placed her hand over his mouth. "Don't say anything else," she begged him, her eyes bright with unshed tears. "I can't—It's all so . . . I've never heard such wonderful things. But I—Saber . . ."

When she tried to roll away from him, Saber held onto her, turning her face up to his. Wariness mingled with the tears in her huge amber eyes was what he saw. The sight filled him with comprehension and compassion. "This isn't a dream, Goldie. Touch me," he commanded, picking up her hand and placing it over his heart. "I'm real. I'm not some dream that's going to vanish if you blink."

Skepticism tainted her earlier happiness. She bit her bottom lip, struggling to hold back a flood of fresh tears. "I want to believe you, Saber."

"Then do. Believe what I'm telling you, Goldie. Say it. Say you believe me."

"Yes. I believe you."

There wasn't a shred of conviction in her answer, he noted furiously. She said it only because he'd forced her to. Battling his anger, he thought about her feelings of unworthiness. Her belief that her dreams wouldn't come true until she deserved them.

Dear God, he'd never known a more deserving girl than Goldie.

It tore at him that she thought herself unworthy of love. The very thing she needed, the very thing he wanted so desperately to give her. But what could he do? It had taken years for such feelings to become so firmly rooted. How long would it take him to destroy them?

She'd given him so much of herself, he thought. And if it was selfish for him to want even more, then he was the greediest man on earth. He craved that part of her heart she kept guarded from him. And he knew in his own heart that he would never cease trying to earn it.

"Very well, Goldie, we won't talk about it. Not until you're ready. But do something for me, poppet."

Her emotions were so tangled, she could barely understand what he was saying. "What do you want me to do?"

Reaching for the bedcovers, he drew them over her and himself, then settled her comfortably in his arms. "Cry. Cry for me, Goldie. I won't be infuriated. I won't tell you to stop. If you cry all night, I'll keep holding you. I'll not let you go until you ask me to."

She frowned at him. "But why?"

His answer was slow in coming, not because he didn't know what to say, but because it was a moment before the words in his heart rose to his lips. "Because, Goldie, no one else has ever let you do it."

His answer folded around a place so deep inside her, she knew it could only be the heart of her soul. Its very poignancy awakened the sorrow he'd asked her to release. Pressing her face against him, she bathed his bare chest with her warm tears, and felt all her painful secrets escaping her. "It all goes away," she sobbed, her entire body shaking. "Every nice thing," she squeaked, unable to stop the words from coming. "Every wish, every dream . . . everything. Saber, it all goes away before I can hold it!"

"I know, poppet," he cooed, brushing her hair with his fingers. "I know."

"I try," she sputtered. "I try so hard to hold onto it before it disappears! But I never can! Oh, Saber, all I can do is touch it, feel it, and want it more than ever. And then—Then it's gone."

He said nothing to her, but only let her cry and tell him what she would.

"Almost everyone I've ever known has made fun of me, been mean to me," she whispered through her tears. "It hurt. So much. But at least those people weren't my family. At least they were only strangers. But Uncle Asa— He—"

She broke off for a moment, struggling unsuccessfully with more tears. "I was eight when Mrs. Granger gave me the tree." She wept piteously. "Mrs. Granger was one of the only people I can remember who never said anything ugly to me. The tree—It was only a saplin', but she promised me it would grow. It was a magnolia. And magnolia blossoms—They're so big, so creamy. They smell

sorta like lemons. I planted the tree, Saber. I planted it
right, too. It never even wilted. I watered it every day,
and I talked to it. It began to grow.

"And then," she continued, crying harder, her slight
body quivering, "one night Uncle Asa got mad at me. He
was drunk and couldn't find his red shirt. He said I'd lost
it. But Saber, I had no idea where it was! Uncle Asa said
I was bad. He got his axe, and . . . and he chopped down
my tree! He—He said that until I started behavin' myself
I couldn't have anything that made me happy! He—Oh,
Saber, he killed my little tree!"

Saber was enraged, but tempered his fury. He didn't
move, he said nothing. He merely waited to hear more of
her wrenching memories.

"The next day," she cried, "he said he was sorry. He
even tried to mend my tree with a strip of cloth. But it
was too late. The tree never came back. I never got another one."

"Oh, Goldie," Saber whispered, his heart twisting at
the thought of all she'd loved and lost.

"And then, when I was ten, I found a hurt bird," she
told him, grief saturating her voice. "His wing was broken, but I fixed it with two sticks and a bandage. I even
made a cage, and put him inside so it could heal. I loved
that bird, Saber. I named him Woodrow, and he was more
than a pet. He was my best friend. He even ate worms
right from my fingers. But Uncle Asa—He hated Woodrow. He said Woodrow kept him awake at night with all
of his squawkin' and flappin' around. He . . . He let
Woodrow go. I didn't know he'd done it until I came home
from shoppin' and found the cage in the yard. Woodrow—
My poor Woodrow, Saber. Hoppin' around somewhere,
with no way of gettin' the sticks and bandage off his wing.
He died. I know Woodrow died.

"I cried so hard. I cried for days. Uncle Asa was so
sick of my wailin', he left home and didn't come back for
a week. When I saw him again, he apologized. But he told
me that fancy things like birds in cages were only for rich
folks anyway. I couldn't understand that. Couldn't understand why folks with money were the only ones who could
have nice stuff. Besides, Woodrow was only a wild bird.

I hadn't paid for him, and his cage was made of twigs. But I couldn't have him. I— Uncle Asa wouldn't let me.''

She dabbed at her eyes with the sheet. ''I wanted to stay mad at him, Saber. I wanted so much to hate him for everything he did to me. But he always said he was sorry, and I knew he really was. I only wish, though, that . . .''

''What, Goldie? What do you wish?''

''I—I wish I could forget the bad things about him. I've tried so hard not to remember 'em. But even after I've forgiven him for the things he says and does, I can't forget the hurt. I've wondered what the good thing is about his mean side. I keep tellin' myself some kind of good comes from his screamin' and all the things he does to me. But I can't. Can't find the good thing no matter how hard I try.''

Anger boiled inside Saber, but he refused to let her see it. ''Let's try to understand the good about it,'' he told her gently. ''Let's—''

''There's nothin' good about it. For all my talk about findin' the silver linin'—I'm sorry for lyin' to you, Saber. Sorry for actin' like there wasn't anything wrong in my life. But I didn't want you to pity me, y'see. I would have hated that, and I hope it's not what you're doin' now.''

He knew full well what it had taken for her to admit to the bad things in her life. She was so proud, his little poppet called Goldie, and it meant the world to him that she'd confided in him tonight. ''Goldie, love,'' he began softly, ''how was it possible for you to keep loving a man like your uncle?''

''He was the only thing in my life that didn't go away,'' she murmured. ''The only thing that stayed with me. He was the one thing I could reach for, touch, and hold onto. The other mean people I've known, they've come and gone. But Uncle Asa was always there.''

''But what about Big? He's stayed with you, Goldie. He hasn't left, and he hasn't—''

''You and Big are my best friends. But Big—Saber, Big feels like my father. But he's not my father, and I'm not his daughter. I know I mean a lot to him, but one day he's gonna leave me. I know in my heart he will. He's not tied to me in anyway, y'see. He's gonna find a job, a woman, or a place he loves. And when he does, I've got to make him go. I can't stand the thought of him stayin' with me out of loyalty. Or pity. I could never let him do that.''

He held her tenderly when another wave of tears came. He felt terribly helpless and thought about telling her he loved her again. But he knew in his heart she wouldn't believe him. He realized then the time for words was over. What she needed most now was rest.

''Go to sleep now, Goldie. Close your eyes and go to sleep.'' While he sheltered her trembling body next to his own, a lullaby came to him from the deepest recesses of his mind. He hadn't sung in years, but he did now. For her. For Goldie. Quietly, soothingly, he sang until her tears ceased, her body relaxed. He remembered the peace he felt as a child when his mother sang him this lullaby, and hoped he was bringing Goldie the same tranquility now.

When her breathing slowed, he realized she was asleep. In the pools of her tears, the violets, and his own frustration, he lay silently beside her, his hand still smoothing her curls. ''Diamond dreams,'' he remembered aloud, thinking about the irony of it all. ''The one thing you want most in the world is love. The kind of love that never wavers, not even for an instant. You long for enduring love. *That* is your diamond dream, isn't it, poppet? And the night you were lost in the maze, when you told me you planned to have twelve children—you didn't mention a husband because you have no belief whatsoever you will ever have one.''

He closed his eyes. ''And you don't believe me either. I love you, and you refuse to believe me. But then I don't really know if it's *my* love you want. You said I was your best friend. But is friendship all you feel for me, Goldie?'' he asked, his heart constricting. ''Does it go any deeper?''

He held her for a while longer, but knew he couldn't stay. The aunties would see him in here with her. With a great sigh, he rose and dressed. ''I love you, Goldie,'' he whispered to her before leaving. ''I love you, and I will never cease trying to make you believe that.''

Turning his head, he peered out the window. Cynicism rose within him as he stared at the heavens. ''Dream Giver,'' he muttered to the star-sprinkled sky. ''She said that's who You are. But You've never given her anything. You've allowed heartache after heartache to befall her. I'm going to change that. With or without Your help. If You won't live up to the name she calls you, then *I* will. *I* will be her dream giver.''

His vow spoken, he left her room, closing her door quietly behind him.

# Chapter 17

D iggory grabbed Og's shirt, slamming him against the blackened wall of the fetid East End alleyway. "Wot do ya mean *ya didn't get 'er?*" he demanded. "Wasn't she the one? Dammit, Og, ya said ya'd seen 'er! Ya said ya'd met a yellow-'aired girl wot talked like she weren't from 'ere! Ya said ya followed Rosie an' learned where the girl's livin'! Ya—"

"Diggory—"

"Ya said ya could do the job, Og! So wot the bloody 'ell do ya mean *ya didn't get 'er!*"

The rage in Diggory's eyes chilled Og down to the very marrow of his bones. "I *did* follows 'er! She's at that big 'ouse on the corner o' Pickerin' an' Landon! I tell ya, Diggory, I was closer to 'er than God's curse is to a 'ore's arse, I was! But—But I missed! The swell with 'er, 'e pushed 'er down afore I—"

"Then why the bloody 'ell didn't ya shoot the scabby swell too!"

" 'E 'ad a dog!" Og yelled "The mongrel—"

"Wot?" Diggory roared. "Ya let the bitch get away because ya was afeared of a *dog!* Ya friggin' prick!"

"I'll goes after 'er again! I'll—"

"Ya thinks I got a case o' the flamin' simples, Og?" Diggory exploded. "I'll take care o' the skirt meself, ya twaddlin' looby!" With petrifying speed he pulled out his knife. "Wot's me name?"

Og went rigid. "Diggory. Diggory Ferris."

"Wot's me other name?"

"The—The Butcher."

Diggory smiled and lifted the blade.

Og never even had time to scream.


"Come away from the window, my dear," Clara instructed Goldie. "Saber had business to attend to this morning. It will be several hours before he returns. Come sit down, and we will continue discussing cards and calls."

"He's been gone all day for four whole days," Goldie murmured, watching the street from the drawing-room window. The last time she'd seen him for more then ten minutes, she mused, blushing, was the night they'd made love.

When Saber had told her he loved her.

"I'm sure his activities are important ones, Goldie," Lucille stated, giving her sister a secret, knowing smile.

Clara caressed her reticule. "*Very* important," she agreed, returning Lucille's mischievous grin.

Goldie turned away from the window. Absently, she walked around the room, trailing her finger along all the elaborate furnishings she passed. *From the moment I met you, Goldie, you have been a part of my life.* She stopped in front of a mirrored cabinet, Saber's whispered words drifting through her mind.

"Social cards are always engraved in fine copperplate, Goldie," Lucille informed her. "Printed ones are absolutely forbidden."

"They are usually snowy-white," Clara elaborated, "But cream-colored ones are acceptable. However, if you leave your card with a family who is in mourning, the card must be edged in black. This is a message of sympathy. A lady carries her cards at all times. If you should be invited to a social engagement such as a dinner at someone's home, you may leave your card in the card holder in the entryway as you leave their house. This is an invitation for your hostess to call on you."

*I'm lonesome for you when you're not with me.* Goldie closed her eyes, remembering. She wondered if Saber was lonesome for her now, and longed with all her heart to believe he was.

"And if you should go calling on someone, you arrive at the house during the acceptable calling hours and knock politely," Lucille continued. "When the butler answers, you ask him for your hostess and hand him your card. Do not fidget or wander around the entryway while he is gone to see if the lady is at home. Stand still and quietly until he returns. If the lady is at home—that is, if she is receiving callers—he will escort you to where she awaits. Do not remove your wrap or gloves, and leave within twenty minutes. Acceptable conversations during a call might include a discussion about a recent gathering you have attended, or you might tell her about something amusing that has happened to you. You might even talk about the weather. Just remember the conversation must be kept light and brief. And do not expect refreshments unless you have called upon your hostess on her official at-home day."

*You're like sunshine, Goldie.* A profound pang of yearning surged through her. If only it could be true, she wished silently. If only it wouldn't all go away this time. Did she dare to dream that it wouldn't? And if it didn't, what would happen after Saber played the duke? Surely he realized he had to leave after the masquerade was over.

"You will know if it is the lady's official at-home day, Goldie, if you have been given one of her own cards," Clara instructed. "In the lower left-hand corner a day of the week will be engraved. If the card says Wednesday, for instance, you may be assured she will be at home receiving callers."

*I love you.* Saber's declaration filled Goldie with yet more desperate longing. The words were so sweet. So wonderful, it almost stole her breath to think about them.

Her heart turned over. She had to leave London soon. She couldn't put off her departure for much longer. The thought of never seeing Saber again left her feeling emptier than she ever had before. Lord in heaven, what was going to happen between them?

"But if it is not a Wednesday, and the butler returns to you and says the lady is not at home," Lucille explained, "you announce your name to him, and leave your card in the card holder he will offer you. If he does not offer you one, look around the entryway for a small table and leave your card upon it before departing."

*Dear God, I love you.* Goldie's eyes filled with tears as Saber's words continued echoing through her.

"Now, is all of that clear to you, my dear?" Clara asked.

"Goldie," Lucille said crisply. "Have you heard a word we said?"

Goldie wiped her eyes and turned to the women. "I . . . cards. Deep black cards with copper on 'em. I knock on the butler politely. I have to have a card to get into twenty-minute dinners that are held on Wednesdays. But maybe I won't get dinner if the day isn't the official dinner day. I stand still, waitin' on the butler. I can talk about the weather with him when he gives me a card holder. I look for a small table and after I've found one, I can leave."

Lucille's face fell; Clara shook her head in her hands.

Goldie sighed deeply. "Miss Lucy, Miss Clara. I'm sorry if I got it all wrong, but I don't even have any of those cards y'all are talkin' about. If I had some, I'd try real hard to hand 'em all out the way I'm supposed to, but—"

"Goldie, my dear," Clara said gently, "you must pay attention. We shall review the subject of calling cards again soon. Now we will discuss titles. We will not go into great detail today, as there are many, many nuances to be considered. Now listen well, Goldie. In the matter of titles and the correct form of address it is imperative that you make no mistakes whatsoever."

"The Queen is referred to as Her Majesty the Queen," Lucille began.

"A royal duke is His Royal Highness the Duke of . . . the Duke of Tristan, for example. A non-royal duke is simply His Grace the Duke of Tristan. His wife is a duchess, and when you are referring to them together, they are Their Graces, the Duke and Duchess of Tristan."

Lucille twisted her bracelet. "The eldest son of a duke has the highest family title under his father's. He is a marquess. His wife is a marchioness."

Goldie's mind spun. "March?"

"The eldest son of a marquess is an earl," Clara continued. "His wife is a countess. The eldest son of an earl and his wife is a viscount. The wife of a viscount is viscountess. The son of a viscount is referred to as *honorable*. Shall we say, the Honorable William Tristan.''

Goldie nodded and glanced at the window.

''And then there are barons, my dear,'' Lucille added. ''A baron is never addressed as 'Baron,' but as 'Lord.' Lord Tristan. The wife of a baron is—''

''Miss Lucy,'' Goldie broke in, ''I—I can't keep all this straight in my mind. Would it be all right if I just called everybody His Royal Mister or Her Royal Ma'am? It's simple to remember, and sounds respectful to me.''

''I think Royal Mister and Royal Ma'am are splendid,'' Saber said from the doorway, smiling.

''Saber!'' Goldie exclaimed. ''Where—''

''Saber, your presence is not appreciated at this moment,'' Clara scolded. ''We are trying to teach Goldie proper etiquette.''

''It appears to me that she has had enough for one day,'' Saber answered, noticing the lines around Goldie's eyes. He gave his aunt a slight nod.

Clara understood his silent message immediately. ''Yes. I do believe you are right, Saber. Goldie has had sufficient lessons for today.''

Saber walked into the room and stood next to Goldie. ''You look sad, poppet. What's the matter?''

''I—Nothin'.'' She looked up at him, fluttery feelings spinning through her at the sight of the softness in his beautiful green eyes.

Saber cupped her chin in his hand and looked at his aunts. ''If I may ask, why is my study filled from ceiling to floor with boxes?''

''Boxes?'' Lucille asked, feigning ignorance. ''Why, whatever do you mean?''

''There are literally dozens of boxes in my study,'' Saber continued. ''They are all wrapped, and I didn't see a single one that did not have ribbons and bows. Since I must use my study, I have asked the servants to bring the packages in here. I have no idea what they are, but I do not care to have them in my workplace.''

Goldie wrinkled her nose, her curiosity piqued. She watched in amazement as a stream of servants began bringing in a vast array of gaily wrapped boxes.

Clara stood and examined the small card attached to one of the packages. Pretending bewilderment, she looked at several more cards. "Goldie, my dear, all these gifts are for you."

"For me?"

"For her?" Saber repeated, struggling not to laugh at how wide her eyes were. It seemed to him they would pop out of her head at any moment. "Goldie, who do you know who could have sent you all these—"

"Nobody!" Goldie hurried to a nearby mound of boxes, reading their cards. "Oh! Oh, they really *are* mine!" she squealed. "Miss Clara, Miss Lucy, they're all—Every single one of 'em is—"

"What happened to laughing with quiet delight?" Saber teased.

"I think in this instance, my boy," Lucille informed him, "squealing is just the thing."

Clara smiled. "Quite right."

"Who in the world could've sent me so many presents?" Goldie exclaimed, shaking a small box next to her ear. "What do you think they all are? Why do you reckon I got 'em'? How—"

"The giver must prefer to remain anonymous," Lucille pretended to speculate while examining a few of the cards. "There is no name other than yours."

She frowned. "But who—"

"Maybe it was the dream giver," Saber guessed, trying to sound as though he were teasing.

Goldie looked up at him. "Saber, God doesn't do stuff like this."

*He doesn't, but I do,* Saber informed her silently. "Goldie, why don't you just open them?" he suggested out loud.

"I—" She broke off, still staring at the huge piles of pretty presents. "But there's so many, Saber," she said tremulously. "I—"

"You may as well accept them though," he told her quickly, knowing full well she was having a difficult time doing that. "After all, you don't know who sent them, so you can't very well send them back."

Lucille nodded. "He's right, Goldie. It would be rather silly not to accept and enjoy them."

"And you're not a silly girl, Goldie," Clara added. "Open them, my dear, and we shall watch."

Goldie deliberated. They were right, she realized. She couldn't send the gifts back. And if she didn't accept them, what would happen to them? "Are y'all sure *you* don't want 'em?"

"Splendid idea!" Saber exclaimed, still trying not to laugh at her utter astonishment. "There very well could be something in the boxes that we might want. Open them, and we'll tell you what appeals to us." He watched her carefully, well aware of the fact that she'd try and give all the gifts away before accepting a single one of them.

Goldie nodded, her yellow curls jumping all over her head. "All right. Saber, sit down, and I'll open 'em."

When Saber was seated, Goldie pulled at the ribbon on the small box she held. Careful not to tear the beautiful paper, she removed it. Her hands shaking, she lifted the top of the box.

A topaz necklace shimmered up at her. "Oh, Lord! Oh, Great day Miss Agnes, Saber, *look!*"

Joy burst inside him at the delight radiating from her beautiful face. "Why, it's the same color as your eyes, poppet!"

She caressed the topaz gems, telling herself repeatedly that they really *were* the same color as her eyes. Topaz eyes. She loved the way that sounded.

"I certainly have no use for a topaz necklace," Saber announced, trying to sound disappointed that the gift wasn't something he could keep for himself. "Aunties, would either of you like to have it?"

"I already have a topaz necklace," Clara said. "I really couldn't use another."

"I don't have one," Lucille stated. "But then, I don't wear topaz. It makes my skin look yellow, and I really don't care for going around with yellow skin."

"Then I suppose you may keep it, Goldie," Saber told her, rising to clasp it around her slender neck. "There." He allowed his hands to linger around her throat, his fingers caressing her lightly.

His touch made her tremble. She reached up, fondling both the jewels and Saber's hands. His nearness sent desire coursing through her.

Her brow raised, Clara watched the scene, and cleared her throat. "My dear, you are dawdling. We are anxious to see the remainder of the gifts. A lady does not keep people waiting. Remember your manners." She glared at Saber. "And I'll thank you to remember yours also," she snapped.

Saber cast his aunt a look that expressed his displeasure with her interference. But his irritation faded when Goldie began tearing open the next package and started squealing again.

"Saber! Saber—The dress—Lace and pearls and ivory satin and— Oh, Saber, *look* how purty!" Holding the gown to her body, she spun in a small circle, the creamy satin rustling and wrapping around her legs.

"Well, it's much to small for me," Clara said. "And it won't fit you either, Lucille."

"I don't wear gowns, and I'm not about to start," Saber said, grinning. "I suppose you may keep that gift, too, Goldie. Open the next one, please."

To Goldie's uncontainable delight, the next one was an exquisite crystal flask filled with French perfume. It so thrilled her that she spilled some of it on her brown frock. But the horror she felt at what she'd done disappeared when she opened more packages and found other bottles of scent. At Saber's urging, she opened gift after gift, each one making her so excited she couldn't keep still, but instead danced around the room holding the presents out for everyone to see.

As the afternoon wore on Saber and the aunties used every excuse in the world to explain why they didn't need or want any of the gifts she opened. Nothing Goldie said could convince them to accept a one of them.

When at last she'd unwrapped them all, she sat in the middle of the floor, overwhelmed by all the beautiful things around her. "There must be at least fifty gowns here," she said, eyeing the gorgeous fabrics and colors. "And wraps too! And the stuff to go with the dresses! Shoes, gloves, and purses! Ribbons, fans, muffs, umbrellas! And hats! Lord in heaven, how will I ever wear so many *hats?*"

"Change every hour," Saber suggested, resisting the temptation to pull her from the floor and enfold her in his arms. "And those are not umbrellas, poppet. They're parasols."

"And the jewelry!" she squealed, staring at the dozens of velvet cases. "I don't even know what half of it is!"

"Why, there are rubies, opals, and pearls," Clara informed her. "Amethysts—"

"And sapphires," Lucille cut in. "And coral, emeralds, cameos, and—"

"Necklaces, bracelets, combs, and tiaras," Clara added. "All set in gold."

Gold, Saber mused. *Just like your eyes.* He watched her pick up another bottle of perfume. "Goldie, I realize you're fascinated with scent, but if you put on one more dab of it, I'm afraid we won't be able to stand you. You're already wearing at least ten different kinds."

Clara laughed softly. "Well, Saber, it's obvious to me that Goldie has a secret admirer. Some young and very wealthy swain has seen her and sent her all these tokens of his affection."

"What do you mean?" Saber asked, pretending astonishment.

"Saber, surely you realize these gifts are from some gentleman who has taken a fancy to Goldie," Lucille said. "Who else would have sent her such beautiful and expensive things? They are certainly not the sort of gifts a lady sends to another lady. I'm not even sure they are the kind of gifts a gentleman sends either," she added, eyeing the many gowns that would reveal half of Goldie's bosom.

"Well . . ." Saber hedged, silently applauding his aunts on their magnificent performances. "Goldie, who have you been seeing behind my back?"

Her mouth dropped open; she stared at him. "Saber, I haven't seen—"

"You know very well how I feel about you," Saber cut her off. "And what do you do? You flirt with another man! You've gone out and made another man fall in love with you, and now the blackguard has sent you all these—'

"Saber, I swear I've haven't done that! I hardly ever leave the house! Daddy's honor! I don't see how any man could have seen me and decided to love me! I—"

"You are always hanging out of your bedroom window," Clara scolded lightly. "I have caught you doing it more times than I can count. It could be that the gentleman who sent you these gifts has caught you doing it also."

"And you have raced out of the house many times," Lucille pointed out. "Every time Itchie Bon escapes, you go tearing after him. We have all asked you repeatedly not to resort to such behavior, but you do not listen. At any rate, it's possible your admirer has seen you doing that. And it is obvious he has a good eye, too. All the things he sent will fit you perfectly. Yes, it is apparent to me he has studied you very carefully."

"You're a very beautiful girl," Clara said. "The gentleman who bestowed these lovely things upon you obviously believes that a beautiful girl deserves pretty things."

Goldie worried her bottom lip. "But how could he have known my name?"

Clara laughed. "My dear, a name is very easy to learn! I've no doubt your gentleman found out through the servants. Domestics are not as discreet as they should be, I'm afraid."

"It's not uncommon for a gentleman to send a lovely young girl a present, Goldie," Lucille explained. "And he doesn't always let her know he sent it. I remember receiving a lovely book of poetry. I never discovered who sent it. Someone sent me a lace shawl once, too. It was so beautiful." She closed her eyes, pretending to remember things that had never happened.

"And *I* have received flowers from a secret admirer," Clara announced, her hand over her heart. "It was most romantic."

"Well, I don't see anything *romantic* about this at all," Saber growled, frowning outside and smiling inside. "This is the most ridiculous thing I've ever—"

"Hush, Saber," Clara commanded. "The gifts are for Goldie, and you have no right to become belligerent over them. I must admit it is rather unusual and not a little shocking that the gentleman in question sent things as intimate as clothing, but I suppose we can bend the rules just a bit in this matter, don't you, Lucille?''

Lucille pushed her spectacles back onto her nose. "I do indeed. If we knew who sent them, Goldie could return them. But since we do not know, I see no reason why she should not keep and enjoy them.''

In a gesture of feigned irritation, Saber folded his arms across his chest. "Blackguard," he muttered, just loud enough for Goldie to hear.

Goldie looked at the three people staring at her. "Do you really think some fella saw me from the window or when I was outside? Do you really think he might have . . . liked me?" she asked disbelievingly.

"*Liked* you?" Saber snapped. "Goldie, it's obvious he spent a veritable fortune on all these gifts! I believe it's quite safe to say he's *enamored* of you! And as Aunt Lucy said, it is painfully obvious that he has been examining you extremely closely! For him to know your size, he had to have—"

"Saber, you are shouting," Clara said. "Remember yourself."

Goldie saw Saber's distress. It made her feel terrible to know he was so upset, and she tried to think of how to soothe him. But as the seconds passed, and she continued pondering his extreme irritation, she decided it wasn't the most awful thing she'd ever seen before. In fact, it made her giddy with pleasure! Saber was acting jealous! Even if he wasn't *real* jealous, it was obvious he was a little bit!

It was the first time in her life a man had felt that way about her.

She smiled, feeling a touch of smugness. Oh, it was wonderful, this small power she had over Saber! And to think someone out there in that great big world actually thought her worthy of such beautiful gifts . . . Well, it was just the most astonishing and wonderful thing that had ever happened to her! "Now, Saber, you just have to grit your teeth and bear this," she told him crisply, gathering a multitude of gowns in her arms. "It's not like I'm gonna marry the man, y'know. I don't even know who he is!"

"Well, that doesn't change the fact that he sent you all

these presents," Saber complained, loving every second of pretending he was jealous. "The man is obviously trying to win you over before ever even meeting you!"

"I didn't set out to make him—To make him . . ."

"Enamored," Saber supplied.

"Enamored. He just saw me, got enamored, and that was that," she told him flippantly.

"Really, Saber," Clara admonished, trying not to smile. "Control yourself." She rang the bell that brought the servants back. "Take these packages upstairs to Miss Mae's room," she instructed them when they arrived. "And Goldie, you go, too. Lucille and I will be right behind you."

Saber chuckled quietly when Goldie swept past him, her nose tilted to the ceiling.

"Do you think we fooled her?" Lucille asked when Goldie was gone.

"Completely," Saber said. "She's quite gullible, which is an aspect of her character that I happen to like very much."

"However did you manage to visit the seamstresses, shoemakers, and jewelers without being seen all over town, Marion?" Lucille queried. "I realize Lord Chittingdon has already seen you, but it seems to me that you would want to avoid being seen again. After all, one of your acquaintances might be inclined to follow you here."

Saber remembered all the darting around he'd done. All the clandestine meetings he'd held with the men and women who'd made Goldie's wardrobe. That, combined with the nagging impatience he felt over not having heard from Tyler Escott, had made the past few days extremely difficult ones. "It wasn't easy, but I managed."

Clara beamed. "It has finally happened. You cannot know how long I have hoped and prayed that you would fall in love again, Marion. And Goldie is such a fine girl. Granted, she is a bit unpolished here and there, but Lucille and I will see to that."

Saber tapped his fingers upon the sofa arm. "Do not polish her so completely that there is nothing left of her," he said, a note of warning in his voice. "I love her because of the way she *is,* not for what she could be. I'll not have the two of you turning her into one of those pretentious women I abhor.''

Clara sighed. ''You would do well to leave her to us, Marion. We—''

''I know what I love about Goldie, and I mean for her to stay the way she is,'' he stated in a voice that dared his aunts to argue.

''Very well,'' Clara said. Taking Lucille's arm, she led her sister out of the drawing room. ''Marion is right, you know, Lucille,'' she admitted as they swept into the entryway and headed for the staircase. ''We can and should teach Goldie good manners, but her natural exuberance should not be tampered with. Let us be careful. However, as for the way those two look at each other . . . Don't you think we should keep a closer eye on them? It is quite obvious to me that there is a strong attraction between them,'' she hinted quietly, blushing.

''Yes, I've noticed it also, Clara,'' Lucille said, twisting her bracelet. ''Not that there is anything wrong about a handsome man and a beautiful girl being attracted to each other, but—Well, you are quite right, sister. We mustn't allow them to lose their heads. We *are,* after all, their chaperones. As such, it is our obligation to see that strict morals are upheld.''

''I don't imagine we will have much success with our Marion, though. He has been well out of our reach for years. Goldie, however, is in our hands. We will teach *her* about what is allowed and what isn't, and then Marion will have no other choice but to respect her wishes.''

Lucille nodded in absolute agreement, then began to dwell on the afternoon's activities. ''Goldie truly loves the gifts. It did my heart good to see the happiness in her eyes. She's really such a lovely person, Clara.''

''I must admit I was distressed when Marion would not allow us to help him choose the gifts. But he really did a splendid job by himself. Everything he picked out suits Goldie's coloring and small stature. What a clever idea he had taking her frock and a pair of her shoes with him to the seamstresses and shoemakers. They used the dress and shoes to determine her sizes, you know.''

''I know. And I must confess it was terribly difficult

keeping a straight face when she discovered the dress and shoes were missing," Lucille said, smiling. "I even pretended to help her look for them!"

Clara laughed. "But do you know, Lucille, that there was one thing missing from the wide assortment of gifts he bought for her?"

"What is that?"

"Well, it's certainly not our Marion's fault," Clara said as they reached the upper landing and turned down the hallway. "It's not his place to—Well, what I mean to say, Lucille—Marion is a man. He cannot be expected to consider such a thing. But the dressmakers should have thought of it."

"Clara, whatever are you talking about?"

"My dear Lucille, not a single one of the dozens of boxes Goldie opened contained a thread of *underwear!*"

Dusk had fallen before Tyler was able to get away from Asa Mae long enough to scurry behind the dense hedgerows on the outskirts of Hallensham. "Damn the man!" he cursed to Ingram, one of the detectives who'd accompanied him to Ravenhurst. "What the hell is his problem? He follows me around like some overgrown, adoring puppy! I could understand his attachment to me if he knew about my connection with his niece in London, but he knows nothing at all about that! And he's not at all the drunken ogre Lord Tremayne described him to be. I almost wish the man *would* drink! Drink himself into oblivion so I could carry on my investigation without him acting like my second shadow!"

Ingram smiled, hunkering down beside his employer. "From what I've noticed, sir, Asa Mae doesn't have many friends here. Besides the midget, no one pays much attention to him. Since you were very polite to him when we arrived, I imagine he sees you as someone he could possibly strike up a friendship with."

Tyler muttered another curse and looked through the branches of the hedgerow. He had a perfect view of the Tremayne manor house. "There she is, going into the house again. Dora Mashburn. During what free time Asa has allowed me, I've been watching her. It's all a lie, Ingram. Hutchins is not sick in his bed. He's not even here."

Ingram watched Dora disappear into the mansion. "How do you know?"

"Dora's been in and out of the house, but the only room she ever bothers to illuminate is that one she's lighting up now. Judging by its location, I know full well it's not a bedroom. If Hutchins were sick, he'd be in a bedroom. Dora is only visiting the mansion to keep the villagers from guessing Hutchins is gone."

"She did act rather queer when Dickinson and I told her we wanted to speak to the estate manager about employment."

"Well, she hasn't seen me yet. I'm going up there to talk to her. You and Dickinson continue chatting with the villagers. I realize they've told us naught so far, but it's important to keep trying. Maybe one of them will remember something. And for God's sake, keep that Asa Mae character from looking for me. The last thing I need is for him to interrupt my time with Dora."

When Ingram was gone, Tyler took a moment to concentrate on his plan, then walked to the house. As he reached it, an old woman waved to him from the yard. He returned her greeting, and knocked on the door.

Dora opened it. "Who are ya, an' wot do ya want? I've got a sick man ter care fer, an' I can't be bothered now."

Tyler removed his hat and bowed his head. "You must be Lady Hutchins," he said, taking hold of her hand and pressing his lips to it. He saw no ring on the fingers he held to his mouth, nor did he see one on her other hand.

Dora blushed with pleasure. "Yes," she said, her nose tilted, "I'm Lady Hutchins. Wot can I do fer ya?"

Tyler smiled. "My name is Mr. Tyler. I'm aware that Lord Hutchins isn't here. You see, I've been sent by him, milady. May I come in?"

Dora hesitated. "Do ya have a message fer me?"

Tyler prayed his plan would work. It was risky at best, but it was the only one he had. "I'm to see to the master bedroom, milady. Lord Hutchins said that for the past five years, you've been wanting to redecorate it." Tyler's palms began to perspire as he waited for her reaction.

Dora's entire face lit up. She pulled him into the house. "Oh! Yes! Did ya bring all the materials with ya? Can I see—"

"Oh, no, milady. I must do much concentrating before we get to *that* point. For today I will see the room. Study it. Take measurements. Will you take me to it?"

Once in the bedroom, Tyler pretended to examine its size. "It's an impressive room. Perfect for a duke and his duchess."

Dora affected an imperious nod. "I want wallpaper. Lots o' rugs. An' all new furniture. I hate this wot's in here."

Tyler took out his notepad, jotting down her instructions. He knew by the look on her face that she could read nothing at all of what he wrote. The knowledge gave him an idea. "You hate the furniture?" he asked, ambling to the superbly carved desk by the window. He opened a few of the drawers, smiling when he saw the many papers inside. "Ah, yes. I can see why you don't care for it. It's cheaply made. The drawers squeak terribly."

He scanned the papers on the tops of the piles, his eyes drawn to a soiled scrap. Hiding his actions from Dora, he picked it up and read the name written on it. *Diggory Ferris.* Where had he heard that name before? Something began to nag at the back of his mind, but he couldn't understand what it was.

"Wot are ya doin' with milord's things?" Dora blurted.

Deftly, Tyler slipped the scrap into his pocket and picked up another paper. "What a beautiful name you have, Lady Hutchins."

"Wot makes ya say that?" Dora asked, joining him at the desk.

Tyler showed her the paper. "This appears to be a love letter. Angelica. Yes, what a beautiful name. Forgive me for reading this, milady, but I confess to being a romantic at heart, and I don't remember ever having read anything so romantic. Lord Hutchins must love you very much."

Dora stiffened, her face wrinkling into lines of rage. "Wot's the letter say?" she asked, her voice shaking.

"Oh, you mean he hasn't given it to you yet? Perhaps I should return it to the drawer and—" He broke off, lifting another stack of papers from the drawer. "Good heavens! *Look* at all these love letters! Why, they date back to some five years ago!"

"Read one," Dora ordered.

Tyler looked at a bill for farm equipment. "My darling Angelica," he pretended to read. "Before knowing you, my life was dismal and empty. I searched long and hard for a woman like you. You fill my every thought, and you must know, my darling, that Dora will never take your place in my heart. She is but a willing wench from the village, unfit to be under the same roof as you. It is you I love, Angelica. You, always and for—"

"That bleedin' bastard," Dora hissed. "Friggin'—"

"Lady Hutchins!" Tyler exclaimed, feigning horror. "What a thing to say about your own husband! Look at all these beautiful letters he's written to you! For five whole years he's been pouring his heart out to you—"

"Not to me. I'm Dora. Dora Mashburn," she cried, losing all control and sobbing into her hands. "And he ain't me husband! He's done me wrong from the very beginnin', he has! A couple o' nights ago, he even called me by her name! I fergave him. I *always* fergave him, but the letter ya read—All those letters—They prove wot he really thinks o' me, they do!"

Tyler allowed her to cry for a moment longer, then put his hand on her shoulder. "But he must have changed his mind about you, Dora. He did, after all, send me to redecorate your bedroom, did he not?"

Sniffling, Dora looked up from her hands. A shred of hope came to her. "Did he say wot colors ter do it in?"

"Oh, he did indeed. His orders were that I was to do the entire room in your very favorite shades—green and gold."

Dora staggered backward, wailing loudly. "But I wanted crimson an' white! Green an' gold be *her* colors, not mine! Her! Always her!"

"Angelica?" Tyler pressed.

Dora shook violently. "He's always pretendin' she's still alive! He shuts his eyes an' makes believe I'm her!"

"Are you saying this Angelica woman died?"

"Fell down the stairs one night an' broke her bleedin' neck!"

"Oh, how dreadful."

"It weren't dreadful! It were a blessin'! I hated her on sight the day she got here! She lost her ring, an' she said I took it! I never even *saw* the flamin' thing! Well, *dead's* wot she is now, an' I'm glad!"

"Oh, my! I certainly hope you didn't have to witness her death!"

Dora clenched her fists. "I weren't here in the house when she fell. It was me mum's birthday that night, an' we gave her a party in the village. Angelica died whilst the party was goin' on. But I can tell ya that if I'd been here, I'd have *cheered* when the bitch took her last breath!"

*The birthday party.* Comprehension dawned on Tyler. It clearly sounded as if Dora was innocent. At any rate, it would be easy enough to see if many of the villagers remembered seeing her at her mother's birthday party on the night of Angelica's death. If so, she'd have an ironclad alibi. Still, he mused, she might be able to tell him *something.* "Oh, miss, please forgive me for distressing you so. I didn't mean to do this at all. I'm well aware that discussing Lord Hutchin's betrayal must be agonizing for you. But look at it this way. He got his just desserts when he found that Angelica woman with her neck broken. Surely the pain he must have felt at seeing her lying there—"

"He didn't find her," a man said from the doorway. "I did."

Tyler recognized him immediately. "Doyle," he said tonelessly, glancing at the gun the man held in his hand.

"It's been a long time, Escott," William Doyle said, walking into the room. "The last time I saw you . . . it was at a dinner party, was it not?"

Dora wiped her tearstained face with the back of her hand. "Mr. Doyle, wot are ya doin' here? An' wot are ya doin' with that gun?"

"I only just arrived," William explained to her. "And it would seem I got here just in time. Now step away from Mr. Escott, Dora."

"Mr. Escott?" Dora repeated, confused. "This is Mr. Tyler. Dane sent him to redecorate."

"*Sent* him?" Doyle demanded. "Dane's not here? Where is he?"

Dora's eyes narrowed with anger. "I heard him tell the coachman ter take him ter London. But I don't know wot kind o' business the bastard has there," she spat.

At Dora's announcement, Tyler scowled. Dane Hutchins was in London. So were Lord Tremayne and Goldie Mae. Tyler felt a deep wave of apprehension spill through him.

Doyle's brow creased too. He'd come to Ravenhurst to dispose of Dane, and the idiot wasn't here! Dammit, what was the imbecile doing in London? He struggled with his fury, realizing he had to concentrate on the problem at hand—Tyler Escott. He'd deal with Dane as soon as Tyler was out of the way. And he'd have to kill Dora, too. She'd seen and heard entirely too much for his liking.

"Dora, this man is Tyler Escott," he explained. He walked to Tyler, quickly finding the gun in Tyler's belt. Tossing it across the room, he backed away again. "Escott is a detective, and I have a sneaking suspicion he's here on Tremayne's orders. You are about to die with him, my dear."

Dora's mouth opened to emit a silent scream before she crumpled to the floor.

Tyler realized she'd fainted. He looked back up at Doyle. As he did so, he saw a shadow move in the hallway, and knew one of his men had come. He must have seen Doyle arrive. Tyler almost smiled. "So you found Angelica's body. That means Hutchins is the one who pushed her down the staircase."

Doyle sneered. "Why are you so certain she didn't fall all by herself? She was wearing a long night rail, and it was dark. She might have tripped."

"She didn't trip, and you know it."

"For a man who is about to die, you are absurdly brave, Escott."

Tyler saw the shadow move again. "Let us say that I prefer to go to my grave having solved my last case."

Doyle laughed, then ran a finger over his stiff mustache. "Angelica would have spoiled everything," he began, waving has gun as he spoke. "She was almost successful at doing just that. She wrote a letter to Tremayne. Thank God I saw her give it to a traveler on his way to London. He died, too. It was a drowning accident. I thought at first I would have to cause an accident to befall Angelica's companion too. But the old hag saved her own skin by sleeping day in and day out. I'm rather good at arranging accidents.''

Tyler raised a brow. ''Indeed.''

William nodded, smiling smugly. ''Twenty years ago, Marion Tremayne father began asking me questions I didn't care to answer. He had a hunting accident soon thereafter. His gun misfired.''

''But it wasn't an accident. You shot him.''

''You've a brilliant mind, Escott. As perhaps you've guessed, over the years, I have been using the Tremayne fortune for my own purposes and am now a very wealthy man. Of course there are still a few obstacles in my way. A few accidents yet to arrange. You don't, by any chance, know why Dane Hutchins is in London, do you?''

Tyler thought of Goldie and Marion Tremayne again. Foreboding almost strangled him, but he kept his wits about him. ''Hutchins is one of your obstacles?''

''He and Tremayne. They'll both die, as will you and that bitch on the floor there. No one who knows anything about me can be left alive, you see. Now I ask you again, Escott. Do you know why Dane is in London?''

''Do you really think I would tell you?''

''Then I damn you to hell.''

Tyler watched as William raised the gun, and felt the beginnings of panic. Why hadn't his man overtaken Doyle yet? What was he waiting for?

''Good-bye, Escott,'' William said. Slowly, he curled his finger around the trigger.

Tyler took a sudden dive toward William's legs, and saw the gun drop to the floor. He made a wild grab for it, but Doyle reached it first. Belly on the floor, Tyler froze, waiting to feel the bullet end his life.

But it never came. Instead, Tyler heard a thud and watched his assailant crash to the floor beside him. He looked up, saw his savior, and frowned. It wasn't Ingram or Dickinson.

Asa Mae stood before him, clutching a heavy silver candlestick in his hand. "God Almighty," Asa whispered. "I've done a lot of things in my life, but I ain't never killed a man."

Tyler looked at William Doyle. "He's not dead, Asa. And Dora isn't either. How did you know I needed help? Did you see this man arrive?"

Asa shook his head. "I just wanted to ask you if you wanted to have supper with me and Big, is all. I couldn't find you at first, but ole Miz Crawton? Well, she come to the cottage with a pie for us, and she said she seen you goin' inside this house. It's a damn good thing I come up here, ain't it?"

Tyler nodded, rose from the floor, and strode quickly toward the door, anxious to start back for London. He had to find Dane Hutchins. Had to warn Marion Tremayne that the deranged man was in the city!

Asa threw the candlestick down and grabbed Tyler's arm. "I heard everything while I was in the hall. Do—Do y'know my Goldie Mae? She went to London to find the duke. Has the man said anything about meetin' her? Did he tell you anything at all about a real tiny girl with blonde hair and freckles?"

Tyler looked into Asa's worried eyes. He hated lying to the man who'd saved his life, but until Hutchins was caught, Tyler didn't want anyone to know a thing about Marion Tremayne or Goldie. "I'm sorry, Asa, but no, he didn't say a word to me about meeting any girl. I—"

A loud knock at the front door cut him short. "Stay here and watch Doyle." He gave Asa Doyle's gun, retrieved his own pistol, then rushed downstairs. Opening the door slowly, he saw the outline of a man in the shadow of one of the pillars. He raised his gun.

"Sir, it's me," the man said. "Jensen. I've just arrived from London. You left orders for us to inform you of everything—"

"Jenson! What the hell are you—God. Has something happened—Has Dane Hutchins—"

"Sir, is it all right to talk now? I've been hiding out here because Ingram and Dickinson said you were with that Dora—"

"Dammit, Jensen, stop your wittering and tell me why you made a three-day trip from London to find me!"

"It may be nothing, Mr. Escott, but—Sir, Lord Tremayne and Miss Mae were shot at in front of their house. Neither was hurt. His lordship described the assailant as a coster. The men and I found no leads to follow."

"A coster?" Tyler scowled, trying to understand. "Could have been attempted robbery. Maybe . . ."

His voice trailed away as a glimmer of understanding came. "A coster," he murmured uneasily. "Or perhaps an East Ender." Slipping his hand into his pocket, he withdrew the dirty scrap of paper he'd found in Dane's desk and read the name again.

*Diggory Ferris.* Tyler felt cold dread slither through him when he finally recognized the name. "The Butcher," he whispered.

Dear God. Diggory Ferris, the most feared assassin in the city, and Dane Hutchins, a dangerous madman . . .

Gut instinct told Tyler that Ferris was probably in Hutchins' employ. Together they were hunting their prey in London.

A three-day journey away.

# Chapter 18

Addison took a seat by the fireplace, dropping his hand over the arm of the chair to rub Margaret's ears. "Saber, the night you asked me if you could live here I mentioned the robberies I'd heard about. If you had listened to me, that shooting incident never would have happened."

"Addison, I have lived for thirty years without listening to you. I daresay I'll live another thirty without doing so." Saber sat in the settee across from Addison.

Addison gave his friend an irritated look. "What do Tyler's men think?"

Saber dragged his fingers through his hair. "They could find no leads. One man left for Ravenhurst to notify Tyler about it, but none of them thought it logical to try and connect a mere coster to Hutchins and Doyle. They, too, believe it to have been attempted theft."

Finally satisfied, Addison nodded and crossed his legs. "Are you aware that every member of polite society knows you are in London?"

"I thought it would happen. But thank God, no one knows where I'm living. If and when Doyle returns, he won't be able to find me either. How did you come about the news that I've returned from Scotland?"

Addison smiled at the absurd question. "I was at White's last night, and your name was on everyone's tongue. There is also talk about the vivacious young woman you are escorting about. A writer from America who is researching the English nobility for a book she is writing. The women in question couldn't possibly be our Goldie, could it?'' he asked, chuckling.

*Goldie.* Saber mused. There was no need for him to bring her image to mind, for it never left.

*Goldie.* When was the last time he'd held her? he tried to remember. Kissed her?

Made love to her?

He frowned. Aunt Clara and Aunt Lucy were never far from Goldie's side. They were like two fierce, sharp-beaked hens watching over their innocent little chick. Why, he couldn't even send Goldie a suggestive look without one of them pecking at him! Dammit, they'd gone so far as to put Margaret in her room at night, and the confounded dog barked every time someone walked past her door!

Considering all that, what was a rooster . . . er, *man* to do?

"I say, Saber,' Addison said. "The look in your eyes could crack a rock in two. Why are you pulling such a face?''

Saber brought Addison into focus. "Let us just say I was pitying a rooster's lot in life.''

"Rooster? What—''

"As for the gossip about the vivacious girl I am escorting about, yes, it is indeed our Goldie. The entire thing happened just as she hoped it would. Lord Chittingdon spotted me, and called me 'Marion.' Goldie was with me, and of course launched into one of her famous bouts of *vivacious* chatter. She nattered on and on until I was finally able to stop her. Anyway, the fact that Lord Chittingdon called me by my real name reinforced Goldie's belief that we can fool everyone into thinking I'm the one and only Lord Tremayne.''

Addison laughed loudly. "Yes, well, it is also known you will be attending the Chittingdon affair tomorrow night. There's been much speculation about that. People are quite amazed that you accepted the invitation as it's been years since you attended a single gathering.''

"Their amazement will fade very soon. I have no intention of going. Goldie will be very disappointed, but—''

"Goldie is not the only one who will be disappointed.

Jillian Somerset will be, too. She's called on you, Saber. She went to your house, only to be told by your butler that you were not in residence. Since she'd already heard that you'd been seen in London, she knew you had to be somewhere in the city. Hence, she came to me for information. I told her I was not your keeper and had no idea where you were. She knew I was lying, and left my house in a rage."

Saber tilted his head back, staring at the ceiling. "I'm to see her shortly. I sent a message to her earlier, advising her that I'd be calling on her."

"Why are you seeing her?" Addison asked, none too nicely.

Saber smiled at the ceiling. "I—"

"Marion," Clara said as she entered the room. "I have been assisting Goldie with trying on a few of the gowns you gave her a few days ago. While we were doing that, she brought it to my attention that you have objections to taking her to the Chittingdon affair. I have heard the whole story from her, and I understand it from beginning to end. However, I don't see why you cannot play along and pretend to be Lord Tremayne, who, in truth, you *are*."

"Aunt Clara—"

"Morever," Clara continued sternly, "most people have undoubtedly heard that you are in the city, so what further need is there to continue hiding away from everyone? It would mean the entire world to that sweet child to be able to attend the assembly. And the Chittingdons are lovely people. I can assure you they will treat her as an honored guest. Lucille and I, unfortunately, will be unable to attend as we have a previously accepted engagement elsewhere. But Goldie has made wonderful progress with her etiquette. Provided you teach her how to dance and she remembers what we have taught her, she should have not a speck of trouble."

"Aunt Clara, the fact that I am not attending the affair has nothing whatsoever to do with her manners," Saber announced.

Addison noted the adamant expression in Saber's eyes. "As Miss Clara said, everyone already knows you're in the city, Saber. So I see no reason why you—"

"This was to be between Goldie and myself," Saber growled. "But since the two of you are obviously not about to cease badgering me, I may as well tell you."

"Yes, you may as well," Addison agreed, leaning forward in his chair.

Saber cast him a withering look, then turned to Clara. "Auntie, you did not see a single ring in the jewelry I gave Goldie a few days past, did you?"

She took a moment to think. "No, I don't believe I did."

"Nor did you see a single diamond."

Clara frowned. "No."

"I did, however, buy her a ring. With diamonds." He waited for his meaning to sink in.

Addison leaped from his chair. "You mean . . ."

"I do. I am going to ask Goldie if she will do me the honor of becoming my wife. The diamonds I bought her are very special ones, and are being cut to my exact specifications. When the jeweler has completed that task, they will be set in a ring of my own design. I've promised the man a tidy sum for his cooperation in getting the ring to me as soon as possible, but I've yet to hear from him."

Clara began to cry. "You're finally going to have a duchess!" she sniffled, digging into her reticule for a handkerchief. "And soon . . . Soon, you and Goldie will have children, and Lucille and I will be great-aunts! Oh, what a beautiful thought, Marion!"

Saber rolled his eyes. "Aunt Clara, get hold of yourself."

Slowly, Addison sat back down. "You love her," he whispered, as if he couldn't quite believe it.

Saber felt a tender warmth filter through him. "Yes."

Addison remained silent for a long moment. "But Saber, what does a ring have to do with your not attending the Chittingdon assembly?" he finally asked, completely unable to stop grinning. "It seems to me you would be anxious to introduce Goldie as your fiancé."

Saber tried to control his anxiety. "I haven't proposed yet, Addison. She might not accept."

Clara dabbed at her eyes. "Well, of course she'll accept, Marion. She loves you."

"Did she tell you so?" Saber demanded. "Did she say—"

"Well, no. But why wouldn't she? Every unmarried girl I can think of is in love with you. They have been for years. You're the most eligible and desirable bachelor in—"

"But they all know me to be the Duke of Ravenhurst," Saber said softly.

Clara fell silent, realizing the significance of his statement.

Addison's heart went out to his friend. "You want her to accept Saber West's proposal, and not Lord Tremayne's."

Saber stared at the rug. "I—You could never understand how important it is to me."

Clara's tears began again. "I think we do, my boy."

Saber stood. "If I attend the Chittingdon affair, something may happen that will reveal my secret. Someone might say something that would make Goldie suspicious. I realize she wants desperately to go, and I cannot stand the thought of disappointing her. If she agrees to marry me, I'll take her to *court* if she wishes to go. But for now . . . I—The ring. I want to offer her the ring first."

And if she accepted it, he reflected anxiously, he would make Ravenhurst their home. She would be his duchess, and as such she'd belong on his ducal lands. Ever since he'd come to the realization he loved her, he'd dwelled on his possible return to Ravenhurst, soon discovering the idea wasn't painful anymore.

After all, Goldie would be by his side, and that made all the difference.

Addison saw the faraway look in his friend's eyes, and wondered about it. "Saber?"

Saber blinked, jolted back to reality. It took him a moment to remember what he'd been saying. He raised his chin when he recalled that Addison and Aunt Clara had been trying to talk him into taking Goldie to the Chittingdon assembly.

"Too, there is the matter of keeping Goldie safe," he argued. "I have told the two of you and Aunt Lucy about what Tyler Escott has learned. I confess to becoming more and more agitated over the fact that William Doyle hasn't turned up. I was positive he would have returned to the city by now, and I can't fathom where the man might be. Every time I turn a corner, I half-expect him to be standing there. And Hutchins, madman that he is . . . Until those two are in custody, I refuse to take any more chances with Goldie's safety. Therefore, she and I will not be joining the Chittingdons, and that is all I will hear on the subject. Now, by your leave?''

He left the drawing room before Addison or Clara could say another word. Walking into the hallway, he looked up the staircase, feeling a profound need to be with Goldie. But after a glance at his watch, he realized he had no time to see her. Aunt Lucy was more than likely on guard by Goldie's door anyway, he thought irritably. With a great sigh, he left the house.

Jillian Somerset did not like to be kept waiting, he remembered as he stepped into his coach. Not that he cared a whit about her impatience.

But he was anxious to see her, too.

From her bedroom window, Goldie watched Saber get into the carriage, and wondered where he was going. Frustration welled when she tried to remember the last time she'd spent any time alone with him. Though she was truly grateful to learn all Miss Lucy and Miss Clara were teaching her, she wished the many lessons did not include those that affected her intimate relationship with Saber.

''I miss you,'' she whispered down to him, pondering the fact that the day of their permanent separation would arrive soon. ''Maybe lettin' you hold me is 'highly improper,' but Lord, how I ache for your arms. Maybe kissin' is 'absolutely incorrect,' but great day Miss Agnes, all I can think about lately is the way you kiss me. That soft, let's-not-rush-this way, and that hard, give-me-everything-you've-got way, too.''

And lovemaking . . . She didn't even want to *think* about how positively forbidden *that* was. But even so, her body burned for his. The memory of the night they'd made love was beautiful and torturous at once, leaving her yearning for that which only Saber could give her.

"Oh, Saber," she murmured, watching his coach disappear around the corner. "This proper-lady stuff is pure hell. And I've got to go soon. Our time . . . is comin' to an end." *Just like good things always do,* she added silently. Blowing curls off her forehead, she began to turn away from the window, but just as she did, she saw Rosie coming down the street, a bouquet of roses in her hands. She waved and left the bedroom.

Downstairs, she met Rosie at the front door and got a closer look at the roses. They were way past their prime, little more than velvety black things stuck on the top of thorny stems.

"Rosie, my dear," Clara greeted the girl warmly. "What have you brought today?"

Rosie grinned broadly, feeling genuine affection for the kindhearted lady. "Brung ya some roses, I did, Miss Clara. They're fer Miss Lucy, too. They ain't real fresh, but they still smell good."

Clara accepted the bouquet, trying not to grimace at the overly sweet odor of the dying roses. "Bennett, put these lovely roses in the finest vase you can find, then set them here in the foyer where everyone may see them."

Bennett handled the flowers with the greatest reverence he could muster. For Rosie's benefit, he even smelled them, closing his eyes as if their cloying perfume was the most wonderful scent he'd ever had the pleasure to enjoy.

Rosie smiled and turned back to Goldie, noticing a sad expression in her friend's eyes. "Let's go upstairs, luv," she said, taking Goldie's hand.

Once in Goldie's bedroom, Rosie sashayed to Goldie's big, plush bed, and made herself comfortable upon it. She waited for Goldie to speak to her, but when Goldie remained silent, she started the conversation herself. "Ya remember Og Drit, Goldie? The bloke wot was botherin' us the day I met ya? The man won't be pesterin' nobody no more. 'E's dead. Somebody bloody well slit 'is throat."

Goldie sauntered to the window again, peering down at the street below.

"Goldie? Ya 'ear wot I said?"

"I've been doin' some hard thinkin', Rosie," Goldie said softly. She breathed on the windowpane, drawing the letter "S" in the circle of fog her breath had left there. "I've been here in London a long time. I reckon Big's worked himself into a frenzy by now, wonderin' what the hell's keepin' me. And great day Miss Agnes, there's no tellin' *what* Uncle Asa's been up to."

Rosie realized the significance of her friend's statement but refused to accept it. "Ya ain't thinkin' about goin' back ter 'Allensham, are ya, Goldie? Wot about Saber? Iffen ya takes 'im to 'Allensham an' lets 'im play the duke, ya ain't never goin' ter see 'im again. Ya said yerself that once them villagers see 'im, 'e can't never go back there again. 'E said he bloomin' *loves* ya! Are ya jest goin' ter let 'im leave yer life like that? Gawblimey, Goldie, don't tell me ya still don't believe the man cares fer ya!"

Goldie turned from the window, ambled to her dressing table, and picked up her gold brush. Every memory she had of Saber, starting from the day she met him, filtered through her mind. "I didn't at first, but . . . Y'know, Rosie, he's never done anything mean to me. And he likes my hair and freckles."

"An' yer gold eyes. An' 'e don't mind yer bein' real little, neither," Rosie reminded her.

Goldie looked down at the beautiful gown she was wearing. "And *someone* likes me enough to have sent me all the gifts. If one man can feel like that, I reckon—Well, maybe Saber can too. Maybe he really meant it when he said he loved me," she said softly.

Rosie smiled a sad smile. She understood how hard it was for Goldie to believe Saber could love her, and said a quick prayer that Goldie would soon completely trust the love Saber offered. "So wot are ya goin' ter do, luv? Will ya still takes 'im ter 'Allensham?"

Goldie sighed heavily. "That's the problem. If I take him, of course he'll have to leave. And I couldn't go with him because someone has to see to Uncle Asa. I can't let Big do it forever. And if I *don't* take him, we'll all get tossed out of town just like we always do. Oh, Rosie, what am I gonna do?"

She plopped into a chair, blowing curls out of her face again. "Y'know, I might have been little when my parents were alive, but I remember how they always got their problems solved. I told you the story about how they both wanted to live in their home states and eventually came to an agreement by livin' on top of the state line. See? Not even a big problem like that was too much for 'em. They came up with an answer. But I guess none of that problem-solvin' of theirs rubbed off on me. Maybe I just wasn't with 'em long enough to learn how they did it.''

Rosie ran her roughened palm over the satin coverlet. "But they 'ad each other, luv. Iffen one 'ad a problem, t'other 'elped solve it. I remember me own mum an' da, God rest their souls. Sometimes they'd stay up all night talkin' about their troubles. There weren't no kind o' problem—no matter 'ow bad it was—wot they couldn't solve together, there weren't. That's one o' the best things about 'avin' a mate, an' I sure 'ope I gets me a good one some-day.''

Goldie nodded, looking at the rug. "Yeah, that's a good thing about havin' a mate. You're never alone with your—'' She broke off; her head snapped up. A flame of hope warmed her heart. "Rosie," she whispered, pausing for a long moment. "I—I don't *have* to be alone. I mean . . . I *do* have someone who might could help me figure out what to do. He's not my mate, but . . . ''

"Yer friend Big?''

Goldie picked up a yellow curl, winding it around her finger and tugging on it nervously. "No, not Big." She stood and began to pace, still fiddling with her curl. "He's never lied to me, Rosie. I can't think of a single time when he's been dishonest with me. And—And I do sorta think he likes me a lot. He . . . might even—Like I said, maybe he even loves me a little bit.''

She stopped at the bed, taking hold of one of the bed-posts. "I'll swannee, I've been so dumb! My mama had my daddy, and he had her. Your parents had each other too, and—Rosie, *I've* got *Saber!*''

"Wot—''

"I can't believe I didn't think of this before! Great day Miss Agnes, here I've been mopin' around, worryin' my-self into a fit as if Saber didn't have anything at all to do with it! And—'' She stopped abruptly, her eyes widening as a new thought burst into her spinning mind. "Oh, Rosie," she murmured.

"Oh, Goldie," Rosie echoed. "Tell me wot the bleedin' 'ell yer talkin' about!"

"I reckon it's really true," Goldie exclaimed, laughing into her hands. "I *trust* him! When and how it happened— Who knows? Who cares?" She flew to the window. "Where the hell is that man? Oh, Rosie, how am I gonna be able to stand it until he gets home! What if he stays gone for hours, and—"

"Goldie! Ya ain't makin' no sense! I can't—"

"But it's so simple, Rosie! My problems aren't just *mine!* Saber's in on 'em too! So why the hell have I been tryin' to do all the decision-makin' by myself? He's the smartest man I've ever come across. And a man that smart . . . Y'see, what I don't think of, he might. And what he doesn't think of, I might. Surely if we talk about all this together, we'll figure somethin' out!"

"Coo, Goldie! Yer right!"

Goldie smiled a faraway smile. "Trust," she murmured, the word filling her with an unfamiliar warmth. " 'Course I don't understand everything there is to know about love, but one thing I know is that a big part of it is trust. The two go together like . . . like biscuits and molasses! Who would ever eat biscuits without molasses, Rosie? 'Cept ole Feenie Spackle back in Koonce Cove, Virginia. Molasses made her lips swell up. They'd swell up s'bad, she couldn't even talk. And Feenie *loved* to talk. Sometimes her mama'd pour molasses down her throat just to shut her up."

Rosie had no idea what molasses were, but laughed anyway. "Ya got offen the subject a bit, luv, but ya know wot yer sayin'? Goin' on an' on about 'ow ya trusts Saber, an' 'ow trust an' love go together . . ."

Rosie's meaning found fertile ground. Goldie's eyes widened again. Astonishment touched each part of her. "My diamond dreams," she whispered.

At the look of awe in her friend's eyes, Rosie smiled. "I'll leaves ya now, Goldie," she said, hopping off the bed. "Looks to me like ya got some thinkin' ter do afore ya talk to yer Saber. An' it's almost dark, anyway. Iffen I don't starts fer 'ome now, it'll be midnight afore I get there. Anything ya wants me ter do fer ya afore I leave?''

Goldie stared at her friend. "Yes," she said softly. "If you've got any faith at all in the Dream Giver, Rosie, put in a good word for me. I need all the good words I can get because what I'm askin' from Him is the biggest diamond dream of 'em all.''

Jillian sank into a plush velvet chair in her parlor, her glacial blue eyes never leaving Saber. He was standing in the middle of the room, his coat still on, his hat and gloves still in his hands. "Why?"

He returned her direct look, thinking about how tall she was. He decided she was *too* tall for a woman. "Jillian, please try to understand. I never made any promises to you. You accepted our relationship for exactly what it was, did you not?''

Her eyes hardened. "No! I was to be your duchess!" she shouted, her chest heaving.

He noticed the generous display of her breasts and the deep, shadowed valley between them. God, he thought. They looked like flesh-colored watermelons. "No, Jillian, you were not to be my duchess, and you never once heard me say that you would.''

"But you love me!"

"No," he said as gently as he knew how. *I love my poppet called Goldie*, he added silently.

Jillian clutched her silk skirt tightly, gathering her emotions. "But you showed me you loved me. In many ways.''

Saber exhaled slowly. "Jillian, why do you insist on making this harder than it has to be?''

"But—But you—Marion, you were going to give me everything I wanted! You were! I know you were!''

He glared at her, thinking about the drastic differences between her and Goldie. Jillian took it for granted that she deserved the world and everything in it. Goldie found it almost impossible to believe she'd received a few gowns and some trinkets.

"It's someone else, isn't it, Marion?" Jillian demanded, hatred coursing through her. "You've a new mistress to warm your bed! You've been with *her* during the many weeks you've been gone! You've been in Scotland with her! Why—Why, she's the writer from America I've heard about, isn't she!''

Saber raised his chin. "I've said what I came to say. I regret any distress I may have caused you, but as I said, I never made any promises to you. Any assumptions you made were entirely your own.''

Jillian rose and crossed to him. "But I love you, Marion,'' she whispered, great tears slipping down her face.

Saber shook his head. "Jillian, you love my fortune. My title. Beyond those things—''

"No! Marion, I love—''

"You don't even know me.''

"How can you say that? Why, I knew you even before Angelica did! I've known you for almost ten years! I've—''

"Did you know I used to make dandelion stew? Did you know that I had a tree house? Did you know that I collected rocks and made yellow paint from pollen? Did you know that I could whistle with two fingers in my mouth? Did you know I was once afraid of thunder? Jillian,'' he said, taking a step away from her, "did it ever occur to you that there is a common man beneath the nobleman?''

"A common man? Marion, you are not a commoner! You're the *Duke of Ravenhurst!*''

He smiled a bittersweet smile. "And to you, Jillian, that is all I've ever been and all I ever will be.''

Sensing defeat, she pressed her body close to his, counting on her ample charms to win him back. "This new woman in your life, Marion . . . this American—Does she make you feel the way I do?'' she purred, slipping her arms around his neck and flicking her tongue along his jawbone. "Does she know all the tricks that I do? Tell me, my darling diamond duke, does she heat your blood the way I do?''

Her heavy rose-scented perfume was sickeningly sweet to him. He couldn't understand why he'd once found it so intriguing. Nor could he comprehend why he'd thought her so incredibly sensual. He felt nothing at all for her now. "Good-bye, Jillian.'' he removed her hands from around his neck, turned, and left her standing there.

When she heard the front door close, fiery anger shot through her. "No, Marion," she hissed. "There will never be a good-bye between us. You *did* promise to make me your duchess. Your vow was unspoken, true, but you swore in a thousand ways. Every time you kissed me, I heard your pledge. Every time you held me, made love to me, I felt you give me your word. And if it is the last thing I do on earth, I will hold you to your troth."

As Saber stepped inside the house and handed his coat, hat, and gloves to Bennett, he noticed the vase of blackened roses in the foyer. "Why are those in here?"

"Miss Rosie Tetter brought them this afternoon, sir. I was going to dispose of them, but Miss Mae asked me to leave them here for a few days in case Miss Tetter should return. She doesn't want her friend's feelings hurt. I—If you don't mind me saying so, sir, Miss Mae is really one of the kindest persons I've ever had the good fortune to know."

At Bennett's words, Saber warmed with pride. "She is at that," he agreed, heading for the staircase. Taking the steps three at a time, he reached the upper landing and walked toward Goldie's bedroom, his quick, confident stride evidence of his exhilaration. Not only had he gotten the ordeal with Jillian over and done with, but he'd also stopped by the jeweler's and received good news from the man. The ring would be ready early tomorrow evening. By tomorrow night, Goldie might very well be his intended, the future Duchess of Ravenhurst. That thought was uppermost in his mind as he arrived at her open door.

She was sitting on the edge of her bed. He lost his breath when he saw her. Her flaxen curls lay in wild disarray upon the shoulders of her deep green gown, making him think of pure, sweet sunshine pouring down on a carpet of grass. He loved the contrast of the beautiful colors.

"Poppet," he greeted her, his entire body aching to rush in and sweep her into his arms.

Goldie looked up from the lacy bonnet she held in her lap and saw him standing in the threshold. He looked devilishly handsome in his snug black pants and ivory cambric shirt. Sable curls framed his face, one of them touching the corner of his eye. And he was smiling that crooked, boyish grin she so loved to see.

She longed to jump off the bed, throw herself into his arms, and tell him about all the wonderful discoveries she'd made earlier. But remembering the stern lecture the aunties had given her a while ago, and recalling also that the two women were just down the hall, she struggled to subdue the urge. Instead, she lifted her chin, trying to contain her wild impatience. "Saber, I need to talk to you."

He recognized her attempt at propriety and decided to see if he could coerce her out of it. "Indeed. Tell me, Goldie love, is *talking* all you'd like to do with me?"

His question jolted her with desire. "Saber, please be serious. I really do need to talk to you."

"As you wish." He put his foot forward.

"Not here! Miss Lucy and Miss Clara were just in here, and they said I can't let you in—"

"Saber!" Clara exclaimed as she arrived. "What are you doing in Goldie's bedroom?"

He stiffened. "I'm not in her bedroom. I'm standing in the hall. To my knowledge, that is not a breach of etiquette."

"We were only talkin'!" Goldie added loudly.

Clara raised a brow. "You may talk tomorrow. It is getting late, Goldie. A proper young lady should be preparing to retire, and a *gentleman*," she said to Saber, "should allow her privacy in order to do so. Say good night to Goldie, Saber, and then go do whatever it is you do at this hour. I shall return shortly with Margaret." With that, she left.

Saber waited until his aunt disappeared, then turned back to Goldie. "We can talk for a few moments. I would, however, prefer to be closer to you while we converse."

She tried to swallow, but couldn't. Lord, it had been so long. Oh, to feel him close to her! "I—Saber, you—Miss Clara and Miss Lucy have been so good to me. I get ill sometimes with all the lessons about bein' so proper, but Saber, I just couldn't disappoint 'em. I—You *can't* come in here."

"Very well. then you come to me."

She was afraid of what his nearness would do to her.

Surely the feel of him next to her would send her over the brink of control. "No. You'll do somethin' you're not supposed to do. I'm tellin' you, Saber, Miss Lucy and Miss Clara are gonna bring Margaret in just a minute!"

Quickly, he glanced toward both ends of the hall, grinning when he didn't see either one of the sharp-beaked mother hens. "They're not coming yet. Let's . . . uh, *talk*."

She heard the sensual tone in his voice. Her desire rose. "You're not in the mood for just plain talkin', Saber."

"No?" he asked, chuckling. "Then pray tell, what kind of mood am I in, Goldie love?"

"You know damn well what mood. You just want to hear me say it."

"True. Say it."

"No."

"Look, Goldie, I'm here for very important reasons. I want to put my arms around you. I want to kiss you. I want to feel your body next to mine. Goldie," he said huskily, "I want to make love—"

"Great day Miss Agnes, Saber!"

"I'm not *doing* those things, poppet. I'm only telling you I *want* to do them."

Heat flowed through her senses. He was looking at her with dark, hooded eyes that saw right through her. She wondered if he knew how very warm his comments had made her. That lopsided grin on his face told her he did. Good Lord, she thought. She had to get him out of here before improper things happened between them! "Saber, you have to leave my—"

"But what about talking?" he asked naughtily.

"We'll talk tomorrow just like Miss Clara said," she told him, hating to wait that long, but knowing full well she had no other choice. "And while we're talkin', you can hold my hand if you want, but that's all. Miss Lucy and Miss Clara said I can't let you do anything else but that. I reckon you can't even kiss my wrist anymore."

Saber fought with the irritation he felt for his aunties. They'd certainly done their work well, the two busybodies! "But you like it when I kiss your wrist. When I start close to your palm and go slowly up your arm."

Goldie felt passion set her cheeks aflame. "You are *so* bad, Saber West."

"True. But tell me in all honesty that you don't like it when I'm bad, and I'll become the most gentlemanly gentleman you'd ever hope to encounter."

Though he was teasing her, she saw the hunger in his eyes. She watched as that sensual gaze of his meandered from her face to her breasts. It lingered there. Flustered, Goldie laid her hand upon the plunging neckline of her velvet gown. "This isn't a proper dress for wearin' around the house. But—Well, I like this one the best. I was just tryin' it on, y'see. I'm not wearin' it for real."

At the sight of her fingers trembling over the lily-white swells of her breasts, Saber smiled knowingly. "Why is that one of your favorite, poppet?"

Her answer came instantly. "Because it's the color of wet seaweed. Just like your eyes."

The love he felt for her threatened to consume him. "Goldie—"

"London's real *fuliginous!*" she blurted, desperate to change the subject before she began begging him to come in and do improper things to her.

A sigh shuddered through him. With great effort, he gathered patience. "Yes, I agree. London is fuliginous."

She felt relieved over her success at changing the course of the conversation, and was determined not to let him switch it back again. Worked up as he was tonight, she knew he'd try. "What do you do in your spare time, Saber? Sit down and memorize the dictionary?"

He chuckled at that.

"I'm gonna test you. Tell me what *fuliginous* means."

"Sooty."

"*Pudibund.*"

"To be ashamed."

"*Monodist.*"

"One who sings or composes monodies, which are odes sung by one voice."

She smiled.

He thought her grin quite mischievous.

"*Thipstrit.*"

Saber frowned. "*Thipstrit?*"

She nodded. "What's it mean? You *are* Mr. Saber I-Know-Every-Word-Invented West, aren't you?"

He shuffled his feet on the floor. "Give me a minute to think, and I'll remember the definition."

"Yeah, sure."

"I will."

"Uh huh."

"Goldie, if you'll only hush, I'll remember what thipstrit means. I know I've heard the word before. Somewhere. I'm sure of it. Just give me a second." Closing his eyes, he pinched the bridge of his nose and concentrated.

Goldie gave him a second. And another. She gave him almost a full minute of seconds. "Give up?"

His shoulders slumped. "Yes, I give up. What does thipstrit mean?"

She tossed her hair out of her eyes. "I'm not gonna tell you."

He felt a mixture of amusement and irritation at once. "Tell me."

"Nope."

"Then you're mean. I'll bet *you* pulled more wings off butterflies than old Raleigh Purvis."

She watched him for a long moment. "I love it when you tease me, Saber."

"Indeed. And what else do you love for me to do?" He took a tentative step into her room.

She tried in vain to swallow again. "Your aunts—They're going to bring Margaret and see you in here."

"Ah, but I'm too big for them to turn over their knees anymore." He took another step toward her.

"They'll—They can still get mad at you, though."

"Perhaps I should close the door?"

"Well!" Lucille huffed from the doorway, Margaret in her arms, Itchie Bon at her heels. "What is the meaning of this?"

Saber saw the look of pure horror and dread on Goldie's face, then turned to face his aunt. "Aunt Lucy, I am testing Goldie's etiquette. As you can plainly see, I am in her bedroom. I took two steps in here and waited for her to dismiss me, as a proper lady should."

Lucille took Margaret into the room. "And did she dismiss you?"

"She did at that."

Lucille smiled at Goldie. "Good for you, my dear." Pushing her spectacles up, she glanced at Saber again. "Well? You were dismissed, were you not?"

Saber gritted his teeth. Spinning on his heel, he turned toward the door and stalked out.

Goldie understood his frustration, for she felt it too. And by the way Lucille was staring at her, she suspected the feelings Saber's presence had engendered were fairly pouring out of her eyes. "Well, I reckon I'll go to bed now, Miss Lucy!" she announced a bit too loudly.

"Goldie, my dear, why are your cheeks so red? Are you not feeling well?"

Her hands flew to her hot cheeks. "I'm—I'm *really* tired. I'll swannee, I'm so tired that I just know I'll be asleep as soon as my head hits the pillow." With shaking hands, she picked up a pillow. "I never had such soft pillows to sleep on," she rambled, her emotions becoming more frenzied by the moment. "In fact, I never had any pillow at all! Made my own. Just folded up some clothes. That worked just fine, but one time I slept on a button. When I woke up I had circle on my forehead. I guess I slept flat on my face that night. It's a wonder I didn't smother, huh?"

Lucille's brow furrowed. "You are talking too quickly, Goldie, and you look feverish to me. Perhaps I should send for a doctor."

"No! A doctor—I'm afraid of doctors. I get faint even thinkin' about 'em. Feel faint right now." In a dramatic gesture, she laid the back of her hand on her forehead for a moment. "My face gets all red like this when—When I'm tired."

"Indeed. Most people become *pale* when tired. And when they are embarrassed and flustered, they become red."

Goldie felt the beginning of panic. "Yeah? Um .. Well, I get red when I'm tired and white when I'm embarrassed. I'm yellow when I'm sick, and greenish when I'm scared. I get blue when I'm too warm, and orangeish when I'm cold. I—I'm a very colorful person. Well, I reckon I'll go to bed now, Miss Lucy!''

Lucille stared at her for a while longer. "So you are sure you're all right?"

"Oh, surely I'm sure. I'm so sure that I just couldn't be any more sure.''

"Good night then, my dear. Clara and I are retiring also, but if you should need anything, do not hesitate to make us aware of it.''

Goldie stood there smiling a fake smile until Miss Lucy left. "Damn you, Saber West. You've worked me into a tizzy, and neither one of us can do a thing about it!''

Desire still stabbing through her, she removed her gown and underthings. The sight of her own bare body deepened her need. "Sleep,'' she muttered to Margaret and Itchie Bon. "I've gotta go to sleep. Unconsciousness is the only way to get over this.''

She chose a silky nightgown from her dresser, and lifted it over head. It fell sensuously over her body, caressing her. She trembled, remembering the way Saber's hands felt when he touched her all over. Tearing the thought from her mind, she marched to her bed and climbed into it.

Laying very still, she closed her eyes and willed sleep to come. It wouldn't. She hummed a dozen lullabies to herself. Thought of exceedingly boring things. Counted two hundred sheep. And remained wide awake.

Her body, mind, and her heart . . . every part of her longed for Saber.

Her eyes popped open. For a long while, she stared at the canopy, Saber claiming her every thought. She became so warm, she kicked off her covers. "Well, there's only one thing to do,'' she told the dogs. "I might get caught doin' it, but great day Miss Agnes, if I don't try, I'll melt, and come mornin' I won't be anything but a puddle layin' here in this bed.''

She gave a sheepish look at the two dogs staring at her from the floor. "Saber and I have to *talk*, y'see. About the problem of goin' to Hallensham and what to do with Uncle Asa. There's nothin' wrong with *talkin'*, y'all, so quit lookin' at me like that.''

Rising, she placed two pillows beneath the covers, giving them pats here and there. "What do y'all think?" she asked as she stepped back to examine her work. "Think it'll fool Miss Clara and Miss Lucy if they decide to look in on me?"

Itchie Bon scratched his ear, then leapt onto the bed, lying down beside the hump that was supposed to be Goldie. Margaret trotted to the bedside throw rug, settling herself comfortably.

Goldie blew kisses to them both and tiptoed to the door. Opening it slowly, she peered out, relieved when she saw no signs of either of the aunties. As quietly as possible, she stepped out into the hall, shut her bedroom door, and proceeded down the long hallway. Every little noise she heard, both real and imagined, sent fear shooting through her, and by the time she reached Saber's room, her heart was pounding so hard, she felt sure it would beat a hole in her chest.

As she stared at the closed door, she thought of all the things that would soon happen behind it. The talking long into the early hours of the morning. The lovemaking . . .

Her hand trembling, she reached for the knob.

# Chapter 19

T he doorknob squeaked as she turned it. She closed her eyes, knowing the small sound could bring the aunties. Every fiber in her body throbbed with the fear of being caught. Her breath came in short pants, and her hand shook uncontrollably on the knob, causing it to squeak again.

She cursed silently, and turned it more firmly. Ever so slightly, she pushed the door open, gratified when she saw the room was softly illuminated. Saber was still awake. That or he was afraid of the dark and slept with a lighted lamp. She smiled at that thought, opened the door further, and saw his bed.

He wasn't in it.

"Dammit, Saber!" she whispered vehemently. "I'm bein' an improper lady for you, and you don't even have the decency to be in bed waitin' on me!" With an angry sigh, she stepped into his room and closed the door behind her. She walked to his bed, running her hand down the dark blue velvet that flowed from the canopy.

"Well, now what the hell am I supposed to do?" she wondered aloud.

No sooner had the question left her lips than the room went completely dark. A scream rose in her throat, but before she could release it, strong hands caught her shoulders. Arms pulled her against a torso that was both hard and soft at once.

Warm lips met hers in a kiss that demanded everything she had to give. Searching fingers fumbled with the ribbons at the neck of her night rail, and a satisfied groan hit

355

her ears when the filmy gown skimmed down her body, pooling at her feet.

"Tell me something, my improper lady," Saber murmured, his lips nuzzling the sweet hollow of her throat. "Do you want me to be an improper gentleman? Shall we cast aside all the rules and make this night highly improper? Shall I do improper things to you, Goldie? And should I do them, may I expect you to do improper things to me in return?"

"Yes." She pulled at the sash of his robe, quivering when the garment fell to join her nightgown on the floor. She ran her hands across his smooth, broad chest, then leaned into him, desire pulsing through her veins when his need for her pressed hotly against her belly. "Yes, yes," she repeated breathily. "But whoever you are, don't tell Saber West. If he catches me doin' this with you, he'll—"

Saber laughed and swept her into his arms. "Minx." He bent his head, savoring the softness of her breasts upon his face. He carried her to the window, and, holding her in one arm, he used his other arm to yank the draperies open. "I love the way silver moonlight looks on your gold hair," he told her as he took her to his bed and laid her down there. He joined her, pulling her to him, his hands traveling over the entire length of her body.

"You smell different than you usually do," Goldie commented, her face in his hair. "You smell like—Like . . . roses."

He tensed, realizing that Jillian's' cloying rose perfume still clung to him. Panicked, he tried to think of what to tell Goldie. "I—It must be those overripe roses in the foyer," he blurted, profoundly thankful that he'd recalled the flowers. "I brushed past them earlier. The things smell sickeningly sweet."

Goldie smiled. "Rosie brought 'em. But the way you smell, Saber—It's different than the roses she—"

"Forget the roses, poppet." He parted her thighs.

She moaned when his fingers slipped intimately into her. "Saber, wait. I need to talk to you first. I've got somethin' important to tell—"

"Later," he told her, his breath coming in ragged heaves. "We talk later."

"But—"

"Goldie, I—I can't wait. It's been so long, love."

The urgency in his voice set her afire. He was right, she realized. Talking could wait. Later, she'd tell him every sweet thing that dwelled in her heart. "Yes," she whispered to him. "It's been so long." She welcomed his weight, gasping when he pushed into her. He filled her leisurely, completely, then began to move, slowly, so slowly, increasing his rhythm and depth with each stroke. Her ecstasy began instantly, and intensified when she realized Saber's bliss had come just as quickly. He pulsed within her, his body hardened and straining over hers.

"I'm sorry," he told her. 'Goldie, I just couldn't—"

"Me either," she admitted, pleasure still shimmering through her. "But Saber, let's do it again."

Her suggestion gave him pause. "I—Can you give me a few minutes?"

"For what?"

"To—I—You see—I'm not ready yet. I have to—"

"I'll ready you. I know how to do it, Saber. Remember the night when you readied me? I'll do that to you, then you'll be ready."

"You'll do that to me?" He slid from atop her, sat, and stared down at her moonlit features. "Really?"

She felt suddenly embarrassed. "Is there something wrong with that?" she asked in a very small voice.

"Well, no, but I—It's just that I never thought you'd want to—I haven't ever asked you to. Never showed you."

"So I'll learn while I'm doin' it. There's nothin' like firsthand experience. Ole Ozzie Worm back in Tater Hole, Tennessee? Well, he told me that. 'Course, he wasn't talkin' about what I'm fixin' to do to you right now, but it's the same principle, don't you think?"

Saber's mind whirled. "Ozzie Worm?"

"Ole Ozzie went to Judge Mudd to get his last name changed, but Judge Mudd wouldn't do it. Judge Mudd said that Worm was a fine name and that he saw no reason for Ozzie to change it. If you ask me, Judge Mudd should've changed his *own* name right along with Ozzie's. Mudd's just as bad as Worm. Anyway, Ozzie said firsthand experience is always the best kind. Don't you think so too, Saber?''

Her proposal made him begin to feel ready for her. He didn't, however, inform her of this. "Yes. I do indeed agree with Mr. Worm.''

"So is it all right with you if I get some firsthand experience on you?'' Without waiting for his answer, she sat up, pushing him back to the mattress. "All right, Saber, you just lay there and concentrate on gettin' readied.''

She turned, looking at that which she was supposed to ready and feeling puzzled over the sight. "It already looks ready to me.''

He wasn't about to let her miss her opportunity for some firsthand experience. "It only *looks* that way. It's not really.''

"But this is the way it always looks when it's—''

"Look, Goldie, it's *my* body we're talking about. I should know if it's ready or not.''

"Well, you don't have to turn into an ill-box over it, do you?''

"I'm not an ill-box. I'm just ready to get readied.''

She took him her hand. "Well, I don't care what you say, it looks ready to me. Feels ready too. Are you sure—''

"I'm sure!''

She smiled at the anticipation she saw lighting up his eyes and knew then that he was as ready as he'd ever be. But she decided to go along with him and ready him to his heart's content.

She bent and kissed the tip of him, wondering what it was she was actually supposed to do. Unsure, she moved her lips down his hard length, smoothing whisper-soft kisses to him as she journeyed. "Saber, what do I do now?''

"It's *your* firsthand experience, not mine.''

"But—''

"Try a little of everything and see what works best.''

His suggestion sounded good to her. She began darting her tongue across him. Up, down. All around. When he groaned at her actions, she became bolder.

Saber shook violently when he felt her take him into her mouth. She went slowly with him at first, then increased her pace, taking more and more of him. "Gold-Goldie," he stammered, trying his best to stem the pleasure. "I'm ready."

She straightened, struggling with the urge to laugh. "Well now, Saber, I don't know about that. You probably need more readyin'." She leaned down again.

He caught her shoulders, lifting her into his lap and arranging her legs so that they were wrapped around his waist. Taking her face between his hands, he kissed her long, gently, and with all the adoration he felt for her. He explored each warm valley of her mouth, savoring the silken feel of her, relishing the sweet taste of her.

And then, abruptly, he stopped. He sat her on the bed, and moved away. "I refuse to do one more improper thing to you until you tell me what thipstrit means."

She smiled. "All right. Don't do anything to me then. I'll do everything to *you*."

When she began squirming closer to him, he moved over again. "I'll have the meaning of thipstrit first, if you don't mind."

"But I do mind." Quickly, she pushed him back to the bed. Before he could respond, she pulled her entire body onto him. Feeling rather daring, she opened her legs, waiting expectantly for him to take advantage of her sensuous invitation.

Saber didn't move a muscle. "Sorry to deny you what you are so desperate to have, my improper Miss Mae, but I really must insist on the definition of—"

"Deny me? Just because you don't offer it doesn't mean I won't get it."

"Oh, really? And how do you propose to have it if I don't give it to you?"

She smiled, and inched her body downward, grasping at the pleasure she felt when she met his manhood. With one smooth motion, she slid him into her.

Saber's moans joined hers when she began to circle her hips. His hands pushed at her bottom, urging her onward. He felt her body tense, and knew her pleasure was building. Grinning rakishly, he seized that exact moment to roll to his side, taking him with her. "Not yet, poppet."

"Saber—"

"What does thipstrit mean?" His hand cupped her femininity, his fingers delved within it. "Tell me."

She couldn't. Her rising bliss defied her will to speak. Saber stilled his hand. "Goldie . . ."

"Dammit, that's twice you messed it up!"

He understood exactly what it was he'd messed up, and smiled again. "But think of how much better it will be when it finally happens. Imagine that, Goldie love. Want it. Yearn for it . . . *wait* for it."

Though her unappeased desire nearly tore her asunder, she couldn't help smiling at the rogue who tortured her so sensuously. "You are so mean."

"Raleigh Purvis and I are cousins. Did I forget to tell you that?" His hand began moving in small circles upon the mound of her womanhood, his palm pressing ever so insistently.

Goldie closed her eyes, sweet, deep pleasure beginning to grow again.

"Think of what's happening to you, Goldie. Think of how good it's going to feel. Think of those things, Goldie. And while you're thinking about them, think of thipstrit too."

She began to laugh. She laughed so hard, tears streamed down her face, and her belly started to ache.

Saber watched her in complete confusion. "Is thipstrit a funny word?"

She couldn't answer. Laughter continued to rumble through her. She shook her head instead.

"Then what's so blasted funny?"

She struggled to breathe, but a long moment passed before her laughter subsided sufficiently. Drawing in a ragged gulp of air, she looked at Saber. "I could have died laughin', and it would have been *your* fault."

"But what a pleasant way to go."

She arched her eyebrow at him. "Two can play at this game, y'know." She laid her hand on top of the diamond birthmark on his left thigh, then walked her fingers higher, all the way up to the tip of his manhood. She lingered there for a moment, running her thumb in a circle around him, then walked her fingers back down again. "Feel good? Y'want me to keep on doin' it?"

He knew her strategy. If he said yes, she'd stop. "No, don't keep doing it. I don't like the way it feels. As a matter of fact, I hate it."

"Liar." She took her hand away.

Saber turned onto his stomach, laughing into his pillow.

Goldie took full advantage of his enticing position, and laid on top of him, loving the way his firm bottom felt beneath her belly. She spread barely-there kisses all over his powerful shoulders, her desire growing to such heights, she felt she would burst if it was not soon satisfied. She began moving her hips, silently showing him what she wanted from him.

Saber's laughter ceased when he felt her moving. Insistently, she pressed her hips into the backs of his thighs, then lifted them, then pressed them to him again. The cadence of her movements was slow, and each time she broke contact with him, he found himself yearning for her sensual return.

"Saber," she whispered to him, her lips still smoothing across his rigid back.

"Yes," he whispered in answer. Turning to his side, he held her in his arms. "Open for me, Goldie love. Put your leg around my waist."

His command sent her spinning. She obeyed.

Pulling her closer to him, he eased into her.

She clasped him tightly to her. "Don't stop this time."

"No. Not this time." He thrust deeper.

She felt the pleasure start. "Promise."

"Promise."

He loved her with deep and steady strokes, her soft whimpers filling him with unmitigated joy. "Yes," he whispered to her when he felt her release. "There, there, now once more."

"Yes, again. With you." She met each of his thrusts, urging him into the deepest part of her, and crying with pleasure each time he found it. She felt him grow harder within her, and knew profound happiness that she could give him the same ecstasy he gave her. The thought increased her own bliss, and she called out his name over and over again when he finally spilled himself inside her.

"Oh, Saber," she said, her voice trembling.

He looked into her eyes. Moonlight and joy shone within those golden orbs he so loved. Her face was flushed with the warm afterglow of lovemaking, and he decided he'd never seen a more beautiful sight in his entire life. "I have a confession to make," he told her quietly, running his finger along her delicate collarbone. "If you hadn't come to my room tonight, I'd planned on coming to yours."

"But what about Margaret? She growls and barks even when Miss Lucy and Miss Clara come near my door."

He smiled, pointing to his beside table.

Goldie looked at it and saw a bone, chunks of meat still clinging to it. She grinned. "It never would have worked, Saber. You only have one bone. Itchie Bon would have wanted it too, and they'd have fought over it. There's nothin' like a dogfight to bring people runnin'."

"So I'd have broken it in half."

Goldie glanced at the bone again. It was at least three inches thick. "Saber, you couldn't have broken that bone."

He pretended to look insulted. Lifting his arm, he flexed his muscles for her.

She pressed her finger into the rock-hard bulges, wrinkling her nose. "They're not all that big," she teased.

He flexed them harder. So hard a vein popped out on them. "What do you think now?" he grunted, his face tight with exertion.

She touched them again. "I've eaten oatmeal that was harder than that."

His arm plopped back to the bed. "I was wrong. *I'm* not Raleigh Purvis' cousin. *You* are."

Goldie giggled, squirming closer to him. "I'm only teasin', Saber. Why, if Hercules could see your muscles, he'd hang his head in shame. And ole Samson? Well, it wouldn't matter how long he grew his hair, he'd never—"

Saber laughed loudly.

"Shhh!" She clamped her hand over his mouth. "Great day Miss Agnes, Saber, y'want the aunties to come?"

He removed her hand from his mouth, and took a long moment to kiss her inner wrist. "If they do, I'll just tell them the truth. That you stole in here, tore off my clothes, and ravished me."

She sighed with pleasure when he began pushing his fingers through her hair. Snug and warm in the soothing shelter of his arms, she began thinking of how to tell him all the truths she'd discovered earlier.

"Saber," she began, pausing to pepper his chest with little kisses, "I—There's somethin' I have to tell you. Somethin' real important."

"Is it the definition of thipstrit?" he asked excitedly.

She smiled. "No, it's even more important than that."

He heard something odd in her quiet voice. Something that made him think she was about to tell him a grand secret. Lifting her chin, he gazed deeply into her eyes, astonished by the luminous expression within them. "What is it, Goldie?" he asked tenderly. "Tell me, love."

The name he'd called her made her heart skip a beat. She prayed she'd hear him call her his love every day for the rest of their lives. "I—Saber, today while you were gone, I thought of somethin'. Lord only knows why it took me so long to realize it, but at least it didn't take *years* before I did. That would have been just awful, don't you think?"

He took note of the way her voice had begun to tremble, and felt a true concern then. "Goldie, is something upsetting you? Has something bad happened that I should know about?"

"Oh, no, Saber. It's not bad. It's wonderful."

"Then why are you keeping me in such suspense?"

"Well, I've never told this to anyone before. Because it's the first time I've ever felt this way, I want to do it right."

He began to feel impatient to hear the all-important secret. "Goldie, the right way is just to come out with it. What is it?" he asked anxiously.

She reached up, laying her hand upon his cheek. "You've been so nice to me, Saber. You're different from any other man I've ever known. I—One time I told you how important honesty is to me. Saber, you've been so honest with me. You've never lied or tried to trick me into anything. I've known boys who did that, y'know. Ole Fred Wattle? Well, he made me believe he really liked me. When I found out it was all a game . . . it really hurt,

Saber. And one time—One time when I was livin' in Alabama, a boy named Gordie Floot asked me to a fish fry. I was so excited. I wasn't in love with Gordie or anything, but it made me so happy that a boy had invited me somewhere. I raced home and spent near about three hours gettin' ready. I waited and waited for Gordie to come get me.

"He didn't come," she continued, her voice fading to a whisper. "I—I was sure somethin' had happened to him. So I went to the fish fry, lookin' for someone who might have known where he was. Gordie was already there, Saber. He and his friends . . . they laughed at me when they saw me. It was all a trick, y'see. I was so glad when Uncle Asa got us kicked out of that town. I couldn't stand seein' Gordie and all his friends laughin' at me all the time.

"Gordie and Fred, they weren't the only ones. I guess because I was so little, and I had strange eyes and wild hair—I was the perfect target for their cruel games. But you, Saber. You've never done anything mean to me. You've never misled or deceived me. You always tell the truth, and—Saber, I trust you. I trust you with all my heart."

Saber couldn't respond. The words he'd waited so long to hear . . . She'd finally said them. And he had no right to hear them. Guilt tore through him, robbing his mind of every thought but the fact that he had, indeed, misled her. Dear God, he'd told her more lies than he could even count!

"I believe you love me, Saber," Goldie announced softly. "And . . . Saber, I love you, too."

He was stunned, unsure that he'd heard her correctly. "What?" he asked in total disbelief.

"I love you. Saber, I love you so much, that just the thought of it makes me ache all over. But it's not the hurtin' kind of ache. It's the kind that feels real good. The kind that sends tingles all over you. I love you, Saber."

Wave after wave of the purest happiness he'd ever known broke over him. Speechless, he hugged Goldie to him, burying his face in her mane of thick curls and knowing in his heart that this night would be branded on his soul forever.

"I'm sorry it took me so long to understand it all," Goldie said, her words muffled in his chest. "But Saber, I was so afraid to trust. My dreams—Saber, they've never come true. They always disappear right when I think that maybe they're really mine. I'm sorry. So sorry for takin' so long to believe you love me and for understandin' that I love you too."

Saber shuddered with anticipation. If only he had the ring right now! he fumed, wondering what her reaction would be when she saw the unique way he'd had the special diamonds set. God. *She loved him!* Tomorrow night, after she accepted his proposal, he'd explain his reasons for all the pretenses. He'd tell her about Hutchins, Doyle, and Dora Mashburn. About his fear for her safety. And he'd pour out everything concerning his overwhelming desire for her to love the comman man, Saber Tremayne, and not the nobleman, the Duke of Ravenhurst. He'd make her understand every motive behind all the lies.

And then he'd begin making her every dream come true. Whatever she desired, he'd give her. God, if she asked him for the entire world, he'd lay it at her feet.

Tomorrow evening, he thought, impatience clawing at him. Tomorrow evening would mark the end of all the deceptions and the beginning of their life together.

"Goldie, I—How can I tell you what this means to me?"

"You don't have to. I feel the same way. I—I never thought somethin' this wonderful would ever happen to me, Saber. It's the most beautiful thing I've ever had in my whole life. My diamond dreams are almost all the way true."

"Almost?" he asked, curiosity rising. "What else—"

"Well, that's one of the things I wanted to talk to you about," she said shyly. "Saber, y'know you have to leave Hallensham after you play the duke." She said no more, but waited to see what he would tell her.

Saber pondered what she said, suddenly realizing what her worry was. *Ah, but I won't be leaving, poppet.* he told her silently, struggling not to smile. *And neither will you.*

Goldie thought his silence meant he didn't understand the significance of what she'd told him. "I live in Hallensham, Saber," she stressed. "In my Aunt Della's cottage."

*But you will soon live in the Ravenhurst mansion.*

"Saber, can't y'see what the problem is?" Goldie asked, totally confused by his silence. "What are we gonna do?"

*Get married, have a dozen children, and live happily ever after.*

"All right, Saber, you never struck me as dense, but I reckon you might be just a tad." She disentangled herself from his arms, sitting up straight. "I know how you feel about Uncle Asa, but no matter what he's done, I can't forget what he did for me when my parents died. If not for him takin' me, I'd have been stuck in some orphanage somewhere. He didn't always do right, but Saber, I didn't starve while I was with him. Somehow or another, he always managed to feed me. Sometimes he'd forget, but— Well, I can't just leave him, Saber. He's family."

"The black sheep of it," Saber muttered, still unable to forgive the man.

"But he's still my kin," she responded, her voice quaking. "My flesh and blood, Saber."

"I know," he said gently, pulling her back into his arms. "I know, Goldie."

At his continued hedging, she began to feel a shred of anxiety. "I—Saber, don't you want to be with me?" she asked, her eyes stinging.

"Oh, Goldie, yes. More than anything."

"But—Saber, I've tried to explain all the problems to you. It's not that I expect you to help me with Uncle Asa— I—I could never ask that of you. I love you too much to do that to you. But I was hopin' . . . I thought if we talked about this together, we'd figure out a way to fix the problem."

Saber knew full well how he'd fix the problem. As soon as he returned to Ravenhurst, he'd handle Asa Mae himself. For Goldie's sake, he'd go gently with the man, but Asa *would* change his ways. If it was the last thing Saber ever did, he'd turn Asa into a man Goldie would be proud to call her family.

When Saber still offered no ideas, Goldie's apprehension increased. "I could do it all by myself," she blurted uneasily. "Take care of him, that is. I've already been doin' it for years. I know how. Saber, I was wonderin'—Well, maybe we should forget all about you bein' Duke Marion."

"Forget it?"

She nodded. "We—Uncle Asa, Big, and I would get tossed out of the village, but—Saber, at least you and I could be together. I wouldn't care about how mad the villagers got as long as I knew I had you. And I could find a place for Uncle Asa. I know I could, Saber. Somewhere close by to where you and I live, Big won't bother anybody, so we don't have to fret over him at all. But Uncle Asa—I'll do all the worryin' over him, Saber. You wouldn't have to do anything. I'll even get a job and pay for all his expenses. And if he makes trouble, I promise to handle it. Daddy's honor."

Her consideration for him wrapped around his very soul. God, she was so good, his poppet called Goldie. Always thinking of others. Always shouldering burdens for the sake of those she loved. He could barely wait to remove every burden she carried and erase every shred of worry that tainted her happiness.

"Saber?" she asked, her heart pounding violently.

"I still think I should be the duke." He pressed his mouth into her hair so she wouldn't see his broad grin. "The villagers have been waiting for many weeks to see Lord Tremayne. It wouldn't be very nice to disappoint them. And I've been practicing for so long, Goldie. I'd hate to think all those hours of duke lessons were wasted."

She pondered that, realizing he was right. Many of the villagers were mean, but perhaps some of the ones she hadn't met yet were kindhearted. And there were lots of them who really and truly believed she would bring back the duke. Some had even begun planning a festival in honor of his return. The thought of letting them down made her feel guilty.

"Goldie, after I've masqueraded as His Grace, we'll think of something. I promise you, poppet, everything will be fine."

"But—"

"You said you trusted me," he reminded her. "Do you take that back?"

"No," she hurried to tell him. "I do trust you."

"In all things?"

"Yes, but I—"

"Then trust me now. Trust me, Goldie."

The tenderness in his voice melted away every concern she had. She recalled how a large part of love was trust. And she and Saber loved each other. She knew then that they would, indeed, think of something. And once they had, they'd discuss it, just like her mother and father had always done. She lapsed into a contented silence, pondering all the wonderful things that were just beginning to happen in her life.

Saber, too, was in deep concentration, imagining the day he would take her to Hallensham. She wouldn't go back as Goldie Mae, the destitute and despised girl she was when she left. She'd return as Goldie Tremayne, the Duchess of Ravenhurst.

He'd organize a procession, he decided, excitement fairly exploding inside him. After having sent word of his and his bride's impending arrival, he'd have his assemblage of splendidly uniformed and mounted attendants, and his own elegant coach make a grand tour of the Tremayne lands. He would have his dark green pennants displayed, the Tremayne crest glittering in gold upon them. The people would pour out of their homes, lined up to wave and cheer as the parade passed.

But the grand spectacle, the sheer pagentry would not be for him. It would be for Goldie. From now on every single thing he did would be for her.

"I love you, poppet," he whispered, his voice shaking with both excitement and the impassioned truth of his pledge to her.

"And I love you," she answered, savoring the way the words felt as they left her lips. "And wish I could stay the night with you, Saber. I can't think of anything I want to do more, but—"

"I know. The hens will find you in here."

"Hens?"

"Never mind." With a tremendous sigh, he rose and

helped her out of bed. After finding her night rail on the floor, he put it on her, disappointed when her beautiful body was once again hidden from him.

Goldie slipped her arms around his bare waist, laying her cheek on his chest. "Soon," she began timidly, "we won't have to sneak around like this anymore. Isn't that right, Saber?"

He smiled. She certainly wasn't very subtle with her hints about marriage. But he didn't mind. He was just as anxious for the wedding as she was. And what a magnificent wedding it would be! The most sumptuous wedding London had ever witnessed. He sighed again, thinking of what a beautiful bride she would be.

Goldie heard and felt his sigh, noting he'd failed to answer her question. Distress rose up in her, but she refused to let it overcome her. *Trust me, Goldie.* he'd said to her. *Trust me.*

She did. He wasn't sighing because he didn't want to marry her, she told herself firmly. He was sighing because . . . because the thought of wedding her was wonderful to him. Yes, that was it.

It was her turn to sigh. She did so, in utmost pleasure. The man holding her so tenderly had never let her down before, and he wouldn't now either. Her dreams . . . all her diamond dreams were really coming true this time.

"I have to go now, Saber," she said, smiling up at him.

He ran his finger over her grin, then escorted her to the door. Opening it slightly, he peered down the hall, seeing no one about. "If either of the aunties catch you, pretend you're sleepwalking."

She nodded and stepped into the hall. After giving him a last kiss on his chin, she began the trek back to her bedroom. But she'd only taken a few steps, when she turned to him again. "Saber," she whispered.

"What?"

"About thipstrit," she murmured, grinning.

"Yes? What does it mean?" He strained to hear her answer.

"Anything you want it to. I made it up."

With that, she scurried down the hall, successfully making it to her bedroom without being seen.

Saber watched her, his shoulders shaking with silent mirth. "Oh, Goldie," he sputtered merrily as he went back into his bedroom, "life with you is going to be . . . Well, there will never be a dull moment. God, how I love you."

Ambling to his dresser, he lit a lamp, looked at his watch, and saw it was one o'clock in the morning. He was to pick up the ring tomorrow evening at six. That was seventeen hours away. Then there would be the hour he would need to make the trip back. Eighteen hours would have to pass before Goldie would become his betrothed.

Eighteen eternities.

Dane stood in the shadows of the tall shrubbery on the corner of Pickering and Landon. The chilly night breeze swept past him, making him shiver. He pulled his hat low over his eyes, drew up the collar of his long black coat, and continued watching the house across the street.

Why was Diggory taking so long? he wondered impatiently. The man had left to investigate the outside of the house fifteen minutes ago! Surely it didn't take that long to discover the best way to break in.

He calmed when he finally saw Diggory hurrying toward him. "Did you find a good way to get in?" he demanded, taking a step away from the stinking ruffian. "Do you foresee any problems?"

Diggory shook his huge head. "There ain't never no problems fer me, milord. The job'll be easy an' over real quick."

Satisfied, Dane reached up to smooth the hair at the nape of his neck, then began to turn toward the coach he'd rented and left down the street. But a sudden movement at an upstairs window of the house stilled him. Though the room was dark, the moon provided sufficient light for him to understand that someone had opened the draperies. He strained to see the person, but could make out little more than a shadowy form. In the next instant the person moved away.

Dane smiled. Perhaps it had been Goldie Mae. Even if it hadn't been, he knew the bitch was living in the house. Tomorrow night she would die in it.

\* \* \*

Saber sat in the corner of the drawing room, watching Goldie. He felt sorry for her, but couldn't think of a way to help her out of her predicament. The aunties were explaining the positions of servants this afternoon, and it was apparent to Saber that Goldie couldn't have cared less. Feeling a touch of deviltry, he winked at her.

Goldie's eyes widened. Her heart began to flutter like a leaf in the wind.

"All right, Goldie," Clara said. "Lucille and I must be leaving for our engagement shortly, but we have a few minutes to go over this once again. Now if you are living in a country estate, tell me about the servants you would employ. Start with the most important of those, and work your way down."

Goldie twirled a curl around her finger, then began fidgeting with the fragile lace at the cuff of her sleeve. "Miss Clara," she hedged, resisting the urge to look at Saber, "I'm never gonna live in a country estate. Why do I have to learn about the servants who—"

"Because it is something every proper young lady should know," Clara answered.

Her mention of a proper young lady made Goldie think of last night. Daring to cast a shy glance at Saber, she remembered all the improper things they'd done, wishing they could do them again right now.

Saber read her thoughts and blew her a kiss.

Goldie squirmed in her chair. Great day Miss Agnes, if she didn't stop looking at him, the aunties would surely figure out what was going on between her and Saber.

Oh, but it was impossible not to watch him! Lord, he was so handsome. And so naughty, too. He knew full well what his crooked grins, sly winks, and sexy looks were doing to her.

The thought brought her a slight grin. If he could do this to her, she could do it back. Slowly, as if she were completely unaware of her actions, she lifted her hand to her breast. Laying her palm lightly upon it, she ran her thumb over it, then leisurely moved her hand down to her tiny waist. Finally, she allowed it to rest on her upper thigh.

Seeing she had Saber's full and undivided attention, she lifted her other hand to her chin. With her index finger, she touched her parted lips before smoothing her tongue over them. She almost laughed out loud at the desire that leaped suddenly into Saber's wide eyes.

Clara clapped twice. "The butler, housekeeper, and head cook lead the indoor staff, Goldie," she snapped, glowering at Saber, who was watching Goldie with eyes that were far too hungry for Clara's liking. "Under them are the footmen, assistant cooks, parlormaids, housemaids, nurserymaids, kitchenmaids, scullerymaids, dairymaids, laundresses, bootboy, a doorkeeper, and a watchman. Female domestics come under the housekeeper's authority, and the male servants are under the butler's."

"And there is the lady's maid, too," Lucille added, also glaring at Saber. "She is in charge of her mistress' wardrobe. She lays out clothes and helps her mistress dress. She washes, irons, mends, packs, and unpacks the clothes. Her other duties include lighting fires in the dressing room and bedroom, and also keeping those rooms tidy and wellswept. A lady's maid should have the talents of a milliner, dressmaker, and a hairdresser. And it doesn't hurt if she is a bit of a chemist. If she is, she can prepare cosmetics and remedies."

Goldie nodded without hearing a word. *I love you, Saber,* she told him with a look.

Understanding her silent message, he inclined his head, then shifted in his chair when the aunties gave him another disapproving look. "I'm sorry," he told them. "but can you not see how terribly bored Goldie is? It's almost five o'clock, and the two of you have been at this for three hours already. Don't you think it's time—"

"We've one more subject to cover, Saber, and cover it we will," Clara announced. "Why don't you go—"

"I'm staying." He looked at his watch, seeing that it was almost time for him to leave for the jeweler's. Still, he had to think of some way to free Goldie from the henhouse.

"Very well, Saber, but do behave yourself," Clara chided, then turned back to Goldie. "My dear, let us discuss what is one of my favorite subjects—the Season. The

Season, my dear, begins in May and ends in July. Most of Society is in London during the Season. People come for the gay round of social events, and to see friends they have not seen in months.''

"One of the most important reasons for the Season," Lucille explained, "is to give young men and women an opportunity to meet. It is quite exciting!''

"Of course the men and women are *strictly* chaperoned," Clara went on. "Chaperones see to it that a young man is allowed only to dance with a lady and escort her to her carriage. Beyond that, there is no other physical contact.'' She gave Saber another well-aimed glare.

"Young ladies at balls should never dance more than two dances with the same gentleman," Lucille stressed. "At private balls, a lady may *not* decline to dance with a gentleman who has asked her, but at a public ball, it is considered quite proper for her to dance only with those gentlemen she knows. Is that clear to you, my dear?''

Goldie began to imagine how it would feel to be in Saber's arms while he whirled her across a ballroom floor. She'd never learned to dance, but didn't think it would be too difficult if Saber led her to do the right steps. "What if you're at a dance with a man you love?'' she asked, her gaze never leaving Saber's. "What if just the thought of bein' held by another man makes you sick to your stomach? What if—''

"Goldie!'' Clara exclaimed, aghast.

"I think," Saber began, standing, "that if a young lady is in the situation you describe, poppet, she should heed her instincts and pay not a speck of attention to any man other than the one she loves.'' With that, he strolled to her, and picked up her hand. "Dance with me, Goldie love.''

"Saber, this is ridiculous," Lucille flared. "You—''

"Just put your arms around me, poppet, and let me show you.''

"But—But there's no music," she responded, mesmerized by the softness in his voice and eyes.

"Ah, then let us make our own.'' When she slipped her arms around him, he held her in a slow waltz, dancing her toward the drawing-room door.

"Saber!" Clara called angrily. "We are not finished with the lessons!"

"Yes, Auntie, you are. I am rescuing Goldie from your clutches."

Clara stood. "And just where do you think you are taking her, may I ask?"

Saber looked down into Goldie's eyes. "I'm going to sweep her into the foyer. And there, aunties, I am going to kiss her. If you don't care to see such an immoral act, I suggest you remain in this room."

At his aunts' astonished gasps, he waltzed Goldie into the entryway, stopping at the front door. As he promised he would, he bent to kiss her.

When his lips met hers, she quivered in his arms. It was such a tender kiss, she thought. So sweet. It was as if it were made of light, like the twinkle in a baby's eye.

"I love you, Goldie," he whispered, spreading more kisses across her cheeks. Releasing her, he looked at his watch, excitement charging through him when he saw it was finally time to leave for the jeweler's. "While I'm gone, I'll miss you. I have an errand to run, you must understand, and I have to go right now. I'll be back in a few hours."

"But Saber, I—Saber, tonight is the Chittin'don party. Please—"

"Goldie, I already told you that we will not be attending." He put on his coat and gloves.

"But you said you still wanted to go to Hallensham and be Duke Marion. Saber, listen to me. Ever since last night when you mentioned how disappointed the villagers will be if they don't see the duke, I've been thinkin' about how right you were. Some of those villagers are real mean, but other ones aren't. That farmer who tried to sell me his baby cow was real nice to me."

"Goldie—"

"And before I left, lots of people were gettin' together and plannin' a homecomin' festival. Hell, they've probably got the whole thing ready to go by now. And I bet they've spent their lifes' savin's on it, too. It'd be so ugly of us to let 'em down. Your bein' the duke will be the last time they ever set eyes on their precious Marion, because the real duke's not ever goin' back there. It would mean so much to those people to see you. I owe 'em a duke, Saber, and you're him. You're gonna be everything they're hopin' to see. This Chittin'don thing is the best chance we've ever had to do the final part of the duke research! We're gonna go, and that's it."

"No, we aren't, and that's it."

"But—"

"I can't take you, poppet," he said, tugging one of her curls. "I've something very important to do right now. However, when I return you and I will do something special together. I could arrange for us to have our own private party here if you like. It can be as elegant as you want it to be, and you may wear your new finery. Would you like that?"

"Saber, *please* take me to the—"

"We are *not* going to the Chittingdons' tonight."

Frustration and fury fairly smothered her until a new thought came to mind. It so thrilled her, she was hard-pressed to keep Saber from seeing her excitement.

"Is that the beginning of a smile I see?" he asked.

Her grin grew broader by the second. "I—It's all right, Saber," she reassured him, swiping a speck of lint from the collar of his coat. "You go on and do your errand."

"So you truly don't mind missing the get-together?" he asked, confused by her sudden pliability.

She realized the necessity of acting upset and tried to cry. No tears came. Dammit, she usually cried at the drop of a hat, and now that she really needed some tears, she couldn't find any! "I—Well, 'course I mind," she said, casting her eyes downward. "And I'm really mad at you, too. Mad as mad can be. But—But maybe I can get us invited to another party before we leave for Hallensham. Promise me here and now that if I can, you'll go to it."

"We'll see. Now, why don't you get ready for our special night? Fern can be your lady's maid. I'll be back in about two hours."

She nodded and waved good-bye to him when he left. Grinning, she raced back to the drawing room. "Saber's gone," she informed the aunties. "And don't go gettin' all upset over the kiss he gave me. It was a *sweet* kiss, not the other kind. Well, I'm gonna go upstairs now. Have a good time at your engagement. 'Bye!''

With that, she tore into the foyer and bounded up the staircase. Once in her room, she closed her door, skipped to her closet, and began rummaging through her new gowns. "I'll get ready all right, Saber West," she mumbled to herself. "For *my* special night."

With a contented sigh, she brought forth a gorgeous gown of rich, honey-colored satin and russet lace. She thought it perfect for the Chittingdon dinner-dance.

And since Saber wouldn't be there to smile at her, she was positive she wouldn't spill any food on it.

# Chapter 20

As his coach stopped in front of the house, Saber took one last look at the gorgeous ring encased in the black velvet box. The jeweler had outdone himself. The ring exceeded Saber's expectations, and he knew in his heart Goldie would adore it. Snapping the box closed, he slipped it into his waistcoat pocket, and quickly alighted from the carriage. Such excitment pounded through him that he could barely contain himself.

Bennett met him at the door. "Good evening, sir," he said, taking Saber's coat.

"Bennett, I want the fire stoked and lamps lit in the drawing room. See to it that there is a bottle of wine— No, *champagne*. Yes, bring champagne in there also. Miss Mae and I will be celebrating tonight, and I want no interruptions once I have escorted her into the parlor. Is that understood?"

Bennett scowled. "Quite understood, sir, but . . . I— Was Miss Mae aware of the celebration?"

Saber didn't like the uncomfortable look on the butler's face. "Why do you ask?"

"Well—She's not here, sir."

*"What?"*

"No, sir. She left a little over an hour ago."

Instant fury left Saber speechless for a moment. "Where did she go?" he asked in a very low voice, already knowing full well where the wayward minx was.

Bennett realized something was amiss, and wished he didn't have to tattle on Goldie. "She said you could meet her there, sir," he replied helplessly.

Saber shuddered with rage. "She went to the Chittingdons', didn't she, Bennett?"

"I—Yes, sir. She did. And allow me to tell you how beautiful she looked!"

Saber closed his eyes, fighting foreboding.

"Sir?" Bennett asked, wondering what his employer was thinking.

Saber opened his eyes, grabbed his hat, coat, and gloves from the butler and stormed back outside, thankful that his coach and driver were still there. He snapped out instructions to the man, then jumped into the carriage, slamming the door so forcefully that the conveyance rattled.

The coach jolted forward, the driver urging the horses into a fast canter. Saber glared at the passing streets, feeling more frantic by the moment. One question hammered repeatedly through his mind, filling him with wild, gut-wrenching apprehension.

*Who,* exactly, would Goldie see when he arrived at the Chittingdons?

Saber West, the common man she trusted?

Or Marion Tremayne, the nobleman who had deceived her?

To Goldie's way of thinking, dinner was proceeding smoothly. True, an extra place setting had to be provided for her at the last minute since she had failed to formally accept the Chittingdons' invitation. But no one had seemed to mind too much. Lady Chittingdon, in fact, had gone on and on about how glad she was that Goldie had been able to attend, echoing her husband's sentiment that any friend of Marion Tremayne's was a welcome addition to their gatherings.

Slipping the last bit of her fruit compote into her mouth, she noticed one woman staring at her from across the table. She smiled at the lady, discomfited when her gesture of friendliness was returned with an icy, hateful look.

Jillian Somerset decided the American girl was the most repulsive human being she'd ever had the extreme misfortune to meet. Why, the ignorant little thing had used her oyster fork for the entire meal, proclaiming the small utensil was the first one she'd ever used that fit so perfectly into her mouth! What Marion saw in the short, ugly, and mannerless chit was beyond her, but whatever it was, Jillian was determined to see to it that Marion's interest quickly waned. She would begin bringing about those ends tonight. And the fact that Marion wasn't here would make it all the easier.

"Miss Mae, I have heard that you were able to interview Lord John Russell," Lord Chittingdon said for the benefit of the twelve other curious guests, many of whom gazed respectfully at Goldie upon hearing the announcement. "Word of it filtered my way from Her Majesty's court, no less! When I heard that the girl who had spoken to him was a lovely and petite American, I knew she could be none other than you. Tell me, my dear, what did our Prime Minister have to say to you?"

Glad to be able to turn her attention away from the rude woman across from her, Goldie smiled at her host. "Well," she began, patting her mouth with her napkin, "we talked about all he likes to eat, mostly. I was real interested in that. Uh, folks in America want to know what kinds of food dukish people like."

"Indeed," Jillian commented in a syrupy voice. "And what was his reaction to you?"

Goldie stiffened, irritated by the mean way the woman had asked the question. She raised a brow. "He liked me so much he told me to call him Johnny."

Lady Chittingdon laughed at what she suspected was a bald-faced lie. She couldn't condemn Goldie, however, for she had witnessed Jillian Somerset's animosity during the meal and knew full well it was jealousy that prompted it. She found the situation highly amusing. "Actually, Jillian," Lady Chittingdon said, "he was quite taken with Goldie. Word has it that every time he related the story, he became so amused that he laughed uproariously. It's my opinion that he would welcome another opportunity to see her again."

"Humph!" Horatio Alders growled. "He's supposed to be looking after the best interests of our country, and he wastes his time laughing over useless anecdotes!"

Lady Chittingdon gave the sour man a despairing look. "Ladies," she said, rising, "shall we retire to the drawing room and allow the men to enjoy their cigars and port before we begin dancing?''

All the women, save Goldie, rose, gathering around Lady Chittingdon. "I'm stayin' in here with the men," she announced, picking up her notepad and pencil from her lap. "I have a lot of questions to ask 'em. Y'all sit back down," she told the men, who had all risen out of their chairs in deference to the ladies' departure.

"Oh, they'll be along shortly, my dear," Lady Chittingdon assured her. "Come with us, Miss Mae. I'm sure I'm not the only one who would like to hear the story of how you and Marion Tremayne came to meet."

"Well, all right," Goldie acquiesced. "But y'all men come on purty soon," she told them. She allowed the butler to pull out her chair for her, smiling graciously at him.

Once in the elegant drawing room, the ladies' inquistion began immediately.

"Where did you meet Marion Tremayne, Miss Mae?" Lady Ainsworth asked.

"Where?" Goldie repeated. She pulled at a ringlet.

"Was it in Scotland?" Lady Baldwin queried.

"Uh . . . Yeah. It was in Scotland," Goldie said, relieved. "I saw him in a little town there. He was doin' one of those Scottish jigs. Had on one of those skirts and everything."

"Marion was dancing a jig?" Lady Chittingdon asked. "My! I would have like to have seen that. Tell us more, Miss Mae."

"I wish y'all'd call me Goldie. *Miss Mae* sounds so fancy."

Lady Roth smiled. "But you are quite . . . *fancy*, my dear. Your gown is simply gorgeous."

Goldie smoothed her satin skirts. "And do I have it on right? Fern and I had us a real time tryin' to understand which was the front side and which was the back. They both looked the same. 'Course the back usually has buttons, but Fern said she'd seen some dresses with buttons in the front. We finally put it on like this because it didn't make much difference. And I have on eight slips, too. I'm not really talkin' about underwear, though. I'm just sorta lettin' y'all know in a real casual way that I have some on over my you-know-whats.''

Lady Ainsworth frowned. "Your *you-know-whats?*"

Goldie leaned forward in her chair and whispered. "My *legs.*" Straightening, she sipped the champagne a maid had offered her, wrinkling her nose as the bubbles tickled the back of her throat. "Yeah, I like this dress, but I'm not used to showin' this much of my other you-know-whats. This gown shows nearly everything I've got. I don't have much as you can plainly see, but I usually cover up what little I've got. Fern said it's all right to show your you-know-whats at night, though." At the look of confusion on the women's faces, she leaned forward again. "My *ninnies.*"

"Oh, my!" Lady Baldwin exclaimed, whipping out her fan. "Oh, my goodness gracious!"

Goldie patted the woman's shoulder. "I wouldn't have said the word if y'all had known what I was talkin' about. It's a mystery to me how y'all can discuss stuff without sayin' what it is you're discussin'. What do y'do? Point?"

Lady Chittingdon smothered laughter. "Why, Goldie, it's very simple. We don't discuss it at all," she explained gently.

Goldie nodded. "Do you talk about chicken parts? I was wonderin' about that the other day. Myself, I like the thighs. 'Course then there's chicken legs, too. What do all y'all dukish folks do when you want a chicken part? Can you ask for a breast at the supper table?"

Jillian sneered. "Tell us, Goldie. What does Marion have to say about the way you act?"

"The way I act?" Goldie echoed in a very tiny voice. "What's the matter with the way I act?"

Jillian refrained from answering, but merely gave Goldie a horrible look.

"Goldie, my dear," Lady Chittingdon said, realizing a change of subject was most definitely in order, "have you heard about our newest project? I'm sure you will want to include it in the book you are writing. We've recently begun adopting street urchins. We bring the waifs into our homes, where we begin teaching and grooming them. They will stay with us until we are satisfied that they have become properly educated in all respects. When that time comes, we will use our influence to find them honest, well-paying jobs.''

Lady Roth smiled excitedly. "We call the undertaking our mission of mercy, and we are sponsoring only the most pitiful and ignorant girls we can find. My girl's name is Elsa, and she's seventeen years old. Not all of our waifs are necessarily children. Some are young women. After Elsa was cleaned up and dressed, I discovered her to be quite pretty. She was very frightened when she first arrived at my home, but my husband and I have showered her with lovely things, and now she is much more confident with us. She's making splendid progress, too.''

Lady Ainsworth smoothed her hair. "My girl's name is Faye. She is eighteen. One of my servants found her selling dog meat! Well, I was absolutely horrified to say the very least. I took the poor child in immediately.''

"And my little urchin," Lady Alders began, "is fifteen. Her name is Netty. She's only been with my husband, Horatio, and me for a week and is still quite shy. But yesterday she succeeded in reciting the entire alphabet! I was so proud of her that I bought her a gold hand mirror. She's never had a mirror of her own and was quite happy to receive it.''

"And how is Horatio taking to the idea of having Netty in his home?" Lady Chittingdon asked, feeling rather sorry for the street urchin who had to live under the same roof as the belligerent Horatio Alders. Why, the man was the stiffest, most cantankerous man in all of England!

Lady Alders' face fell. "Not very well, I'm afraid. I take great care to keep Netty out of his way.''

Goldie sat back in her chair, listening to other women describe *their* waifs. When the last one had finished, she smiled. "Y'all are sure compassionate folks. I think this new project of yours is real nice. Y'know, maybe y'all could even find noble husbands for those girls. I bet any one of 'em would be tickled pink to be able to marry a dukish man.''

"Oh, but that would never do," Lady Ainsworth explained. "It would be quite unseemly for a titled gentleman to marry such a girl.''

"I should say so," Jillian agreed, fondling the huge emerald on her necklace. "Take Marion Tremayne for example. As the Duke of Ravenhurst, it would be in very poor taste for him to actually *wed* a girl so far beneath him. He may dally with such a girl, but marry her? Never."

"Jillian," Lady Chittingdon began, struggling with anger, "please—"

"And what are you beautiful ladies discussing, may I ask?" Lord Chittingdon asked as he entered the drawing room. "Whatever the conversation, I hope you don't mind if the gentleman and I join in. We missed the pleasure of your company so much, we decided not to linger over our port."

Goldie grinned at the cluster of men, some of whom were elderly, and some of whom were as young as Saber. "Y'all pull up a chair. We're talkin' about how it's not right for dukish men to marry poor, ignorant girls. Before that we were talkin' about chicken parts, and before that we were—"

"We have been discussing many things," Lady Chittingdon finished for her. "Do be seated, gentleman."

As the men accepted Lady Chittingdon's invitation, Goldie noticed one of them frowning into empty space. Great day Miss Agnes, the man looked angry with the whole world. "What's your name again?" she asked him. "I forgot."

Horatio snapped out of his irritable daze. "I am Horatio Alders, and I do not want to be included in your book."

Goldie wondered if the man had ever been happy in his entire life. *What an ill-box,* she mused with a tiny grin. "Well, that's just a shame. You look like just the fella who could have answered a very important question for me."

Horatio lifted his chin. "And what question is that?"

"There's no use in askin' it if you aren't gonna answer."

"Nevertheless, I would like to know the question."

"Well, all right. What was your favorite thing to do when you were a little boy?"

Horatio frowned. "What bearing would that possibly have on anything?"

"I'm not real sure yet. But I'm gonna tie it in somehow. Maybe I'll have a chapter called 'Dukish Kids.'"

Horatio turned away, but Goldie noticed his scowl had turned into a thoughtful look. She grinned again.

Lord Baldwin cleared his throat. "I'm very disappointed that Marion was unable to join us tonight, Miss Mae. The last time I saw him was at Angelica Sheridan's funeral. He—"

"You know, now that you ask, Miss Mae," Horatio interrupted, crossing his arms upon his chest, "I *did* enjoy making paper boats."

"Can you still make 'em?" she asked.

Horatio saw that all eyes were upon him. "I have no idea and no wish to find out," he flared.

Jillian turned her glacial blue gaze to Lord Baldwin. "What a pity you haven't seen Marion in so long," she said, casting a swift and hateful glance at Goldie. "*I* have seen him on countless occasions since the funeral."

"I don't imagine one forgets how to make paper boats," Horatio commented. "If you will be good enough to give me a sheet of your paper, Miss Mae, I will endeavor to show you how."

She smiled and gave him the paper.

"Horatio," Lady Alders said to her husband. "What in the world are you doing?"

Horatio grunted an answer no one could comprehend, and remained busy folding the paper.

"Goldie, my dear," Lord Chittingdon said warmly, "are you enjoying our gathering?"

"Oh, Duke Chittin'don, you just can't know what bein' here means to me. And I'm ready to start takin' notes on y'all. I only need stuff about dukish *men*," she explained to the women. "I've enjoyed y'all's company and all, but I mostly came for the men."

"Indeed," Lady Baldwin murmured, eyeing the delighted look on her husband's face.

"It's all the folding, you must understand," Horatio mumbled as he continued to fashion the paper toy. "If the creases aren't exactly right, the boat will sink."

Goldie grinned at him, and picked up her pencil. "All right, y'all. There's really just a few things I want to know.

For one, what do dukish men talk about? Since I had to leave the dinin' room while y'all were in there, I didn't get to hear. I'm purty sure y'all talk about different stuff than the men I know in America.''

"What do they talk about?" Lord Roth queried.

"Well," Goldie said, trying to remember as much as she could, "the young ones usually talk about how great it'd be to *get* a woman, and the old ones talk about how great it'd be to get *away* from the ones they got."

Horatio Alders' lips twitched.

"Ole Cecil Bean down in Squattin' Junction, Kentucky, didn't ever talk about anything but the rattlesnake bite that cost him his arm. Yeah, they had to cut his arm off back in 1833. Cecil had everybody carve their names into his wooden arm. He even had President Andrew Jackson's name carved on it. He told everybody he'd met that president, but anybody who'd had a speck of schoolin' knew he was lyin'. We knew because the name was spelled A-N-D-R-O-O J-A-K-S-I-N. Ole Cecil carved that name himself. No one ever accused him of lyin' about it though. We all figured that a man with one arm deserved whatever pride his wooden one could give him.''

Horatio Alders smiled.

"And ole Vern Odle back in Willy Wally Way, North Carolina? Now, he was a character if you ever wanted to meet one. All he ever talked about was how bossy his wife, Mabelle Ann, was. But he did everything she told him to. Yeah, Mabelle Ann'd say 'Frog,' and Vern'd jump. I'll swannee if she'd have said 'Cloud,'' he'd have tried to rain. You didn't ever meet up with ole Vern when he didn't tell you about how mean Mabelle Ann was. Y'know, Vern didn't even have a job. He stayed home almost all the time because leavin' would've meant he'd have to kiss Mabelle Ann good-bye.''

Horatio's shoulders began to quake.

"And I remember a man by the name of Able Poots, back in Babbitsboro, Alabama. He—Y'know, folks there were always fightin' over the name of that town. Some said it was *Babbitsboro*, and others insisted it was *Rabbitsboro*. Y'see, the town's papers weren't written too clear. You couldn't really tell if the first letter of the town's name was a 'B' or an 'R.' There was even bloodshed over it. Yeah, old Barnaby Babbit shot ole Lem Smedley in the foot. Barnaby claimed it was his grandfather, Farley Babbit, who established the town. Lem said anybody with an ounce of brains knew the town was *Rabbitsboro* because of all the rabbits that were there.

"Anyway, ole Able Poots? Well, he was the chitchattin'est man God ever made. He didn't talk about any one thing, but any subject could get him off on another one. If you told him it was gonna rain, it'd make him think of water, y'see. So then he'd tell you about the time he almost drowned when he was seven. One time I told him how purty the crepe myrtles in yard his were? Well, in the space of less than a minute, he went from crepe myrtles to the story of why his beard only grew on one side of his face.

"Y'want to know how he did it? Crepe myrtles reminded him of this girl he knew once. Her name was Myrtle, and she made the best collard greens Able ever tasted. Collards reminded him of the time he broke his collarbone when a tree branch fell on him. The branch reminded him of what he was doin' by that tree at the time. He was gonna cut it down to get some wood to fix the leakin' church roof. Church reminded him of the time when he was kneelin' by his bed, sayin' his prayers. He was prayin' so hard, he didn't notice how close his lighted candle was to the curtains. They caught on fire, and Able burned one side of his face tryin' to beat out the flames. Never could grow a beard on that side of his face again."

Horatio could contain his laughter no longer. In a great loud burst, it exploded from him. He doubled over, his body shaking violently. His paper boat floated to the floor.

His wife, Lady Alders, jumped from her chair, frantically fanning her husband. "Oh, my! He's having an attack!"

"Looks to me like he's laughin'," Goldie commented.

"Send for a doctor!" Lord Chittingdon barked at a young maid.

"He's just laughin'," Goldie said again. "He must've really liked the story about Able Poots."

Lady Roth shook her head. "Horatio Alders never even

*smiles,* much less *laughs,* Goldie! There is something definitely wrong with the poor man!''

Goldie cocked her head, watching the guests fuss over Horatio. Bending at the waist, she looked at his face, which was almost between his knees. She saw tears clinging to his whiskered cheeks, and a huge smile on his thick lips.

''Look what you did to Lord Alders with your ridiculous stories,'' Jillian hissed. ''You've shocked him to such an extent that he is suffering some sort of terrible seizure!''

Goldie glanced at all the other guests. When she saw no one but Jillian was looking at her, she stuck her tongue out at the catty woman, giggling at the horrified expression on Jillian's face.

''Horatio!'' Lady Alders cried, kneeling and pushing at his shoulders. ''Speak to me, husband! Horatio, tell me what—''

''Barnaby Babbit,'' Horatio sputtered, ''shot Lem Smedley in the foot! All because of the name of the town!'' His face reddened as more laughter rumbled through him. ''And Poots! Able Poots! I've—I've never heard a funnier name in all my life!''

Lady Alders stood, still staring down at her husband. ''He's laughing,'' she murmured, her face a mask of pure disbelief.

All heads turned toward Goldie.

''Lord Marion Tremayne,'' the butler announced from the doorway.

As Saber stepped into the room, his eyes widened at the sight before him. Horatio Alders was leaning over his knees, and the other people in the room were staring at Goldie. His first thought was that she'd said something that so upset Lord Alders, the man had died.

''Marion!'' Jillian exclaimed, rising. Disregarding the fact that he'd ended his relationship with her, she smiled and started for him.

He swept right past her, arriving at Goldie's chair. His hand on her shoulder, he looked at Horatio Alders. ''What has happened here?'' he asked anxiously.

''Able Poots!'' Horatio tried to explain.

Lord Chittingdon shook Saber's hand. "Quite a girl, Miss Mae is, Marion," he said, grinning. "It—Well, it was the most incredible thing I've ever seen. She actually had Horatio making a paper boat, and then sent him into a fit of laughter! I was just saying earlier that Lord John Russell is extremely amused by her, also. She is a very lovely and entertaining person to have around, and I've no doubt you have thoroughly enjoyed her company since meeting her."

"I have indeed." Saber was relieved to understand that Horatio Alders was fine, but remained uneasy about what the evening had taught Goldie. He looked down at her, steeling himself for whatever she might say to him. "Goldie," he said quietly.

She tried to read the look in his eyes. The softness wasn't there. But then, neither was anger. Worry was. Lines of anxiety creased his forehead, too. She realized then that being in the midst of so many dukish people was making him nervous. After all, she mused, smiling up at him, this was the real and final test. Fooling Lord Chittingdon was one thing, but deceiving a whole *room* full of noble folks was quite another.

She had to give him some encouragement. Standing, she wrapped her arms around his waist, her fingers caressing his back. "I'm so glad you decided to come, Marion."

The sweetness in her voice and the twinkle in her eyes convinced Saber she hadn't learned the truth of who he was. "Have you had a good time, poppet?" he asked, wondering what the best way would be to get her out of here.

She laughed with quiet delight. "Yes, but now that you're here, I'll have an even better time. We were just gettin' ready to start dancin', y'know."

"We were at that," Lady Chittingdon said. "In fact, I hear the quartet now. I saw no need of an orchestra, what with only the few of us dancing. Shall we, dear guests?" she asked, gesturing toward the door.

Before Saber could object, Goldie was pulling him along. "Saber," she whispered, "remember that festival I told you the villagers were plannin'? Well, what if you have to dance at it? Now listen, pay real good attention to all the dukish dancin' these folks are fixin' to do. Try and remember every move they make."

Saber's mind whirled as he tried to think of a way to dissuade her from staying any longer. But before he'd come up with a good excuse, they'd arrived at the small ballroom. "Goldie—"

"Marion," Jillian purred, sidling up next to him. "Remember the way we used to dance?"

When Saber's body suddenly went rigid, Goldie grew alert. He had no idea who the woman was, much less how to answer her. "Surely you remember *Jillian*, don't you, Marion?" she hinted loudly.

"Well, of course he remembers me!" Jillian snapped.

Saber felt apprehension curl through him. Of all the people here, Jillian was the one most likely to reveal his identity. "Would you please excuse us, Jillian?" he begged off, taking Goldie's hand.

Rage made Jillian's eyes glitter ominously. "Of course," she seethed. "But I must insist on a dance with you before the evening is over." She turned to Goldie, smiling. "Marion and I adore dancing together. It doesn't even make any difference if there is no music. We always made our own, didn't we, Marion?"

Goldie frowned at what Jillian had said. How strange, she thought. Just this afternoon, Saber had told *her* that they'd make their own music. She looked up at him, noting the deep distress on his face, and realizing once again how nervous he was masquerading as the duke.

She had to help him before Jillian sensed there was something wrong. Somehow, she had to get the woman to leave him alone! "Jillian, I'm sure Marion remembers every single thing he's ever done with you. It's probably branded in his brain. But we didn't come here to talk about memories. Besides that, he's not here with *you* tonight. He's here with *me*. 'Bye."

" 'Bye," Saber echoed, leading Goldie quickly away.

"Y'know, Saber," Goldie whispered. "I think the real Marion and that Jillian woman used to be lovers. It all makes sense now. She's been givin' me mean looks all night, and she just said how she and Marion made music together. Dukish men *always* have lovers, y'know. Mildred Fickle told me that. Anyway, I think it's been a while since Marion and Jillian have seen each other, though. If they were still carryin' on, she'd have noticed you aren't him.''

Saber tugged at his collar. ''Goldie—''

''Marion, my boy,'' Lord Roth said, taking Saber's elbow. ''It's been years since we've had one of our deep discussions. Why, the last one I recall having was some seven years ago! We talked about *The Economist.*''

Saber wondered what to do, answer correctly for Lord Roth's sake, or pretend ignorance for Goldie's. *''The Economist,''* he repeated lamely.

Lord Roth frowned. ''Why, you act as though you don't even know what it is.''

Saber felt Goldie nudge him in the ribs, urging him to give an intelligent response. ''Of course I know what *The Economist* is, Lord Roth.''

''Yeah, of course he does,'' Goldie agreed, wondering if Saber was going to have to make something up. ''He— He just would rather talk about somethin' more recent. After all, y'all had that talk seven years ago. Don't y'think it's old news by now?''

Lord Roth nodded. ''It is at that, but we were terribly excited by the weekly financial paper, weren't we, Marion? Why, we even sought out its founder, Sir James Wilson, and discussed it with him.''

''Yeah, Marion here remembers that just like it was yesterday,'' Goldie went on. ''Just the other day, he was goin' on and on about how ole Sir Wilson finally found that paper. How long did you say it'd been lost, Marion?''

Despite his dismay over the situation, Saber smiled. ''Goldie,'' he said tenderly, *''founding* something means to give it origin. Sir James Wilson created *The Economist.*''

''Tell me, Marion,'' Lord Roth continued, giving Goldie a puzzled look, ''what did you think about our defeating the Sikhs at Chillianwalla and Gujarat last year?''

Saber wished the man would suddenly disappear. How was he to answer these intellectual questions without tipping Goldie off? ''I—Well, of course, I was . . . I was very glad.''

"Yeah, he was real glad," Goldie said. "He was just sayin' that those Shicks got exactly what they deserved over there in Chilly Walls and Grat, weren't you, Marion?"

"Shicks?" Lord Roth repeated.

Goldie realized she'd made some sort of mistake, although she had no idea what it was. "Well, it was real nice talkin' to you, Duke Roth, but Marion and I were just headin' for the dance floor. 'Bye!"

As they made their way across the room, they were intercepted once again, this time by Lady Baldwin and Lady Ainsworth.

"Marion," Lady Baldwin said, "my granddaughter, Isabelle, told me to convey her salutations to you. I spoke to her briefly before coming tonight, and I must say she was positively delighted to know that you are out and about now. She recalls very fondly her sixteenth birthday party. You do remember attending her party, do you not, Marion?"

Saber resisted the urge to roll his eyes. "I do indeed remember Isabelle's party, Lady Baldwin, and please give her my warmest regards."

"Where are you residing, Marion?" Lady Ainsworth asked. "I called on your aunts several days ago, and—"

"They wanted to redecorate the house," Saber blurted, desperate to cut the woman off before she mentioned his aunts' names. "In order for that to be accomplished, we decided to leave the house. We are renting another now, but will be back in our own very soon. I shall inform my aunts that you would enjoy seeing them again."

"Yeah," Goldie declared, nodding. "They bought all new stuff to go in their house, too. It's gonna be so purty. Well, we're gonna go dance now. 'Bye!"

"Goldie," Saber said as she pulled him along, "let's leave. We—"

"Saber," she broke him off, "how did you know all those folks' names? I never did get the chance to tell you that was Duke Roth. And I didn't ever tell you about those ladies, Miz Ainsworth and Miz Baldwin, either.'

"I—I heard their names being spoken when I arrived,"

he stammered. "Goldie, I really must insist that we leave now."

"But—"

"*Now,*" he pressed, taking her hand and leading her to the corner where Lord and Lady Chittingdon were standing. "Thank you for the invitation," he told his hosts, and pressed a kiss to Lady Chittingdon's hand.

"But surely you aren't departing!" Lady Chittingdon exclaimed. "It's early yet, and Goldie hasn't had the pleasure of even one dance with you, Marion."

"Nevertheless, we must leave," Saber responded, feeling more anxious by the moment. "Isn't that right, Goldie?"

She saw the stubborn gleam in his seaweed eyes and knew then he would not stay another minute. For a moment, she felt like arguing, but as she continued looking up at him, she began to imagine the things they would do after they left. The ride home was a long one, and the coach would be dark and very private. And the aunties were out, she remembered. Realizing the intimate possibilities of the night, she blushed, suddenly deciding it didn't matter whether Saber learned dukish dancing or not.

" 'Bye, y'all," she told her hosts a bit breathlessly. "I had a really good time, but Marion and I have to leave now. I enjoyed all the food. 'Course, I didn't know what most of it was, but none of it looked like guts so I did the proper thing and ate all of it. Did y'all notice that?"

Lady Chittingdon laid her hand on Goldie's cheek. "We did indeed, my dear."

"Miss Mae," Horatio Alders said as he arrived at her side. "My wife and I will be hosting an informal luncheon next week. Would you do us the honor of accepting our invitation? I would dearly love to hear more of your stories about the people you've known in America. You may come too, Marion," he added, his twinkling eyes never leaving Goldie.

Saber felt pride well within him. Goldie would have little trouble being accepted by the nobility. She was already well-liked by the Chittingdons, Lord John Russell himself had spoken highly of her, and Horatio Alders, the most peevish man in the country, had just extended her an invitation to his home. "We will be in touch, Lord Alders," he responded, his fingers caressing Goldie's palm.

"Caroline and I will escort you and Miss Mae to the door, Marion," Lord Chittingdon announced.

In the foyer, Saber helped Goldie with her wrap. After thanking the Chittingdons once again, he began leading her outside, relieved beyond belief that nothing untoward had happened during the course of the evening.

"Wait!" Goldie exclaimed, turning back to the house. "I left my notes in the parlor!" She hurried to retrieve them.

Saber started after her, but was detained when Lord Chittingdon began a conversation concerning the German scientist Rudolf Clausius. Saber had no choice but to stay by the door and listen to Lord Chittingdon drone on about Clausius' study of the law of thermodynamics and the kinetic theory of gases.

Goldie skipped into the parlor, finding her notes lying on the chair she'd been sitting in. As she picked them up, she heard the parlor door close.

"I'm glad to have found you alone at last," Jillian said caustically. "I would like to speak to you."

"Well, I'm really sorry about that, Jillian," Goldie said, sashaying toward the door, "but Marion's waitin' on me, and I—"

"What, exactly, is your relationship with Marion?" Jillian demanded, moving in front of the door and barring Goldie's way.

Goldie stopped before the hateful woman. As she did, a familiar scent wafted around her. It smelled like roses, but not fresh ones. She couldn't remember where she'd smelled the strong fragrance before. "My relationship with Marion isn't any of your business, Jillian, so get out of my way."

Jillian tapped her rouged lips with a long, tapered fingernail. "Has he said nothing at all to you about *my* relationship with him? Oh, but of course, he wouldn't have, would he? After all, Marion is the sort of man who enjoys a variety of women. He doesn't, however, know that I am aware of his trysts. I allow him this for now. But I've warned him that as soon as we are wed, it must cease.

And since we will be living at Ravenhurst, it will be easier for me to keep my eye on him. He loves me as he did Angelica, you see. He promised *her* to make Ravenhurst their home, and he has made the same oath to *me.*"

"You're marryin' the Duke of Ravenhurst?" Goldie asked, astonished over this incredible information.

Jillian held out her hand, upon which glittered the magnificent diamond ring she'd inherited from her mother. "He came to see me last night and presented this to me as a token of his love. He spoils me so!"

Goldie blinked several times. Confusion such as she'd never known before seized her. "I—Jillian, did you say you'd been with Marion *last night?*" she asked, her voice almost a whisper.

Jillian gloated. "Yes," she said, her chin raised. "And we had a most romantic evening."

Goldie felt paralyzed. If Jillian had been with the real Marion last night . . . How was it possible that the woman who was to marry the duke didn't recognize Saber as an imposter? Yes, Saber resembled Marion Tremayne, but surely Jillian, who'd been with the duke only last night wouldn't mistake her own fiancé!

She groped for words, but her confusion was so thick, she couldn't speak.

Jillian saw the bewildered expression on Goldie's face and took full advantage of it. "Surely you noticed how reluctant he was to speak to me tonight. He wasn't expecting to see me here. When he did, he knew he'd been caught. But I'll forgive him, of course."

Goldie recalled how terribly anxious Saber had been earlier. He'd wanted to leave as soon as he arrived. Things she didn't want to believe began darting through her mind, leaving her sick with foreboding.

"You aren't the first, you know," Jillian continued silkily, savoring the look of horror in her adversary's eyes. "Marion has had a long string of women since Angelica's death," she lied. "I realize you believe that he is sponsoring your research here in London, but that is merely a ploy he has dreamed up. He goes to extravagant lengths to entice women into his bed, and then dismisses them as soon as he becomes bored with them. Your time will come.

Take my advice, Goldie. Have a care with your pride and leave him before he demands that you do so. Your relationship with him will come to naught, for he is to marry *me.*''

Goldie's breath came in short pants. ''But—But he said he loved me,'' she whispered, each word a tremendous effort.

''Love *you?*'' Jillian scoffed. ''You're a *commoner!* Surely after all your research concerning the nobility, you have learned that a man like Marion Tremayne would never stoop so low as to actually *care* for a girl of your background. No, Goldie. I can assure you that my darling diamond duke belongs to *me,* heart and soul.''

Goldie's mind continued to spin. ''Diamond duke,'' she repeated absently, assaulted by a horrible sense of dread.

Jillian sneered. ''My pet name for him. I named him that years ago when I discovered the diamond-shaped birthmark on his left thigh.''

Goldie's throat suddenly closed up completely, making breathing impossible. The familiar fragrance she smelled . . . roses. The same cloying scent she'd noticed on Saber last night when she'd stolen into his room.

Jillian's perfume.

She staggered backward, clutching her neck. Her entire world was shattering right before her eyes.

Jillian began to laugh. ''Don't take it so hard, my dear. You'll find someone else. Someone more like *you.* I suggest you look in the East End. After all, you're no better than those repugnant street girls the matrons are adopting. Why, there's an idea for you! Perhaps you could convince Miss Clara and Miss Lucy to adopt you! Then you could go back to that godforsaken country that hatched you and attempt to teach all those other backward Americans what you learn about the proper mode of decorum! Which brings me to a question. Where did you get that gown you are wearing? And those jewels. They are far too expensive for a girl of your means to be able to afford. Did Marion give them to you?''

''Gown?'' Goldie looked down at her luxurious satin dress. Reaching up, she touched the topaz necklace.

''Marion gave them to you, didn't he?'' Jillian pressed.

"He fairly showers his doxies with expensive gifts before casting them away. And such charm he uses! I imagine he plied you with honeyed words, didn't he? He told you how incredibly beautiful you are, and made you believe that everything about you is exactly what he wants in a woman. Ah, my dear Marion. He has such a way with words. Why, I've no doubt he could seduce the Queen herself if he had a mind to do it!"

Goldie began to shake so violently that she was forced to grab the back of a chair to keep standing. From the depths of her heart rose the truth. All the many presents she'd received hadn't been from any secret admirer. They'd been from Marion Tremayne. Payment. Payment for her services.

And the lessons. All those hours and hours of lessons on manners! It was true . . . Miss Clara and Miss Lucy had adopted her! *She* was their pitiful, ignorant waif!

And their nephew had brought her to them. He'd found her and taken her to them. He'd seen her as a girl who could both warm his bed and satisfy his aunts' desires to have a needy, uncultivated girl to educate.

She felt as though she were being sucked into a sea of bottomless grief. "Jillian," she whispered almost inaudibly. "Who is Addison Gage?"

"Addison? He's the Earl of Aurora Hills. He and Marion have been friends since they were lads. Myself, I don't approve of their relationship at all, and will end it as soon as Marion and I are wed. When those two are together, they are almost always up to no good. They take great delight in childish pranks, which I find highly unseemly."

Pranks, Goldie thought, her eyes stinging with unshed tears. She'd been the unknowing victim of yet another prank. Saber and Addison . . . they were just like the boys who'd played such cruel tricks on her. "And Leighwood?" she asked with what breath she could find.

Jillian closed her eyes in ecstasy. "Ah, Leighwood. That's one of Marion's four country estates. Leighwood is where he and I go when we want some private time together. Why? Has he taken you there?" she demanded.

Goldie couldn't answer. Memories of the many weeks she'd spent with the man she'd thought was Saber West came hurtling back to her. Oh, how he must have laughed inwardly at her attempts to turn him into a duke! How he must have secretly ridiculed her tremendous ignorance!

Horrible pain ripped through her, making her feel as if she'd been torn wide open. Tears blinding her, she ran to the door, snatching it open when Jillian stepped aside. "Is there a back way out of the house?" she asked a young maid in the corridor.

The maid showed her the way. Goldie dashed through the small garden in the backyard, quickly finding the door in the fence. There were no street lamps to light her way as she fled down the narrow path that ran parallel to the backs of the row of town houses. Tall trees shrouded whatever moonlight might have helped guide her steps.

She stumbled, falling face-down. Her cheek began to ache, and she realized she'd cut it on something sharp. She lay there for a moment, remembering the things Jillian had said.

*He goes to extravagant lengths to entice women into his bed. Your relationship with him will come to naught.*

Goldie felt as though her heart had been snatched from her breast. Staggering to her feet, she continued on until she'd run as far away from the Chittingdon house as her legs and lungs would allow before heading for the front street.

*Marion Tremayne would never stoop so low as to actually care for a girl of your background.*

Hot humiliation burned into her very soul. Sobbing, she reached the street, spotting a cab immediately. Tears, blood, and dirt staining her face, she yanked off her topaz necklace, holding it up for the driver to see. "I need to get to the corner of Pickerin' and Landon as fast as you can take me, but I don't have any money," she choked. "Will you take this instead?"

The man examined the jewelry carefully, recognizing its value. "Get in."

No sooner had she pulled herself inside and shut the door, than the coach jerked forward. Unprepared for the sudden jolt, Goldie pitched out of the seat and fell to the floor. She struggled to rise, but fell again as the coach hit a rut in the road. On the floor, she lay her head on the seat, her tears staining the upholstery.

*I imagine he plied you with honeyed words, didn't he?* Jillian had guessed. *He told you how incredibly beautiful you are, and made you believe that everything about you is exactly what he wants in a woman.*

"Yes," Goldie whimpered. "Yes, he did all those things."

*Trust me, Goldie. Trust me.*

She heard his voice. It came from the air. From nowhere.

*I love you, poppet.*

"Saber," she moaned, her fist at her mouth, her body quaking as her agony pounded through her. "Lies. So many lies. You must have laughed at me . . . just like all the others. I thought—I thought you were different. You made me believe. For the first time—I trusted—I loved— Saber, I loved you."

Broken. Her trust in the man she loved. Her heart.

All her diamond dreams.

She'd been allowed to touch them. Hold them for a time before they were snatched from her. But everything was gone now. Over.

Just like always.

# Chapter 21

When Saber arrived at the doorway of the parlor, he knew he was witnessing his own nightmare. Goldie's pad of paper lay ruffled on the floor. Goldie herself was gone.

And Jillian was sitting on a velvet settee, her brow raised high, a smug grin tugging at the corners of her red mouth.

"She left," Jillian purred, smoothing a slender finger across the top of one of the pale breasts straining from within the tight confines of her scarlet gown. "I doubt seriously that you will ever see her again."

Saber stopped breathing. He was numb with rage, regret, and an all-consuming fear that Jillian spoke the truth.

"You belong to *me*, Marion," Jillian continued, licking her lips. "You have for almost four years, and you always will."

Saber heard the roar of his pumping blood in his ears. He clenched his jaw, his fists. His entire body went rigid. "You sicken me, Jillian." Fury turned his voice into a low and frightening growl.

Apprehension writhed through her like a slithering snake. "You don't love her, Marion. You're merely intrigued by how *different* she is. That will pass. She is only the second woman you have looked at since Angelica's death, but remember, Marion, it was into *my* arms you fled after that tragedy. It was *my* attention you sought, and *my* loving ways that helped you to mend. You will come to your senses and realize that *I* am the only woman who could ever be the Duchess of Ravenhurst. I am gentle-bred. I am a true lady, my darling diamond duke."

"You were but a willing body. Someone into whom I could pump my frustration and rage. You were a temporary and physical remedy, Jillian. And if you were really gentle-bred . . . if you were a true lady, you never would have done what you did tonight. You are no lady, Jillian. You are little more than a fortune-hunting doxy. A bitch who will spread her legs for any man wealthy enough to satisfy your boundless greed."

Molten rage sluiced through her. "If I cannot have you, no other woman will either. I swear to destroy any future relationship you might ever hope to have with anyone else."

Saber drew himself up to his full height. "There will never be anyone else for me but Goldie. And you, Jillian Sommerset, are not fit to utter her name. God willing, I'll find her tonight and mend what damage you have done. And if I am successful, you will never have the opportunity to hurt her again. I am going to use every possible means at my disposal to make certain that you are immediately and permanently banned from society. You will never be welcome among the nobility again. And don't doubt for a moment that I cannot do it, for you know full well that I can."

His sharp gaze crucified her to her seat. She couldn't move. "You wouldn't," she whispered, horror stealing her voice.

"Consider it already done."

Goldie pounded on the front door, but Bennett failed to open it. Confused, yet desperate, she raced to the back, finding the kitchen door wide open. Taking not a second to ponder the oddity of that, she flew upstairs to her bedroom and ripped off her gown and underthings. She found her old brown frock wadded up in the back of her closet and hastily put it on. After slipping into her old slippers, she dragged out her tattered bag from beneath the bed, stuffing her dictionary and spare dress into it. For a brief moment, she wondered where her Aunt Della's diaries were before remembering Saber had taken them.

"To learn more about bein' a duke," she choked, feeling a fresh wave of mortification break over her. Staggering into the corner, she retrieved her claymore. As she passed the dressing table, the rich gleam of the gold brush caught her eye. Her broken heart couldn't bear the memories the sight of it brought, but recollections, like a raging river, flooded through her nevertheless.

"The dandelion stew," she murmured, pain weaving through every part of her. "The bread. The maze. Eyes like dancin' coins, and freckles painted on by cherubs. The first kiss. The softness in your eyes. The—"

She broke off, a torrent of tears escaping from her. "Lies! All lies!" Sagging against the table, she willed the veil of memories to lift and disappear, but knew in her soul they never would. Like phantoms, they'd haunt her forever.

With what strength she could find, she swayed toward the door, the heavy claymore slowing her considerably. "Itchie Bon!" she called to her dog. "Itchie Bon!" When he didn't respond, she realized he and Margaret had taken advantage of the open kitchen door. She prayed she'd find her dog somewhere outside.

A sudden noise in the hallway startled her. Believing it to be Bennett or Fern, she rushed toward the staircase before either of them could see and try to stop her. Just as she reached for the banister, a foul odor caught her attention. A putrid mixture of stale sweat, urine, and something rotten, it made her gag. Foreboding skated down her spine; instinct shouted that she wasn't alone.

Someone was watching her.

Her skin grew clammy, her mouth went dry. Slowly, she turned, her eyes wide, her lungs burning for the breath of air she couldn't draw.

"Ya ain't goin' nowhere, ya ain't, chickabiddy," Diggory Ferris declared as he stepped out of the black shadows of the corridor. "I been waitin' fer ya, an' I don't like ter be kept waitin'. Jest fer that, yer goin' ter suffer a while afore ya die."

At the sight of the glittering dagger in the man's hand, Goldie screamed so loud, she felt it rattle her own bones. Her bag and sword dropped from her hands, both plunging down the staircase.

The man stepped closer to her. So close she could see

the dirt-filled pockmarks on his greasy face and the red
streaks in his small, lashless eyes.

She watched in stunned terror as he raised his blade to
her throat, and knew then that not only had all her dreams
come to end, but her life had also.

Saber nearly tore the coach door off, trying to get it
open as the conveyance came to a rattling halt in front of
the house. He bolted out and flew up the steps. The door
was locked, and Bennett did not respond. His hands shaking, he fumbled with a ring of keys, infuriated when he
couldn't find the one that would open the door.

"Dammit, Bennett, open the door!" he shouted. "Bennett—"

Another shout cut him off. *Goldie!* Her screaming turned
his blood to gel and his mind into a seething mass of fear
and horror.

Adrenaline spinning through him, he took a step away
from the threshold. Drawing up his leg, he kicked the door
with every shred of might his body possessed. He heard
the crack of splitting wood, but the door remained shut.
Taking a deep, shuddering breath, he braced himself and
rammed his shoulder into the door.

It rattled loudly, then gave way with a splintering crash.
He dashed madly inside, utter panic whipping through him
when he saw Goldie at the top of the staircase. A brawny
man had her crushed in his arms, restraining her with a
knife poised at her slender throat.

*Saber.* Goldie tried to say, her voice subdued by her
riotous terror.

Her plea remained soundless, but it fairly thundered in
his heart. Fury such as he'd never before known slammed
into him when he saw the barbarian drag her into the dark
hallway. He charged up the stairs, slowing only to snatch
Goldie's claymore from a step. When he reached the upper
landing, Goldie and her captor were nowhere to be seen.
His fist wrapped tightly around the hilt of the great sword, he
moved cautiously, silently through the dim corridor, every
fiber in his body straining to hear the smallest of noises.

As he passed his own bedroom, he saw a silver stream
of moonlight on the dark blue carpet. A shadow slithered

across the pale pool of light. The point of the claymore leading his way, he stepped into the room, every nerve in his body pulsing with apprehension.

The door suddenly banged shut behind him. Spinning, he heard Goldie's choking sob and a low, guttural laugh. His stomach knotted, immense waves of panic passed over him. The man who held Goldie captive was now pressing the tip of his dagger into the soft swell of her left breast. Her neck was bleeding. The crimson smear on her pale flesh almost sent Saber to his knees.

"Ya shouldn't orter 'ave come up 'ere, guv," Diggory sneered, giving his blade a slight twist when Goldie tried to move. "Tender'earted bloke that I am, I was goin' ter stick 'er away from where ya could see. Now yer goin' ter 'ave to watch."

Saber held the claymore steady. "How much do you want for her life?" he demanded, sweat pouring from his brow. "Whatever your price, I'll pay it."

Diggory snickered, his smile revealing blackened teeth. "So yer another flamin' nob, eh? Be ya richer'n the one wot 'ired me ter do this job? 'E's some sorter nobleman, 'e is. Makes me call 'im 'milord.' Wears a ruby at 'is throat wot's almost as big as me bleedin' fist."

*A ruby. A ruby. Angelica's engagement ring. Her ruby ring.* Saber's mind whirled with sudden comprehension. "Dane Hutchins is not a nobleman! He works for me. I am Marion Tremayne, Duke of Ravenhurst. Let the girl go, and I'll give you—"

"Ya thinks me balmy?" Diggory blasted. "I'm Diggory Ferris, an' there ain't nobody 'ere in London-town wot can outwit me! Ya ain't no duke! The bluebloods ain't in this part o' town!"

Saber sucked in a ragged breath when the ruffian pushed the knife further into Goldie's chest. Horror permeated every inch of his rigid body when he saw a spot of blood seep through her dress. Her pain-filled groan tore at his very soul. "Dammit, I am who I say!"

Diggory spat a long stream of spittle on the floor. "Prove it then, guv. Show me the kind o' wealth wot only a bleedin' duke would 'ave. Iffen it strikes me fancy, I'll give ya the girl."

Saber knew the man called Diggory was lying. He knew the bastard would kill them, steal everything of value from the house, and then collect whatever payment Hutchins had promised him. Desperate for some sort of scheme, he watched Diggory intensely, taking note of the light in the man's eyes. Saber recognized it immediately. It was greed. If he could play on it, he might just stand a chance of saving Goldie.

That in mind, he strode to his dresser, his eyes never leaving Diggory's. His hand folded around the top of a large wooden box. With a jerk of his wrist, he threw it to the floor. It crashed at Diggory's feet, scattering its contents in wild disarray.

Diggory's eyes widened at the sight at his boots. In the wan moonlight, gold, silver, and diamonds glittered. He saw pearls. Emeralds. He'd never laid eyes on such an awesome fortune. "Gorblimey, ya weren't lyin', ya weren't," he whispered in amazement.

"There's more." Saber tossed a huge wad of bills atop the shining heap of jewelry. He watched the man tremble, knowing that greed would keep the bastard mesmerized for a long moment.

A moment. It would be all he had to save Goldie's life.

He took full advantage of those precious seconds and lunged toward her. Grabbing her arm, he tore her out of Diggory's clutches and threw her well away. As his left hand released her, his right hand tightened around the hilt of the claymore. Then he drew the great sword up with one swift, powerful motion.

Diggory never understood what happened when the blade impaled his heart. He made no sound at all, only fell, his body twitching for a few moments before it became still.

Huddled on the floor by the bed, Goldie stared at her captor's corpse, unable to take her horrified gaze away from it. Revulsion crawled through her.

"Goldie."

She looked up. "You're the duke," she whispered raggedly. "Marion Tremayne."

He took a step toward her.

"Don't," she murmured, her tears dripping to the carpet. "Don't come near me."

He stopped. "You're hurt," he said, his voice breaking. "Your cheek and breast . . . Goldie, you're bleeding."

"I'm not hurt."

"Let me—"

"No." Clutching the bedpost, she pulled herself up. Part of her yearned to be in his arms, where she would be safe and warm. She longed to hear him tell her sweet things, and wished she could see that special softness in his eyes just one more time.

But another part of her ached, the part his betrayal had wounded and made bleed . . . She swayed with grief and pain. "Now," she began, trying in vain to moisten her dry lips, "I understand. It's—It's all so clear. You . . . would have been ashamed to be seen with me. That's why—That's why you never wanted to take me anywhere. That's why you kept me hidden away in this house. It's why you made me stay in the coach."

"You're wrong. Goldie—"

"Last night," she whimpered, choking on a sob before she could continue. "It was Jillian's perfume I smelled on you. You were with her. You—"

"I was with her because I—"

"And when I asked you what we would do about Uncle Asa—You had no answer. You didn't answer because you knew my problems would never be yours. And when you sighed . . . Right before I left your room last night, I—I hinted at marriage. You sighed. Deeply. You sighed with revulsion, didn't you? You—The duke. Marry me . . . I'm only a commoner. I'm not fit to breathe the same air as you."

Saber's heart lurched. "No! Goldie, that's not—"

"I trusted you," she whispered, her body quaking. "So much so that I gave you the only thing of value I've ever had. And when I did, I became your whore. But—But—*I didn't know!*"

Saber had never seen such profound sorrow on anyone's face. Her agony poured from her huge, golden eyes, and shook her slight form. That she believed such terrible things about him made him want to die. Every muscle he possessed coiled with the readiness to go to her and enfold her in his arms. But he hesitated. She would fight him. She'd be a wild thing in his embrace. He knew she would. Dammit, he had to make her understand! "Goldie, listen to me. Let me tell you the reasons for—"

"I trusted you," she told him again, edging toward the door. "You—You made me believe you loved me. I loved you back. All my dreams . . . you made them seem so true. You offered me every diamond dream I ever had. And then . . . When I touched them—When I allowed myself to believe they were really mine—They weren't real," she sobbed. "They weren't real, Sab—*Your Grace!*"

When she flew out of the room, Saber followed her. But his chase was delayed as she turned and knocked over every piece of furniture she passed. The corridor was littered with fallen tables, chairs, paintings, small shelves, and knickknacks. Saber stumbled several times in his haste to catch her.

By the time he'd reached the staircase, she was already scurrying through the foyer downstairs. "Goldie!" he screamed, bounding down the steps. "Wait!"

She was gone as he leapt off the last step. Realizing she would go for Dammit, whom she kept secured in a small shed in the back, he raced toward the kitchen, where the back door was located.

But as he sped down the narrow hall that led there, Margaret came bounding toward him. She stopped in front of a small closet, yapping and digging at the door. Saber slowed, and heard moaning coming from within. Two distinct voices groaned for help. He knew immediately they belonged to Bennett and Fern.

Snatching the closet door open, he saw them lying on the floor amidst a pile of damask tablecloths and linen napkins. They were both bleeding from head wounds. "Dear God!" he shouted, bending down to them. "Bennett! Fern! What—"

"We were taking tea in the kitchen," Bennett explained, "We didn't see him until it was too late."

"He hit us, sir," Fern added weakly.

Saber helped them both to their feet. A battle of desires

waged inside him. He longed desperately to go after Goldie, but he couldn't leave the two servants until he was certain their injuries weren't severe. Biting back his raging frustration, he led them back through the hall and into the drawing room, assisting them onto the soft sofa.

With shaking fingers, he examined their wounds, relieved when he saw they were not deep. He knew then Bennett and Fern would be fine. "Stay here," he ordered them both. "Goldie—I've got to find her. She—I'll be back. Stay here!"

His race to the kitchen was so fast, he could barely remember the trip there. When he reached the room, he saw the door was wide open. Fear for Goldie still pumping through him, he bolted toward it. The unmistakable click of a gun hammer being pulled back stopped him short. The gun suddenly materialized from the threshold. Held in a stark-white hand, it was pointed directly at his chest.

The man who brandished it stepped out of the night fog and into the kitchen. Saber stared at him. There was something hauntingly familiar about the man.

"Good evening, Tremayne."

Saber stood riveted, watching the large ruby twinkle at the man's throat. "Hutchins." The name left the taste of poison in his mouth.

"I'm impressed," Dane said, his lips twisting into a smile. "You remember me after all these years. Where is Diggory Ferris, might I ask?"

"Dead." Hatred for Dane ravaged through Saber but his fear for Goldie was stronger. Dammit, she was getting away! She was going to ride through London at night, alone! "Get out of my way, Hutchins."

Dane smoothed his free hand across the side of his head. "The mist out there is utterly nasty," he commented, leveling the gun again. "Why, it's not even a *clean* mist! It's filled with London grime. I fear it has ruined my clothes. I detest the city. I prefer my country estate." He lifted his pistol a bit higher, aiming it at Saber's forehead.

"You'll not escape, Hutchins," Saber warned. "I've a slew of detectives trailing you, and every one of them knows the extent of your crimes. You may kill me if that's what your twisted mind tells you to do, but you will still lose all you believe to be yours. And that includes your very life. You're going to hang.''

Dane smiled again. "I killed her, you know.''

Saber's knees almost buckled. He reached for the kitchen table for support. "Goldie.''

"Goldie? No, not her. I will though. Yes, I certainly will. But I am speaking of Angelica. Sweet Angelica . . . It was nighttime. I found her in bed, exactly where I wanted her to be. I explained to her that by visiting her I was doing her an honor. I was going to allow her to share her charms with me, you see. But she refused. She raced out of the room, but I caught her at the top of the staircase. She fought me, calling out your name. I forgave her her ignorance, but I realized then that she would never understand the privilege I offered her.

"I consider her murder as a mercy killing of sorts,'' he continued calmly. "I took pity on her, you see. Given my extreme compassion for her, I could not allow her to marry you. She would have been miserable. And a woman as beautiful as she . . . Death was infinitely better than a life with you. Wherever she is, I know she's thanking me for delivering her from such a fate. And now, this is all I have left of her.'' He reached up, caressing the ruby nestled within the folds of his milk-white neckcloth.

Saber never knew such wild dread existed! If Dane escaped tonight, the man would, indeed, go after Goldie. He would succeed where Diggory Ferris had failed. "I won't let you do this, Hutchins,'' he gritted between clenched teeth. "Do you hear me, you murderous bastard? *I won't let you take anyone else away from me!*''

"Allow me to commend you on your courage, Tremayne,'' Dane taunted. "There you stand quite defenseless, and here I am, pointing a gun at your head.''

Saber did not respond, but only continued watching the barrel of Dane's pistol, waiting for the opportunity to overcome the deranged man.

"You always had everything, didn't you, Tremayne?'' Dane continued.'' I hated you from the first time I saw you. As a baby, you were swaddled in silk and lace, as a little boy, dressed in the finest clothes your father's money could buy. The pony you rode cost more than everything

I owned put together. My small house was sparsely furnished, and day after day I saw you taking fine and expensive things into that cursed tree house the villagers built for you. Silver candlesticks! They were worth more than several months of my wages! And yet you had them in your *tree house!* It wasn't fair, Tremayne. It was wrong. I knew that. Knew in my soul that the estate and everything on it was supposed to be mine.

"Heaven as my witness, if you hadn't left Ravenhurst when you did, I would have killed you. Twenty years have passed since that day, but as I look into your eyes, I know my loathing for you hasn't faded. If anything, it's increased, and I realize now that only your death will bring me the peace I deserve. You have to die, Tremayne. And once you're dead, I'll find that little bitch who dared to try and spoil my dreams. She'll go to Hallensham. I know she will. She'll go to collect her uncle and midget friend. Oh, how I will relish punishing her for trying to ruin my life."

The thought of Goldie in Dane's hands filled Saber with fury. Before he even realized what he was doing, he hurled himself at Dane, taking his opponent off-guard. He heard the gun drop to the floor before he smashed his fist into Dane's jaw and heard the crack of breaking bone. He then lunged for the pistol.

So did Dane. They fell upon it at the same time, each of them getting a firm hold on it. Rolling on the floor, they struggled for sole possession of it.

The explosion of gunfire ended the fight. Saber became motionless, feeling no burn, no pain. He pulled away from Dane, his eyes drawn to the crimson stain blossoming on the front of the man's snow-white shirt.

"Lord Tremayne!" Tyler Escott raced into the room, followed by several of his detectives. He stopped short when he saw Dane's body. "What—"

"Tyler!" Saber jerked to his feet, grabbing the detective by his shoulders. "Did you see her anywhere? Did you see Goldie?"

Tyler frowned. "She's not here?"

"Dammit!" Saber dragged his fingers through his hair. "Tyler, I've got to find her!" He flew toward the door.

"Lord Tremayne, wait!" Tyler shouted. "Listen to me. We got Doyle. He—"

Tyler's sentence died unfinished in his throat. He watched as his distraught client disappeared into the thick mist outside.

The cold fog defied Saber's efforts to find Goldie. Mounted on Yardley, he rode down street after street, but the heavy haze prevented him from seeing more than a few feet ahead of him. He might very well have come within yards of her, never noticing her, he raged.

As he searched on through London, he tried to convince himself that wherever she was, she was all right. His heart refused to believe otherwise.

But his mind, his intellect, reminded him repeatedly that she was wandering around in a city that fairly oozed with perils. Even if she managed to find her way out of London, the countryside was rife with danger. Assuming she'd found him, Itchie Bon would be her sole source of protection.

She would head for Hallensham, he knew. But even on a superb mount, the journey was a three-day ride away. Dammit would need twice that to make it, provided the old horse was able. Moreover, Goldie had no idea how to get there.

He realized his only recourse was to go to Ravenhurst and wait for her, for he knew he'd never be able to find her this way. But dear God, there was no telling where she'd end up or what would happen to her before she arrived.

*Dear God.* The words echoed through his mind, heart, soul. *Dream Giver.* Saber stopped Yardley and peered up at the heavens. He could see nothing of them, the fog spitefully veiling his view. "Are You there?" he demanded loudly, his throat aching from so many hours of screaming Goldie's name. "Don't let it happen again! Don't take her from me! And Goldie—She thinks You believe her to be unworthy! Haven't You let enough heartache happen to us already? Let me give her her dreams! Do You hear me? Are You listening? Dammit, are You there?"

His eyes and soul strained to detect some sort of answer. When none came, he knew he was completely alone.

"Goldie," he murmured, staring down at the reins in his trembling hands. He remembered every single thing about her. Her fresh scent, sweet, bubbly voice, and the profound allure of her beauty.

But mostly he recalled her character. Her simple way of looking at things. Her determination to deal with her own pain so as not to burden others with what she thought she could handle herself. Her outrageous ideas and the deep faith she had in them.

Her dreams. All her innocent and beautiful diamond dreams. He'd made none of them come true for her. Instead he'd hurt her. She'd wept, and now she was alone, cold, and without a shred of protection. His agony was so sharp, he felt as though a sword were slashing into his heart.

"Poppet," he whispered, pain clutching his throat. "My poppet called Goldie." His eyes stung. A tear rolled down his cheek. Another joined it. And another. He watched them splash onto his hands, the reins, and Yardley's mane. A loud moan escaped him as he leaned over his horse's neck, memory after memory sweeping achingly through him.

His head bowed, he rode on, never seeing the momentary parting of the fog. Through the patch of clear sky it revealed, one lone and brilliant star smiled down upon him.

# Chapter 22

With only Dammit, Itchie Bon, and sorrow for company, Goldie looked down the long, winding dirt road stretched out before her. Surrounded on both sides by vast, windswept fields, she could see no end to it.

"Do you think that man was lyin' to us, Itchie Bon?" she asked the panting mongrel. "He said Ravenhurst was right over the hill, but where the hell's the hill? Lord, we've been wanderin' around lost for so many days that I'm beginnin' to think we'll never find Hallensham."

She felt tears coming, but stubbornly held them back. Upon leaving London, she'd sworn never to shed another tear over her misfortune again, and she'd succeeded. She would not break her oath now.

Her shoulders sagging, she closed her eyes, reliving the past ten days. Ten twenty-four-hour nightmares was what they'd been. Her small bag of belongings had been stolen from her before she'd even found her way out of London. She'd thought to fight to get it back, but when she'd seen the gaunt and filthy face of the child-thief, she'd lost the heart to do battle with him.

Without money, she'd been unable to buy anything. She'd slept outside, huddled next to Itchie Bon for warmth. If not for the few compassionate peasants she'd met during her journey, she would have starved. But even so, the food she'd been given had barely been enough for five days, much less the week and a half she'd made it stretch out over. She shared it with Itchie Bon, who added bugs, reptiles, and rodents to his half. The loyal dog had even offered her a freshly killed field mouse two days ago.

Thank God the countryside itself fed Dammit, she mused, smoothing her hand down his coarse mane. She mashed grass, roots, seeds, and water together for him. But though he'd eaten well, his gait slowed by the hour, each step a real struggle for him. Her breath caught in her throat as she dwelled on the efforts the old, stouthearted horse had expended for her sake.

That in mind, she slipped to the ground, deciding to walk a bit. Without Dammit's warm flesh next to her legs, she shivered. Rubbing her hands up and down her arms, she felt hunger gnaw at her belly. Her entire body trembled with exhaustion.

But cold, hunger, and weariness were nothing compared to the ache in her heart. In fact, she welcomed the discomforts. Anything was better than the horrible pain thoughts of Saber brought.

She lifted her chin, looking down the endless road again. With a gentle tug on Dammit's reins, she began to walk. "I won't think about him," she murmured to her animals. "I won't. I can't. I'll think of dandelions. They don't stay smashed down. Crush 'em, and they spring right back. We'll get to Hallensham, get thrown out, and then we'll go somewhere else. It'll be all right. I'll *make* it be all right. I will. I will," she vowed. "And I'll never think about him again. Never."

She trudged onward. The wind smoothed across the fields, causing the long grass to sway. Goldie couldn't help noticing how green it was. Green as fresh seaweed.

Her traitorous memory summoned recollection after recollection. She saw him.

Saber.

His image, like a bolt of lightning, seared into her mind, stubbornly refusing to leave. It remained, so real to her that she felt as though she could reach out her hand and touch him.

She pushed her shoulders back and quickened her pace. A large blackbird sailed overhead. Black as coal. Just like his hair.

Saber.

She shook her head, trying to clear it of all memories. Running her hand down Dammit's neck, she forced herself to concentrate on how soft his coat was. "Soft as silk," she told him. "Just like silk sheets."

She could smell him. Sandalwood. Warm, silk sheets. And something simmering.

Saber.

A breeze floated past her, picking up her curls. As if the gentle wind carried the song of his voice, she could hear him. *Trust me, Goldie.* he whispered to her. *Trust me.*

The words he'd told her with such sincerity continued to waft through her, despite her best efforts to forget them. She walked on. Faster, as if she could leave all the memories behind her. An hour passed. The memories followed.

He was with her. She saw him, smelled him, heard him. He stayed with her every step of the way, and it had been so since she left him in London.

She dropped the reins and began to run. *Trust me, Goldie. Trust me.*

"Saber," she moaned, her legs aching and trembling as she struggled up a high hill.

She didn't see the rut in the road until she felt herself falling. Down she rolled, sharp stones and sticks bruising her every inch of the way.

When she finally stopped she opened her eyes. She was at the bottom of the hill lying in a soft bed of dandelions. The bright yellow blossoms made a pillow for her head and caressed her face. Their fresh scent filled her with yet more memories, more heartache. She could hold her tears back no longer. In a great flood, they escaped her, and she lay amidst the butter-soft, golden flowers, drenching them with all her pain, and mourning all her broken dreams.

Asa looked up from the armful of firewood he carried. Like he did every day, every hour on the hour he swept his gaze over the countryside, searching in vain for some sign that his Goldie had returned. He saw nothing. Nothing but old, gnarled trees, hedgerows, and never-ending fields. His heart heavier than the tremendous stack of wood in his arms, he turned toward the cottage.

As he reached the yard, he heard a distant sound. Facing the field again, he searched intently once more, spying a stray dog. The barking mongrel raced toward the village, stopped, then turned to yelp at something behind him. Curious, Asa continued to observe him.

A horse plodded into view and began pawing the ground. Asa watched the dog run in a circle around the horse then speed out of view, all the while barking. The horse turned its head and let out a long, loud whinny. Asa then saw the dog return.

By its side was a person. A little girl, Asa mused, noting how small the child was. He squinted, trying to see the distant form better. Sunlight glinted off her hair. Her hair of bright gold.

Asa's heart began to bang. His load of firewood crashed to the ground. "Goldie," he whispered, joy surging through him like a rush of cool water upon parched earth. "God Almighty! Big! Big, it's Goldie! She's back!"

Big almost killed himself trying to get through the front door of the cottage. As he scurried into the yard, he looked everywhere for Asa, finally spotting him running into a field. "Goldie," he murmured, spying the tiny, yellow-haired girl in the distance. A mixture of relief, happiness, and excitement scampered through him. "Goldie! Goldie! Gold—*Saber!* Good Lord, I've got to tell *Saber!*"

Spinning around, he looked at the manor house. His short legs moving as fast as they were able, he raced toward the mansion, shouting the news of Goldie's return to all he passed, and waving frantically at the field in which she could be found.

The people spilled out of every building in the village. Shouts filled the air, men, women, and children alike cheered the return of the girl who'd somehow coerced Lord Tremayne to come back.

Vaguely, Asa heard the cheering, but could concentrate on nothing but the sight of his Goldie. Tears streamed down his freshly shaven cheeks as the years fell away, and he saw her as the little girl who'd been given into his keeping. "Goldie!" he screamed, his long legs pumping to get him to her.

Goldie stopped when she saw the man running toward

her. Who was he? she wondered, her tired mind unable to function. He was calling her name, so he obviously knew her. Frowning, she watched him near her.

He was tall, trim, and well-built. His face was clean-shaven, and his clothes were neat and looked to be freshly laundered. Even his boots were spotless.

"Goldie!" Asa shouted from the distance. "It's me, darlin'! It's your Uncle Asa! God Almighty, Goldie!"

Her heart skipped several beats before seemingly dropping down to her toes. Disbelief enveloped her before tremendous joy chased it away. Before she'd even thought to do it, she was running to meet him. "Uncle Asa! Great day Miss Agnes, Uncle Asa!"

He reached her, crushing her to him. Weeping unabashedly, he groaned her name over and over again. "I'm sorry," he sputtered. "God Almighty, Goldie, I'm so sorry!"

"Uncle Asa," she sobbed into his chest, relishing his fresh, clean scent. "You aren't drunk. You aren't drunk. Oh, Uncle Asa, you aren't—"

"And I ain't never gonna be again, darlin'," he promised, sweeping her into his brawny arms. "We're startin' over, Goldie. You and me. And Big. We've got us a real home now. The duke's back. He told all of us how you went and found him, Goldie. He—"

"Back?" Goldie repeated, hot pain searing through her heart.

Asa nodded and began the trek back to the village, Dammit and Itchie Bon following closely behind them. "Yeah, he's here. I never knew too much about dukes, but I'm learnin'. See them little green flags flyin' around the mansion? They mean the duke's on his lands. Me? Well, I ain't talked to the man very much because he don't hardly ever leave his house. I ain't seen him do much but stand out on that big ole balcony, lookin' over his lands. He's out there every day doin' it. It's almost as if he was huntin' for somethin'. Big's been up there near every day. I keep askin' Big what all he talks about with such an important fella like the duke, but Big, he won't tell me. It's like they got some sorta secret, or somethin'."

Goldie heard nothing at all of what her uncle was saying

to her. She could concentrate only on the fact that Marion Tremayne had returned to Ravenhurst. "Back," she murmured on a raspy breath. "He's here."

"Yeah, and y'wanna know what happened the very day he got here? He throwed that bitch, Dora Mashburn, right outta Hallensham! Told her that if he ever saw her anywhere near his lands again, he'd—"

"Uncle Asa, we can't stay here!" Goldie exclaimed, her body shaking uncontrollably. "We have to pack and—"

"We'll never move again, darlin'," Asa assured her, thinking her trembling came from the dread of having to leave. "We got us a real home now. You're a heroine to the villagers, Goldie. You got their duke to come home, and they ain't talked of nothin' but you since he got here. And now that I don't drink no more and I got me a decent, honest job at the blacksmith's, they're warmin' up to me, too."

Goldie scanned the village, then looked up the hill behind it. Up to the mansion. Ravenhurst. Saber was there. Her throat threatened to close. "Uncle Asa, listen to me. We can't—"

"And guess what else, darlin'? The duke's got him a sweetheart, and he's gonna make her his duchess! The day after he got here, he announced his engagement and promised to introduce her to us real soon. Nobody's seen her yet, but everybody says she's probably real delicate and that she's restin' up after her trip here from London. Ain't that somethin'?"

Foreboding clawed up Goldie's spine. She couldn't answer. She could only remember Jillian's words. *He loves me as he did Angelica, you see. He promised her to make Ravenhurst their home, and he has made the same oath to me.*

Marion Tremanye, the duke. Jillian, his future duchess. Here at Ravenhurst. Goldie realized then the extent of Saber's love for Jillian. Only true love could have brought him back to the estate that had been the scene of so many tragedies.

"Like I said," Asa continued blithely, "I ain't set eyes on the girl he's gonna marry yet, but I reckon she must be purty as all get-out. 'Course I ain't never seen a real duchess before, but I got 'em figured out to be real—''

"No!" Goldie screamed, consumed with panic. "I don't want to live here, Uncle Asa! I want to *move!* Please—''

"But Goldie, why?"

She could find no words to explain her violent opposition to living in a place where every day she would be forced to see Jillian and Saber together. Where day in and day out she would witness their love and see its evidence in the children they would soon have. The thought was the most agonizing thing she could think of.

Asa saw the blaze of anxiety in her eyes and felt true concern. "Goldie, why—''

"Goldie!" several of the villagers chorused as they arrived in front of Asa.

When Asa set her down, Goldie felt the urge to run. Abandoning herself to it, she turned and began to flee back toward the field, crying out in anger and frustration when a few of the village men caught her.

They lifted her from the ground, holding her up for all to see. More people arrived, crowding around the men who carried her.

A cacophony of "thank-you's" hit Goldie's ears. Everyone she saw was smiling at her, reaching out to touch her, and expressing their gratitude to her for convincing the duke to return. "Let me down!" she cried, misery surging through her. "Let me—''

"He's called fer us!" one man shouted, his shoulders heaving with exertion as he ran toward the crowd. "I've jest come from up there, I have, and His Grace has ordered us all ter gather in the courtyard!''

"Oh, wot a day this is!" a woman exclaimed loudly, her hands on her plump cheeks. "This is it! Lord Tremayne is goin' ter bring out his betrothed at long last! Hurry! Let us hurry!''

Goldie began fighting in earnest. She twisted and squirmed so wildly, the men holding her were forced to set her down. When her feet touched the ground, she tried to escape again.

But what seemed like millions of hands grabbed onto

her, restraining her, pulling her along with the great crowd as it moved toward the manor house.

"Come along, lass," a man told her cheerfully.

"No!" She tried in vain to get away.

"A right modest little soul, she is!" someone called over the din. "Here she's got His Lordship ter come back, and she wants no gratitude or recognition fer it!"

The fifteen minutes it took to walk to the estate seemed like fifteen seconds to Goldie. Dragging her feet, she lost both her shoes, arriving in front of the magnificent mansion quite barefoot and completely exhausted from her struggles to escape the insistent villagers. If only she could find Uncle Asa or Big! she raged. Surely one of them would help her get away!

She looked all over for them, soon spying Big on the veranda. "Big! Big!"

He saw her and waved before running into the mansion.

Goldie frowned. "Big, wait! Big—"

"Lord Tremanye!" the people called in unison. "Lord Tremayne! Lord Tremayne!"

Goldie's heart quaked. She tried to melt into the screaming, jostling crowd, dreading Saber's appearance with every fiber in her body. Rising apprehension lent her strength, and she began doing battle with her captors once again.

But they held her steady and pulled her directly in front of the huge portico that opened into the courtyard. Unable to move, breathe, or think, she watched in alarm as the two great doors of the mansion slowly opened.

"Let me go," she begged, her voice no more than a slight whisper. "Please don't make me see him." Anguish pouring from her heart, tears steaming down her face, she turned her head and closed her eyes.

"There he is!" the man next to her screamed. "Goldie," he said to her, taking hold of her chin and turning her head, "look, lass! Thanks to you, there he is!"

By their own accord, her eyes opened. She saw him. Saber. Dressed in the most elegant clothes she'd ever seen him wear, he was standing at the top of the marble steps, his seaweed gaze sweeping over the mass of cheering villagers. Her banging heart stopped altogether at the sight of him.

And then his gaze roamed no further, but settled intently on her. At his piercing stare, her knees buckled, and she sagged between the two men holding her.

A thousand emotions swept through her when he began his descent of the marble steps. His stride was quick, purposeful; his eyes never left her. She tried to flee, but her muscles refused to work. She longed to scream, but her voice wouldn't come. She could do nothing but stand there and watch helplessly as he neared her. What was he going to do? Why was he doing this to her? The questions reverberated through her mind.

A hush came over the shouting villagers as he moved off the last step. Goldie could hear nothing at all but the deafening thunder of her heart. The crowd parted, making way for him when he began walking toward her.

*No, God.* she prayed desperately. *Don't let this happen! Please don't!*

Her prayer went unanswered. Saber stopped before her. Her head bowed, she saw the tips of his shiny shoes through the blur of her tears. The men who held her released her, and she stood there, trembling so hard she could see the skirt of her dress shake.

Swallowing and trying to find a shred of courage to see her through her torturous situation, she raised her gaze. Slowly. Up it went, from his shoes to his legs. She swallowed again at the sight, remembering the muscles, the strength of those legs. She saw his slim hips, his flat belly, his broad chest. And then she looked at his face.

The world and everything in it ceased to exist for her. She was aware of nothing but Saber's eyes. Their glow. Their softness.

Very slowly, Saber reached out his arm and picked up her quivering hand. He held it gently in his own for a moment that was an eternity to Goldie. Then, he turned, and increasing his pressure on her hand, he led her to the steps.

In a mindless daze, she trailed behind him, vaguely aware that all eyes were upon her. She felt weightless, as though she were drifting through a cloud, through a dream.

Only when she tripped on a step and stumbled did reality come back to her. Stung with humiliation, she braced herself for the fall.

It never came. Instead, she felt herself being lifted into a familiar embrace. Into arms whose might she knew well. The scent of sandalwood drifted through her senses, making her dizzy with bittersweet feelings. Her head next to his chest, she heard the steady beat of a heart she'd once thought belonged to her. Weak with emotion, she couldn't find the strength to protest when Saber carried her the rest of the way up the steps. She realized then that whatever plan he had for her, she would have to deal with it as best she could. There was simply no escaping.

As if she were made of the most fragile crystal, Saber set her down on the spacious veranda, keeping his arm around her waist. She felt his hand, his long, strong fingers caress her there. When she swayed, that same warm hand steadied her.

Unable to concentrate on any one thing, she looked down, surveying the dense gathering of people below. Her confusion intensified. Why had Saber brought her up here? Where was Jillian? Her mind filled with questions so numerous that she could not distinguish between them. They blended into one seething tangle of bewilderment.

"Goldie."

His voice, so much like sweet, rich chocolate, stole her breath. What was he going to say? What was he going to do to her?

"Poppet."

She couldn't look at him. She was afraid. She couldn't understand any of this.

"Goldie, love."

She felt his hand beneath her chin, his fingers bringing her face upward to meet his. She blinked several times, totally captivated by the softness in his beautiful eyes.

When he had her attention, Saber slipped his hand into the pocket of his waistcoat, bringing forth a small black velvet box. His eyes never leaving Goldie's, he lifted the top of it, waiting in breathless anxiety for her reaction.

Lowering her eyes, she looked at what he held out to her.

Nestled within folds of dark green satin lay a gleaming gold ring. She thought the setting the most beautiful thing she'd ever seen. Yellow diamonds, some large, some tiny, were arranged in the shape of an exquisite flower. She knew in the heart of her heart that the blossom of diamonds was none other than a dandelion.

"For so long," Saber began softly, taking the ring from the box, "I wondered what the connection was between a diamond and a dandelion. The answer eluded me until you spoke of your dreams. Your diamond dreams. In one's dreams anything can come true. And so, Goldie, it is with dreams that I join the diamond and the dandelion. Your dreams. My dreams. By accepting this ring, love, you will be uniting our dreams forever."

She looked up at him, refusing to believe she'd heard him right. "I—Saber . . ."

The awe in her huge, golden eyes made him smile down at her. "I love you, poppet. I want you to be my duchess. Marry me, Goldie Mae."

He held the ring before her. She realized he was waiting for her to draw up her hand to receive it, but she couldn't do it. Fear continued to stab through her. Surely this was going to end. It wasn't true. She *knew* it wasn't.

Saber saw the hesitation, the disbelief in her eyes, and knew exactly what she was thinking. "Goldie," he murmured, his voice as soft as the sweetly scented country breeze, "the dreams aren't ending, poppet. They're only beginning. Marry me. Say yes?"

"Saber, I . . ."

Her mind screamed for her to run. Shouted to her that it was all a prank, and that it would end in her complete and utter humiliation, just like always. Saber would bring Jillian out. They'd laugh at her. The villagers would join in on the merriment. It would be the worst thing that had ever happened to her. *Run, Goldie! Run!* her mind continued to scream.

But her heart . . . From the deepest recesses of her heart whispered a voice so dear to her, it brought tears to her eyes when she heard it. *Trust me, Goldie.* it begged her. *Trust me.*

The quiet whisper in her heart overcame the frenzied

shouting in her mind, and in that instant her decision was made. Slowly, tremulously, she lifted her left hand. Time was suspended as she waited to see what Saber would do. Never in her life had she felt so totally vulnerable, so wide open for hurt.

Warmth seeped through every part of her when Saber took her hand and clasped it in his own. "Saber," she whispered, unable to say more.

"Will you marry me, Goldie?"

Still speechless with wonder, she could only nod.

Saber slid the ring on her finger, his own fingers shaking as uncontrollable joy crashed through him. She was his.

This wonderful poppet called Goldie was his, now and forevermore.

"From this moment on," he began, bringing her hand to his lips and pressing a kiss to it, "I will give you everything you've ever dreamed of."

Tears of the most profound happiness she'd ever known streamed down her face. Every hurt, every confusion, every heartache she'd ever had melted away. "Saber," she squeaked, unable to decide what to look at—the wonderful, sparkling ring, or the beautiful glow in his eyes.

Her tears, so like small diamonds, made Saber smile, for he knew they were not born of sorrow. "Look, Goldie," he told her quietly, his voice trembling with emotion, "look at our home, and see the mere beginnings of all the dreams I will make come true for you."

She cast one last glance at the wondrous ring shimmering on her finger, then obeyed his tender command. Raising her head, she peered up at the mansion.

What she saw sent a rush of pure astonishment coursing through her. From each open window of the house fluttered ruffled curtains of pink and white gingham. She couldn't contain a squeal.

Her squeal made Saber chuckle. His chuckle turned to full-fledged laughter when he noticed she had no shoes on. "My barefoot duchess," he teased. "I take it your *unquiet* delight means you like the curtains? The village women have been sewing for days. The men, too, have been working. Do you see anything else, poppet?"

She examined her surroundings more intently, her hands

flying to her open mouth when she saw the white picket fence. It encircled the entire manor house. "My fence," she murmured. "Oh, Saber, my—"

She broke off at a mewling sound. Looking down, she saw a multitude of kittens, one trying to climb up her skirt. With another squeal, she bent and scooped the wiggling ball of gray fur up into her arms.

Saber thought he would burst from the joy of seeing her so happy. "And inside the house there are—"

"Pink sofas with little white arm pillows that have strawberries stitched on 'em, and a rockin' chair with my name carved on it!" she finished for him.

He nodded, laughing again. "But the parlor—Goldie, it's completely empty. We even took down the wallpaper. It's your tea parlor, poppet, and I want you to decorate it to your heart's content. I'll take you all over Europe so you can find just the right things to put in it. It'll be a thousand times better than Imogene Tully's. And your kittens can sleep all over the furniture, and we won't ever get mad at them," he added. "And we'll plant magnolias, Goldie. We'll plant hundreds of them, and no one will ever cut them down. And look there, poppet. What do you see?"

She looked in the direction in which he was pointing and saw an array of gilded cages, each one holding a brilliantly colored bird. More tears trickled down her cheeks as she recognized the significance of his gifts to her.

"No one will ever let your birds go, Goldie," Saber promised. "They're yours. I've even figured out how to keep the cats away from them. We'll convert one of the rooms into a bird room, and we'll keep it locked all the time. This is your home, Goldie. And no one will ever have the right to tell you to leave it."

"Saber, I—"

"And as for the other dream you told me about . . ." he continued, deliberately letting his voice trail away as he smiled rakishly at her. "Remember those twelve children you always wanted? Well, I must admit that *that* dream is one I'd like to start making come true right now."

His admission made her tremble anew.

"We'll fill the whole mansion with children, poppet,"

he told her excitedly. "Ravenhurst will ring with laughter once more, for by giving you all your dreams, my own have come true. I'm back on my lands, where I belong. Because of you, Goldie. All because of you."

She could find no words to describe how happy he'd made her. Relying on actions, she set the kitten down, then threw herself into Saber's arms.

Holding her close, Saber turned to the silent, awestruck crowd below. "People of Hallensham!" he roared. "I present to you Goldie Mae, the future Duchess of Ravenhurst!"

The cheer that went up was deafening. Goldie smiled, laughed, waved, and cried. She embraced Big and Asa as they joined her, then received yet another surprise when the aunties came scurrying out of the house. Between them, with a huge, bright smile on her face, was Rosie.

"I been adopted, luv!" Rosie exclaimed. "An' not jest fer a while, neither, but *ferever!* Saber says I'm part o' the family now, I am!"

"Rosie!" Goldie shouted above the din of the villagers' applause. "Miss Lucy, Miss Clara!" Glowing with radiant happiness, she turned back to the man who had made her every dream come true, and held his face in her hands. "Saber—Great day Miss Agnes, I love you!"

He took her hands from his cheeks and kissed each of her wrists. "And I love you, Goldie. Now, tomorrow . . ." He looked up, casting an expression of the deepest gratitude to the heavens. "I'll love you all the hours God sends." Taking her into his arms, he bent to kiss her.

Right before his lips met hers, Goldie caught sight of the estate garden. What she saw sent her joy to the highest pinnacle.

The roses were blooming.

# Avon Romances—
## *the best in exceptional authors and unforgettable novels!*